A TIME TO LIVE

Vanessa de Haan is an author and journalist who writes for various newspapers, magazines and podcasts. She was a columnist for the *Western Morning News*, writing under the name Zoe Kenyon.

A Time to Live is her second historical novel. She lives in Blackdown Hills on the Devon/Somerset border, where she is also learning to lay hedges.

Also by Vanessa de Haan

The Restless Sea

A TIME TO LIVE

VANESSA DE HAAN

HarperCollins *Publishers*

HarperCollins*Publishers* Ltd
1 London Bridge Street
London SE1 9GF

www.harpercollins.co.uk

HarperCollins*Publishers*
Macken House, 39/40 Mayor Street Upper
Dublin 1, D01 C9W8

First published by HarperCollins*Publishers* 2023
This paperback edition published 2024
1

A catalogue record for this book is available from the British Library

ISBN: 978-0-00-822983-2 (PB)

Typeset in Meridien LT Std by HarperCollins*Publishers* India

Printed and bound in the UK using 100% Renewable Electricity by
CPI Group (UK) Ltd

MIX
Paper | Supporting
responsible forestry
FSC™ C007454

*For everyone who has felt torn between duty and freedom.
And for Richard Tyrell-Kenyon, the father I never
got to know.*

PROLOGUE

Bristol, 1914

Edward cannot resist. He is leaving for France tomorrow. He will be at the Front within the next few days. He is filled with an urgent desire to seize every opportunity that presents itself, and this is certainly one of those.

The maid has been flirting with him since he arrived three weeks ago. She has dark hair and pale skin, a combination he's always had a weakness for. His heart beats a little faster when he sees the shine of her pink lips against the porcelain white teeth of her smile. She is a brazen young thing – speaking in a way that the staff would never dare to at home. But his uncle's house is run differently to Coombe, and what harm was there in passing her friend's name to the adjutant? God knows, they need more volunteers, and so much the better if the man is good with horses. Edward doesn't usually feel the need to exchange a favour for some fun. He could pick any girl he wants, but staring at his own mortality must have softened him.

She is waiting for him in the corridor. He reaches for her in the darkness, hears the crackle of the cheap fabric covering the slender hips, smells the laundry soap and beneath it something more animalistic. She pulls him closer. She is an English rose, opening up to his touch.

He hears her gasp. He uses the wall to steady himself as he enjoys the familiar feeling of release. He sees her pulse quicken

1

in the slender neck, feels her push back as her hand comes up to caress his face.

He pulls away. He does not want to be caressed. She starts to say something, but he puts his hand against her mouth to indicate she must keep quiet. He is disappointed by her boldness. He prefers the ones that keep their gaze averted; it is so much easier to get on with things. She tries to take hold of his hand. He takes a step backwards. He hopes she isn't going to cause a scene. Not that his uncle would care; it's just he's gasping for a drink, and a fuss might delay that.

They both jump as there is a movement by the door to the drawing room. Edward spins around. 'Freddie, you little devil!'

His younger brother backs away. He's such a po-faced, dishevelled boy; sometimes Edward can hardly believe they are related. He grabs hold of Freddie's arm, twists it so that he is forced to turn to face him. 'Why are you lurking in the shadows? Or is that how you like it? I can arrange another show, if you want?' He laughs as Freddie wrenches free and retreats down the corridor.

Edward does not look back, to where the maid is smoothing her uniform. Now he has had her, his desire is spent. He flings open the drawing-room door, and steps back into his world, the girl already forgotten.

2

CHAPTER 1

England, 1918

Freddie cannot stomach much breakfast – no bacon, no porridge, not even Cook's marmalade – only a dry piece of toast and some black tea. He glances around the dining room. It is the same as it ever was. Food steams on the side, next to the warm plates, the pot of tea, the milk leaving its creamy rim around the jug. His father nods and grunts behind the newspaper. His mother eats gracefully. His sister Ginny rubs at her bleary eyes; she needs more than tea to recover from last night's party. She catches him watching, and the look prompts a stab of guilt in his gut, but then the ancient housemaid Jennings calls to say the car is here to take him to the station, and they are all manoeuvring their chairs back from the table, and following him out on to the steps.

It is late summer, and the air is warm, the sun already high above the trees, lighting the leaves so that they glow various shades of green: the wide-spreading cedars, the exuberant beeches, the burgeoning elms. In the distance, beyond the ha-ha, Freddie can see the fallow deer grazing the yellowing parkland beneath the twisted oaks. He breathes in deeply: it is the perfect day on which to start the rest of his life.

Jennings and the driver battle to get the trunk on to the roof of the car while Mrs Foley shouts instructions. Freddie's parents and sister watch from the steps, toy figures against the backdrop of the vast house. He smiles. The truth is he cannot wait to leave. He has been working towards this moment for a year, and dreaming of it for far longer.

The trunk is secure. Jennings hobbles back into the short line of servants who wait expectantly. Mrs Foley dabs tears from her eyes. Freddie shakes their rheumy hands, nodding and saying a few kind words to each, trying to keep the excitement from his voice, trying to retain the same veneer of propriety that keeps their faces expressionless: but they must be aware of how he has longed for escape; they have known him all his life.

He moves from the two housemaids to the decrepit gardener Dibble, to Cook, to Jennings, and finally to Mrs Foley. 'You've done well to keep the place going,' he says. The housekeeper glances at her fingers, uncharacteristically lost for words. 'Edward will return any day now: the war's as good as over; the Allies are making huge advances. And when he does, he will employ an army of staff once more, and with you at the helm, it won't take long to restore Coombe to its former glory.'

Mrs Foley nods and lifts her handkerchief to her eyes again, and he could reach out to give her a comforting pat, but that would never do. It is a relief when Ginny throws her arms around him with a sob. She is the only one happy to display her emotions, where even a shake of the hand can seem overdramatic. 'I'll miss you most of all,' he mumbles into her dark hair.

'Rot,' she sniffs, stepping back. 'You'll forget all about us as soon as we're out of sight.' But she smiles wryly through her tears.

Freddie's mother moves as if to embrace him too, then thinks better of it, and squeezes his hands instead. Her fingers are ice-cold, her sapphire earrings splashes of midnight blue against her skin, a colour that matches her eyes.

And finally, he stops in front of his father. 'Good luck, son,' says the earl, gripping Freddie firmly with one warm hand, and clapping him on the shoulder with the other. They stare for a moment, the grey eyes of each searching the other.

'Come and visit?' It is a question they both know the answer to. His father would never abandon his seat here for the weeks it takes to cross the ocean to Ceylon.

Freddie regards them for one last time: his family, his home, his life. His *old* life. He glances once more across the park. The top lake is sluggish, the water low and choked with weed, barely lapping at the dry, cracked mud at its edges. The lawns are patchy and unkempt. Even the great house, Coombe Hall – home to the Hemburys since medieval times – seems to be flagging, some of the chimneys leaning dangerously, the window frames rotting.

He shakes his head. It was never his problem.

He opens the passenger door, turns to wave, a foot, a leg in the car, the click of the door closing. He hears the crunch of gravel beneath tyres as the car begins to move. He twists for one last look at the people on the steps, silently whispers his last goodbye.

But they are not looking at him any more. They are looking beyond the departing car, along the drive, eyes wide, faces rigid. Freddie cranes his neck to see what they see.

The car grinds to a halt. In front of it, a boy is dismounting from his bicycle, mopping his brow as he looks up and surveys the tableau in front of him.

Freddie swallows, a loud sound in the silence of a world stood still. He grips the handle of the door fast, as if to keep it shut. He wants to shout to the driver to keep going, to order this boy out of the way, to fly on as fast as he can.

But the boy's arrival forces Freddie to do the opposite, to step back out into that balmy Devon air, to take a deep, deep breath as he straightens his back, squares his shoulders, turns to face whatever is coming.

The messenger boy, face flushed, advances self-consciously, until he is only a yard away from Freddie. He fumbles in his pouch as he finds the envelope.

'Earl of Hembury?' he asks.

Freddie shakes his head. 'His son.' He has to force the words out of his dry mouth. He cannot take the telegram, because that will make whatever is inside it a reality. He wants to stop time. He wants to go back to yesterday, to lighting a cigarette, to playing croquet, to anywhere but this moment.

Then somehow his sister is by his side, her hand on his arm, tethering him to reality. He reaches out to take the envelope.

'Thank you,' says Ginny. The tone of her voice is curt and dismissive; the messenger knows that there will be no reply. He nods smartly and turns around. He wheels a safe distance away and then mounts the bicycle for the downhill, his relief tangible.

Ginny looks at her brother. Freddie looks at the envelope. His fingers work automatically, as if spurred on by some sense of duty. It is not addressed to him, but perhaps by opening it, he might protect his father from what is coming. He cannot read the words out loud. Instead he shows them silently to his sister, the letters crashing around his head, sharp like broken glass, shattering his dreams of freedom.

CHAPTER 2

'But it leaves on Friday. I've rebooked my passage . . .' Freddie tries not to let disappointment dissolve into anger.

'You cannot take it.' The earl is pale beneath his garden-browned skin, his body deflated like a spent balloon.

'But I can't miss another one. Matthew is waiting. I'm already three weeks late.'

'Then a couple more won't matter.'

'It's a crucial time . . .'

'What could be more crucial than the whereabouts of your brother?'

The room falls silent, apart from the sound of Ginny biting her nails. Freddie bites his tongue, for what can he say, apart from that his world has always hinged on the whereabouts of his brother.

His father frowns. 'We must prepare for the worst.'

'Papa!' Ginny reaches for his hand. 'Don't speak like that. The telegram says he's missing, only missing.'

The earl opens his mouth, then closes it again, as if he has forgotten what he was going to say. Freddie turns away. The last three weeks might as well have been three years, the seconds dragging slowly, relentlessly onward. Missing. Only missing. Well, if only Edward would hurry up and be found, so that Freddie can be released. And then his spirits plunge further; he hates himself for this resentment.

The clock on the chimneypiece chimes. The earl releases his daughter's hand, reaching instead for his pipe which he places in his mouth. He tamps it down, the movements automatic. He speaks from the corner of his mouth: 'Frederick, why don't you come to the estate manager's meeting this morning?'

Freddie is surprised: he has never been party to such meetings before. 'Of course. If you really think I can help,' he says, a bubble of pride lifting his shoulders, making him stand taller.

The earl strikes a match and holds its tiny flame close to the tobacco. 'Not really the done thing. But desperate times . . .' He peters out, sucking on the pipe as he leans his head back in the chair and stares into space.

There is a commotion in the hall. Downstairs, the servants' bells are ringing, sending footsteps pattering, and dogs barking. Freddie readies himself for Arthur Mulligan, the estate manager, but instead he hears a familiar voice, loud, abrupt, matching the clamour of the dogs. His father's younger brother, Maurice, sweeps in with a flourish, flinging his hat at Jennings, whistling at his valet to collect the cases from the car. The greyhounds lower their heads when they see who it is, and slink away into the shadows. Maurice strides up to Freddie and Ginny, kissing the latter's cheeks, shaking Freddie's hand. His grip is strong, confident, as if he has been waiting for this moment all his life.

'Any news?' But Maurice is already talking before either of them has a chance to answer. 'That poor boy. We grew so close in the weeks before he left.'

Maurice has a small estate, Parkfield, on the southern edge of Bristol. It had been Edward's home while his regiment mobilised for France. Freddie was taken to visit his brother there before Edward left for the Front. The memory makes him shudder; his uncle's home is the antithesis to Coombe Hall – filled with gaudy trinkets and ostentatious parties – but neither way of life appeals to him. He is after something new, fresh – an adventure in a place where he is not simply Hembury's Other Son.

8

Maurice slaps him on the back. 'I thought you'd be abroad by now? Sugar cane, isn't it?'

'Tea.'

'Of course. A splendid idea. It's important to have a project. Now. Where's your father? Needs galvanising, no doubt. I know how he likes to brood . . . Take this, won't you, dear girl?' He thrusts his coat at Ginny – even though Jennings is hovering in the background – and begins to make his way down the corridor towards the study. Freddie watches uneasily. It is not just his uncle's house that makes him uncomfortable; there is something unsettling about the ease with which Maurice imposes his will on others.

Arthur Mulligan arrives shortly afterwards and joins Freddie in the library. The land agent is gangly and walks with a limp, an injury sustained early on in a war that has wounded everyone, visibly or not. He sits awkwardly at the table, setting out his papers, adjusting and readjusting the piles. They both stand to greet the earl and Maurice as they enter from behind a hidden door in a bookcase that adjoins the earl's study. The atmosphere settles as they sit and get down to business.

Mulligan starts with the list of accounts due and paid, then moves on to discuss which tenanted farmers are succeeding, despite shortages of labour, to be productive, and which are not. Freddie tries to concentrate, but a lifetime of being shut out has left him clueless. It should be Edward sitting here, making decisions about the future of his estate – an estate handed down to him by a long line of firstborns. How ironic that after all this time of wanting to be party to these meetings, he finds it not in the least interesting.

Freddie glances at Maurice, who is in full flow. It is a good thing, after all, that his uncle is here. Maurice already has a handle on things; he can stay and help the earl until Edward is found. If Freddie leaves soon, he can still help Matthew clear the rest of the land before the monsoon, and together they can make plans for the first planting.

9

'Frederick! What do you think?' His father is calling to him. 'Where will food and land prices go next? Surely the government will have to raise taxes when this war is finally over . . .'

Freddie tries to focus. 'I'd need to have a look at the papers,' he begins.

His uncle interrupts. 'I wouldn't waste the boy's time. He has his own fish to fry in the Sudan . . .'

'Ceylon.'

'Wherever. The point is that all of this is irrelevant, as I've been trying to explain. You have nothing to worry about. Edward saw to that. Before he left we were working on an exciting project together. One that will guarantee the future of this place.'

Freddie perks up. Now this *could* be interesting: to hear what his brother has in store for Coombe.

The earl furrows his brow. 'Edward said nothing to me . . .'

'He couldn't until he was sure the others were on board. And things have moved so slowly with the war on. No one was willing to commit.'

'What others?' asks the earl.

'Lucky Monkton, Thomas Hampden, and Rupert Granville.'

'On board with what?' asks Freddie.

Maurice takes a deep breath. 'We're close to agreeing a deal to build a racecourse . . .'

'A racecourse?' Freddie almost chokes with laughter. 'Here? At Coombe?'

Maurice glares at him. 'I've been busy tying things up while we wait for the war to end and your brother to return.' Maurice pats a stack of papers. 'It's all here . . .'

'But you'd need stands and stables, paddocks, parking . . .' Freddie looks from his uncle to his father, expecting the earl to join him with incredulity.

'Yes, yes. I'm aware of all that,' snaps Maurice.

'And how will people get here? The lanes are barely wide enough for one motor car . . .'

'It has all been worked out. Thomas Hampden . . .'

Freddie snorts. 'Of course he'd be in the thick of it.' Their neighbour is always looking for an excuse to expand his empire. 'What does he know of racing? What does Edward know, for that matter?'

'If you read the proposal . . .'

'I'd be happy to.' Freddie holds out his hand in readiness.

But Maurice ignores him and turns to the earl: 'All that's left is for Coombe to deliver its part of the capital.'

The earl sighs. 'But we have no capital.'

'But you do!' Maurice brandishes the papers triumphantly. 'Mulligan, tell him . . .'

Mulligan clears his throat nervously. 'It is true that the Honourable Mr Thorneycoombe and the viscount have come up with a way of making this work . . .'

Freddie looks at his father, who has taken the sheaf of papers and is beginning to flick through them. He sighs. 'At least let me have a look,' he says. 'I've had experience of writing a business plan.'

'If it's what Edward wants . . .' says the earl absently, running a finger along a page.

'He might have missed something.'

'It's not your place!' says Maurice briskly.

And Freddie wants to respond, *Nor yours*, but instead he leans both hands on the table and pushes himself to his feet. 'I'd better let you both get on with it, then.'

'Frederick!' His father glances at the land agent. 'You can't walk out halfway through a meeting. Your brother would never behave in such a manner . . .'

'As I've just been reminded, I'm not my brother.'

'Sit down!'

But Freddie steps away from the table and pushes the chair neatly in place. 'Papa, as has always been made clear to me, Coombe is Edward's future. Not mine. I have another path to follow. One of my own design.'

'One funded by Coombe.'

'An advance on what you would have given me anyway

11

when I'm 21. And I will pay you back in spades once the plantation is up and running.'

'That's not what I meant . . .'

Maurice claps his hands together. 'Hush, hush,' he says. 'Emotions are running high. It's understandable. Why don't you let the boy have a break while we go through the details?'

Freddie looks at his father, but the earl is lost in thought, and Freddie knows he will not push for his second son to stay. He slams the door on his way out.

Freddie takes the stairs two at a time. When he reaches the top, he is a little out of breath, partly because of his rage, partly because the staircase is so very long. Rain has started to patter against the large window above the front door. He pauses and looks through it, across the parkland, towards the lakes. There are five in all, each dropping away from the other down the valley, though from here he can see only the top one glittering in the fading light. Once they were a feat of engineering. Now they are neglected and overgrown, havens for the coots and moorhens that hide in the tangles of weeds. Beyond them is the woodland, where Freddie and Edward used to scale the branches in search of birds' eggs. Despair spreads through his body like the fungus that grows where so many of those trees have fallen. He will decay too if he stays any longer.

He continues to his room. He will be on that ship on Friday, no matter what his father says. He crosses to the trunk, flings open the lid. Inside, his clothes are still neatly folded; he has not let Mrs Foley unpack. He moves to the dressing table, leans on it with both hands as he bows his head. Outside, the wind heralds the approach of autumn, making the branches bend and snap, throwing shadows on the windowpanes, distorted by the raindrops. Inside, Freddie allows images of his future to colour the room, imagining the house he will build, the long verandah framed by bright exotic flowers.

He snatches up the brushes and combs and thrusts them into the trunk. He throws the mirror in on top, as well as three boxes of his favourite cufflinks. He starts to rummage through the clothes that are still hanging. He has no idea how to fold them, so he stuffs them in too. He tries to close the lid tight enough that the clasps will snap into place, but the trunk is too full and they will not reach. In frustration he stands on the lid. He hears something snap. He retrieves the broken mirror.

'Well that's seven years of bad luck.' He starts as Ginny appears at the door.

'Can't be any worse than the last seven years,' he says, miserably.

'What are you doing?'

'I'm going.'

'You can't. Not yet.'

He waves his arms in the air. 'Do you know what they're planning? A racecourse! And they think a tea plantation is ludicrous!'

'They don't think it's ludicrous.'

'They don't understand it. Papa's simply relieved I've got somewhere to go that isn't here. Edward teases me, and says it's all very bourgeois. And Maurice can't even get the crop right, let alone the country. I'm not surprised he and Edward have always got on so well. They both believe the world revolves around them, that the rest of us are their playthings, and everyone lets them get away with it.'

'You don't mean that.'

'And that's what's even more unfair: we can't say anything bad about Edward because he's a missing bloody hero.'

'And we love him . . .'

'Sometimes I'm not so sure.'

'Freddie! You adore him. You always did everything to-gether.'

'No. He did everything, and I got the blame. Remember the summer house? How I was banished to the nursery for six weeks, fed bread and water.'

'It was a dangerous thing to do . . .'

13

'I didn't set fire to it. Edward did!'

'Why didn't you say?'

'I did. Nobody listened.'

'You shouldn't dwell on such things. Life is too short.'

'Exactly.' He grabs hold of her arm. 'I'm suffocating. Trapped . . .'

'I know,' she says, looking at him with eyes the same cerulean blue as their brother's and mother's. 'I really do understand. I feel it too. A daughter's not exactly a priority around here.'

He lets go of her, turns away. 'At least you can bugger off and get married. I don't know what they want from me. For nineteen years they've expected me to go. Now they're forcing me to stay.'

'Just a few more weeks, Freddie. Please. For the parents. For me . . . Until we know he's safe.'

14

CHAPTER 3

W eeks turn into months. November brings the news the world has been waiting for: the signing of an armistice, and the church bells, silent for so long, ring out across the village. The notes jar in Freddie's ears, as he waits glumly in the Great Hall, staring at another note from Matthew. His business partner sends regular updates: this time a postcard, with a picture of a line of elephants in a river, natives astride their wide backs, long-stemmed palm trees wavering in the background. 'Bathtime for the elephants from the temple in Kandy,' Matthew has written: 'Can't wait to show you. We see it every week when we drive to the town!'

Freddie folds the card and tucks it into his breast pocket. These frequent telegrams and cards constantly remind him of what he is missing. He walks one length of the Great Hall, tracing with his finger the coats of arms that have been painted on to the panelling. Griffins and feathers, stags and armour that illustrate the Hembury ancestry: unbroken from the thirteenth century to the present day. He turns away, for this is where his own life ends, where the blank panels wait for Edward's wife, and for their children, and their children's children. He flushes with a sudden rush of guilt, for deep down he knows that the probability is that his brother is no longer missing, but dead – and there are further twists to be painted into the Hembury futures – ones that involve him, no matter how much he wishes it was otherwise.

The countess and Ginny appear, their footsteps echoing on

the polished floor, their long skirts rustling like the dead leaves blowing outside the door. Freddie follows them to Maurice's car. The worry about his missing son is eating away at the earl, and he is unable to muster the strength to read a dedication at a service of thanksgiving to the men who left the village to fight; Maurice is happy to stand in his stead.

On the way down the hill to the church, they pass not only the servants, but, it seems, everyone from the surrounding area: grey-haired couples in carts pulled by ragged ponies, wiry men with dogs at their heels, neat women with babies on their hips; they all squeeze against the hedges as Maurice's horn blares. How jealous Freddie is of their simple lives: war is over for the nation, but how much longer must he live in limbo? Why does he feel duty bound to a place that has never wanted him anyway? He should be far away, watching the temple elephants swaying through the river.

The village has been transformed with bunting and banners: red, white and blue garlanding the little cottages. The streets are teeming: tweed-suited farmers rub shoulders with labourers in their Sunday best, youngsters have been scrubbed until their rosy cheeks glow. Sheriff, a Clydesdale once-famed for regularly ploughing the most acres in the parish, is buffed and shining, ribbons in his mane, five small children astride his broad back. In the centre of the village, the church bells still peal in the tower.

Maurice twists in his seat to look at them. 'I know it is difficult to rejoice without news of our boy,' he says, 'but the village needs to see us holding our chins high, celebrating our heroes and the end of this goddamned war.'

In the passenger seat, the countess exhales loudly. She is dressed in purple, rich against skin as pale as ash from a fire that once burned too brightly. She steps from the car, and they follow her through the parting crowd to the gloomy interior of the church and their family pew at the front. Freddie slides along the wooden bench next to his mother. The bells fall silent, and now he can see that so many of the congregation

16

are dressed in mourning that the service could be a funeral. A wheelchair blocks the aisle. The church is cold, the people's breath coming from their mouths like spectres. Freddie shudders, and presses the postcard in his pocket, picturing the bright plantation, warmed by a mellow sun, the neat rows of tea bushes stretching away across the hills.

Afterwards, the family mingles in the churchyard, shaking hands and moving among the villagers, a ritual that Freddie used to enjoy before it became a schedule of loss. He acknowledges the Stonemans who run the bakery, and the blacksmith Alfred Hartnell with his scarred hands. But he also notices the absence of others, the freckled twins who used to scrap in the back pews, the gangly lad who jumped off the boathouse one summer, boys with whom Freddie and Edward swam in the lakes at Coombe or scrumped apples from the surrounding orchards – before childhood became duty.

He is distracted by Dibble, the old gardener, who is saying, 'I hope his lordship is feeling better today. Please tell him our rabbits are growing good and fat on the carrot tops from the walled garden.'

'He will be cheered to hear that,' answers Freddie. 'And you must continue to help yourself. We have no need for them.'

'You're very kind, sir.'

Mrs Arrowsmith bustles forwards: 'And please thank her ladyship for the fruits for the children.'

'You can thank her yourself,' says Freddie, indicating his mother, who is deep in conversation with the blacksmith's wife.

'I wouldn't like to interrupt. The Hartnells are talking of a visit to the battlefields in France. To see where their Bernard fell.'

'Well, you know my mother is always pleased to help. We recognise things must be hard with your husband's injury.'

'We are lucky to have the post office to run.'

Walter Prescott, the wheelwright, steps in as she moves away. 'I believe you'll be hearing from the viscount any day

17

now,' he says. 'You know, we thought we'd lost our Michael, and then he turned up in that prisoner-of-war camp.'

'I trust he is doing better?'

'It is hard to tell some days . . .'

Freddie has seen Michael only once since he returned, when the countess sent him to their cottage with some fresh vegetables and cut flowers. The memory of that man haunted Freddie for days – not much older than Edward, and with a wife and a baby to support – sitting dribbling and speechless like a child himself.

With relief he focuses on a young man with broad shoulders and ruddy cheeks. At last someone he can talk to properly. 'Albert! Have you finished ploughing the long fields beyond Littlecombe yet?'

Albert looks surprised. 'Oh no, sir. I were told to delay.'

'But I thought you were going to try and plant oats there this year?'

'There were talk of us not being able to use that land . . .'

'Why on earth not?'

Albert glances awkwardly at Prescott.

'Not this infernal racecourse?' Albert looks away, embarrassed, and mutters something unintelligible. 'Has my uncle, Lord Thorneycoombe, been talking to you?'

Albert shifts from one foot to the other. Prescott comes to the rescue, speaking bravely into the silence: 'I suppose the young master'll be staying now . . .'

Freddie shakes his head, irked at the avoidance of his questions. 'Oh no. I plan to leave as soon as the viscount is located.'

Their second surreptitious glance, indicating that they are surprised by this, annoys Freddie further: even the villagers have some say in his life, some expectation of how he should behave. It is all so stifling that he feels like throwing his head back and shouting at the top of his lungs.

He feels Ginny's hand on his arm. 'If you want a lift, Uncle Maurice is heading back,' she says.

He touches his hat politely, and leaves.

18

CHAPTER 4

The next day, Maurice insists on a convivial atmosphere at a lunch to celebrate the end of war. Jennings hangs a Union Jack in the hall, wobbling awkwardly as she balances on a chair to reach higher, one swollen ankle dangling. The murmur of guests fills the dining room. Freddie blows smoke into the air, watches it curl and dissipate around the silver jugs and salt cellars, the crystal glasses. The bubbles in the champagne rise relentlessly upwards, miniature fireworks that resemble those still being set off across the country. He wonders if there are celebrations in Ceylon.

Someone laughs, and there is the glug of more wine being poured. Freddie glances around the table. Tom Winterbourne is deep in conversation with Sybil FitzRoy, while his father – Sir Richard – is talking about the return of their other son, a highly decorated officer, with Mrs Dearing. Harriet Grafton is listening to James Euston describe a recent visit from a prominent MP, while Mr Dearing is amusing Tom's mother, Lady Sarah. And presiding over them all is Maurice, as if he has always sat at the head of this table opposite the countess, who is pasty and drawn, but at least present.

'It's so late that we should perhaps be having tea instead of wine, don't you think?' Mrs Dearing chuckles into a lull in the conversation.

Outside the window, dusk is indeed falling, and Jennings begins to tug the curtains closed while Mrs Foley places lit candelabra along the table.

19

'We could offer you all manner of tea: it's Freddie's thing, of course,' says Ginny. 'He's got endless varieties of leaves.'

'I still don't understand, why tea?' asks James. 'I thought they grew coffee over there.'

'They did thirty or forty years ago,' says Freddie, 'but the coffee crops were destroyed by blight, and the growers eventually threw in the towel. Now it's all about tea. Perfect climate for it. There's money in rubber, cinnamon and coconuts too. We've already built accommodation for more than one hundred workers, with enough for another hundred planned.' Freddie enjoys the lightening of his senses as he indulges himself in the detail.

'Golly. It's a big operation . . .'

'It will take a while to develop to the scale we want.'

'We?'

'I've gone in with Matthew Carrington. He's already out there.'

'Wasn't he a friend of Edward's from university?'

Freddie nods curtly. 'His family have an estate just outside Kandy – in the middle of the country. He stayed with us one Christmas rather than going all the way home.' He omits to say that Edward abandoned his serious young friend for the usual Christmas festivities of heavy drinking and hard riding. It had been Freddie's gain: the first time he had met someone who had ideas, plans, a life beyond a British stately home and ornamental gardens – the first inkling that he could shape his own future.

'I remember Matthew,' says Harriet, who is as good as Edward's fiancée. 'Wasn't he a scholar like Edward?'

Freddie laughs sharply. 'Edward was never a scholar!'

Harriet blushes. 'I'm sure he told me . . .'

'I don't think he's ever read anything – unless you count a game card . . .' Freddie pauses as there are chuckles of agreement from around the table.

'I hardly dare ask,' says Sir Richard. 'Any news?'

Freddie shakes his head. He is feeling groggy after the lengthy lunch, and cannot shrug off a mild irritation that another conversation about things that he is interested in has returned to his brother.

Mr Dearing speaks up briskly. 'He'll be holed up somewhere in France,' he says. 'We all know he has a habit of getting out of scrapes intact . . .'

'The ice-well's my favourite one,' says Sybil.

'What? He left me down there for twenty-four hours,' says Freddie, grinding his cigarette into the silver ashtray and replacing the lid. 'I could have died.'

'But you didn't . . .'

'You two were always at loggerheads,' James laughs. 'I've never forgotten that fight at your eighth birthday party. Didn't you stab him with an arrow? He's still got a scar on his palm . . .'

'It was an accident . . .'

'Wasn't it something to do with a pony?'

Freddie flushes: 'Pyramus.'

'I'd forgotten about that scruffy little skewbald,' says Tom. 'You two were made for each other.'

'Edward thought differently. He just had to try and take over . . .'

'That's not fair,' says Lady Hembury.

Freddie can't prevent the old resentments rising. 'You always take his side.' He tries to make his voice light, but he knows it sounds petulant.

'That's enough, old boy,' says his uncle, calmly lighting a cigar, and sucking on it until the tip glows red and orange.

This interference also annoys Freddie more than it should. 'I spoke to the ploughman today,' he retaliates. 'Did you tell him not to plough beyond Littlecombe?'

Maurice leans back and lets the smoke trickle out of his mouth. 'Why do you always seem so disappointed in everything? Can't you lighten up? Be more like your brother . . .'

Freddie feels his cheeks burning. The guests do not know where to look. 'Perhaps I don't want to be like him,' he says. 'Like you . . .'

21

'Freddie!'

But Maurice is nonplussed. 'You can be whoever you want . . .'

Freddie scrapes his chair back. 'I can't. I'm stuck here . . .' His voice is rising.

'Enough!' The command comes from the doorway, where Freddie is surprised to see his father standing, a letter in his hand. The room falls silent, save for the thumping of Freddie's heart.

They are in the earl's study. The guests have slipped away, the guilt bearing down on them as they clambered into their cars and disappeared into the night. Maurice is behind the earl's desk; the earl is in his seat by the fire, his wife standing above him, one hand resting on the back of the armchair, a casual pose except her knuckles are white. She addresses her husband: 'Are you going to read it to us, Richard?'

The earl does not appear to have heard; he just stares at the flames flickering in the grate. Maurice sighs, and moves to pluck the paper from the old man's hand. Too late, Freddie wonders if he should have been the one to take it.

Maurice clears his throat. 'It's a telegram from Buckingham Palace, signed by the Keeper of the Privy Purse.' He smoothes the sheet out. 'The king and queen deeply regret the loss you and the army have sustained by the death of your son in the service of his country. Their majesties truly sympathise with you in your sorrow.'

'They found him?' asks Ginny.

'Not exactly,' says their uncle, scanning another piece of paper. 'Major General Rawlins has written with more details of the battle. It appears it was during the last major offensive, very close to the German line. Edward's battery were keeping up the pressure, bombarding the Hun heavily to sustain momentum. Unfortunately when their gun jammed, the enemy was able to land a blow that took out three quarters of Edward's battery. A second shell landed on the gun, and that took out

22

the rest. The only survivors at the time were Edward and another man, a Private Bolt, who apparently dragged our boy to safety, despite heavy retaliation from the Hun.'

'Safety?' The countess's voice is a whisper.

'Yes. But it seems Edward had sustained such heavy wounds that he died either before the ambulance got to the field hospital or shortly afterwards.'

'Why did they not know this before?'

'It seems they . . . mislaid . . . his body. They have his identity disc, which would have been removed at time of death. But the dear boy must have gone into an unmarked grave. I'm afraid it is common.' He swallows into the silence. 'There's a letter of condolence from the brigade chaplain too.'

The countess draws herself up tall. 'I don't believe it,' she says, and moves to snatch up the letters from Maurice. 'It's a mistake.'

Freddie glances across at his father. The old earl remains motionless.

'It's been months,' says their uncle, 'and no sign of him. We have to face facts.'

The countess's gaze rests briefly on her husband. 'If you hadn't encouraged every man in the house and village . . .'

The earl does not answer, but slowly gets to his feet and starts to make his way to the door, shuffling, as if he has aged another decade in the last few minutes. Freddie feels torn: he wants to defend his father; he wants to comfort his mother. 'You can't blame Papa,' he says, 'Edward was determined . . .'

She whirls to glare at him. 'Your father should have stopped him.'

'Wild horses wouldn't have stopped him.'

'What do you know? You were still at school!'

His father stops in the doorway. Freddie looks from one parent to the other: his father's stooped back, his mother's eyes glimmering like the taxidermy creatures in the library.

'Frederick is right, Katherine.' Maurice speaks quietly, as if he is trying to calm an infant. 'Edward wanted to fight more than anyone I have known. He had a keen sense of duty. He was a credit to you all.'

Lady Hembury covers her mouth with her hand. A tear rolls down Ginny's face and on to the carpet, making a tiny dark stain on the woven silk. The old earl steps into the corridor and disappears.

Freddie cannot make sense of what he feels . . . is this pain for his brother, or for himself, for the life he feels slipping away? He feels a traitor for even wondering.

Maurice sighs. 'I wish that I was wrong, but Mrs Foley informed me two days ago that Cox's had returned Edward's kitbag.'

'Why didn't you tell me?' cries the countess, looking around wildly. 'Where is it?'

'You cannot see it in your state.'

'You can't stop me.'

'For your own sake I can.'

Freddie's stomach turns as he thinks of what that kitbag will contain: Edward's compass and diary, trench maps and boot polish, even his shaving kit. When Harriet's brother's things were returned, his riding breeches were there, still caked in mud and horsehair.

'You are a cruel man,' the countess hisses, leaning across the opposite side of the desk. 'You cannot understand. You've never felt like this about your children. You don't even know half of them.' She seizes the letters from the desk before beginning to back away from Maurice, towards the door.

'Katherine! This is no time for female hysterics. I'll have to call the doctor.'

'My son is still alive,' she hisses. 'I'll prove it somehow.' She waves the papers in the air, then throws them at Maurice. 'The major general said there was one other survivor, this Private Bolt. I'll find him. He's the last link to my boy. He will know where Edward is.'

Maurice tries to grab her, but she sidesteps and runs past him into the hall, Ginny racing after her. Freddie is pinned to the spot, unsure of what to do. He has never seen his mother behave in such a way; her pain is so palpable that it is as if he is suspended in it, like a specimen preserved in a jar.

Maurice sighs and clicks his tongue in disapproval. 'Drink?' he says. But Freddie ignores him, and his uncle too departs, shaking his head, and leaving Freddie alone in the study, surrounded by empty chairs and shadows.

The wind whines in the chimney. Freddie's heartbeat slows and a wave of nausea breaks over him. He steadies himself on the desk. After all these weeks of waiting it is impossible to believe that this is it: Edward will never return. Never run down the stairs, a smile on his face, covered in mud from a day in the saddle. Never slap him on the back when they're winning at doubles, or slam his muddy spurs on the dining-room table. Freddie knows he would put up with always being the one in trouble if only he could see his brother one more time.

He feels a hand on his back. 'Are you all right?' His sister's voice, quiet, concerned.

He nods.

'She's in bed. Hopefully she will sleep once the doctor's been.'

Freddie turns to her: 'Isn't she right? Wouldn't we know if he was dead? Wouldn't we sense it somehow?'

Ginny shakes her head miserably.

He stares down at his hands. 'I feel so guilty for the things I've said, the things I've thought.'

'Don't. He's our big brother. Of course he annoyed us. But nobody's perfect, and we loved him for who he was.'

'I'm not like him. He's a natural leader. People don't follow me . . . I'm not that person.'

'You don't have to become him. Be yourself. You have your own strengths.'

Freddie doesn't sleep. He lies curled on the edge of his bed, staring into the darkness. He is hollow, an empty shell. Matthew's latest telegram sits on the table by the bed. The first tea has been planted, the first workers are installed in their homes. Matthew apologetically asks for the final instalment of money to be sent to the bank in Colombo. Freddie is happy to do it – it is part of their plan, to use his advanced inheritance to build up the business. He knows they will make it back, but he wants to be there to see the bushes growing, to witness the fruits of their labour. If he does not, then what is he? Simply an investor.

Dawn is breaking. He feels as if he is watching himself from a long way away. He sees the trunk on the floor. He sees the room he has slept in all his life. Is he really destined to move only a few doors along to his parents' room? To stare into the mirror in his father's dressing room as he straightens his tie, just as his father and grandfather and great-grandfather did before him?

Freddie stands and crosses to the window. He can just make out the stables, the top lake, the ghostly shapes of the trees in the half-light. He did adore Edward. Of course he did. He remembers the thrill of rising at this hour with his brother to saddle up to go off on some adventure. In the distance he can see the summer house. That was both of them really: Edward struck the match, but Freddie stole the box. Did Edward abandon him in the ice well, or was it a plan they both came up with to frighten the nanny? He will never know for sure, never be able to talk to his brother about it. And now that arrogant, perplexing, idolised older brother is gone. Wiped from the face of the earth, as if he was never there, without any chance to live his life, to have a family of his own, to pass Coombe on to his oldest son. And how could Freddie resent his brother when he is dead, and Freddie is the one who will get to wake every day and see the dawn break across these hills?

Ginny is right. He must step up to the mark; he is the same age as Edward was when he joined up. It is light enough that Freddie can see his faint reflection in the windowpane. He stares at the shadowy figure: I am the Viscount Damerel now, he thinks, whether I like it or not. There is only one way forward: to rise to his family's expectations, and so say goodbye to his dreams of carving out his own life.

Freddie crouches, and starts to unpack his trunk.

CHAPTER 5

Freddie has far more practical ideas than a racecourse to get Coombe back on its feet – he wants to reconfigure some of the farms, the fields, increase crop production. And he plans to have an auction, which so many other families have had success with, including James, whose mother sold all her family jewellery and replaced it with clever imitation. Not that Freddie could imagine his own mother doing such a thing.

The winter darkness begins to recede. Buds appear at the ends of bare branches, and the mean croak of the rooks is replaced by something more hopeful: the smaller birds of woodland and field calling in the spring. The curlews are searching for hiding places on the heathland, and the lapwings with their fine chieftain headdresses are swooping and tumbling through the air.

'I won't hear of it.' Lady Hembury is in the morning room, feigning sewing a tapestry, but instead staring at the oriental wallpaper.

'But the men are here, ready to start cataloguing.' Freddie's voice betrays his exasperation.

'Well tell them to go away. Edward will be distraught to find his home plundered when he returns.'

Freddie clenches his jaw. There is no swaying her from the belief that her oldest son is alive – which must mean she believes Freddie has no purpose. He cannot bear the way she will not catch his eye. He longs for her to take his hand or smile at him the way she smiled at Edward – or even to shout at him, to throw something at him, to tell him she wishes it had been Freddie instead.

He returns to the familiar smell of dusty books and pipe smoke in his father's study. On the desk is a new pile of documents, written in his own hand. He crosses to the armchair, and stands before the earl. 'Mama wants me to send them away.' His father does not answer. In the silence Freddie's frustration begins to dissolve. 'I know she misses him, but even if Edward was still alive he'd need to do something. This auction will just about keep our heads above the water for a few months . . . And then we've got to look at diversifying. Crop prices are high. I still want to try growing oats beyond Littlecombe. The soil is better there. This auction will raise enough for us to buy seed, and to sort out the worst of the cottages. There might even be a bit left over to update the house – install running water upstairs, or electricity in the west wing. Perhaps then there will be time to have a look at Edward's racecourse plan, if you really think there's something in it . . .' He stops to scrutinise his father. Sometimes he is not sure the old man can hear him. 'But for now, I need to issue instructions to the men from Christie's.' Still no response. 'Look. Either you trust me or you don't. I can help get the estate back on its feet. Or I can just go to Ceylon now, and not come back until . . . when . . . when I'm finally needed.'

He stops again, embarrassed to mention something so delicate. But this is what they do: survival of the line is all.

Suddenly his father leans forward, and grasps both of Freddie's hands. He is surprised not only at the physical contact, but at the strength in the knobbly fingers. The earl's eyes are fixed on his, and it strikes Freddie that this is the only time his father has looked at him – really looked at him – since they first heard that Edward was missing. The old man tightens his grip still further. 'I do understand,' he says. 'Whatever you have thought in the past, or you think now or in the future, remember that. I wanted you to have the life you sought. There is freedom in being the second son.

29

There is a freedom those of us who are born first can only dream of.' He sighs and stops, collapsing back with the effort. 'Sell whatever you see fit, but leave Edward's personal effects for your mother.'

Maurice returns from Bristol for the auction, and to discuss their next steps. Freddie is confident that with his new plans for the farms his uncle will see the estate could turn a profit: it will be tight, but he's sure it can work without the need for a racecourse.

It is a grey day. A relentless drizzle spatters against the window panes and pools in the uneven dips in the drive. But the queue of cars stretches to the lane, and the park is dotted with figures shielding off the rain. Ever the jovial host, Maurice stands at the entrance to greet them.

Lady Hembury watches as they drift into the Great Hall, mouths agape, as intent on examining the carvings around the fireplace and the paintings of early Hemburys as the Georgian silver, Venetian glass, Chippendale chairs. 'I can't bear it,' she says. 'It's just a day out for the village. They might as well have laid on a charabanc.' She is dressed in another shade of purple, still refusing to wear any form of mourning, no crêpe, no black jewellery, no armband.

'Why don't you go somewhere else until it's over?' Ginny touches her arm gently.

But the countess cannot tear herself away. She lingers in the shadows, her pale fingers fluttering at her long neck.

Freddie keeps his distance from his mother's disapproval. He is grateful for the company of Tom and Sybil, who are here for the day to lend their support. They too mingle with the crowd, reporting back to each other, trying to find answers about provenance and dates for interested buyers, making it up if they have to.

Freddie does not want to watch when the bidding begins, so they retreat to the dining room, where Mrs Foley has left a cold lunch of game terrine and ham. They help themselves, sitting haphazardly at the table, in the way that close friends do. Maurice and the countess remain in the hall.

'How is your mother?' asks Tom. 'She seems . . .'

'On edge?'

'Very.'

'She spends half her time trying to convince us that Edward's not dead.'

'I fear it's quite common.'

'It's not having a body to bury,' says Sybil. 'It makes it so much more difficult.'

'But everyone's in the same boat. They're all buried abroad.'

'I can't bear to think about it. All those men and boys never returning . . .'

'I think there will be a national memorial built in London.'

Ginny shudders. 'It's too depressing.'

'Have you thought of building a memorial here? A stone for the church in Hembury? It might help.'

'Mama won't allow it. Not while she believes he's alive.' Freddie stubs out his cigarette, putting an end to the conversation. Talking about his brother, and thinking of his mother's recent behaviour, make him uncomfortable.

Ginny gets to her feet. 'Come on,' she says. 'It sounds as if it's finished.'

The crowd has indeed thinned. Many of the items are labelled as sold. Through the open door Freddie can see the damp cars roll back down the drive, sending splashes up from their wheels that spray those on foot. Ginny is talking to the auctioneer. The smaller lots have been scooped up by their new owners and the hall is already emptier. The countess drifts between the spaces, lost in thought.

There is a noise at the door, and a short rotund man clatters in from outside, shaking out his umbrella so that it spills droplets across the stone floor, and over the slight girl with auburn hair who is following him.

Freddie approaches them. 'I'm afraid it's over,' he says, ready to send them packing.

'What?' says the man, whose round belly makes up for his lack of stature. 'Nothing left at all?'

'Well . . . a few things.' Freddie cannot stop his eyes lingering on the girl, who is still wiping the rain from her face. She is fine-boned, delicate, like a bird, but there is also something defiant in the tilt of her chin, and her meeting of his gaze. He looks away; unlike his brother, he has never been good with girls. He finds them confusing, hard to read.

'Would you mind if we had a peep?' says the man, craning his neck to see past Freddie's shoulder. 'We meant to get here earlier, but we seemed to be going against the flow of traffic.'

Freddie finds himself irresistibly drawn back to the girl as she adds, 'We would be very grateful.' There is in her voice a softer hint of Bristol than the man's.

Her grey-blue eyes flash as she smiles, and to his surprise Freddie finds he cannot help smiling back. He has an inexplicable feeling that he wants to know her better. It's not something he's felt before, and it momentarily unsettles him. 'I suppose so . . .' he stutters.

'How kind,' says the man. 'You won't regret it,' he adds, with a knowing wink, which disarms Freddie further.

'Come, Father,' says the girl, and she threads her arm through his as they take a turn around the room.

The countess moves to Freddie's side, bristling with irritation. 'Why didn't you send them away?'

'We might as well sell what we can,' stammers Freddie, 'now that we've got it all here . . .'

He watches the pair of them walk, the way the girl bends slightly to her father, the way her small hand rests gently in the crook of his elbow. He could not imagine walking through a room in such a way with either of his parents.

The man stands back to admire a pair of enormous antique Chinese vases on either side of the fireplace, running a hand around the rims. He raises himself on his tiptoes to squint inside, then around the back. Lady Hembury tenses.

Ginny digs Freddie in the ribs. She knows the vases are not for sale. The man summons the auctioneer. The auctioneer tries to summon Freddie. The countess glares. 'This is the last straw,' she says. 'Tell them to go. Tell them all to go now.'

'I can't do that,' says Freddie.

'Then I will.' Lady Hembury sweeps across the floor. 'Would you mind?' she says imperiously at the man's shoulder.

He turns to face her. 'Aha! Lady Hembury,' he says, his smile breaking into a beam.

'They're not for sale. Please don't touch . . .'

Most people fade away in the presence of the countess, but the girl also seems unperturbed. 'It states in the catalogue that everything in the room is for sale,' she says, holding the booklet aloft. '"Coombe Hall contents",' she reads, '"being a sale of the surplus Hembury family antiques and modern furnishings found in the Great Hall." Surely that includes these vases.'

'I can only repeat that they are not for sale.'

'Then that should have been indicated in the brochure.'

Freddie is transfixed; few people ever stand up to his mother. He watches the colour rise in the countess's cheeks. It is matched by the colour in the girl's.

Meanwhile, the gentleman is still trying to attract the countess's attention, lifting his hat on and off his head. 'Lady Hembury, please allow me to introduce myself . . .'

'I don't want to be introduced to you . . . and certainly not by yourself . . .'

'I'm very sorry but it's simply a misunderstanding.'

'It's not a misunderstanding,' says the girl.

'You must be idiotic if you can't see that these vases are too heavy to be moved . . .'

'Please, ladies,' says the man, this time so loudly that his voice brings everything in the hall to a stop, as both the women turn their furious eyes on him. He clicks his heels together and holds out a hand. 'Delighted to meet you,' he says. 'I'm Joseph Cottam. And this is my daughter, Celia.'

Lady Hembury looks blank.

'We bought Littlecombe Farm. We're your new neighbours . . .'

The countess is not the only person who responds in shock. Freddie's reverie is broken: he had no inkling the farm had been sold; he had his own plans for it. Tom and Sybil look at each other. Even Ginny's mouth falls open. But Joseph Cottam carries on, seemingly oblivious. 'We've been looking forward to meeting you, haven't we, Cee?' The aside causes his daughter simply to raise an eyebrow as she scans the surrounding faces. Her eyes settle on Freddie in a challenge. Even in his confusion, he feels another stab of admiration at her brazenness. Mr Cottam continues to address the countess: 'I'd love to pick your brains, so to speak. We're not exactly country folk like you . . .'

Ginny gives a gulp of laughter as Lady Hembury's eyes widen.

'I mean, two heads, or four heads . . .' his voice begins to peter out '. . . or however many are better than one, eh?'

Lady Hembury glances at Freddie, a frown darkening her features. He feels his own cheeks burning. He wants to say he knows nothing about this, but before he can open his mouth, Maurice strides up to the man. 'Joseph!' he says, turning to bow to the girl. 'And the illustrious Miss Cottam.'

'Maurice. You're right. What a lovely place this is. A real corner of England.' Joseph Cottam regains his enthusiasm.

Maurice beckons to Freddie. There is no apology, only a wide grin. 'Come, nephew: Frederick Thorneycoombe I'd like you to meet Joseph Cottam.'

But the countess lays a hand on Freddie's arm, holding him back. The girl with the auburn hair watches, her anger apparently turned to mild amusement, as Freddie grapples with what to do next. His rage at Maurice is growing, yet he doesn't want to appear an oaf in front of this girl.

'What is he talking about?' says the countess with icy calm.

'I'm sure it's a mistake,' is all Freddie can think to say.

'There's no mistake,' says Maurice. 'Mr Cottam has bought Littlecombe and has great plans for it.'

'I'd like to think so.' Joseph Cottam pats his belly. 'But I'm a fish out of water at the moment . . .'

Freddie feels sick. Everyone is watching them: the auctioneers, their staff, the servants, the stragglers.

'But . . .'

'We'll discuss it later,' says Maurice. 'For now, I think you should go and pour your friends a drink and toast a successful day. You've done very well. Now off you trot.' He puts his arm around Mr Cottam's shoulder and they move through the room, the daughter alongside.

At last Freddie comes to his senses. 'I'll kill him,' he seethes.

'Not if I get there first,' says his mother.

'Feel free to do that later,' hisses Ginny. 'Just not now. Please.'

It takes all of Freddie's self-control not to shake her off as she steers him and their mother from the room.

Freddie waits at the window in the study, watching dusk fall over the park. He focuses on the rain dripping down the glass on the outside of the pane; it sparkles as it catches the warm glow from the electric lights inside. His father sits in his chair, staring at the newly stoked fire. Freddie knows that it won't be long until Maurice arrives in the study, the cuckoo in the nest.

Sure enough, the door opens and his unrepentant uncle appears. Freddie stands, placing his hands firmly on the desk. His uncle hovers for the briefest second, then crosses the room to pour himself a drink.

'How could you?' Freddie blurts out.

'We need capital – we all agree on that,' says Maurice. 'I told you it was in hand. Cottam was so desperate to buy a house in the country that he paid well over the odds. He's got more money than sense. Thinks a little estate will give him a bit of class.' Maurice rolls his eyes and laughs.

'How much land did you sell with it?'

'A few acres.'

Freddie raises his voice. 'How much?'

'Three hundred acres.'

Freddie gasps. 'That's almost a third of everything!'

'Don't be overdramatic.'

'Overdramatic? You do realise that the land around Little-combe is some of the most fertile we have? I'll bring in a lawyer. Stop the sale.'

'You can't. It's too late.'

'But I am the rightful heir now.'

'Yes. But your father is the current earl, and his signature is on the documents.'

Freddie runs his hands over his face. 'You just don't understand what you've done . . .'

'I do understand that you won't need to farm when the racecourse is up and running.'

Freddie runs his hands through his hair, and gives a bitter laugh. 'Ah yes. The racecourse. Have you even read the proposal? It places the course mainly on Hampden's side of the lane, with him owning more acreage, and therefore firmly in control.'

'Do I need to remind you that it was something that Edward was planning for the future of this place? He had ideas far beyond the odd little jumble sale.'

'What care you of the future of Coombe?' says Lady Hembury from the doorway, where she has appeared with her daughter. 'No doubt you're looking to pay off more debts.'

'You do me a grave dishonour, Katherine. I stand to gain nothing from the sale. I love this place as I love myself. You forget that I grew up here.'

'As did I . . .' says Freddie.

'That may be, but . . . well . . . Come on, Freddie . . . You've always been . . .'

'What?'

Maurice laughs self-consciously as he looks at the others in the room. 'Let's just say you've never shown a desire to be involved.'

'Because there was no role for me here' – Freddie glances hesitantly at his father – 'until now.'

His uncle snorts derisively. 'Learning to run a place like Coombe takes a lifetime. Your brother spent years being groomed for this role. It was his life, his future, and he was the kind of man who took it in his stride, yet even so was prepared to give it all up to fight for king and country. And all we hear from you is how imperative it is that you get away to inspect some coffee plants . . .'

Freddie grits his teeth. 'If I've learnt anything in the last few months, it's that communication abroad is becoming easier. I can help run the plantation from here. And if I have to visit for a few weeks a year, then so be it.'

'But do you even like it here?'

'Yes,' he says quietly. 'I just never thought I would end up staying.'

'You'd better be damned sure, because it will consume you as it consumed your father . . .'

They all turn to look at the earl, who clears his throat as he pushes himself upright in his armchair. 'Maurice was right to suggest selling Littlecombe,' he says.

Freddie crouches down by him. 'Why do you say that?'

The old earl gazes at him with watery eyes. 'I thought it might buy you some time to follow your dream . . .'

'I don't understand.'

The earl sighs deeply. 'None of you knows how very dire the situation is . . . apart from Katherine, of course . . .' The countess crosses the room so that she can lay a hand of support on the old man's shoulder.

Everyone is quiet now, straining to hear what the earl is saying. He addresses his brother: 'It seems that dum-dum bullet I took at Spion Kop has been working hard to finish me off.'

Ginny and Freddie exchange glances, while their mother fiddles with her engagement ring.

'But that was years ago,' splutters Maurice. 'I know it caused abdominal damage, but you've always said it was nothing worse than an inconvenience.'

'It was. But now the doctors believe the poison from the shrapnel's spread around my body. The prognosis isn't good. I'm afraid I'm dying . . . and with Edward gone too, you really will have a fight on your hands.'

Maurice seems too shocked to speak, lost for words for the first time Freddie can recall. Ginny kneels next to her brother on the floor at their father's feet. 'How . . . how long?' she asks.

'It is impossible to say. Some days I feel stronger than others.' He takes hold of his children's hands, but he addresses Freddie: 'I am sorry I have been so distracted. I do not know what else the world will throw at us, but what is of no doubt is that you are going to have to bear its weight on your shoulders. There are so many people relying on you: your mother, your sister, the staff, the village . . . And you will all need to work together if Coombe is to survive.'

CHAPTER 6

Celia has finished her final rounds. She is going to collect her coat and bag, so that she can meet her father at the entrance of the hospital. He always insists on walking her home after a late shift, despite her protestations that she is capable of doing it alone – especially now that blackouts are no longer in operation.

The hospital has that soporific evening feel. On this ward in particular, where the most neurologically damaged of the men stay, it is such a contrast to the bursts of noise and uncontrollable movements that mark the daytime.

The lights in the corridor are dim, and the rooms are dark – all except for Major Lewis's. He has been restless these last few days, perhaps ahead of his wife's long-anticipated first visit. Celia stops outside his door, where a sliver of light spills over the threshold. She knows she is not meant to go in alone, but she always enjoys their conversations, and he is only weeks away from being discharged. What harm can it do to pop in and encourage him to bed?

A night porter turns into the corridor, stopping when he reaches her. 'Do you need any help, Miss?' he asks.

She shakes her head. 'I'm just going to remind the major that it's lights out.'

'Probably best if I do that.'

The insinuation that she's not capable rankles Celia. She's worked here for two years; she may be a volunteer, but she's

39

as experienced as most of the nurses. Besides, the porters can be indelicate; they are not always aware of the subtleties required with different patients.

'Thank you, but the major is particular about who visits him. It'll just take a moment.' Still, the man lingers. 'There's no need to wait,' says Celia briskly. 'I'm sure you've got plenty to be getting on with.'

The man nods curtly before moving on.

Celia waits for his shoes to squeak away to silence, and then knocks lightly as she enters.

The major seems peaceful, writing by the light of the lamp. At the click of the door, he looks up, snapping his diary shut. His eyes seem to glitter, for a moment she fancies with tears.

'How are you this evening, Major?' she asks.

He smiles stiffly, as if having to force his lips into a crescent. 'Jonathan, please,' he says.

She acknowledges the familiarity with a brief nod, and goes to turn down his bed. 'You must get some rest before tomorrow,' she says. 'Your wife . . .'

He is suddenly agitated, picking at his fingernails. 'She shouldn't see me like this. I'm not ready . . .'

Celia holds up a hand to stop him. 'You are so much better. And she has been looking forward to seeing you for weeks. I should know. I've spoken to her enough times.'

He shuts his mouth and blinks at her. He is a handsome young man – only a couple of years older than she is at twenty-two – and certainly younger than most of the other men of his rank that are here. She does not want to dwell on why he rose so quickly or the things that he must have seen on the way up.

'Now come on.' She indicates the bed. He is almost childlike in his dressing gown and pyjamas.

'You're very severe this evening.'

She frowns. His voice has taken on a strange tone, almost mocking. 'I think it would be prudent to get some sleep,' she replies, taking a step backwards.

'Won't you tuck me in?'

A shiver of discomfort rolls up her spine, but she doesn't want to offend him. 'Goodnight, Major Lewis.' She smiles politely, her hand on the open door.

He is across the room and gripping her arms so quickly that she does not even have time to cry out. His breath is hot on her cheek: 'I did say, call me Jonathan . . .'

She tries to twist away. She can feel every muscle in his body rigid against hers. She wants to scream, but no sound comes out. He pulls her from the door, managing to close it at the same time. She tries to grapple for the handle, but he is far stronger. He pins her against the wall with one arm while undoing his dressing gown cord with the other. Stupid, stupid girl, she thinks. Why didn't she listen to the porter? Why doesn't she behave more like she's supposed to?

'Come now.' His words are muffled in her neck. She pushes back, but that only seems to excite him. 'Admit it. We've grown close.' He is fumbling at her skirts, his fingers probing, his breath coming short and fast. Did she encourage him? He uses one hand to try to wrench her face around, so he can kiss her mouth, and as he relinquishes his grip to find a better one, she gasps for air, and her lungs fill with oxygen, and she may be small but she strikes and catches him with her nails. It only makes him bark with laughter, 'You wildcat!'

But she is not finished. The adrenaline gives her strength: her knee makes contact, and this time he shouts with pain and anger. In the moment that he pulls away, she scrabbles for the door, but he has her again, and he drags her towards the bed. 'You whore! You bitch!' And now the fear is pumping so fast around her body that she goes limp and barely registers her skirt is up around her waist and he is thrusting himself against her, and her head bangs against the metal foot of the bed and then just as suddenly he is receding, struggling against the larger hands of the porter she spoke to only moments ago, and she is lying there half-naked and frightened and utterly ashamed, for he can see her exposed undergarments – her exposed flesh – and she knows it is her fault; and she knows he will think the same.

Celia does not remember the walk to Dr Hayne's office, but she must have done it, for here she is, staring at an untouched mug of milky tea. She sits on her shaking hands, takes deep, slow breaths to calm herself. Every time she looks at her lap, she sees her clothes rumpled and torn, and her cheeks flood with colour.

'I shouldn't have gone in there on my own,' she says.

Dr Hayne shifts awkwardly in his seat. 'No point in apportioning blame,' he says. 'We must make sure you are all right.'

'I'm a little shocked. But I'll be fine tomorrow.'

'Your father . . .'

She groans inwardly. 'He does not need to be involved.'

But it is too late. She hears the familiar rushed step of her father in the corridor, his voice as he greets someone outside. The porter. She buries her face in her hands. How will she face him again?

Joseph Cottam bursts into the room, rushing straight to Celia. She shrinks from his touch. Her body is sore, and the noise and energy emanating from his seem to batter her own.

He lets his hand fall, retreats a step. 'The porter said there'd been an incident—'

'Don't fuss. I'm fine. Honestly. He didn't—'

Dr Hayne coughs gently. 'I believe she is shaken, but . . . er . . . intact.'

Joseph Cottam narrows his eyes at the doctor. 'How could you allow her—'

'He didn't . . .'

He turns back to her. 'You must come to Devon with us tomorrow. To Littlecombe. To recover.'

'A splendid idea,' says the doctor.

'I'm not going anywhere.' Celia tries to beat back the memory of a hand crushing her face. 'I can't leave the men.'

She jumps as there is another commotion in the corridor. Then they are all on their feet. The sound of men shouting, heavy footsteps hurtling past. Celia's heart starts to race, her palms grow clammy. The door bursts open. 'Doctor, quickly.' Somewhere there is a bell ringing, and Celia feels the ground sway. She steadies herself against her father.

The doctor runs from the room. She wants to follow, but her father holds her back. His hands burn against the bruises from the major's grip.

An hour passes as they wait for Dr Hayne's return. Her eyelids droop. It is late, and she is bone-tired. The rush of adrenaline has sapped her energy.

'Come. Let me take you home,' he says.

'I must wait for Dr Hayne. I need to show him I'm able to return tomorrow.'

'You can't! I forbid it.'

But she knows she must. If she admits defeat now, it will be all the harder to come back in the future. 'You would never do that.'

He sighs. 'Just take a few days off. Come and help your mother settle in the countryside. I have such high hopes for it all. That fresh air. The peace and quiet.'

She wants to tell him not to rest too much hope on it. She knows how ill her mother has been. But she does not have the strength for that now.

The doctor reappears, his face is ashen, his glasses askew.

Celia grips her father's hand, for there is something alarming in the doctor's manner.

'It's Major Lewis,' he says. And for the first time since it happened, he looks Celia in the eye. 'He's dead.'

CHAPTER 7

The drive to the hall is long, winding between estate parkland dotted with large trees and wandering deer. Celia rests her forehead against the car window. Away to the right, in the distance, the village of Hembury is nestled in the valley, a scattering of thatched cottages clustered around the church spire. It is a bucolic scene, like the pictures they had on the walls of the War Hospital. How she wishes she could travel back in time, to before it happened, instead of stuck in this rural backwater, where time seems to have stood still, and feudal lords continue to rule over their peasantry. She cannot believe they have been summoned to tea by their neighbours – still less that her mother has accepted. Six months they have lived here, and this is their first contact!

The car pulls to a halt in the shadow of the house. Their chauffeur, Watts, who came with them from Bristol, opens the doors. Celia climbs out, offering her arm to her mother, who leans on it heavily. A dour-looking old maid appears at the top of the steps to show them in. Even the staff look down their noses at everybody else.

They enter through the vast front door, just as Celia did with her father at the auction almost a year ago. Her heart yearns again for the past, for the person she was. Sometimes her current mood swings exhaust her. As she steps over the threshold into the entrance hall, Celia shivers: despite the sunshine outside, inside it is cold as a grave. They follow the maid through the Great Hall – empty now, which makes the space seem even bigger – and then along one corridor, and then another one, and another, through passages with no defining features, apart from a musty smell and a gloomy ambience. They move slowly, for Mrs Cottam struggles to keep up.

At last the maid steps aside to announce them into another expansive room. Celia blinks in the light that streams through the windows. Dust dances in the rays beneath an ornate ceiling. Her eyes are drawn to an arrangement of sofas and armchairs around a large bare fireplace, where a pair of women are seated, one of whom now moves forward to greet them. The other remains motionless.

As she draws nearer, Celia sees the girl is her age, though significantly taller and broader. Her hair is dark, but her twinkling eyes are the same blue as the wildflowers that dot the hedges in the lanes, and she seems to glow with vitality. She grins as she holds out her hand. 'Celia? I remember you from the auction.'

Celia blushes. She is no longer that pluckier version of herself.

'I'm Virginia Thorneycoombe. Commonly known as Ginny.'

'Pleased to meet you,' says Celia, her voice sounding loud in her ears.

Ginny makes her introductions to Celia's mother, as she encourages them both towards the fireplace. 'How are you finding Littlecombe? I can't believe we haven't got to know each other yet. But you must have been busy . . . it was almost a wreck . . . Did you know the last tenant we had allowed his livestock to live in it? Cows and sheep wandering willy-nilly through the rooms. Can you imagine? We had to kick him out . . .'

They have reached the large sofa, and the stiff figure perched at one end of it. 'My mother, Katherine Hembury,' says Ginny. The countess's head nods almost imperceptibly, an acknowledgement more than a greeting. For a moment Celia fears her mother might curtsey, but instead Margaret Cottam steadies herself against the back of a chair as she finds a place to sit. The countess remains rigid as her eyes follow her new neighbours. Celia feels defensive about their last meeting, wonders whether the older woman holds a grudge, but the countess is impossible to read.

The two older women enter into small talk, about the weather and the local topography.

Ginny leans towards Celia: 'And what about you?' she says. 'Are you finding it very different to the city?'

'Very,' she says.

'I'm sure you'll grow to love it as much as we do . . .'

'Actually, I'm planning on returning to Bristol as soon as possible . . .'

'You're not staying? Why not?'

'I'm going back to work—'

Lady Hembury turns abruptly. 'Work?' she says. 'How unique.'

'She's certainly that,' says Margaret Cottam proudly.

The countess twitches. 'I can't get used to this new generation of women.'

'They are no different to how we were . . .'

The countess raises an eyebrow. 'And what is it that you do, Miss Cottam?'

'I was a VAD at the war hospital for two years . . .'

'Admirable. And now that war is over they have no need for you?'

Celia glances at her mother. 'It's complicated,' she says.

'It's not really,' says her mother swiftly. 'She needed a break. It is a taxing environment.'

Celia knows her mother won't go into details, but she also knows her mother is keen to open up, hoping that it will create a web of friendship. She listens as Mrs Cottam talks proudly about Celia's work, their breakthroughs in the treatment of men returning from the Front with unaccountable ailments, their behaviour – often irrational, sometimes peculiar, even dangerous . . .

The countess watches Celia with eyes that give nothing

46

away – not surprise, or disgust, not interest or boredom. It makes Celia uncomfortable. She is sure the countess is filled with disdain, but she hides it well. It is probably something they teach in finishing school. Talk of her past work makes Celia impatient, but she has been unable to elicit a response from Dr Hayne, and she has been rejected by every other institute she has applied to. She has heard that many women are struggling to continue with work they did during the war, but she cannot help worrying that the rumours of her own personal circumstance have spread beyond the hospital – that her lack of judgement led to her near-violation . . . and far worse. A familiar melancholy settles in the pit of her stomach.

'I'm afraid no good comes of women trying to do men's work,' she hears the countess say. 'It always ends in tears.'

A terrible thought strikes her: does the countess know? Has news of her transgression spread this far?

Celia feels her cheeks burn as her mother mounts a defence of working women. She glances at Ginny Thorneycoombe, who is looking at her with compassion. Her chest tightens. She doesn't need a rich girl's pity. She stands abruptly, and the room spins.

'Are you all right?' Ginny rises too, concerned.

Celia nods. 'I need fresh air . . .'

'Let me show you—'

'No. I'd rather be alone.' She sees the hurt written plainly across Ginny's face, but she can't help it.

'You'll find the quickest way is through the ballroom,' says Ginny. 'Go down the hall the way you came in, but take the first left, and then the first door on the left. The French windows will be open . . .'

Celia swiftly excuses herself. The house is like her nightmares: long corridors leading to dead ends. She tries the first door on the left, and is sickened as hot air and the smell of pipe tobacco hit her face. She can see the tips of someone's cotton-white hair sticking above the back of an armchair. She reverses and stumbles on, along another hallway. She

47

opens another door, and this time finds herself in another vast, empty room, with a piano in one corner, and – to her relief – large windows opening up to the outside.

On the terrace, she realises she is no longer at the front of the house, but at the back, and the car is nowhere to be seen. She hurries on, down the steps, towards an overgrown yew hedge . . . anywhere to be out of sight of the large windows. She slows as she enters the garden, and lets the sounds of the outdoors fill her ears – the birdsong and the buzzing of insects – pushing her way onward until she finds herself standing by a large, round pond. Statues peer at her in stony silence from among the scraggy hedge. There is a lichen-patterned bench, and she sits and watches pond skaters glide between the white clouds reflected in the water.

'Miss Cottam! What a pleasure!' She jumps up, heart racing again. She recognises Maurice Thorneycoombe, who owns the land that her father's colliery stood on; Ginny's uncle who told them of Littlecombe. He steps closer, hand outstretched. There is something about him that sets her on guard, though she feels the same about being alone with all men now. She wishes it wasn't such a visceral reaction; it is impossible to trust her instincts any more. Everything is tangled up: a fear of giving a wrong impression, of making a wrong decision. Is it her imagination that he holds her hand for a few seconds longer than he should?

He sits down on the bench, and pats the seat next to him. 'Come, come,' he says. 'Let us get to know each other better.'

Celia suddenly feels very alone, out of sight of the house, and probably beyond calling distance of anyone. She backs away.

'My dear, what's wrong?' Maurice is on his feet again, and moving towards her. 'Do sit down. You're white as a sheet . . .'

She doesn't want to cause a scene, but must he really stand so close? And his voice, with its upper-class edge of assumed authority, just like Major Lewis's . . . Maurice licks his lips, and Celia is overwhelmed with the urge to flee. She starts to walk as fast as her legs will carry her, in the direction of the house, but the yew hedge suddenly seems to press in on all sides, and she realises she is in an overgrown maze, and Maurice Thorneycoombe is hurrying along after her, and she keeps expecting to feel his hand grip her arm at any moment, and she has no idea which way to go.

She stumbles into an opening, and he brushes against her as she comes to a stop. She is trapped.

'What's going on here? Uncle, really . . . Give her some space.' Another voice, loud and firm, as a young man steps into the clearing. She recognises him immediately: Ginny's brother, Frederick Thorneycoombe, with his unsettling grey eyes that seem to dig into her soul.

'I'm escorting young Miss Cottam here back to the house. She appears to have had a funny turn.'

Frederick Thorneycoombe glances at Celia, and she knows he can read the fear in her eyes. She feels foolish, for Maurice has not behaved inappropriately, but she is relieved to hear Freddie say, 'I'd be happy to take her from here.'

'But—'

'Uncle, please. We're meant to be building bridges, not burning them.'

Maurice mutters. 'You young . . . too forceful. Good day, Miss Cottam.' And he disappears off towards the house, which Celia can now see is closer than she realised.

Freddie turns to Celia. 'Are you quite well, Miss Cottam?'

'Yes, thank you.' She has had time to regain her composure and is glad her voice does not quaver.

'Your hair . . .' He points and she lifts her hands; the hair that was loose before has come out and tumbled over her shoulders. His grey eyes are concerned. 'I hope my uncle . . . ?'

'Oh no . . . It was already coming out . . .'

They walk together towards the house. He keeps his distance, seemingly lost in thought, and she takes comfort in his

49

apparent disinterest. She sees that no harm will come to her, and berates herself for being so weak. She needs to get a hold of herself, or she will never be able to go back.

Ginny appears from behind a hedge. 'There you are! Goodness, what have you been doing? You look as though you've seen a ghost.'

'Uncle Maurice was in the garden,' says her brother.

Ginny rolls her eyes. 'Worse than a ghost. I hope he didn't upset you? He can seem quite a bully, but he's really rather harmless. It's all bluster.'

'I'm fine, honestly. I don't need looking after.'

'But I forgot you already know him, of course! And I forgot to introduce you two! Celia, this is my brother Freddie, and Freddie, this is Celia, whose father bought Littlecombe.'

'Yes, I know.' The change in Freddie is instantaneous, a darkness that creases from his forehead and into his eyes. He starts to walk away.

'Aren't you going to stay and talk?' Ginny calls after him.

'I have more important things to attend to than afternoon tea.' He scowls over his shoulder before disappearing.

Ginny grabs Celia's hand. 'Apologies. Freddie's been having a tough time lately, but it's no excuse for such rudeness.'

Rather than taking umbrage, Celia finds she is sorry to see Freddie go. But she is impelled to lighten the situation, especially as Ginny look so cross. 'We can't be held responsible for our brothers' behaviour,' she forces a small smile. 'Mine can be just as bad . . .'

Ginny tugs her on to the front of the house, arm entwined. 'You'll have to come and meet Fred properly. He's not that awful once you get to know him, and I'd love you to visit again soon. I'm desperate for some female company. Any company . . .'

Celia detects something unhappy in her voice. 'I'm sure—'

'How about tomorrow? Say you will? Please?' Ginny gathers herself, and her eagerness is hard to resist.

'Yes,' Celia laughs, feeling the tension drain at last from her body. 'All right. Tomorrow.'

They have reached the front drive. 'It's all arranged, then. We'll go for a ride. See you at ten.'

Celia wants to tell her that she can't ride. Has never sat on a horse in her life – but Ginny is already yelling at the dogs, and there is her mother, waiting for her in the car.

CHAPTER 8

Celia cannot get used to Littlecombe, with its square, functional furniture, and art deco design, in the same way that she cannot get used to the countryside. She misses their Georgian house in Clifton, elegant and homely, the motor cars and carts rolling by, people's hats, faces, bobbing past the window, the noise and chatter of the city.

Dr Rogers arrives punctually, and is brought to the bright living room that overlooks the garden. In his plain, dark suit, his pallid face hidden behind thick-rimmed spectacles, he is so different to her exuberant father, with his lightly oiled moustache, his bald head shining almost as brightly as the waistcoat stretched across his round belly.

The doctor greets Celia with a bow. 'Radiant as ever,' he says. 'Everyone at the hospital sends you greetings.' He does not meet her eyes at this last comment. Instead, he settles himself on the sofa next to Mrs Cottam, reaching out to take the frail wrist, checking her pulse against his pocket watch.

Joseph Cottam fusses around the room. 'I had her chair put here especially,' he says, running a hand along the comfy armchair with its pile of cushions. 'She loves to sit in it, with the windows open. Plenty of fresh air blowing in.' He indicates a table with small drawers, starts pulling them in and out. 'There's room for her art paper and sewing. A compartment for paints and pens . . .'

Mrs Cottam raises a hand. 'I think the doctor has more

important things to do than discuss my chair, however perfect it is. Celia, take your father outside while Dr Rogers finishes his examination.'

Celia and her father stand in the sunshine, listening to the soft rustle of leaves in the trees. Joseph Cottam has transformed Littlecombe to a new glory, employing the best architect and interior designer to reinvent the fifteenth-century farmhouse. All trace of the wreck that they bought has disappeared. The crumbling walls have been rebuilt in chert, the flint-like local stone. The rotten thatch has been removed, and a new roof of slate has been brought up from Delabole.

Celia winds her arm through her father's as they take in the view: an Arcadian vista of fields rolling down into a goyle. She had not known there were so many shades of green: the lush pale fields, the chiaroscuro of the hills, the darkness of the woodlands.

'Beautiful, isn't it?' says her father. 'Our very own slice of England.'

'Yes, but what are you going to do with it?'

He pats her hand. 'What are *we* going to do? I want us all to be involved. I shall call a family meeting to discuss it.'

'You know I have my own vocation. And George won't come. He disapproves of you buying Littlecombe.'

'He is wrong to think that those who work hard cannot enjoy the fruits of their labour. Besides, your mother's health is more important to me than anything.'

'Don't you miss Bristol?'

'I'm glad we got out when we did. Mining in the city is all but over. The last collieries will close soon, and then I fear there will be much unrest – and it won't be only Bristol that suffers.'

In the distance a sheep bleats. The black pits of industry seem a world away.

'Well, I'm looking forward to going back,' says Celia, with what she hopes is conviction.

Her father sets his jaw. 'Your mother said you had a turn yesterday.'

'I just needed some air. It was horrible in that house.'

'And you are sure it has to be the war hospital?'

'I like working with Dr Hayne. He knows what I am capable of . . .'

'I still believe they were negligent.'

She sighs. 'Father, Major Lewis was ill. Very ill. He didn't know what he was doing.'

'They shouldn't have left you alone with him.'

'They didn't. That was my fault.'

He squeezes her hand. 'None of it was your fault.'

She squeezes back, but does not answer.

'You know I will always worry about you,' he adds, 'but I will never stand in your way.'

They return to the living room. Mrs Cottam has moved back to her chair, and is dozing peacefully. Dr Rogers joins them at the window. 'She'll be lucky to make another year,' he says.

Her father frowns, and seems to shrink a little. 'But you said the fresh air would do her good.'

'And it will, as much as it can. Her windpipe was severely damaged by the force feeding, not to mention the mental scars she bears in relation to food. Her liver is not functioning properly. I believe her heart is also weakened; her blood pressure is extremely low.'

Celia tries to think of her mother as a patient, not a parent: 'She is very thin and her bones are brittle too – the wrist fracture at Easter took a while to heal. She's struggled to eat ever since prison. The smell of bread and milk still makes her retch.'

Dr Rogers nods. 'You know better than many how fragile the nervous system is.'

Celia glances at her father. He turns away, straightens his waistcoat, goes to adjust his wife's cushions.

Celia turns back to the doctor. 'And Dr Hayne?' she says. 'How is he?'

'He still talks about you. You were one of his protégées.'

'That's good to hear.' She takes a deep breath. 'Because I've been trying to contact him.'

Dr Rogers starts to pack his things into his Gladstone bag rather too quickly. 'You know how busy the department is. Your position had to be filled quickly. But there are other places?'

'I've tried everywhere.'

The doctor stops. 'Look, it seems very nice here. If I were you, I would make the most of it. Settle down and put the past behind you.'

Celia reddens. 'You're not me,' she snaps. She hates to think of them all knowing, discussing her like they discuss their patients. She wonders what they say. She has a flash of memory of the porter pulling the major free; her body laid bare. She feels her cheeks burn even more. She wants the chance to restore her reputation, but maybe it's too late and one mistake will colour her future.

Dr Rogers picks up the bag and clutches it to his chest. Celia takes up the letter she has left on the side table. 'Could I ask you to give this to Alan, please? Directly into his hands?' She smiles in what she hopes is a winning way, and thrusts the letter into his unwilling fingers.

Mrs Cottam murmurs. Mr Cottam is already at her side. She waves him away. 'Won't Dr Rogers be late for his train?' she asks.

The men take their leave, and Celia drags the card table and a chair over to her mother, running her hand over the green baize before dealing their hands. A faint, warm breeze carries the scent of spring through the open French windows. Her mother catches her breath. 'Shall I close it?' Celia asks.

'No, no. It's only a flutter.'

Celia frowns. Her mother often suffers palpitations, but they are becoming more frequent. 'Really. I'm all right. I'm more

55

worried about you. But I am so proud of you for not giving up.' She clutches Celia's hand, and Celia tries to remain composed, for part of her wants to give up, to hide here for ever. But she knows she must go back or she will never regain control over her life.

Her mother reaches out to tuck a loose strand of hair behind her daughter's ear. 'Now what did you think of our neighbours yesterday?'

Celia pulls a face, relieved to move on from the subject of her mess of a life. 'We are not suited in class or temperament. Like Maurice, the countess displays every bit of the false charm I expect from the aristocracy—'

'But the children?'

Celia hesitates as Freddie immediately springs into her mind. She has to admit he didn't seem false. But then, he didn't go out of his way to be charming . . .

'The daughter seemed nice,' says her mother.

'I hope so. I've agreed to spend time with her.' Celia groans as she glances at the clock on the mantelpiece, sees it is almost ten. 'I'd better leave!'

This time Celia walks to Coombe Hall. She stops for a moment to investigate the dilapidated lodge house by the gates on the lane, the ivy swarming across its walls, and creeping in through the broken windows, the brambles scratching at the door. She knows that many of these old families have had to sell parts of their estates to survive. It is a good thing: it is unfair for such a small percentage of the population to own so much of this island.

She continues on through the park, past the oak trees and the nearest lake, towards the enormous house. She thinks of Maurice Thorneycoombe and shudders. The drive suddenly seems extremely long. She steels herself. She must be strong: she will need to be close to her patients again one day, the majority of them men. Her mind drifts to the hospital. She does not need to read the poems that are being published to

56

know what lies beneath the public veneer. She has seen first-hand the damage, the twitching and grimacing, heard the nightmares, the screams.

Somewhere dogs are barking, and she spots their small shapes streaking across the lawn towards her, past a pony that glances up for a moment before resuming its lazy grazing. It appears to have cloths tied around its feet, but she is distracted by the terriers sniffing the hem of her skirt and chasing each other around her feet.

Ginny is waving from the front door, flanked by a pair of lithe greyhounds. 'I thought you weren't going to come,' she calls as she bounds down the steps. 'Welcome!'

They skirt the house. Ginny points out the rooms that they pass: study, drawing room, library, music room, ballroom. It goes on for ever. She points at the pony too. 'Our lawnmower,' she says. 'In lieu of an under-gardener. He has to wear socks so he doesn't mark the lawn.'

Finally they enter the stable yard via an arch. The clock in the tower chimes ten, sending up a flurry of white doves that flutter in the air before landing on the roof. 'It's never on time,' says Ginny, showing Celia into the tack room, which is lined with the trappings of horses: work and carriage harnesses, all manner of saddles and bridles hanging beneath oil paintings of horses that would not look out of place in an art gallery. There are shelves and cabinets lined with silver cups and plates, and rosettes wedged in various spaces. Everything is covered in a thick layer of dust.

'Those are mainly Edward's,' says Ginny, when she sees Celia examining the prizes with the most recent dates: 1912, 1913. 'He was our older brother. He didn't come back . . .' Her face clouds over. She starts to rifle through a cupboard in the corner. 'We'll have to find you something to wear,' she says. 'You can't ride in that.' She points at Celia's long skirt.

'Actually, I can't ride at all,' Celia answers.

Ginny looks at her, astonished. 'I thought everyone could ride.'

'There's not much call for it in Bristol.'

'We'd better teach you, then. Otherwise you'll be stuck.' Ginny holds pairs of breeches against Celia until she settles on one. 'There you go. These were Freddie's when he was about ten.'

There is no getting out of it. Celia clambers into the new clothes while Ginny stands guard at the door. 'Perfect fit,' says Ginny, looking her up and down. 'Lucky you're so minute.'

'Meet Aztec,' says Ginny, as Celia looks nervously up at the towering horse. 'He's part Clydesdale. He's an absolute honey. Perfect for a novice.'

Celia approaches the mounting block, her heart in her mouth; the horse is a mountain, with hooves like dinner plates, but it seems placid enough. She reaches out to grab hold of its mane. 'Go on. Left foot,' says Ginny. 'You'll be fine.'

Celia tentatively reaches out, and the horse shifts. She lets go and steps back, stomach lurching. She feels a hand gently support her arm as she regains her balance. The shock of the touch makes her flinch, and she turns to see Freddie Thorneycoombe's grey eyes looking back. He frowns, before saying, 'How do you do, Miss Cottam?' He moves away, giving her space. 'Fetching breeches,' he adds, and as he smiles his face opens up. 'They certainly suit you better than me.'

'Now, my sister may have a heart of gold, but she's a hopeless teacher,' says Freddie. 'You need to take a firm grip on the saddle. There.' He points, and as she leans forward, he reaches to support her, and again, she hesitates, though does not step away. He removes his hand and encourages her to breach the gap between mounting block and animal, explaining where to hold the reins, where to balance her feet in the stirrups. He takes care not to touch her again, until he has to press her knee to show the correct pressure.

From the back of his own horse Freddie explains how to stop, how to start, demonstrates the posture Celia should adopt. There is so much to remember that she forgets to be self-conscious, and soon the three of them are riding abreast along the back drive, Freddie offering encouragement, Ginny talking nineteen-to-the-dozen, the dogs sliding along beside them, the horses languorous in the heat.

'You're a natural,' says Ginny. 'How does it feel?'

The horse's gait is smooth, rolling. 'Not as bad as I'd imagined,' Celia replies.

'There's nothing to it,' says Freddie. 'Damn,' he reins in his horse, and jumps to the ground. On their left a walled garden lies only just perceptible through a tangled thicket of brambles. Someone has hacked a path to the iron gate, and Celia catches a glimpse of beds burgeoning with vegetables, and along the far wall, a greenhouse, though many of the panes of glass are missing. 'The wretched man never shuts the gate. Now the deer have got in, and no doubt the rabbits.'

He gives a short whistle and the dogs follow him up the path. '*Hi-lost*,' he calls, and the terriers spread out, noses down, tails wagging. Before long, they start to bark, and a rabbit is flushed out of the vegetable patch, and another, and another. The greyhounds give chase, ears back, teeth bared. The rabbits zigzag, the dogs turn with them. The rabbits dodge, and break for the undergrowth. One, two, make it. The third is snapped up in the jaws of the closest dog, and within seconds another has hold of it too, and they are tearing and growling as the creature is torn apart.

Celia looks away, feeling queasy. Freddie closes the gate, pulls himself back into the saddle.

'It seems you may not be cut out for country life, Miss Cottam,' he says sardonically.

She clenches her jaw and returns his gaze. 'I don't have to be. I'll be back in Bristol soon.'

For a moment, she thinks she sees fleeting disappointment in his face, but then he asks, 'And what about Littlecombe? What does your father plan to do with it?'

Celia shrugs. 'That will be up to him.'

CHAPTER 9

Two weeks later, and there has been no reply from Dr Hayne. Ginny suggests they ride to the village. They have spent many hours together, enough for Celia to have grown quite proficient on horseback, and Ginny wants to show her the school. Celia has enjoyed their time together – better than worrying at Littlecombe – and she looks forward to seeing Freddie, who often accompanies them on their forays around the fields. The siblings have a dry wit and a casual confidence that Celia finds refreshing, if a little disconcerting. She is not used to people exhibiting such casual entitlement – it is not so much arrogance as assertiveness – and the assertiveness is catching: she finds herself growing more confident by the day.

It is the first time she has ventured off the estate on a horse. On the road the animals are lethargic, snatching mouthfuls of the succulent green shoots that are sprouting around the gates they pass. Their hooves thud in the lane, occasionally catching a stone and sending it flying. Noisy clouds of sparrows rise out of the hedge ahead, chattering crossly as they land further along.

A sprinkling of cottages appears, their low stone walls draped in curtains of purple aubretia. The centre of the village is a mixture of thatched and tiled roofs, cottages and larger buildings. A pub sign swings in the breeze: a pair of heavy horses straining against the plough. The door is open, and someone is whistling as they sweep the floor. Celia catches the earthy scent of drink and sawdust.

'There's the school,' says Ginny, pointing at a small stone building. 'It's a lovely little place. We pay for the upkeep. But they could do with a good schoolmistress.'

'Perhaps you should encourage Miss Cottam to take the position,' says Freddie. 'Then she won't forsake us for Bristol.'

Celia feels a warm flush of pleasure at the comment, and risks a glance at Freddie, but he is staring nonchalantly ahead.

'I have higher aspirations than schoolmistress,' she says, trying to reassert some authority, and she is sure she glimpses the ghost of a smile before she too turns back to view the world through the horse's ears.

'Are you going to train to be a nurse?' asks Ginny.

'Actually I'd like to study neurology.'

'I don't even know what that is,' says her friend.

'The study of diseases of the nervous system.'

'Is that what you did when you were a VAD?'

Celia nods. 'I worked under a brilliant man who treats shell shock in a new way. A kinder way. And his results are good. I'd like to work on it further. Perhaps become a specialist . . .'

'Are women even allowed to do that?' asks Freddie, and she can tell he's only gently mocking.

'I'm sure you know it was a woman who established the first hospital for nervous diseases sixty years ago in London,' she retorts.

'Women tend to be the ones suffering from such diseases, I suppose.' He raises his eyebrows as he finally looks at her again, his eyes dark and unreadable.

'That's a piggish thing to say,' says Ginny.

There is nothing mean-spirited in Freddie's laughter – quite the opposite – it's warm and conspiratorial, and Celia laughs too. 'So why don't you go to medical school?' he asks.

'It would seem somehow like a step backwards. I learnt more in those two years at the hospital than I could anywhere else – new treatments that aren't even being taught yet.'

* * *

61

They alight outside the village shop, tying their mounts to the bench beneath a spreading horse chestnut. The women sit while Freddie disappears inside. He returns with a selection of sweets in a twisted paper cone: sherbet lemons, humbugs and peace babies. Celia savours the sugar, rolling the sweets on her tongue. A cart trundles down the street, large milk churns clanging against each other in the back. A man on a bicycle stops to move out of the way of an oncoming sea of sheep, their feet pattering against the ground as their eyes roll. A collie snaps at their heels, its tongue hanging pink between the white enamel of its teeth.

'Morning, sir,' says the cyclist, touching the front of his cap.

Freddie leans back on the bench. 'Morning, Quicke. Not busy on the farm today?'

'I got to see the reverend about something, sir.' He starts to dust nervously at the wisps of hay that are stuck to his shirtsleeves.

Freddie stretches out his legs. 'I hear beef prices have shot up again.'

'Aye, sir.' Quicke grimaces, and Celia sees that one of his teeth is missing; the others are dark with decay.

'Cheese as well?'

'Aye.'

'How are the Christmas calves?'

'They's coming on fine this year.'

'Perhaps you could pay your rent on time, then.'

The man looks embarrassed and shuffles from foot to foot. 'It be on its way, sir.'

'It's three weeks late. You promised that it would be on time this month. From now on, I will send Mulligan to you at the end of every week and you will pay him what you can afford until you are up-to-date. If you refuse, then you will be out. Consider this your final warning.'

The farmer squirms. 'Yes, sir.'

'Send my regards to Mrs Quicke, and to the children.'

'Thank you, sir.'

Quicke touches his cap again, nods at the two women, and wheels his bicycle away.

'The poor man,' says Celia when he is out of earshot. 'He seems to be struggling.'

'He has no reason to be.'

'Sometimes people have difficulties we cannot know about.'

'Sometimes they do. But not in this case.'

'Have you no compassion?'

'I have compassion, Miss Cottam. Have you?' His grey eyes settle on her, a calm challenge.

'I don't understand.'

'Let me explain. Quicke's family have rented the Home Farm for three generations. His father and grandfather worked hard. They built up a good herd, and they always paid their rent on time. Quicke unfortunately is more fond of ale than he is of farming. Every time he makes any money at market, he stops at the Plough on the way home and spends it all. He has seven children, none of whom have shoes in the winter unless my mother provides them. If he loses the farm it will be even worse for those children, not to mention Mrs Quicke, their stockman, the wheelwright and the blacksmith, who all rely on Quicke's business. You see, we are symbiotic, land-owner, farmer, labourer, consumer. We all rely on each other, and we need Quicke to farm our land to the best of his ability. If he can't, then we will put someone in who can. And then where will his children and wife be?'

There is an awkward silence as Celia considers his words.

Eventually, Freddie adds, 'I should think it not dissimilar to one of your father's coal mines. A farm and a coal pit are both businesses. No doubt your father has had to make diffi-cult decisions that you don't know about with regard to efficiency and output.'

'Actually, he discusses most things with me.'

'Then you will know that when people won't help them-selves one has to step in. And one must do that before they become desperate. Desperate men will do anything. They can cause all sorts of problems for one's business. It's all a matter of judgement.'

Celia feels the crimson start to creep up her neck. It feels as if Freddie is aiming his comments at her. But surely he can't know about her own failures of judgement that ended in the death of a man.

Celia swallows. Her mouth has gone dry. The siblings are looking at her expectantly. 'I suppose I can see the similarities,' she says, quietly, willing herself to stay calm. She must divert the subject. 'How many tenants do you have?' she asks.

Freddie sweeps his hand around the village. 'We own pretty much everything you can see.'

'The whole village?' she gasps.

He shrugs. 'Not the church, of course. And not the pub, more's the pity, as that turns over a good shilling – especially on pay day, and especially from men like Quicke.'

Celia looks again at the cottages, past the emerging spring flowers, and the swept thresholds, to a network of hidden alleyways that lead to the village refuse dump, and the smaller, more dilapidated cottages, where the creeping damp chews away at the walls and the roofs have fallen in. Three children are staring back at her from a dank corner. They are barefoot, and their pinafores that must once have been white are now a dirty shade of grey.

'And what about the people down there?' she indicates. 'Do you own them too?'

'There are people beyond even our reach,' says Freddie. He glances at her, watching her closely with his strange mixture of thoughtfulness and arrogance. She does not retaliate. She thought the countryside was meant to be green and pleasant, but she is realising there is more to it than that.

They ride back up the hill, soporific in the sway of the horses and with the sun on their cheeks. Celia is dimly aware that she hasn't had dark or irrational thoughts for the whole day – only perfectly rational ones, driven by debating with Freddie.

As Littlecombe comes into sight, Freddie rises in his stirrups and squints into the fields below the house. 'Is that your father?' he asks. Joseph Cottam is walking the hedges. Every few steps he squats down and peers at the ground before standing and turning in a circle to look up at the sky. 'What is he doing?'

'I don't know,' Celia replies.

'Why is he testing the ground?'

'I really don't know. He is full of ideas . . .'

'I thought he told you everything,' he teases, although Celia detects an edge to his voice, and his horse begins to act skittishly, searching for things to shy at, pulling at the bit, dancing in the lane. By the time they reach the stable yard there is a lather worked up along the animal's neck.

Freddie slides to the ground. Celia's muscles are sore from the adventure, and she is not sure her legs will support her when she dismounts, but Freddie is there to hold the horse while she makes it on to the mounting block.

'I can't believe you've only been riding for a couple of weeks,' says Ginny. 'You were brilliant.'

Freddie loops his horse's reins over its head. 'So you really have no idea of your father's plans for Littlecombe?'

'Not yet,' says Celia, 'but he isn't one for sitting around.'

'You own three hundred acres and you don't even know what to do with it!'

'Freddie! It's theirs now,' says Ginny. 'It's up to them . . .'

Celia is taken aback by his abrupt tone: 'Why does it matter to you what we do?'

'You're not the only one who doesn't want to be here,' he answers quietly.

'Why don't you leave, then?'

Freddie glowers at her over the horse's withers. 'Because I have no choice. My brother had the good sense to die in France, and left me lumbered with all this.'

'There are worse places to be . . .'

'And everyone has lost someone, right?' His eyes are locked

on hers, daring her to answer back. But she doesn't, and frustrated, he looks around and shouts, 'For God's sake, where's the damn groom?' before thrusting his horse's reins at Ginny and striding away to the house.

'I'm so sorry,' Ginny mumbles as she tries to comfort Celia. 'That's the second time you've witnessed his temper flare. He never used to be like this. It's the estate: it's in a bind, and our father is getting worse . . . and Freddie really hasn't come to terms with Edward. But he won't admit it. We're all meant to carry on. Stiff upper lip and all that, particularly the men . . .'

Suddenly Celia has had enough of men and their suffering. She too throws her horse's reins at Ginny and flees through the wood, away from the drive and the possibility of people watching. The trees grow denser, and the branches begin to pull and tear at her clothes and scratch at her arms and her face, and she is moving blindly now, not sure which direction home lies, disoriented by the echoing call of birds and the croaking of the rooks that wheel above the canopy. She stops, gasping for breath. The smell of decades of rotting matter fills her nostrils. As her eyes adjust she suddenly realises that the sharp, spiky conifers are hung with the bodies of dead animals: the dull fur of a rat, the large pink hands of a mole, the glassy eye of a crow, the soft stiffness of a rabbit tied by its ears – glimpses of death twisting and turning in the dim light.

CHAPTER 10

Summer comes and goes. Celia spends much of her time walking, getting to know every twist and turn in the hedgerows, every corner of the patchwork of fields, and where the morning mist takes longest to disperse from the valley. She still rides with Ginny, but Freddie no longer accompanies them. It annoys Celia that this upsets her, and she is confused: his behaviour had been so out of character for the man she had thought she was beginning to know.

As the days shorten, and there is still no news from Dr Hayne, she spends more time in the old buildings that surround the house, pulling the ancient farming equipment from the cobwebs with her father, discovering what the strange shaped implements are used for, clearing piles of torn sacks, spoiled feed, pieces of timber, anything that the previous tenant had collected and stacked away in case it might one day be needed. Sometimes she forgets she was ever in the hospital: the landscape is beginning to eradicate her memories; the clinical precision of the ward is harder to recall, and so too is that dreadful evening.

Ginny visits to tell her the family is going to London for a few weeks. They spend the afternoon playing cards, watched by Mrs Cottam, when she is able to stay awake. As Ginny deals the hand, she chatters indiscriminately. 'Have you seen the lawyer who's moved into our old coach house yet?' she asks.

Celia frowns. 'Is he the one that almost ran over those boy scouts?'

Ginny laughs, nodding. 'He's a dish, don't you think?'

'He's not the sort of person I can see myself with . . .'

'And what sort is that?'

Celia recognises the look in Ginny's eye. There is no point evading her questions: she loves to exchange confidences, and Celia has grown to trust her. She sighs, and tries to sound insouciant. 'I'm not sure. I don't have much experience . . .'

'You must have had masses of beaus?'

'Two or three. No one special.'

'But you're so pretty. I'd die for your complexion.'

Celia blushes. 'The men I like – the sensitive ones – are always so shy. And the ones I don't like – the overbearing ones – want to protect me.'

'It's because you're so delicate-looking. Not like me.' Ginny giggles. 'Most men run a mile. They're terrified.'

'Do you think you'll ever get married?'

'I know I will. It's my destiny. That's why I hope Freddie manages to make a go of Coombe – I want to have more of a choice than be foisted on someone with pots of cash.'

'Can't you say no?'

'What would I do instead?'

'Work? Perhaps at the school?'

She means it to be light-hearted, but Ginny gives an uncharacteristic sharp bark. 'I'd love to, but I didn't really have an education, so I'm no good for anything much. What about you? Do you think you'll marry?'

Celia shrugs. 'I'm not sure I'll ever be close to a man—' She stops, unsure whether to continue. Celia has never told anyone outside the family what happened, but Ginny is so uncomplicated that the words begin to find a way out. 'There was a man,' she starts. 'One of our patients. He developed an unhealthy attachment to me. One evening, I was working late . . .' she stops and swallows. 'He tried to force himself on me.'

Ginny frowns. 'You poor thing.'

Celia feels a lump in her throat. She says she doesn't want

68

sympathy, but really it's just that she can't cope with people being nice. 'I tried to fight him off, but he was far stronger . . . If it hadn't been for the night porter, then he would have . . . well . . .'

Ginny shudders. 'How utterly vile.'

'But that's not the worst of it,' says Celia, taking a deep breath. 'That same evening he hanged himself with the belt from his dressing gown. He was so ashamed . . . you see, he hadn't meant to do it. He was ill . . .'

'Now stop right there,' says Ginny, banging her cards down on the table. 'You can't think like that. I can see you're blaming yourself, but it's not your fault. Not at all. No matter how ill, one can't behave like that. You can't go about assaulting people.'

'You make it sound so black and white.'

'It is.'

Ginny stares at her, shoulders shrugged. Celia stares back. She wishes she had the other girl's confidence. She dares to clarify: 'I shouldn't have been alone in his room in the first place. It was against hospital policy.'

'That still doesn't mean you're to blame. I had a piano tutor once. He used to share the stool so he could put his hand up my skirt. I slammed his fingers in the piano lid and broke two of them. That wasn't *my* fault. It was his fault, for behaving like a toad.'

Celia smiles. 'It's not quite the same.'

'Perhaps. But you can see my point, and so would anyone else.'

'You won't tell anybody?'

'Of course not. Cross my heart and hope to die.'

'Not even your family.'

'Definitely not them. Now, unless you've got a trump hidden away, you lose. Want to play again?'

And Celia feels a sense of relief – because Ginny is so plain-speaking, and because it is good to have unburdened herself to someone other than her parents, whose unerring sympathy does not seem to make her feel better. And because Ginny still wants to be her friend – even after what she's confessed.

Too soon, it is time for Ginny to leave. She stops on the doorstep, and squeezes Celia's arm. 'You know, Freddie was an idiot that day,' she says. 'I wish he'd say sorry.'

'There's no need.'

'He's still angry that Maurice sold Littlecombe. But I'm not. I'm glad. And he'll get used to it.'

She takes a step back. 'And when I am married off to Lord So-and-So, and surrounded by a bunch of screaming children, please remember that we are friends, and allow me to carry on living the life I might have had through you?'

Celia continues with the long, solitary walks in the country-side. She learns to recognise the sharp bark of a fox and the trundling of the knife sharpener's cart. She is no longer afraid of the silence in the lanes; there are often people in the fields and byways, checking drains and ditches, women visiting friends, people out riding, ponies pulling traps. During the harvest, it is as busy as a town, with labourers and locals traversing the well-trodden footpaths from homestead to homestead, wherever the work pulls them. Since confiding in Ginny, her nightmares have begun to ease, along with the panic of being trapped. She is learning to control the fear as well as the shame.

And then it is Christmas.

Reverend Bridges sends invitations to the entire parish to attend the house for mulled wine and carol singing. Watts drives the Cottams down to the village, parking in front of the tall house. Their breath flows in plumes into the chilly night. Mrs Cottam is wrapped in furs, leaning against her husband as they crunch over the gravel. Music and light spill from every window, and the scent of cloves and oranges, cinnamon and pine needles lingers in the air.

Celia is hit by a wave of heat as they open the front door. The guests are gathered in the hall. There is a tall Christmas tree lit with candles and decorated with gingerbread men and delicate glass baubles. Reverend Bridges spots them as they enter, opening his arms. 'The Cottams!' he cries, and everyone turns to stare. 'You're last but one,' he says. 'I'll take your coats. Tonight is a night off for the maids.'

Celia glances around the room. She recognises many of the faces: villagers and domestic servants, farmhands and shopkeepers, the Arrowsmiths from the post office and the Stonemans from the bakery. Mr Smithson the schoolmaster finds a chair for her mother, who is happy to sit and listen to the choir. Joseph Cottam is in his element, at ease with anyone who wants to converse as he beetles through the crowd.

The door opens again, and a blast of cool air briefly interrupts conversations. Celia's heart skips a beat as she sees Ginny and Freddie breeze in with their parents. They are immaculately turned out, but the veneer, the aloofness that is like an aura around the family is back. She notes the farmhands and staff give them a wide berth; others see a chance to ingratiate themselves. Celia tries to catch Ginny's eye, but Ginny has been drawn into conversation with the schoolmaster. Instead, Celia finds she is locked in Freddie's gaze. He fights his way through to her, grabbing a glass from a tray on the piano.

So much time has elapsed since their last encounter, that though Celia tries to present a frosty demeanour, she finds that she can't. Freddie clears his throat. 'I believe I owe you an apology for how we last parted,' he says. 'I'm an ass. I don't know what came over me.'

Celia is immediately taken aback. For a moment she wonders if Ginny divulged her confidence, but she dismisses the idea as quickly as it came; she trusts Ginny implicitly. Freddie's eyes are troubled, and, with disquiet, Celia realises that the fluttering in her stomach may have nothing to do with anxiety, and all to do with pleasure at seeing him again. It gladdens her too that he has been dwelling on their last meeting for all these weeks.

71

'Am I forgiven? It is the season for peace and goodwill, after all.' At last she glances up, and smiles back. He looks relieved, and leans in to be heard better above the din. She catches the faint smell of saddle soap and tobacco, and finds that it pleases her too. 'You know, we're actually quite similar,' he says, the grey eyes lightening.

She cannot help laughing out loud. 'How do you work that out?'

'Neither of us wants to be here, but we've both got to make the best of it.'

They stand companionably as they watch the revelry going on around them. Reverend Bridges tries to encourage them to join the singers, but they decline. Freddie lifts two mince pies from a plate, offers Celia one. 'While we were away,' he says, 'I discovered that a friend of the family gave one of their houses in Exeter over to the military to treat patients with neurological problems. I thought I could put you in touch?'

Celia wipes a crumb from her hand. 'It must be very nice being someone like you,' she says.

'Someone like me?'

'A rich and well-connected man with the world at your fingertips.'

'Ah. I see Miss Cottam may have arrived at the wrong conclusion.' He does not sound angry, more amused. 'Actually I'm not rich. Not at all.'

Her eyes widen. 'You live in a house as big as Buckingham Palace, with a whole village at your fingertips, not to mention acres of land, and you think you're not rich?'

'I thought you were broader minded than that. You need to look beyond that very sweet little nose of yours.'

She blushes. 'I'd thank you not to comment on my nose.'

'There's no need to be like that . . .'

'How would you like me to be?'

'Believe it or not, I would like you to be you. I find you intriguing . . .'

There is no irony in the grey eyes, and her heart gives

another leap. She curses herself. Why is she so easily swayed by this man? 'If that is the case, then what was it you found so offensive about us buying Littlecombe?'

'It was more to do with being upset that it was sold. But now you mention it, I suppose I wondered what on earth people like you would do with it?'

She shakes her head. 'You actually have no idea how rude you're being.'

'None.' His smile is wolfish. 'But I do know that you know nothing about farming, and Littlecombe has some of the best pasture for miles—'

'I can learn.'

'I thought you were going to study diseases of the nervous kind.'

'It seems the world thinks otherwise.'

'Still no news from that doctor of yours?'

She shakes her head.

'I'm sorry. Perhaps we both need to adapt . . . not be so stuck in our ways?'

'I'd like to see you try.'

'Very well. I promise. I'll stop being such a dolt. And let's see if we can both survive here. I'll make a go of it if you will?'

Celia grins; she has always liked a challenge.

Freddie grabs another passing drink, swapping his empty glass for a full one. 'And now I've got to get out of here,' he says, holding the glass up to the light and studying its contents.

'But you've only just arrived.'

'I didn't want to come at all. I can't stand all these people staring at me, desperately hoping we'll be as generous as we were before the war, and go back to giving them all brooches instead of books for Christmas.'

'Where's Ginny?' she says, suddenly realising that her friend is no longer among the crowd. 'I was hoping to see her.'

Freddie frowns as he scans the room. 'Damn. She didn't want to come either. We had to show our faces to keep the parents happy. I fear this reminds her of the good old days, with my brother. We used to throw a party every Christmas for the tenants and the villagers. They probably think I've put the kibosh on it. The truth is, we simply can't afford such extravagance these days.' He knocks back the glass of wine. 'Bugger this,' he says. He turns to go, but then stops and bends closer so she can feel his breath on her ear: 'Look. It's good to see you. Have you been invited to the Boxing Day meet?'

She shakes her head.

'Please come.'

'Oh no . . . I couldn't . . .'

'Come on, remember to look beyond this . . .' He taps his nose. 'You did just agree to adapt, and you cannot make judgements if you don't see how we live.'

'It's not that. I don't want to be a figure of fun.'

'You won't be. I'll look after you.' And for the briefest moment he reaches out to intertwine a finger with one of hers, and she feels a flare of heat travel up her arm, and it is hotter than the rectory's roaring fire.

CHAPTER 11

It seems that the whole county has turned out for the Boxing Day meet at Coombe Hall. The lawn seethes with hounds, their tails whipping from side to side as they pour from one end to the other. There are horses of every shape and size: great shining chargers with Roman noses, fine thoroughbreds patterned with veins, fat ponies with tiny children bouncing on their broad backs as if they are being jiggled on a grandmother's knee. There are women, some riding side-saddle, but plenty riding cross-saddle like Ginny and Celia, smartly turned out in their dark hunting jackets and pale breeches, hair held back by neat ribbons beneath bowler hats. Men in top hats and bright scarlet coats rub shoulders with ruddy-cheeked farmers and dour landsmen. And at their feet mill the locals, some of whom will follow on foot.

Everyone is making the most of the Hembury's hospitality, sipping the port, hoping it will revive their fuzzy heads after yesterday's revelries. The air echoes with the call of the hounds and the chink of harness and the chomping of bits as man and horse blow puffs of warm air into the cold grey morning.

Celia is on Aztec. Her heart is hammering in her chest and her legs are like jelly. She hopes no one will notice. A man she recognises as Major Thornberry rides alongside her. 'Top of the morning to you,' he says. 'You look wonderful.' She notes the way his eyes linger over her legs and nods in what she hopes is a courteous yet confident way. At least she is safe up here.

Ginny barges through on her exuberant mount, and Major Thornberry wanders off. 'Sometimes it's a bonus to have a horse that kicks,' she grins. The horse bangs against Celia's leg, and for a moment they are entangled. 'Sorry,' says Ginny. 'He's so full of beans, I don't think I'll be able to keep back with you.'

'Don't worry. I'll be fine.'

'As long as you're sure? I could swap with Freddie, but he does love that horse.' They both look at Freddie on Tybalt, the model of composure, as Ginny's horse skips backwards, neck arched, spitting foam.

'I'll be fine,' says Celia, gripping the saddle. She is sure Freddie has forgotten his promise to look after her.

And then the master, resplendent in his scarlet coat and white breeches, hunt buttons glinting, sounds the horn, and the people and animals fall silent for a second before there is another cry, and they are off across the park. Celia tries to hold Aztec back, away from the hooves of the horse in front. Ginny is flying ahead of the field, and there is Freddie, trying to rein in Tybalt, who is already glistening with sweat. The hounds give tongue, the whipper-in calls to them, and all Celia can do is cling on for dear life.

The day passes in a blur of mud, sweat, and terror. Celia glimpses things she will never forget: the flowing of the field of dogs and horses across ditches and over hedges, squeezing through gaps like running water. The two small flat-capped boys like twins on a matching pair of Shetland ponies. The lengthening of the pack as it streaks across a field. The baying of the hounds as they pick up a scent, and the electricity that fills the air at the kill, which mercifully she does not witness. And surprisingly, there is Freddie, always at her side, checking she is safely over hedges, finding a way through for her if she needs it, opening gates, taking detours.

When she falls, it is unceremonious. She feels Aztec gather himself. The hedge looks huge, and the horse crashes through the top of it with his front legs. Somehow they make it over, yet she is unbalanced, and loses the grip she had, feels herself slipping, as if in slow motion. The blackthorn scratches and tears at her legs, and before she can even cry out, she thumps against the muddy ground, her bones jarred, the wind knocked from her lungs. She glimpses the underbelly of another horse leaping above her and she instinctively curls into a ball. Still they come, the round bellies and feet and spurs and a tangle of reins and bridles as they stream over her, spraying water and mud.

When she finally dares to uncurl, when the thunder of hooves has subsided, she can see Aztec standing patiently, head down, reins dangling dangerously close to his knees. She tastes soil in her mouth and there is water in her ear and the cold is seeping through her clothes. Her whole body is trembling and she tries to get to her feet, but she is too weak. Then she feels strong hands lifting her and there is Freddie, carrying her out of the mud, calling her name.

He sets her down gently, and she leans against him, legs shaking as she tries to stand. 'Are you all right?' he asks. 'Are you sure you haven't broken something?'

She is abashed by his genuine worry, and the way he placed her so carefully upright, as if she might break. 'I'm fine.'

'You know what they say? Straight back in the saddle . . .'

She groans. She is not even sure that she can stand unaided.

'All right,' he laughs. 'Let's sit for a moment.' He helps her hobble to a tree, propping her up against the trunk. He reaches out to brush the dirt from her face. His fingers are strong and warm.

'I don't understand why you do it,' she says.

He grins. 'It's fun.'

He stands to fiddle with his saddle, removing a leather flask. He sits back down, and removes two cups that are neatly stacked inside. He pours some liquid into each. 'This will help.'

She takes the little silver cup, feels where the heat from his fingers has warmed the cold metal. She sips the liquid. It is warm and treacly, slipping down her throat easily and making her cheeks glow.

'Better?'

She nods. A pleasant sensation begins to creep into her bones.

Aztec and Tybalt stand quietly next to each other, heads down, snatching mouthfuls of grass. They are caked in mud. Freddie and Celia watch them, listening to the hypnotic chewing, the tearing of the grass. She feels warmth seep through her shoulder and realises she is leaning against Freddie. They stay like that for a while; as her shaking subsides, the heat between them increases.

Celia feels an urge to break the silence. 'Well. I've tried to adapt,' she says, 'and failed . . .'

'Nonsense,' says Freddie. 'You haven't failed. You'd never believe how many times I've fallen off.'

'What about you? Have you tried anything new?'

His arm flexes against hers as he shrugs. The grey eyes grow dark again. 'I suppose I've been indulging my mother. We're not exactly close . . .'

'It must be hard for her – to have lost a son.'

He snorts. 'I'm still not sure she believes he's gone. I found out she's been writing letters to a man – a soldier – from my brother's regiment. He was the only survivor. My mother wants him to come and talk to us about Edward, about how he died.'

'And you don't want him to?'

'I don't think it's helpful to rake up the past. I don't want my father or Ginny to be upset again.'

'Tell me about Edward,' she says.

He rests his head back against the tree, looking up at the gathering clouds. 'Edward? He was better than me in every way. He was the good-looking one, the easy-going one, the well-dressed one.'

She understands well that lack of confidence; he's like me, she thinks, hiding a whirlwind of emotion beneath all that bravado.

He offers her another drink, but she declines. He pours himself one. 'You know, he was younger than I am now when he went to France. I can't believe he's never coming back. I really miss him.'

She sits motionless, not wanting to throw him off as he starts to open up.

'He should be here. He was born to this. It's his life, and he loved it, suited it – it's what he was bred for.'

'You make him sound like one of your horses.'

'You wouldn't understand. You couldn't. It's different for your sort . . .'

Now it is her turn to snort. 'My sort!'

'I'm sorry. That was rude. It's just . . . my life has changed – or the life I thought I was going to have.' He turns to her, and his grey eyes shine for a moment. 'I was going to get away, make something of myself.'

'I understand that . . .'

'I know you do.' He is staring at her with such intensity. 'I was going to build a business. A tea plantation in the sun. None of this mud and rain. Blue skies and leopards! Somewhere I could make a name for myself without deferring to my brother. And without people thinking it's all been handed on a plate. I want to build something to be proud of rather than drifting through endless dinner parties . . . And now . . . now I don't know if I'll have to give it all up.'

Celia feels as if they are balancing on the edge of an understanding deeper than she has felt with anyone: she shares his ambition to be something more than what is expected of her. She understands what it's like to have the ground pulled from beneath you.

Suddenly the sound of the hunting horn pierces the air, and Freddie's face clouds over. 'Listen to me,' he says abruptly, 'moaning like an old woman. We must head back.' And before she can stop him, he is knocking back his drink, and packing the cups away.

'But—'

'They'll be turning for home.'

She does not protest further; she knows there is no point

when his mouth sets in an unbreakable line. He helps her into the saddle, cupping his hands together to use as a step. She grits her teeth as her joints grumble and creak. Her sore body somehow settles back into position.

The light is beginning to fade. Pheasants call in the woods where they are settling to roost. The air is chilly, but they are warmed by the exertion of the day, and the heat from their mounts. Celia glances across at Freddie, and when he sees her, he smiles, and she smiles back, and she knows there is a connection and he feels it too, as if a spider has spun a silvery strand of silk between them. It lifts her soul and gives her hope.

Freddie helps Celia dismount, and she hands the horse over to the groom. The yard is beginning to fill with other returning riders, and in the clatter of hooves, and chaos of people relinquishing their mounts to their own grooms, Celia feels a powerful surge of belonging. The dark has fallen quickly, and the lamps in the yard throw a warm light on the steaming bodies of horses and riders. Celia runs her hand along Aztec's flank and thanks him silently for conveying her safely for most of the day.

Someone calls her name, and Ginny appears, windswept and mud-spattered. 'Why don't you stay for supper?' she says. 'I'm sure we can persuade Mrs Foley to lay another place at the table.'

'Splendid idea,' says Freddie.

But now Reverend Bridges is coming up behind her. 'There you are!' he says, mopping his hatless brow with a handkerchief. 'I promised your father I'd drop you home.'

'Worst luck,' says Freddie, before he and Ginny are swept along by their houseguests.

Celia turns to the vicar. 'Thank you,' she says, although she could happily throttle him.

They head towards the village in his trap. The cold air bites at her cheeks, but she has the image of Freddie's grey eyes smiling to keep her warm. She persuades the reverend to drop her at the top of the drive. She wants to walk the last bit alone, savouring memories of the day. She hears the vicar's cart creaking away. Then silence. The moon is a haze behind the clouds, just enough to light her way. Ahead of her, the windows at Littlecombe glow invitingly.

When she reaches the front door, she suddenly realises how tired she is. Every limb is aching. Her hips and legs are sore and her muscles are throbbing. But she is also exhilarated. It is liberating to know that her body is capable of such treatment. She is not a precious flower that should be kept under a glass. It dawns on her that it is not only the countryside, but also spending time with Freddie Thorneycoombe that has helped to heal her. She is so nearly back to where she was, so ready to face the future.

The house billows heat into the chill winter night when she opens the door. She can hear fires crackling in the grates. She removes her gloves, smiling at the mud that reminds her of Freddie.

And then Frances is there, fussing. 'Let me take your coat, miss. Aren't you a fright, miss? Are you harmed?' Celia tries to shake the maid off; she finds the staff here more intense than they were in Bristol. Though they do not live in-house as they do at Coombe Hall, they might as well do, for they seem to be at Littlecombe all the time, and always on the periphery of her vision.

Once Celia has reassured the maid that she is all right, Frances turns to her with wide eyes. 'It's very exciting, miss. He's turned up at last.'

'Who? Who's turned up?'

'Your brother!'

'George?' Celia runs towards the sitting room, where she spies a broad-shouldered man leaning against the chimney breast. He is talking in earnest to her father, but when she calls his name, he turns and holds out his arms.

George. Her brother. She kisses his freckled cheek and stands back to survey him, beaming. They share the same auburn hair, the same grey-blue eyes. He seems pale, which she puts down to city living. He has filled out; he is a real man now.

'What in God's name have you been doing?' he asks, looking down at her filthy clothes and torn breeches.

'You won't believe it . . .'

Mrs Cottam clucks over her daughter. 'She's been out hunting!'

The smile fades from George's face. 'Hunting?'

And suddenly Celia feels a fool. A blush spreads across her face and she stammers, 'It was a bit of silliness. I'd better go and get cleaned up . . .'

She cannot bear to meet his eye. She doesn't belong to Freddie's world, and she is fast losing touch with her own.

'Before you go.' Her father moves towards her, a letter in his hand. 'George brought this. It seems it was sent to our Bristol address.'

She takes it, knowing without looking that it is from the hospital.

They all fall silent, and she turns her back on them, tearing it open, and scanning the contents, her heart in her mouth.

It is signed by Alan Hayne, but does not sound like him. It thanks her for her interest, but regrets that at the moment all positions are filled, and they do not see that the situation will change for a while. She crumples it into a ball and throws it on the fire, watching the hungry flames consume it until all that is left is ash.

CHAPTER 12

France

Edward moves away from the road, towards the pock-marked hill that looks like the moon, the ground blasted white by years of fighting. The morning's raindrops run down the stumps of charred vegetation, pooling in the holes left by shells and mortars. Along the crest of a crater, against a gun-metal sky, he can see the silhouettes of the Chinese labourers who form his search party working among the rudimentary wooden crosses.

He climbs towards them slowly, his smoke-damaged lungs struggling to convert oxygen to breath. His side aches where they took the rib to rebuild his jaw. He feels his cap chafing against the bare skin on the half of his scalp where the hair will never grow back. The mask he had made in Paris rubs against his face. He is dressed in the uniform of the ordinary Tommy, mass-made breeches, ill-fitting boots. He no longer enjoys the attention that being an officer commands, and, once the nurses stopped their questions, he became Private James Cooke.

The men work in silence, the tools of their trade scattered across the ground: rubber gloves, pickaxes, wire cutters, canvas, rope, shovels. The search area is staked, ready to be explored grid by grid. The only sounds are the clink of shovel on stone, the squelch of mud. Edward helps Ling battle with a roll of barbed wire. He tries not to let the barbs catch at his clothes, tries not to think who might once have worn the torn strips of cloth that are fluttering in the breeze.

He scans for the telltale signs in the sticky earth: the spike of a bayonet, the curve of a helmet, the way the soil darkens. He catches sight of something: a neat black hole. He moves closer, crouches down. He pushes his hand inside, rummages around. He feels the mud soft against his fingers, and then something harder. He thrusts in up to his elbow, and pulls out the pale length of bone, pushed closer to the surface by the rats that dug this tunnel. He turns it over in his hand, smears the mud from its yellowing surface with his fingers. It feels soft and smooth. He has no doubt that here lies the company of men they have been searching for, who were buried alive as they hid in the cellar of a farmhouse. How Edward wishes it had been him.

He stands, straightens his back, but keeps his head bent, his cap low. He does not have to say anything. He points. Ling and Shan come with the shovels. Their faces remain inscrutable. They are foreign men a long way from home. They know what they must do.

Later, they join the stream of trucks and carts on the road towards Lille. Every few yards a vehicle is parked haphazardly while its driver changes another punctured tyre. The wasteland is strewn with piles of charred timber, the tracks from a ruined tank, while bubbles of gas leak into the poisoned air. They pass a gang of American negroes smashing rubble for the roads. The men are singing strange songs while the sweat trickles from beneath their hats and grows in great patches on their backs. All the misfits, thinks Edward. We are all that is left.

The truck slows and stops. Edward gets out, looking up as the other vehicle carrying the rest of his party rumbles past. The men stare grimly out of the back, the sacks carefully piled behind them. Only Shan holds Edward's gaze for a moment. He places his hands together in a praying position and bows his head, before the truck is absorbed back into the traffic.

Edward walks through the battered town, until he reaches the place he calls home. The grand columns of the large town house still stand, though they are studded with bullet holes. The walls are a patchwork of timber and metal, rags and brick, but much of the rubble has been cleared from the front garden, and Madame Sauveur insists the path is swept clean every day. The door is always open, but she does not get much business now that the officers have left, and the children have moved in. She will not lower herself to the general revelry of a red light brothel.

Some of these children are dancing in a circle by the gate, singing a French nursery rhyme. Their bare feet make no sound in the dirt, but their high voices jar in his head. These are the lucky few who have found their way into Madame Sauveur's affection. They guard the house jealously, living by some secret code that means they allow some children entry, while others are barred.

Monsieur Mercier, their dapper old neighbour, is shouting from his window: 'Keep your noise down, you dirty beggars.' The children laugh and curse. It is a game they play every evening. Monsieur Mercier retreats back into the room, slamming the casement shut. Even if he drove this lot away, another would soon replace them, for there are refugees and orphans wandering the streets in droves, searching for lost parents, relatives, places to sleep.

'Monsieur.' Edward glances down. A scrawny boy with eyes too large for his sunken face holds out the metal casing of a shell, a drawing etched into its surface. 'For your sweetheart . . .' Edward is relieved to see the shell is spent. He has heard of a child pulling the pin on a grenade that was still live.

'*Votre chérie* . . .' the boy says again, then catches sight of the mask, and stumbles back into the road, where he stands, scratching at the bites in his hair. His legs are twisted, malformed, probably from time spent too long hiding in the dark. An old woman lugging a wicker basket on her back shuffles between them, leaning heavily on her stick. The boy chases after her, trying to tug some of the leaves from her basket. His small hand closes around something, and he pulls it clear before hobbling away down an alleyway on his bent legs, as fast as a fox that has broken cover.

Edward crosses the road. Madame Sauveur's children return to their rhyme.

He enters the cool interior of the house. There is a strangled scream, a sound Edward knows well: one of the goats that are tethered in the garden is having its throat cut. He can hear two women arguing. Madame Sauveur is coming in from the back, wiping her hands, looking cross. Danielle is berating her for being cruel.

'Why can't you buy meat from the butcher like everyone else?'

'That butcher charges too much, and now we are many mouths to feed.'

'Then you must stop taking in those filthy youngsters. They are taking over. I found some in my room—'

'You do not have to live here. Find somewhere else.'

They both glare at Edward.

'I thought you were leaving anyway,' says Danielle. 'Going to your château in the country.' She says this with a snort of disdain.

'Laugh if you want. But it is true. I will be leaving soon enough. And I will be taking many of those youngsters with me. But not you. You are old enough to stand on your own two feet.'

Danielle stares at Madame as she brushes angrily at her hair, tugging at the knots.

Madame Sauveur has been threatening to move back into her old home for months; no doubt she will be saying it for years to come. She claims her family home near Arras was sequestered by the army in the early days of the war, then by the advancing Germans, and then left to ruin while the war raged on. Ever industrious and able to spot an opportunity, the madame left for the town and set up her *maison tolérée* – a blue light for the officers only. When the war ended, she began to rent out four of the bedrooms, keeping three for her prostitutes. Now Danielle is the only prostitute left, and the children have filled all available spaces.

Madame Sauveur is still angry. She turns her beady eyes on Edward, like an inquisitive blackbird. 'And you, *Anglais*. You will have to go. You must return to wherever you come from. I will be selling the house to pay for supplies.'

Danielle starts to jabber with anger. 'You cannot turf us out on to the streets.'

Madame shakes her head. 'You will have me turf out innocent children, but you wish to stay? You have had a good life here. Now you must make your own destiny.'

Edward starts to edge towards the door. He will not go back to Coombe. He didn't even go when he had leave during the war. It was too far removed from the reality of his life. He couldn't face his mother fussing, or his father discussing estate maintenance, or his brother and sister gazing in adulation. He couldn't even stay with Maurice in Bristol. He preferred instead to enjoy the comfort of prostitutes and the company of men in France.

And now he could never return. Not like this. He is glad they will believe him dead.

He leaves the two women to bicker.

Edward's room is in the attic. It is an arduous climb, but worth it to have the space to himself. On the way up he passes more children, making themselves comfortable on blankets, guarding their precious squares of floor. Danielle is right; it is becoming intolerable. The children are taking over. He reaches the top, breathing heavily. A large section of the roof is missing, but Edward has rigged up a tarpaulin to keep off the rain and the dew. The snap of it flapping sometimes wakes him with a start in the night, but at least he is alone: no one else would sleep in such a place. He has a straw mattress on the floor, a low table which serves as a chair. Apart from that there is nothing to set him apart from the next man: a change of clothes, a book from the market, a comb, but no shaving kit. He thinks briefly of the monogrammed one he used to have, which of course would have been returned to Coombe, along with all his other effects. Anyway, he no longer shaves, preferring instead to let the beard hide what it can where it still grows. Madame Sauveur keeps it trim for him, because he has no looking glass. He will never have a looking glass again.

Carefully, he removes the mask, lifting the arms of the spectacles that fix it in place, feeling the thin galvanised metal peel away from his raw skin, before placing it carefully back into its box. It is more than two years since he was injured. The wound has healed, but it is still painful, the skin stretched tight, the damaged sinews aching. No one has seen it since the portrait studio in Paris, when it was covered by the plaster, so that he could be reborn. He remembers the other moulds hanging there, hundreds of ravaged faces like his, swollen and deformed, noses, mouths, eyes missing, a gallery of the macabre.

He places the box next to the lamp on the floor. He unties a corner of the tarpaulin, pulling it back to reveal a nightscape of smashed roofs beneath a darkening sky. There is no moon. Soon it will be pitch black, how he likes it best, as it was behind his bandages. He unlaces his boots, blows out the lamp and stretches out on the mattress, hands behind his head. He feels nothing. He is hollow, inhabited by ghosts and shadows. He wonders why he is still here, why he couldn't have died that night. He curses the man who dragged and carried him to safety. Bolt. After all he'd done for him.

He allows the darkness to swallow him up. Images from the day chase through his mind. The slippery disintegration of an arm falling from a half-buried body. The slimy oozing of a ribcage opening up, the sudden movement of the maggots inside. But none of it is as hideous as his own face. The scar still oozes, the skin is weeping and puckered, the grisly hole of his mouth the stuff of children's nightmares.

He wakes to a strange sensation. With a sudden ache that hits the pit of his stomach, he realises it is a human touch. His eyes flicker open. The hand retracts into the darkness. There is a gasp. He knows his eyes are strange, naked without their eyelashes, one with barely an eyelid. He reaches out and grabs the arm. It wriggles and tries to pull away. He grips more tightly. It is small and bony. He pulls it, and a small child appears in the dim light. Danielle is right; the damn children are everywhere.

It must be five or six in the morning. A pale light spills from the open sky, and the air is fresh and cool. The child stares at him but does not recoil as he expects her to. Her eyes are narrow and fierce, and she grunts as she tries to wriggle free.

'You must find somewhere else to sleep,' he says.

She struggles again, hisses and spits like an alley cat, but says nothing.

'This is my room—' He yelps and lets go as she bites his hand. She scrabbles to the edge of the room, back up against the wall.

From her position, the little girl watches him. The dawn light is bright enough to outline the belligerent tilt of her chin. It is also bright enough to reveal the horror of his features. But the girl does not flinch. She continues to stare. Edward squares up to her, displaying his disfigurement in all its glory. She shrugs and glares back. And he experiences another forgotten sensation: a smile trying to break across his mutilated face.

CHAPTER 13

England

The blinds in the village are down. The shop and the pub are closed out of respect. The church bell has tolled. The verges and lanes are blocked with an unusual number of motor cars. The morning sun falls in biblical streaks through the windows, lighting the tombs of Freddie's ancestors. His father's funeral has arrived too soon, just a week after he died in his armchair by the fireplace.

The vicar is speaking: 'The Right Honourable the Earl of Hembury will now read from . . .'

Freddie feels his sister's elbow in his ribs, and suddenly realises that the vicar means him. He walks to the front of the church, barely taking in the rows of faces. Somehow he manages to utter the words on the sheet, and to thank everyone for their kind wishes, before a lump in his throat prevents him from continuing and he returns to the pew. There is a hymn, and then Lord Brixham walks to the front, stopping to nod at the altar before he steps up to the lectern. He gazes out at the congregation. The golden eagle glints beneath his hands. The air is full of the scent of flowers cut from the garden. Freddie closes his eyes and listens.

'The grief of these last years, after his beloved Edward's sacrifice in France, must not allow our memories of him to be tarnished. No parent should lose a child. It is not the natural order of things. Richard Hembury was an extraordinary man, a beneficent employer, a kind friend, and a much loved husband and father. He saved Coombe Hall, battled to keep it going against the odds, thus saving the village and the area from falling to rack and ruin, sometimes to his own detriment. He was a forward-thinking man but inherited an estate that his own dear father had neglected after sacrificing his health to the Boer War. The selflessness of such men as the Hemburys – whether abroad or at home – in protecting our nation and its fine values must not be overlooked. Richard was blessed with luck in finding his match in Katherine, whose beauty and wit were, and still are, renowned. Eyebrows were raised at the gap between their ages, but those that knew him well also knew it was necessary for one with as much energy as Richard Hembury to find someone to match it. Our thoughts are with the dowager countess at this difficult time. The only solace we can take is that Richard and Edward are now re-united.'

The cathedral choir that has come from Exeter sings praises to God the Father, and Freddie thinks of his own father, and how he knew so little about him. He feels breathless. He tries to loosen his collar. His mother's head turns towards him, but she is closely veiled, and he cannot see her expression. On her other side sits Ginny, a shadow of her usual self. Freddie has never felt more alone than on that hard wooden pew, with grief and shame in equal measure: grief at the loss of his family; shame that he is still here. It is not the natural order of things to be thrust into one's brother's shoes. He feels a fraud. A usurper who is now head of the family. It's a burden he is not ready to bear.

The organ begins to play. Freddie stands and the rest of the congregation rises as his father's coffin – carved elm from the estate – is carried down the aisle on the broad shoulders of men from the village. The choir follows, still singing. Freddie comes next, escorting his mother past pews overflowing with family and friends who have travelled from as far afield as Ireland and Scotland. Further back, the villagers have kept a respectful distance, heads bowed, expressions solemn, families who have worked on the estate over the decades, families who knew Freddie's grandfather, his great-grandfather. The servants hang in another knot; they too have the morning off to pay their respects.

The bishop of Exeter – a friend of the family – waits at the side of the church, ready to lead the committal, his robes billowing in the breeze. The people cluster around. Freddie stares upwards, at the yew tree that has seeded itself in the tower of the church, at the gargoyles, feeling giddy as the clouds roll across the sky. He does not want to look at the little door to the family vault. He does not want to see the steps leading down to the rows of coffins, to the space waiting for his father. He does not want to think about the space next to that, where Edward should be, instead of in some godforsaken hole in France, and where one day Freddie will lie instead, having stolen his brother's final resting place.

He says a silent prayer to them both, that they will send guidance, for he knows what comes next: a ruinous bill for estate duty; the death tax – a sledgehammer blow that will slam down on them not once but twice – first for his father, and then on the reversion of his dead brother, on whom the estate was entailed.

Back at the house the guests wander from room to room, remembering previous, happier visits, occasionally glancing at each other with raised eyebrows, for Coombe Hall is crumbling, paint is peeling from the walls, and some of the windowpanes are broken. Freddie is relieved they have no cause to go upstairs, where the rain trails brown veins along the ceilings, until it drips into the carefully placed chamber pots. No matter how quickly he plugs one gap in their finances, another appears. The money from the auction and much of the money from the sale of Littlecombe has already been swallowed up. He has reluctantly conceded he must consider the plans for this damn racecourse – which could end up being the answer to their problems – but only if the other investors agree to new terms, and therein lies the problem.

People turn to greet Freddie as he moves through the crowd. He will never get used to this strange feeling of being the one they all gravitate to – the standard-bearer of the Hembury family. He spots Monkton and Granville, standing together. He sees his neighbour Hampden move towards them. They are circling Coombe like rooks around a waterlogged ewe. He knows they think he is weak, and ready to hand his share to them on a plate. But they are wrong. Edward was prepared to give away too much, focusing only on the early reward of cash – and the later one of kudos – and not on the long-term damage. Freddie will only agree to sign up if they bring Cottam in on it, thus keeping an equal share of land either side of the lane, and between the three landowners: Hampden, Joseph Cottam, and Coombe. Then Monkton and Granville can throw as much money as they like at Hampden: he will not be in control. The only problem is, he hasn't discussed it with them – or with Joseph Cottam.

Freddie stops, shakes hands, makes polite conversation with cousins he has not seen for years, will not see until the next funeral. He keeps one eye on the three men: Hampden has reached the other two and they are deep in discussion. 'Now's your chance to introduce them,' Ginny hisses in his ear. 'Joseph Cottam is over there.' She indicates with her eyes, where Mr Cottam and his family are being welcomed into the semicircle of sombre-faced women who surround the dowager countess. Mr Cottam and Freddie's mother are unlikely allies, but their neighbour has been pivotal in raising money for a village memorial for the men lost in the Great War, and has thus earned the countess's respect. Less so Mrs Cottam, who is leaning on her husband's arm; but then, his mother always found men easier to respect whatever their class.

'It wouldn't be right today,' says Freddie, whose eye has travelled to Celia, who is supporting her mother on the other side.

'Well don't leave it too much longer. I've had to put up with Hampden's cat-that-got-the-cream look for far too long.'

Ginny turns to welcome their great-aunt Maud, bending her ear to the wrinkled lady's mouth, nodding her head at the reply. Celia catches Freddie's eye and smiles. He feels his spirits lift. Her dark dress brings out the red tones of her hair, her skin seems to glow. He has enjoyed sharing their ideas and hopes for the future as they ride or walk the area these past few weeks. She has a quick mind – no doubt from her father – and he has found himself confiding in her in the final weeks of his father's illness, valuing her opinion at a time he feels so at sea. He is sure an alliance would work.

Maurice blocks his view. 'Didn't Brixham give a superb eulogy?'

Freddie nods. 'I never knew Papa had spent so much time in southern Africa.'

'You are not the only member of the family with a desire to wander.'

They stand and watch the guests in companionable silence. 'And how are you feeling?'

Freddie shrugs. 'Tired. It's a constant battle.'

His uncle reaches out. 'I know, dear boy. It is so unfair to penalise us twice, when we have already lost so much. But we must keep up the fight. Dare I ask how things are going?'

'I have an idea of how I could revive the racecourse plans.'

'That is good news.'

'The thing is, it involves the bit of land you gave away.'

Maurice frowns. 'I've been thinking about that too. There are ways you could make it difficult for the current owners. Put them off so they want to give it back. You can ruin a harvest, poison livestock . . .'

Freddie shakes his head as he watches Celia move across the room next to her father. 'I was going for a more collaborative approach.'

Maurice eyes him carefully. 'Ah. Yes. She's a pretty little thing!' Freddie finds himself blushing, and Maurice raises an eyebrow. 'You weren't seriously entertaining the idea of going into business with *them*?'

Freddie stammers, 'No . . . I mean . . .'

'You couldn't possibly!' They both stare at the Cottams, who are talking in earnest to the vicar. Joseph Cottam suddenly guffaws with laughter, and a few of the other guests turn to stare before returning to their conversations. Maurice downs his drink. 'Money can't buy you class, can it, old boy?' He smiles at his joke.

Freddie's spirits plummet: if his uncle reacts in this way, then it's unlikely that Hampden and the others will have a positive outlook.

Maurice leans in. 'Damn! I say go for it. Charm the socks off her. Just don't let her catch you out by getting in the family way. Come to your Uncle Maurice if you need any advice on that score.' He guffaws again. 'A dalliance we can condone for the sake of some ready cash, but we couldn't have the future of Coombe resting in the hands of a commoner. Of course, if you can't bend her to your will, then we'll resort to Plan B.'

'Which is?'

'Plenty of fresh debs on the market, or we'll find you a rich American. They're coming over in droves, and they are always hungry for titles.'

CHAPTER 14

The dowager countess is in the nursery. Since she has been in contact with the soldier from Edward's battery, she spends much of her time there, absent-mindedly lining up Edward's tin soldiers in neat rows, running her finger along the horses' backs, holding them up to the light as if she might be able to look back in time and see Edward there, frowning in concentration, tongue half-sticking out as he painted them so carefully.

She looks up from the rocking chair by the window and smiles. 'Darling,' she says, 'do come here and let me hold your hands . . .'

Freddie crosses the room and kneels down, taking hold of the cold, sinewy fingers. She is horribly gaunt, her bones pushing and stretching against her skin. Sometimes he thinks he might hug her, but the reality is he doesn't dare: it is such an unlikely gesture between the two of them, and he does not like to imagine how he would feel if she pulled away. He clears his throat. 'Mr Bolt is here,' he says. 'The soldier . . .'

She is on her feet in seconds, and pushing past, down the narrow nursery stairs. Freddie stands. The smell of wood polish and fusty bears, crayons and lead paint takes him back. He reaches out and runs his hand up the doorframe, over the grooves where the three of them gouged their heights in 1914. He traces Edward's initials, remembers how Edward had teased him then, that Freddie would never be as tall or as handsome as his older brother. Freddie lets his hand fall away. Edward was a foot taller then; but Freddie is now well in the lead.

Mrs Foley is hanging around outside the library, straining to hear what is being said. Freddie knows she is as anxious not to upset the dowager countess as he is. When she spots him, she says, 'I only wondered if the visitor would like tea.'

'Of course, Mrs F. Why don't you come in?'

He has barely uttered the words before she strides briskly over the threshold, eyeing the newcomer distrustfully.

Victor Bolt is standing awkwardly, his cap in hand. He has the same dark eyes and hair as the Romany gypsies who arrive in the summer, though his skin is pale as winter, in contrast to the grime ingrained in the skin of his hands. He is broad, and the muscles in his back and his wide shoulders strain at the cheap demobilisation suit he is wearing.

'Thank you so much for agreeing to see us, Mr Bolt,' says Freddie's mother. 'When we didn't hear from you, we were worried you would never come, but the major-general is a dear friend, and he promised he would reassure you that we meant no harm.'

Blotches of red are creeping up the man's neck, as if trying to escape the tight collar. He waits for the countess to settle herself before perching uneasily on the edge of his own chair. Against the backdrop of the sumptuous curtains, he seems even grubbier.

'If you wouldn't mind telling me about my boy,' the dowager countess prompts. 'You were in the brigade?'

The man nods. 'South Midlands, Royal Field Artillery,' he says, a Bristol burr thick in his low voice.

'Headquarters at Whiteladies Road?'

'Yes, ma'am.'

'We saw Edward on parade there the last time he was on leave. 1917.'

'Then you might have seen me too . . .' He trails off, then coughs into his hand as if realising he has said something foolish.

'And tell me, when did you join Number 10 Battery?'

'That were really thanks to the captain. I wanted to volunteer . . . and . . . well . . . when the captain heard about me, he put in a good word with the adjutant.'

'You became a driver?'

The man shakes his head. 'I were groom first, and then Captain Damerel were kind enough to put me forward after he lost his first batman . . .'

'Poor Gordon Spiller. He was from here, you know. Our head groom.' There is a pause for a moment, while Bolt stares at his feet, as if in a trance, before snapping back when the countess prompts: 'But you didn't remain batman?'

'Oh yes, ma'am. I stayed batman, but the captain said I were wasted and also put me as a driver when there were . . . well . . . another vacancy . . .'

The countess clears her throat. 'Yes. I read about that in his diary. A sad business. So much waste, of both man and beast. But you managed to rescue his beloved Grey, for which he rightly rewarded you. It seems you shared an affinity with horses.'

'I've worked with ponies all my life. In the Bedminster pits. They may not be so grand as the big beasts that pulled the guns, but they speak the same language.'

The countess stands and drifts over to the window. She stares into the garden. Without turning around, she says, 'And that last day in France? I'd like to hear . . .'

The soldier's fingers start to work at his cap. He glances at Freddie, who looks away. 'It were a bad night. We were dug right in. We had our guns on the Jerry trenches, but they knew they were fighting their last battle, and they gave it all they could . . .'

'Go on . . .'

The soldier swallows again. 'Our breech block had jammed. Gunner Jones were trying to pickaxe it open. Captain Damerel were helping when a German shell landed on the barrel. The captain were thrown across the gun-pit.' Victor's teacup rattles on the saucer as he places it safely on the table. 'I managed to get to the captain, and we were both up on our feet when another shell landed almost on top of us. I were out for a bit, for it were awful dark when I came to. I thought everyone else dead, but then I heard Captain Damerel make a noise . . .' Freddie watches Bolt closely. He is tugging at his shirt collar and there is a film of sweat across his face. A vein in his temple is throbbing. 'I managed to get to him. He were injured real bad. I pulled him out of range . . .' He tails off again.

'And then what?' says Lady Hembury.

'And then the stretcher men came . . .'

'And?'

'And . . . well . . . and then . . . and then he . . .' The soldier wipes a hand across his eyes, and looks up. His dark eyes are impenetrable. 'It were muddled. The battle were still going on. It were a bad injury . . . I stayed with him until the ambulance took him . . . but it were too late . . .' He swallows as he comes to a stop. They sit in unbearable silence. Freddie tries to block the image of his brother, injured . . . dead.

Finally, the countess speaks: 'So you were with him? When he died?'

The man glances nervously from her to Freddie, then drops his eyes to stare miserably at his fingers. He gives a small cough, and – barely perceptible – 'Yes. Well, no . . .'

'Which is it?'

'He . . . he were barely conscious. But I were there when he spoke his last words . . . before he were taken away.'

'And what were they? What were my boy's last words?'

The soldier gathers himself, lifts his chin. 'He said he hoped he'd done nothing to be thought badly for . . . and then . . . and then he said he were sorry . . .'

100

'Sorry? For what?'

The dark eyes dart anxiously between the two of them again, and then the final words come out in a rush: 'The captain always looked out for me, your ladyship, since I were his batman and all. He said that after the war – when it were all over – he'd like me to come and work for him. And now it weren't going to happen . . .'

Freddie struggles to make sense of what he has heard. The whole situation makes him feel uncomfortable. Is this man to be trusted? It seems unjust to be suspicious, yet he cannot imagine his brother suggesting such a thing to a man like this. But he has heard the unlikeliest tales of the Front, of the two sides playing football, of ghosts in the trenches, of miraculous escapes, and what does he know of war, how it can change a man?

Freddie glances at his mother, and is surprised to see her smiling, for the first time in many months. 'Well we can do something about that,' she says. 'We have been looking for staff recently. Mrs Foley? You yourself said you'd had no luck with *The Lady* or Mrs Hunt's registry.'

Freddie is so taken aback that he cannot speak. He stares from Bolt to Mrs Foley, who is equally perturbed. 'But surely the soldier would be better suited to work outdoors, ma'am?' says the housekeeper.

'Then have a word with Mr Mulligan.'

Freddie is shaking his head. 'Mother. We don't know this man . . .'

'What about the stables? You're always muttering about Spiller's son.'

'I'm good with the horses, sir.' Bolt is leaning forward, earnestly nodding his head. 'And quick to learn. Captain Damerel knew that . . .'

'There we are,' says Lady Hembury. 'Is there a Mrs Bolt? It always helps if there are two of you available.'

'There is,' says Victor. 'And she's experienced in domestic service . . .'

Lady Hembury claps her hand to her heart. 'It must be fate. Mrs Foley, do I really have to do your job for you? Bolt could have the lodge house.'

'But it's a wreck,' says Freddie.

'Then let the man clear it up!'

'I can do it,' Bolt adds eagerly.

'But . . .'

'It's what Edward wanted.'

Freddie looks imploringly at Mrs Foley. The housekeeper jangles her keys and clears her throat. 'All the same, we would need a character, madam.'

'Character? Were you not listening? He was Edward's man. If Edward could see fit to commend him twice, I can't see you need any better reference.'

Mrs Foley raises her eyebrows but she cannot argue back. Lady Hembury stands, drawing the conversation to a close. 'It really is so very kind of you to have come to see us, Mr Bolt. And more importantly, to have looked after Edward in his last moments. I am glad that he did not die alone. And I am glad that we will be able to repay you. I look forward to meeting you again.' And with that she sweeps from the room with her head held high, leaving Freddie with the ominous feeling that his brother's follies will for ever shape his own future.

CHAPTER 15

It is agreed that Victor Bolt can move into the lodge house immediately. He returns to Bristol only to collect a small case of belongings. By late spring, the derelict home has been transformed: the roof is fixed, the windows have been rubbed down and varnished, the smashed panes replaced, the gutters cleared, the ivy cut away.

Freddie is at the stables with Victor, explaining what he expects, trying to gauge the man's capabilities. He is still suspicious of his motives. He calls to the groom to show Victor around. Ned Spiller scowls. 'I got to put your lordship's horse in the lower meadow first,' he says, leading Tybalt out into the yard with difficulty: the horse is in a stubborn mood, throwing its head around as the groom fights for control.

Freddie is about to berate him for his insubordination, when he is distracted by the look on Victor's face. The soldier's mouth and eyes are wide with shock, and he has to steady himself against the wall. He is staring at the horse. 'Are you all right?' asks Freddie, but Victor walks forward as if in a dream, raising a hand to touch the dappled grey, running the other along the animal's neck. The horse, too, seems to be surprised by the man's touch, and suddenly drops its head and stands quite still while Victor circles it, shaking his head in disbelief.

Finally Victor turns to Freddie. 'He's so like the captain's horse. Grey. I thought it were him.' His voice is barely a whisper.

'They're from the same line,' says Freddie. 'My brother bred them both. He had such success with Grey that he did it again two years later. Tybalt was too young to go when the army came calling.'

'Grey were a fine beast.'

Freddie feels a lump in his throat, and he has to wait a few seconds before he can speak. 'Have you any idea if the horse survived?'

'Without the captain to speak up for him, he were probably sold. Or worse.' Victor strokes Tybalt absent-mindedly.

Within a week, it is clear that Victor can turn his hand to most things, and he is far better with the horses than Spiller. It becomes a habit for Freddie to go to the stables after break-fast and watch Victor work: it is far preferable to fretting at his desk. Victor is immensely strong yet somehow calm and quiet. He doesn't bully or abuse. The horses seem to under-stand his wishes by the angle of his body, the tilt of his head, and through his broad, scarred hands.

Word spreads, and when Lord Hampden asks if Victor could have a look at one of Lady Hampden's hunters, Freddie agrees: it is the perfect way to butter up his neighbour. The horse is as docile as a lamb in the yard, but it transforms into a fero-cious beast as soon as anyone tries to ride it.

Hampden's own groom delivers the animal on foot to Coombe stables, a walk of about four miles, followed by two stable boys carrying the animal's bridle, saddle, and mono-grammed rugs.

'Good luck to you,' says the groom grimly as he hands the horse over to Spiller. Coombe's head groom takes charge grudgingly; he seems to have grown more sullen than he was before Victor arrived, and Freddie is beginning to find his attitude testing.

Freddie watches from the side of the enclosure as Spiller hands the lead rein to Victor with a glare. The horse stands quietly until Spiller approaches with the saddle, when it wheels away. Victor lets it go, and it gallops to the far side of the pen.

Freddie hears Spiller hiss, 'What you do that for?' before resting the saddle on the railings, and going to try to catch the horse.

Victor doesn't answer, just watches with his unfathomable eyes as the animal backs away each time Spiller closes in on it.

'They must have drugged it to get it here, m'lord,' Spiller growls when their dance has finally ended, and man and beast face each other, sweat glistening and breathing hard.

'Finally broken him, do you think?' calls Freddie. He moves to unlatch the gate and enter the enclosure himself: the horse seems spent and he wants a closer look. Spiller's fingers almost close on the rope, but the horse suddenly reels away again. Freddie glances over his shoulder. The horse has been spooked by the arrival of Mulligan, nervous and pale, with his shuffling limp.

Freddie grunts with irritation. 'Damn. I forgot we were meeting . . .'

'I apologise for disturbing you, m'lord, but it is important. Things are rather coming to a head, and I must have a clear picture of how you plan to pay . . .'

'Yes, yes. I've told you it's in hand.' Out of the corner of his eye, Freddie sees the horse kick out with its back legs, narrowly missing the head groom. 'Can't you see you're upsetting everyone?'

'I'm sorry, m'lord.' Mulligan touches his hat.

'I'll be in the library in five minutes.'

Mulligan nods and backs away. The horse lashes out again, and at the same time Spiller grabs a large stick that was propped up against the fence. Victor shouts for him to stop, but the groom ignores the warning, and runs at the horse, bringing the stick down on the animal's head, and splitting the skin above its eye. The horse screams, and spins sideways, towards Freddie, who, having been distracted by Mulligan, is trapped. He grapples to get out of the way, but the horse is

105

coming straight at him. Time slows. Freddie trips and sprawls, bracing for the crunch of flesh and bone, but suddenly the bulk of Victor throws a shadow over the ground. The man has planted himself directly in the animal's path. Still the horse bears down on them, but Victor stands, solid as one of the pillars at the front of the house, and inches from Victor the animal swings around and gallops away, showering them both in mud.

Time speeds up again. Victor turns and offers Freddie a hand. 'M'lord?'

Freddie's heart is thundering so fast that he cannot speak. Victor pulls him easily to his feet. The horse stands to the side, head down, sides heaving, foam and blood dripping from its muzzle.

Victor strides towards Spiller and snatches the stick from the groom's hand. The two men glower at each other.

Freddie recovers his voice. 'Why the hell did you hit it, Spiller? If Lady Hampden sees . . .'

'A horse like that needs to learn a lesson. You'll never control it if you don't tell it who's master.'

'There's never a need to beat an animal,' says Victor.

Spiller appeals to Freddie. 'M'lord, I can fix this horse by the end of the day. You know I can.' He tries to snatch the stick back, but Victor sidesteps out of the way.

'The stables need a change of direction, Spiller,' he snaps. 'You're to work with Mr Bolt . . . listen to what he says.'

'But Mr Bolt don't understand our ways . . .'

'If you won't, then perhaps I'll make him head groom in your place.'

Spiller glares at him in disbelief. 'But that's my job. It were my father's . . .'

'Are you questioning me?'

'And after my father followed the viscount out to France . . .'

'This man too was in France.'

'He stole my father's job there and all.'

But Freddie has heard enough. 'He didn't steal it. He risked

106

his life for his country. I'll tell you again: if you don't like it, then go.'

'Very well.' Spiller kicks the dirt with his boot and grabs his coat from the fence. He spits on the ground, and without a backward glance, he walks away.

The two men watch the figure disappear down the back drive. Freddie glances at Victor. The man's cheeks are red with exertion, but his manner is as calm as always.

The horse snorts. The doves settle to scratch in the dirt. Freddie is back in control. 'Now what does our new head groom think is wrong with the Hampden horse?' he asks.

Victor shifts from one foot to the other, and pushes his cap up his forehead. 'Saddle's not been fitted right, and it's hurt his back. Change the saddle, and reintroduce it slowly. He'll soon learn it's all right. But first we got to catch him.'

The two men stare at the horse. The horse stares back.

Freddie smiles. 'You know, Edward used to practise for the cavalry when we were children,' he says. 'He used to make me the enemy. I'd have to stand there, just like you did, and he'd charge. I usually stood my ground.'

Victor glances at him, his dark eyes giving nothing away. 'Whatever you did worked a treat. He were a fine captain. Never afraid . . .'

'And always immaculately turned out, no doubt.'

'Always.'

And Freddie smiles, because they are both caked in dirt, their clothes rumpled, hair dishevelled, and slowly a smile starts to spread across Victor's face too, and Freddie feels as if he has a link to his brother's life in France: he can even understand how Edward might have grown close to this quiet man, and that makes him feel closer to his brother, and more positive about the future.

CHAPTER 16

The spring is unseasonably dry, the earth cracked and scarred where the cattle have congregated in the park. The fallow deer lie in dappled shade, too lethargic to move, their wide antlers ungainly, their white tails flicking irritably.

Freddie is surprised to see Maurice in the stable yard. His uncle has come to stay for a long weekend, but he has never liked horses or long rides, preferring instead to spend time indoors with a drink and a conversation. But here he is, picking his way across the cobbles, nose wrinkled as he tries to avoid dirtying his shoes.

'What's dragged you out here?' asks Freddie.

'I never seem to get a moment alone with you. I want you to know there are rumours that Monkton and Granville are looking elsewhere. Possibly somewhere near Taunton.'

'I thought Hampden had been more off with me than usual . . .'

'You haven't exactly had your ear to the ground. You're spending far too many hours out here.'

'We're building up the stables again. It's been a relief to have something to take my mind off things.'

Maurice sighs. 'Can't you just sign the damn document before it's too late?'

'No. I've redrafted it. We must go in with Cottam.'

'I thought you were merely hoping to get the land back by cosying up to the girl? Not actually going into business with him.'

'You were the one that sold it to him in the first place.'

Maurice scratches his chin. 'I suppose he does have business sense,' he says. 'He ran the colliery at the Parkfield site very well. In fact, I rather wish he still did. The whole place is going to pot: workers these days make far too many demands . . .' He stops, and brightens. 'It's not up to me anyway.' He smiles at Freddie. 'Whatever it is you're doing, I urge you to get on with it. Would you like me to talk to Cottam?'

'No!' Freddie does not want his uncle heading off on another tangent. 'I'm actually going there this afternoon. Miss Cottam has invited me and Ginny to see the work they've done since Papa was ill. I plan to broach the subject then.'

Maurice suddenly staggers forwards as a horse nudges him over the top of the stable door. He turns to growl at the beast as he dusts down his shoulder. 'I can't understand what you see in these blasted creatures.'

Freddie laughs. 'I'm toying with the idea of moving into breeding them. There must be money to be made. The country lost so many to the war . . .'

'Have you not seen that marvellous new invention: the motor car?'

Freddie rolls his eyes. 'Horses will always be needed for farming, for hunting . . . The new groom agrees. You remember the horse Edward bred? Grey? Victor thought it the finest . . .'

Maurice snorts impatiently. 'First business deals with the Cottams, and now you are taking advice from a man like that?'

'He was a friend of Edward's . . .'

'Like hell. Edward wasn't friends with such people.' Freddie frowns as the old doubts creep in. Who was the real Edward? The kind brother or the cruel one? 'But I must say the country air seems to have done the man some good. He is a fine specimen . . . of his type.'

Maurice is right. Victor is helping the new stable lad fill water. He has changed dramatically: his skin no longer translucent, but lightly tanned, his troubled eyes clear.

'Quite the war hero,' Maurice continues. 'You'd better watch out your young Cottam filly doesn't catch sight of him. They're rather more in the same league . . .'

'Oh uncle, honestly.' But Freddie has to admit feeling a surge of jealousy at the thought. 'Let's go in for lunch,' he says.

As they enter the back door Victor's wife – now employed in the house – is walking towards them with a bucket of fire ash. She is a wan young thing, who might have been pretty once, but is too thin, with a harshness about her mouth that speaks of trouble. She spots them coming, and freezes. Freddie supposes it is because she is not used to seeing her employer using the servants' entrance, but then he realises it is not him but Maurice who has caught her attention. The last remnants of colour drain from her face, and the bucket falls to the ground with a clatter, clouds of ash billowing everywhere.

'Really!' says Maurice, waving his hands in front of his face and coughing as the dust swirls.

The maid curtseys low, head down, eyes averted as she backs away. 'I'm so sorry, sir,' she says, before falling to her knees and trying to sweep the mess into the bucket.

'On second thoughts, I think I'll leave you to the chaos, old boy,' says Maurice, still batting the air.

'What about lunch?'

'No no. It's time for me to return to Parkfield. Write and tell me how it's going. Toodlepip!' And he disappears through the baize door that separates the house from the staff quarters, leaving Freddie staring at the kneeling maid.

Lady Hembury waves Jennings away. 'I'm not hungry,' she says.

Freddie looks at her. 'Is it troubling you? Is it too soon?'

She shakes her head. 'No. The paperwork needs to be done.'

'I'm sure it will be straightforward. And it doesn't need to be all business. We could go to a museum, or the theatre, like we used to. How about the pet shop in Harrods?'

He reaches out to cover her hand in his, but she removes it from the table, giving him a tight smile. 'We can't stay away for long. There's too much to be getting on with here . . . the stone commemorating Edward . . .'

Freddie pushes his own plate away, his appetite lost too. His brother still takes precedence, even now.

'It will be strange,' says Ginny, 'having Papa's title.'

'Edward's title.'

'Your title now.'

'It feels dishonest somehow.'

'You'll get used to it.'

Their mother says nothing, and Freddie stands, bringing the conversation to a close, relieved they have arranged to visit Celia.

The Cottams' housemaid directs them to the old orchard, where they find Celia and someone they don't recognise knee-deep in brambles. Celia waves, and Freddie feels his melancholy recede a little as a smile breaks across his face. He hasn't seen her for weeks, and now he realises how much he has missed her. Behind her the orchard has been cleared, and the rows of fruit trees are covered in fading white and pink blossom. 'Have you done all this yourself?' asks Ginny.

Celia tries to grapple her hair back into shape, pulling and twisting the thick strands, which keep falling across her face. 'Not me,' she says, indicating the other girl. 'It's all Maggie, really.' Maggie stops to wave, and Freddie notes the dungarees and the hair tied in a knotted headscarf. 'My father found her. She worked for the Women's Land Army at that large flax farm near Yeovil. She did a course at Cannington. She didn't want to go back to the city.'

'We didn't employ women on our farms during the war,' says Freddie.

'That's probably why you were so unproductive,' says Celia, wiping her hands on her skirt and grinning. 'Maggie's a godsend. She's learnt everything – from ploughing and

111

harvesting to weaning and milking. It's just as well, since I couldn't get any of the men to show me. I persuaded my father to relinquish the dairy. He can find other places to park his cars. The milk factory in Hemyock says it will take all of our milk. We're planning to make cheese ourselves . . . and restore the orchard, as you can see. Did you know there are more than eighty varieties of apple here? They've got funny names, like Sheep's Nose and Crimson King. Apparently Littlecombe used to produce the best cider in Devon. Or so they say in the village . . . But of course you know that. It used to belong to you.'

Ginny shakes her head, and Freddie says, 'I had no idea.'

'Well, we'd like to grow something, and I don't think tea would be suitable!'

'Ha ha.'

'Come and have a look at what else we've been up to.'

Freddie and Ginny admire the clean yard, the repaired doors, the oiled tools. There are chickens scratching around in the courtyard of the outbuildings. Last year's hay is neatly stacked, and there are calves jostling in the shed. They gaze at Freddie with eyes like the pools of ink in his father's study, stretching out their glossy red necks and licking their wet noses with sandpapery tongues.

Freddie is grudgingly admiring: 'Fine, healthy specimens.'

'It's a start.'

Celia pushes open the doors to the old cider barn, leaning heavily against their weight. Inside, the cider press has been stripped back and cleaned, the great iron screw gleams in the light, the large oak planks have been sanded back. Celia walks to the far end where there are barrels stacked neatly on top of each other, returning with a flagon and three enamel mugs. 'This isn't ours,' she says. 'But it'll give you an idea. We'll press our first batch this autumn. See where it takes us.' They follow her out through the other side of the barn, through matching doors that open up into the fields below the house. They sit, and Freddie feels the stalks and stems tickle and

112

scratch at his skin, the warmth of the ground beneath his fingertips. The sky is clear, the hills are hazy. He could almost be in another country.

Celia pours the cider, releasing its scent of late summer. Freddie takes a swig. 'Not bad,' he says, savouring the taste of sunshine and apples. 'Though it's not my usual tipple.'

'Delicious,' says Ginny.

They sit in amicable silence, enjoying the heat of the sun.

'What news of that brother of yours?' asks Freddie. He met George while he was visiting, and it did not go well. The man was the opposite of Celia – boorish and discourteous, with outlandish ideas about equality in society.

'George was very rude. I'm sorry. There was no need for it.'

'He's not the only one,' says Ginny. 'Celia and I are in agreement that brothers get away with a lot.'

'You haven't had it so hard,' says Freddie. 'Think of me – sent away to Radley while Edward went to Eton. Second-rate education for second-rate son.'

'What rot!' says Ginny. 'You loved Radley. And the pair of you in the same school would have made trouble for everyone else.'

'Were they naughty?' asks Celia.

Ginny laughs. 'Always . . .' She glances at Freddie. 'But it is hard being in an older sibling's shadow . . .'

'Especially when he's the favourite.'

'Think what it's like being sandwiched between two brothers.'

'Being a sister to one is bad enough,' says Celia.

'You women can't gang up on me. I'll go and get Maggie to help. She looks as if she wouldn't take any nonsense.'

The sound of the church bell chiming the hour drifts up the valley from the village. 'Oh dear,' says Ginny. 'I'd better dash. Major Thornberry's coming to play tennis . . .'

'I'm staying right here,' says Freddie. 'I'm enjoying my cider.' He fishes out a thunder bug that is wriggling in the liquid and wipes it on the ground.

113

'Will you be all right without a chaperone, Celia?'

'She'll be perfectly safe,' says Freddie, colouring slightly.

Celia smiles up at Ginny, shielding her eyes from the sun. 'I'll see you when you're back from London.'

'I'll take her swimming down by the boathouse,' says Freddie, regaining his composure.

'You will not.' Ginny eyes him disapprovingly.

'I don't have a costume anyway,' says Celia.

'Neither do I.' He feels a tingle of pleasure as he watches her cheeks burn.

After Ginny has gone they sit silently, listening to the rustle of the grass and the drone of the hoverflies. Celia lies back, disappearing into the wildflowers, and Freddie does too. The sky is the same colour as his mother's eyes, as Edward's eyes. He closes his own, and the world turns dark, and his other senses sharpen, and he forgets about his mother, and his brother, and he can sense only the heat emanating from Celia's body and the beat of her heart. He remembers sitting with her after her fall. She is so different to the usual girls he meets, who either fawn over the fact he is connected to Coombe, or are disappointed that he is not Edward. Celia does not care about Coombe, never knew Edward.

He pushes himself up on to an elbow. He cannot resist picking a bright blue cornflower and putting it behind her ear. It looks so perfect there against the russet of her hair. She puts up her hand and her cool, soft fingers gently brush his, sending a spark of pleasure in the sensation of her touch, as light as a moth.

He falls back on to the grass, and she turns her head to him, stares into his eyes. 'I haven't had a chance to talk to you properly since your father died. How are you? Really?' she asks.

He sees that the sun has scattered freckles across her skin, resists the urge to touch them. 'It's hard. I feel alone.' As always he finds it easy to allow the truth to escape from his mouth when he's with her.

'You're not alone.' Celia holds his gaze until she grows bashful and looks away, giving him a thrill that he has some sway over her feelings. He has never had that with other women – usually finds himself fumbling for words.

'I'm sorry you never got back to the hospital,' he says.

'If those dark years of war taught me anything, it's that we've got to live in the moment.'

'I admire your fortitude.'

'I enjoy learning new skills.'

'Then farming will suit you. It changes all the time. Forecasts never match prices, the weather always does the opposite to what you expect, and then of course the government suddenly do things like repeal the Agriculture Act . . .'

'Did you lose money?'

'Not as much as some. We're lucky we don't grow much wheat. But I never thought a government would go back on a promise.'

'Perhaps you are too used to getting your own way.'

She looks at him again, raising an eyebrow, and he knows she is gently teasing, and he laughs. But then he sighs. 'I don't always get my own way,' he says. 'This isn't the life I chose.'

'You'll still get to Ceylon one day, I'm sure.'

'I hope so. I had another postcard from my business partner Matthew today.'

She sits up. 'Let's see. More elephants?'

He sits too, pulling the card from his pocket. 'No. Monkeys, this time.'

She turns the card over to read. 'Sounds as if things are progressing.'

He smiles as he elucidates. 'Our first crop was a success. So much so that we've been able to purchase a state-of-the-art boiler. Apparently it was pulled to the factory by three elephants.'

115

Celia laughs. 'Imagine that procession making its way through the village here.'

'I just long to see it all myself. I want to experience another country. To live another life. Not to be trussed up in a dinner jacket or a hunting jacket every day of the week.'

'I can't see you going native, Lord Hembury.'

'Who knows what I would do? I just want the chance to try! I love the prospect of things being less formal. There's real opportunity to make something of oneself.'

'It's hard to believe there's anywhere like that – a place without preconceptions and judgement.'

His blood sings again as he warms to the theme. 'Exactly. It would be a clean slate. To be able to prove oneself, to make a life for oneself.'

'I understand. I also dream of somewhere not limited by class and expectation.'

'You must come out and see for yourself.'

'That's the most exciting prospect I've ever had.' Her eyes are shining. And his spirits lift further: it is the first time anyone other than Matthew has seen the merits of his alternative life in such a way.

'We could ride an elephant together. And there are so many exotic plants, and people. Everything is brighter. The colours. The weather. Harvest must be quite a sight: all the women carry their baskets on their heads. One day . . .' He tails off, and his face falls. 'But Coombe must come first.'

'So what are your plans for next year?'

'Well . . .' He takes a deep breath. This is his moment. 'I wanted to talk to you about an idea that might seem a little far-fetched, but . . . it's possible it could work . . . You see, my brother had a plan to build a racecourse. He had drawn up draft plans before he left. But my uncle arranged for the sale of a prime piece of land – now yours – to cover some of the costs, and well . . . if I am to retain any sort of control we need it back, or at least we need you . . . or your father, really . . . on board . . .'

116

She looks apologetically at her hands before answering: 'I'm afraid my father wouldn't like it.'

'But I thought he was into new business ventures . . .'

'He is. But he doesn't like horse racing. He's a Guardian, and he's seen the harm betting can do. Many of the men who ended up in the workhouse in Bristol had lost money to illegal gambling.'

'But a racecourse is the only place you can *legally* gamble.'

She shakes her head. 'He won't want to be involved. But perhaps you could talk to him about other possibilities. He has so many ideas . . .'

'I have my own ideas, thank you.'

'Of course.'

Freddie drains the last of his cider, warm and sweet. All roads lead back to Ceylon.

'It's just such a disaster,' he says, leaning back and looking up at the sky. 'All of it . . . I know they couldn't have predicted what was going to happen, but I wish my father and brother had left Coombe in better shape. I'm ashamed of how awful the situation is.'

'I don't consider you impoverished yet.'

He rolls his eyes. 'I'm the Earl of Hembury. I've got a large estate and a house to run, a family to look after. There are expectations . . . duties . . . I don't expect you to understand.'

'The tea business will help?'

'It might. Except now Matthew wants me to find space in a warehouse in London so that we have somewhere to store our tea when production really gets going. He also has an idea that we could be selling directly to the customer, without having to deal with the tea merchants . . .'

'It sounds sensible.'

'But to sell our own tea. That involves more investment. A factory. Packaging . . .'

'Not impossible . . .'

'And then I have an idea we should be breeding horses. Coombe has had success with it in the past. And it's something

117

I can do right now, here on my doorstep. But all of these things cost money. Money that I don't have.' It's embarrassing to speak about finances like this, but the drink has loosened his tongue. 'We already had so many debts. And there are more to come.'

'I could lend you some.'

He pauses, shocked, as her words sink in. 'You would do that for me?'

'Why not? My father set up a trust when I was born. I've had access to it since I turned 21 . . .'

'I couldn't . . . Matthew and I are joint partners. He has an equal hand in the business. I couldn't offer you that.'

'I wouldn't expect it. It would just be a loan: my father got a loan from the bank to purchase his first colliery. It's the same thing. And I would love to be a part of it; to travel there with you one day.'

Freddie bites his lip. He can hardly believe he's considering it, but she makes it seem so straightforward. 'If I take you up,' he says, 'I'd rather keep it between us.'

'May I ask why?'

'I don't want my family finding out just yet. I can't understand why you would be so kind,' he adds, seeing she is downcast. He cannot think of anyone else who would offer such a thing without a caveat, but then he doesn't have such discussions within his circle. 'Would you mind your name not being registered anywhere?'

She shakes her head. 'Not yet, anyway.' The colour rises in her cheekbones again.

'Thank you. You cannot know what this means to me.'

She nods and her blue eyes flash with pleasure. Her cheek looks soft; her lips are full, and the cider must be going to his head because their hands are touching, and the electricity of her skin against his has set his heart pounding. Nothing seems to matter when he's with her. His insecurities melt away, and he feels as if he could do anything – that he doesn't need some madcap idea of a racecourse to keep the plantation and

118

Coombe running – that he is bursting with a million other ideas that will work. And he is so grateful that he cannot resist stealing a kiss to thank her. Her in-breath of shock mirrors the fluttering deep within his own ribcage, and he backs away, hoping he hasn't offended her. Her eyes are wide, the pupils dilated, but she is smiling shyly as she meets his gaze.

His fingers on her face are gentle, and her lips seek his. His body wants to mould itself to hers. He senses it is the same for her. He separates from her once more, looking down into her eyes with a question, and she pulls him back in answer – and for the next breathless moments, their bodies are consumed by each other, and he believes in a new future: for the earl and the mine-owner's daughter on the plantation in Ceylon.

CHAPTER 17

The house in Cadogan Square is like spring sunshine after a hard winter. The colours are vibrant: gold and green and blue rather than the muted browns and dusty crimsons of the antique furniture at Coombe. People, cars, trams, bicycles, horses and carts clamour past the windows. With Celia's loan, Freddie has refused to bow to pressure from Hampden and the others to go into the racecourse on such unequal footing. The relief at extracting himself was worth Maurice's short-lived tantrum, and now he feels as if he has a real part in the future of Coombe rather than existing only in Edward's shadow. Instead he will make his own mark, breed some fine horses of a type fit for Coombe, whose line will carry their name forward into the future. Her money has already helped with urgent repairs to the stables, as well as with entertaining a couple of tea brokers on his visit to Butlers Wharf at Tower Bridge.

As Freddie's understanding of the business grows, he can see why it would be better to package and sell their own tea than to rely on the brokers. The problem is that it means greater investment – certainly the rest of Celia's loan – and although that should eventually mean a greater return, it would take far longer to come to fruition than a decent pedigree. It is a gamble.

He visits the solicitor with his mother. She does not say it, but Freddie knows she too balks at the irregular turning of the second born son – the Honourable – into the Earl of Hembury. Afterwards, they both throw themselves into a plethora of social engagements: dinners and dances, hotels and houses, taxis and white-gloved servants. It all serves to distract.

Sybil gives a party at Claridge's, part of her delayed season. Ginny and Freddie urge their mother past the dark bundles of men sleeping on the streets beneath pieces of newspaper. Ginny grips Freddie's arm tightly. She reads the scribbled sign next to the upturned hat: '"No home, no job, no future". Too awful,' she whispers.

The blanket moves and a man peers up at them. 'That's what you get for fighting for king and country,' he says.

Freddie throws a penny into the hat and pulls his mother and sister quickly towards the hotel entrance.

Tom is there, and Freddie embraces Harriet especially warmly. She seems nervous of them, and when she introduces her fiancé, Freddie realises why.

'But we're so happy for you, Harriet dearest,' says Ginny.

'Are you?' says Harriet, not looking in the least bit happy.

'Of course. You couldn't have turned into a nun. Edward would never have wanted that. And Charles seems awfully nice.'

Harriet leans in closer. 'We met ice skating in the winter. I was meant to be going to Paris, but I think . . .'

'You think you'll be married soon? How exciting. And well done you. Men are rather thin on the ground these days . . .' Ginny stops, then adds brightly: 'Paris is off the menu for us too.' She drops her voice to a stage whisper: 'We're counting pennies.'

'How is Coombe?'

'Falling apart. But we have faith in Freddie . . .'

They both look at Freddie and he raises a glass, puts on his cheeriest voice. 'All will be well.'

He soon grows tired of small talk, and is relieved to see Tom battling his way through the crowd with a distinguished-looking man in dress uniform at his side, the medals spread across his chest gleaming in the light. 'I'd like you to meet

121

Nicholas Helstrom. He's a friend from Oxford. Returned to his studies after being interrupted by the war. Won a scholarship, you know.'

'How do you do?' says Freddie.

'Very well, thank you.' The handshake is as clipped and curt as Nicholas's voice. 'We have mutual acquaintances: Tom tells me you're related to the Armstrong-Joneses, and old friends of the Weymouths.'

Freddie nods. He regards the medals on Nicholas's chest. 'Looks as if you had an eventful war.'

'I did. And I'll fight to the death to make sure it was worth it.' Nicholas steps aside as they are joined by a woman. 'My sister, Elizabeth,' he says.

Elizabeth is strikingly beautiful, with eyes as green as new clover and skin as pale as the marble statues at Coombe. She holds out a hand, and Freddie takes it.

'I've heard all about you from Tom,' she says.

'All good, I hope?'

'More than good.'

She smiles, a slow, elegant turning up of the mouth, which stretches into her eyes. 'Tom says your home is simply magnificent.'

'Tom hasn't been for a while . . .'

'Is it true you have deer in the park? I do love deer. And I hear you have one of the best hunts in the country. Some challenging fences.'

'Now that *is* true.'

'I hope you'll invite us one day. Nicholas and I both adore a challenge.'

'It would be my pleasure.'

'Now,' she says. 'I hear you've been making life difficult for Lucky Monkton and his pals.'

Freddie flushes. 'How on earth . . .'

'Lucky is my godfather,' she laughs. 'You mustn't be embarrassed. You were absolutely right to reject going into business with him. It would never have worked in your favour. He's a perfect devil. No loyalty to anyone apart from himself. In fact, I have it on good authority that he's already found somewhere else.'

'I know. He was bragging about it at White's the other day.'

At the time, Freddie had been annoyed listening to Monkton boasting about his new plan for a racecourse near Taunton – annoyed because Monkton had appropriated Edward's idea, even though he is still certain the price would have been too high for Coombe.

Elizabeth calls gently to him. 'Please don't look so dejected,' she says. 'It doesn't suit you. You seem more the dark and mysterious type than the sullen and depressed.' Then she smiles as if something is dawning on her. 'You know what? You could have a little fun.' She drops her voice to a stage whisper. 'I hear from Maurice that you're planning to dabble in a bit of breeding?'

Freddie nods. 'Hunters and some heavy horses.'

'How about racehorses?'

'They're not exactly my speciality.'

'How different can it be?'

'Well . . .'

'Think of it: you could be breeder and owner. There aren't many who do that. Imagine what fun it would be to swoop in and watch it win on Lucky's new racecourse . . . And a fitting tribute to your dear brother.'

Freddie smiles. 'Yes. Now that would be quite something.'

'Will you do it? Say you will! I'd love to be involved. I adore racing: the speed, the silks, and of course a spot of gambling. It would be such fun. I know some fine trainers who would love to help bring Lucky down a peg or two . . . and we would make quite a team . . .'

Freddie is quite caught up in the moment, imagining Monkton's face puce with anger as another one of the Hembury horses sweeps past the post.

'You look like you're enjoying yourselves.' Ginny approaches with Tom.

'It's wonderful,' says Elizabeth, taking Ginny's arm. 'Your brother is quite the catch, and you look fabulous. Where have you both been hiding?'

Ginny throws Freddie an unreadable glance. 'Well . . .'

'I'm having a small party later. I shall be mortified if you're not there.' She slips a card into his pocket as she walks off with Ginny. Freddie watches her go. She is clearly aware of his eyes on her back, and waves a hand as they disappear into the crowd.

'I see you're taking my advice at last?' says Tom with a nudge. 'She's perfect for you. No children. Pots of money. Her husband was in my brother's regiment. He died in the war. You know, her family are some kind of foreign royalty. They came over from Europe decades ago, during one of their revolutions, I believe. But you're an ideal match. Made for each other.'

Freddie wants to fend off his words, to say this woman does not light a fire in his blood like another back home. But sometimes it is easier to nod along with what your family and friends expect, so he smiles and raises his glass to Tom before downing the drink.

All too soon it is time to pack their things and say goodbye to Cadogan Square. They have let it for the following year, and Freddie is not sure whether he will see it again. The old heaviness begins to weigh down on his shoulders as they approach Coombe. The countryside is so dark compared to the luminous streets of London. He catches a glimpse of Littlecombe, its cosy light swiftly swallowed up by the night as they sweep past and turn into the drive towards the great house.

A weak, faltering light flickers by the front door. Mrs Foley and Jennings are there to greet them. The house smells musty, of damp and dust, despite the fire that is burning in the hall. 'Everything been all right while we've been away?' he asks Mrs Foley as she fusses over Lady Hembury, chivvying her up to her bedroom.

The housekeeper nods, and collects various envelopes. 'All the letters are here. There's a package on your desk. And this was hand-delivered by Mulligan.'

He takes the envelope with a burgeoning feeling of gloom. 'Thank you. Please see to my mother. I'll be in the study.'

'Very well.'

In his father's study Freddie holds the package against the desk lamp. There is a scroll and a bronze disc, one of the memorial plaques that the government has been sending to commemorate the fallen. He slides it into one of the drawers. He will keep it from his mother for now.

He extracts Mulligan's letter, stares at it bleakly. It is the one they have been dreading. Death duties. Of course he's been expecting it, but in black and white it is a different thing. Forty per cent inheritance tax on his father's death, and then on his brother's. A punishment that will push them to a place from which they will never clamber back.

He puts his head in his hands. And after everything was beginning to pick up – the tea, and the horses – he was just starting to get a handle on it. And now what? Throw it all away? Lose their home? Lose everything? There must be something that can be done. He remembers his conversation with Tom, and a vision of the feline Elizabeth sways through his mind.

Ginny knocks, popping her head around the door. 'You look frightful. Anything I can help with?'

He looks up, forcing a smile as he shoves the letter to the bottom of the pile. He will deal with it in the morning. 'I might just stay here and have a drink.'

'It was such fun in London. I hope you thought so too. You need to relax sometimes. I'm glad Elizabeth and Nicholas are coming to stay. Things could do with livening up a bit around here. Perhaps we could ask a few others, otherwise they might be bored?'

He smiles grimly at the prospect of a house party. 'Let's talk about it tomorrow. Night night.'

Ginny closes the door softly. Freddie moves to the window. A shadow seems to have settled in his heart. A floorboard creaks. The terrier lifts its head from his foot. Freddie moves to stroke it, and it settles. Could Elizabeth be the key to all their problems? She is rich and socially acceptable. With a woman like that he could swiftly restore the house, and his family's prospects. It is what is expected of him. She has the kind of pedigree his family and friends approve of. She certainly seemed amenable. But at what cost?

He opens one of the French doors, shivering as the fresh air sweeps across his skin, for it is ice-cold. The night smells of damp earth and wood smoke. A crescent moon splits the sky, a tear in the universe. He thinks of how in a different world he once had the freedom of a second son. He is someone else now: someone older, alone. He must knuckle down, save the house, and provide another son to follow those that have come before, to be painted on to the panelling in the Great Hall.

The deep sound of cattle lowing in a barn drifts through the darkness. They must be the Littlecombe herd, brought in for the winter, and they are not happy about it. It will be twice as noisy in the Cottams' yard. He wonders if Celia is listening too. He feels a rush of regret combined with gratitude: thanks to her, things have begun moving in the right direction at last. Can he betray what they have? What do they have? A brief flirtation. It can be no more than that when he has a house, a title, a history to preserve. It is all up to him now, no matter the cost. Surely Celia will understand. She will see that he has no choice. In the wood, a tawny owl hoots, and something screeches in reply: a rabbit in a trap.

CHAPTER 18

Before the house party, there is frenetic activity at Coombe. There is no need to open the west wing, but Ginny insists that the staff sweep through the rest of the house, bringing flowers and cuttings from the greenhouse, beating the dust from the carpets and curtains, making everything appear fresh and bright. There is a buzz about the place that hasn't been seen since before the war, since before Edward left.

Ginny is finalising seating plans. 'Caroline Williamson has dropped out. Terrible morning sickness.'

'That's all right,' says Freddie. 'They were only coming for the dinner on Saturday. We'll just move the spaces up.'

'But Harry wants to come. He says he's bored to tears. Feels as if he's in confinement too. I've invited Celia as his other half. I didn't think you'd mind; you're such good pals.'

Freddie feels sick at the thought of Celia meeting Elizabeth. More than anything he would like to keep the two sides of his life separate. But the day of reckoning is inevitable. It might as well be sooner rather than later.

The weekend is grim and rain-spattered, which only makes the house seem more festive. Outside, the last of the autumn leaves twirl from the bare branches, and lie scattered across the lawn until the gardener has time to rake and burn them. The teasels no longer rattle with seeds, for they have been stripped by the goldfinches.

Freddie stands at the top of the stairs. The sombre house is aglow. He has had to employ eight temporary staff from the village to get the place ready. He surveys the hall, the polished silver, the garlanded statues, the flickering candles. There is ivy wound around the columns, and the marble floor has been polished and buffed so that it shines as much as the shoes that crisscross it. A footman stands against the wall with a tray of drinks, and in the far corner below the tapestry is a string quartet.

Nicholas and Elizabeth have descended from their guests' quarters and are mingling with his friends. Nicholas stands head and shoulders above the rest, straight-backed and confident; people gather around him like moths to a flame. Elizabeth's blonde hair has been cut in a fashionable bob, every strand of it straight and perfect. It is the colour of a field of corn in the early morning, and held in place by a band covered in jewels that twinkle and sparkle like the chandeliers. Men and women cannot resist watching her; she moves with the grace of a ballet dancer.

As Freddie descends, the guests look up and some wave, a smattering of satin gloves and pink hands above the colourful dresses and black and white suits. He scans the faces for Celia, worried about how the evening will unfold. Lady Hembury bows her head as he reaches her at the bottom. 'You've pulled it off,' she says.

'With Ginny's guidance,' he answers, smiling as his sister appears at his shoulder.

Freddie wanders among his friends. Tom is there with his new wife, a wide-hipped girl with an exuberant smile. 'I thought you'd grow fusty out here in the sticks,' he says, 'but this is like the good old days.'

James joins their group. He has filled out – there is success in the extra flesh, the success of a desk job. 'Government clearly suits you,' says Freddie. 'Remind me to introduce you to Nicholas later.'

He walks on. There is Harriet, with Charles standing stiffly next to her. Freddie bends to kiss her cheek. 'Dear Harriet.

You look positively blooming.' Charles puts a protective arm around her shoulders and Freddie shakes his hand. 'Congratulations to you both,' he says.

Finally he reaches Elizabeth. She too has been working the room, ending up in conversation with Maurice. 'Such a beauty,' says his uncle. 'Helen of Troy. With as many suitors, no doubt. You'd better get in there quick, my boy.'

Elizabeth smiles and her green eyes soften. She briefly curtseys to Freddie and then holds out a hand encased in a white glove. Freddie takes hold of it and feels the long fingers, the bumps of her knuckles hidden inside. He kisses it and the satin feels soft against his lips as he inhales her rich perfume. He wills himself to feel some attraction. He knows she is sophisticated, urbane; he knows others find her bewitching. Besides, it is a rarity for two people to be passionate when they marry. It is a transaction, and husband and wife can grow to love each other – his parents are a perfect example. One must be practical about these things.

'I hope your rooms are comfortable,' he says. He has ensured that Mrs Foley oversaw the preparation of the finest guest rooms in the house.

Maurice glances from one to the other. 'He's certainly pulled out the stops, my dear. It's been a while since we saw such a happy party of guests here for the weekend.'

Elizabeth turns to greet another guest, and Maurice leans in. 'Well this puts a whole new flavour on things,' he whispers. 'No need to settle for coal when you've got diamonds.' Maurice bumps him with his shoulder. 'You're growing more like your brother every day. Money and class. The only way is upwards from here, my boy.'

Elizabeth turns back and Maurice extends an arm, resting his hand in the small of her back. 'Let me show you the Poussin,' he says. 'One of the few originals we kept. You'll love it.'

They stop as the chill of winter forces its way into the hall. Maurice glances at the clock on the chimneypiece. 'The irony of the neighbour being late,' he says.

Freddie's resolve weakens as he spots Celia.

'What a fish out of water,' says Elizabeth. 'Do go and rescue her, Freddie.'

Celia is looking nervously around as one of the servants takes her cloak. Freddie swallows, and heads to greet her, forcing himself to think of the negatives with each step he takes. She is different; that might be fine in another place, another country, but here, in front of his family and friends, it is too glaringly obvious. And while she has some wealth at her disposal, it is nothing compared to Elizabeth's fortune. The only jewellery she is wearing is a pair of small emerald earrings. The knot in her thick auburn hair is threatening to come loose, and her smooth skin, still coloured by the summer sun, is so much darker than that of the other ladies. Yet when she turns as he makes his way to her, and catches his eye, he sees her relief, and cannot help his heart going out to her. He is a cad. He takes her cold hand, with its rough underneath, and kisses it. Her small, cool hands remind him of that afternoon before he went to London, and he feels a surge of heat flush his face. He lets go. When she glances up, her blue eyes seem to sear right to his soul, and the guilt washes over him again. It would never work. He must not be swayed by emotion. His duty lies elsewhere.

'Can we walk soon?' she asks. 'It's been so long.'

He doesn't trust his voice to reply. He would like to, of course he would. But it wouldn't do. Not when he is going to have to relinquish their relationship. 'I'm so glad you could make it,' is all he can manage, and then, to his relief Ginny whisks Celia away, and immediately he is surrounded by friends eager to talk about Elizabeth, where she came from, who her parents are, how exotic she is, how she must have suffered, poor thing, losing her husband, but how she will therefore understand better than anyone his own losses.

They are called to the dining room. Freddie takes his place at the head of the table; his mother is at the other end; between them the paraphernalia of a party, the crystal glasses and the decorations, the flowers and the fruit. The guilt that he is sitting in his brother's place still tastes bitter.

The starters appear, creamed mushrooms and iced artichokes, elegantly arranged on the plate. Only now does he realise that Elizabeth is seated on his right, with Celia on his left. He silently curses whoever set the places.

The conversation flows around the table, heads turning politely to listen to the person on one side before turning to the other. Jewels glimmer and sparkle in the candlelight. Feathers nod, glasses clink. Sometimes the conversation includes the whole table, especially when Lady Hembury is talking.

Elizabeth leans across, addressing Celia. 'And what is it that you do?' she asks. 'You look as if you must be involved in something. Fundraising for the local needy? Or perhaps working at the local school?'

'Celia is in the process of setting up a successful farm,' says Freddie, getting a hold of himself.

'A land girl? How charming. I've not got the hands for it. I would need to be rescued from all that muck . . .'

'I've never needed rescuing,' says Celia, and Freddie can hear the irritation in her voice.

'Oh, is that right? Because Ginny told me you had to be rescued out hunting.' Freddie grimaces inside, wishes Ginny hadn't mentioned it, though he is sure she intended it in admiration rather than Elizabeth's more negative spin on it. 'I must say,' Elizabeth continues, 'I think you're very game to have tried it at all. It can be hard on amateurs.'

'I won't be doing it again,' says Celia, glaring at Freddie momentarily.

'You're against it then?'

'I'd rather not do it myself.'

'I suppose you're against coursing too?'

'I can't really see the enjoyment of watching hares being ripped apart either, if that's what you mean.'

131

'Don't let my mother hear you say that,' Freddie interjects, glancing at the dowager countess. 'She's the proud winner of the Waterloo Cup.'

'It's city types,' says Elizabeth. 'They don't understand the ways of the country.'

'I thought you were from the city?' says Celia. 'London?'

'Not originally. My father's family came from Belgium almost a century ago, but my mother's family is from Lancashire. Also home to said Waterloo Cup.'

'And Pankhurst country.'

'If you must.'

'Not a fan of the Suffragettes?'

'I think there are better ways of dealing with men. I find a soft approach works wonders.'

'I'm not sure I agree . . .'

'Are you thinking of throwing yourself in front of a horse, then?'

'I hope not,' says Freddie, trying to soothe the situation. 'Our first broodmare from a racing stables arrives this week. I wouldn't want her to come to any harm . . .'

'Racing stables?' asks Celia, her forehead creasing as Freddie avoids her gaze.

Elizabeth nods. 'A multiple prizewinner in her time. But of course we're talking horses and not greyhounds.' She reaches out to rest her hand briefly on Freddie's arm, as if laying claim, before looking back at Celia. 'Isn't it exciting?'

Celia glares at Freddie. 'I should think such a creature costs a bit.'

'Oh dear,' says Elizabeth, retracting her hand. 'You don't disapprove of racing too . . .'

'It's really her father who doesn't approve,' says Freddie, desperately trying to think of ways to move the conversation on. He cannot tell Celia now, but he will assure her later that he does not intend to use her money for the racehorses. He can just about pay for the broodmare himself, and if all goes well, he can see a future where Elizabeth will come in on the rest.

'Can't you breed normal horses?' asks Celia. 'Useful horses?'

'And where would be the fun in that?' Elizabeth retorts.

'It's not the fun that is the point. It's the business. May I ask how are you planning to fund such a venture, m'lord?' She uses the term acerbically. 'I understand that the estate has had problems recently.'

Elizabeth looks at her in horror. 'You can't ask a man about such things.'

Freddie is floundering, wondering how to alter the course of their conversation.

From the other end of the table, Maurice shouts, 'Do you really think you can breed a winner?' Freddie has never been so relieved to hear his uncle's voice.

'He certainly can,' says Elizabeth. 'And I'm allowed to name the first foal . . .'

There is the scrape of a chair and Celia throws her napkin on to the table. Everyone stares. She gets to her feet and all the men begin to rise too.

'No, no,' she says. 'Stay where you are. I hope you don't think me rude, but I must get back. We're expecting some calves to be born tonight and I can't leave it to the stockman. We've lost too many recently.'

The guests glance at one other, embarrassed.

'A veterinarian as well. Is there no end to your talents?' Elizabeth's eyes are wide with false wonder.

The two women's eyes glitter at each other. 'Goodnight, everyone,' says Celia.

And for a moment, Freddie forgets convention, and rises from the table with brief excuses, following her out into the hall, where the housemaid is extracting her coat. Celia barely throws it on as she hurries for the door.

'Celia! Wait.'

She pauses at the bottom of the steps, the warm light from the house spilling on to her upturned face. 'Don't follow me,' she says. 'I wouldn't want you to miss a moment with Miss Bloodsports.'

'I'm sorry.' He tries to get hold of her, but she backs away.

'Who is she, anyway? She seems to believe your fortunes are aligned . . .'

'She . . .' Sweat prickles at the back of his neck. Is he really going to say this?

But there is no need. Celia's eyes widen in understanding. Freddie feels sick to the stomach. 'I . . . Look, it's the damn house . . . the estate. I wish it was different. I don't think you realise how in debt we are. I need her money . . .'

She stares hard at him. 'I gave you money,' she says. 'A fact you seem to have conveniently forgotten.'

'I haven't. Of course I haven't. You know how very grateful I am. It has already helped beyond measure. Ceylon is a real possibility now. But Coombe is something else entirely . . .'

'I don't want your gratitude, Freddie.'

He breaks her gaze. 'I can't give you more than that, no matter how much I wish I could.'

'You would sacrifice your own happiness for your family's?'

'It's the way we do things.'

'And there is the truth of it,' she responds. 'I have less of a pedigree than the horses you plan to breed.' Her eyes are ice-cold.

'Don't say that.'

But she is already moving away. 'Go back to your people, Freddie.'

'Please say you forgive me, that you understand.'

She laughs – a bitter sound – and he can see that she will not give him that – and he feels a sense of panic. 'I don't want to lose you. This doesn't have to end . . .'

'You want me to be your mistress?' she replies with contempt, and he is disgusted with himself. 'Goodbye, Freddie.'

Behind him, he hears Ginny calling, and he turns to see his sister standing in the doorway, framed by the light.

'Freddie! What on earth do you think you're doing?' she hisses. 'You can't leave the table! You're the host. Everyone is waiting for you – including Elizabeth. Please don't muck this up. She may be your only choice.'

Inside he groans. Even his sister expects him to do his duty. He turns back, to Celia, to freedom and true feelings. But Celia has slipped away into the darkness, taking a part of him with her.

CHAPTER 19

Freddie lies awake in the early hours. He has been unable to sleep. He is upset about Celia's departure, but knows he could not have expected her to stay. He groans as he remembers his suggestion they could carry on somehow. It is the kind of behaviour that would have suited Edward more.

The thoughts race around his head like horses around a track. With Elizabeth, he could be the one to secure the future of Coombe – not just in his lifetime, but for generations. He could even pay back Celia with the proceeds from the horses, without having to wait for the plantation to profit. He could pay her interest as a thank you.

He turns on to his side. It still catches him by surprise sometimes when he wakes in his parents' bedroom. The carved headboard looms over him. It is an honour to be head of the family, and he is right to pursue Elizabeth. She is the solution to all. He imagines his ancestors breathing a collective sigh of relief. Celia and he are entirely unsuited. He must stop fixating on her. He owes her nothing but the repayment on a loan.

It is still dark outside. His head is bleary. Someone is scraping the grates clean. No one apart from the servants is up; the guests will not rise for hours. The stale smell of last night's ash, dampened, dead, is being blown away by the morning air, still cool with dew. New fires are being lit.

Freddie's head is pounding. His mouth is dry as sand. He is desperate for water. There is none left in the carafe by the bed. He must have drunk it all. He rises, wraps himself in his dressing gown, makes his way downstairs in the shadows of memories of last night. The candles are long gone. Stale cigarette smoke lingers in the air. He hears the sound of glasses being cleared. The easiest thing would be to collect water from the dining room. There must be some left on the sideboard or on the table. He makes his way there. One of the temporary housemaids approaches with a tray of dirty glasses. She keeps her eyes averted and bobs slightly as she passes him.

Victor Bolt's wife Agatha is in the dining room, clearing the table. He is surprised to see their child is with her. He has only seen the boy a handful of times – around the lodge, and once in the woods, but he is not meant to be here in the house. The child is helping lay silver on the tray, his blond head bent as he looks at his reflection in the polished side of a spoon. Freddie with a sudden lurch remembers watching his brother carrying a tray at a similar age, blond head bent in concentration as he stared at the silver on the tray and the adults ruffled his hair and said how charming it was that he should hand around the cups at the shoot. Freddie had been jealous then, and wanted to do the same.

The maid clicks her tongue at the child. 'Don't touch,' she whispers, shooing him into the shadows. 'Remember. You're not here.' She puts her finger to her lips and smiles.

The boy crouches in the corner next to the sideboard. He must be no more than six or seven years old. There is a toy on the floor and he starts to run it backwards and forwards along the floorboards, tongue half-out with concentration. Freddie catches sight of another figure at the other door. His mother. He is not surprised; he knows she rarely sleeps these days, has often heard the floorboards creaking as she drifts along the corridors between the nursery and her bedroom.

But now she is standing with her hand on the doorframe, watching the child with an odd expression. The maid suddenly notices the countess too. She drops into a curtsey, and backs away, pushing the child behind her. 'I'm sorry, my lady, I didn't mean for him to be here. I don't usually work these early hours, but with the house party and the extra guests. And the boy don't like to be alone in the dark . . . and Victor thought it'd be all right if he came as we were only helping Mrs Foley for a moment . . . and . . .'

But the dowager countess does not seem to hear. She advances towards the pair of them, and Freddie sees a shadow of fear cross the child's face. The boy takes hold of his mother's hand, while the maid grabs the toy from his other and holds it out to the advancing woman, and Freddie sees now that the toy is one of his and Edward's old tin cars. 'I'm sorry, ma'am. I don't know where he found it. It must have dropped behind some furniture.' The maid moves backwards as Lady Hembury draws closer. 'He's not a bad boy. He wouldn't have thieved it. Please take it . . .'

But Lady Hembury bats the car away and it drops to the ground with a clatter. 'Come here, child,' says the countess, extending a hand.

The child eyes the hand in terror. Agatha turns to try the handle on the French windows, keeping the boy safe in the folds of her skirts, fluttering at the door like a butterfly trying to get out. 'I'll send him home . . .' She rattles at the handle, but still it won't open.

'Edward?' says the countess. 'My boy . . .'

The maid shakes her head, her eyes wide with alarm. 'No, ma'am. This is *my* boy. Wilf.'

She pushes at the door with every sinew, and Freddie steps in, putting a restraining hand on his mother's shoulder. 'Mama, that's Victor Bolt's son,' he says. The countess shakes him off, takes another step towards the distressed maid.

'Stop it,' says Freddie, trying to restrain her.

But the countess will not be stopped. 'Look at him, Freddie. Look at his eyes!'

Strange memories are falling through Freddie's mind, of a child carrying a tray, of the look on the maid's face when she saw Maurice, and the hunch that all is not as it seems, but then the French window gives way and the maid and child

138

tumble out on to the terrace, and away through the rose garden. The countess tries to follow, but Freddie holds her back, and she gives up, steadying herself with one hand against the frame of the open door. The maid glances once over her shoulder before pushing the boy on, out of sight.

Freddie bends to pick up the toy car.

His mother gasps as if in pain. 'I'm so sorry, Frederick. I don't know what's wrong with me. For a moment I thought . . .'

'Hush,' he says, reaching out to comfort her, an uneasy gesture, too close compared to the usual distance they keep. 'You're just tired. You should go back to bed and rest.'

But he knows she was not mistaken, for he saw it too. He pushes past her and slowly descends the steps, the car dangling from his hand, as he follows the path down to the lodge.

The dogs are growling, deep, low rumblings of aggression, their hackles up as Freddie calls from the gate.

Victor opens the door. Freddie holds the car up. 'I've only brought the toy. I'd like the boy to have it.'

'I'll give it to him.' Victor's voice is gruff.

'I'd like to do it myself. Can I come in?' Freddie does not wait for an answer, but barges his way into the house. The maid and the child are there, on the other side of the kitchen. Freddie tries to get a clearer picture of the boy, but it is hard to make out detail in the darkness of the interior, and the child is far away. He extends his arm. 'This is for you,' he says. 'We have no need of it up at the house.'

Agatha pulls the child closer. 'No, thank you, m'lord. We have no need of it here either.'

'Don't be discourteous,' says Victor. 'Let the boy take it.'

But Agatha will not allow the child to come forward. 'He don't want it.'

'He do want it.' Victor's voice is very quiet.

'I think I know my own son best,' snaps Agatha.

Victor slams his fist on the table. The noise ricochets around the room like a gunshot. It is so out of character for the man that Freddie is quite taken aback, and the feeling of unease grows. One of the dogs whimpers. Victor snatches the toy from Freddie's hand. 'Thank you, m'lord,' he says. He thrusts the toy at Wilf. 'Now you run along, boy. Go and fetch some wood.' Still, the child does not move, just holds the car in one hand and watches Freddie as if he is waiting for further instruction. 'Go on now.' Victor pushes the boy forward, and he has to edge past Freddie to leave the kitchen. He glances up as he passes, eyes wide, and Freddie feels the same sharp pain squeeze at his heart when the light falls on their cerulean blue, and – something even more disturbing – the unusual way the pupil bleeds into the iris. Then the boy is at the door and calling to the dogs, who are more than willing to escape into the grey drizzle.

Freddie watches the small figure disappear into the gloom. He makes as if to follow, but stops and turns back to Victor. 'Is the child really . . . ? I mean . . .'

Victor and Agatha are glaring at each other motionless, their dark eyes burning with anger. The silence is unbearable.

'I don't understand,' Freddie stammers again. 'There's something . . .' How can he give voice to his suspicions? The couple snap back, as if suddenly remembering he is there. Agatha looks away, but Victor meets Freddie's gaze, and Freddie can see his face is creased not in anger, but in pain.

Freddie swallows. 'Just tell me, is the boy your son?'

Now it is Victor's turn to turn away, while Agatha's eyes flicker towards Freddie, and for a moment he catches in her face the same look she had when she saw Maurice at the back of the house – and he sees it is something more akin to disdain than fear. Could the child be the reason? He would not be the first of Maurice's unwanted progeny . . . But the blond hair . . . the eyes . . . that irregular pupil . . . He has a sickening memory of his brother laughing at him in a corridor, someone behind him, hidden in the shadows. Surely the child couldn't be Edward's?

At last Victor speaks, his words barely audible, but his voice steady. 'Please, m'lord. The boy is mine. I'm his father.'

Aggie still says nothing, but she does not flinch from Freddie's confused gaze. Defeated, Freddie backs away, out of the lodge, into the rain, where a buzzard sits hunched on the fence, and in the rain-spattered lake the world appears upside down.

CHAPTER 20

The horse's back is tantalisingly close. If he leans forward, he is almost astride it. His father's words ring in his head: 'They're not playthings, and they're not ours. If the master catches you, we'll all be out on our ears . . .'

But Wilf can't resist. He looks at them now, from where he is perched on the fence. He reaches out and they amble over, nudging his outstretched palm, sniffing his skin, his hair, their sweet breath tickling so that he cannot help bursting into laughter. He jumps to the ground and walks among them, running his hand along their warm flanks.

Wilf has lived here for more than a quarter of his seven years – so long that he barely remembers Bristol any more. The city is just a set of fleeting images that fill him with a sad yearning: memories of the tiny parlour, smoke tickling his throat, the faces of his grandparents and his uncle grow more ephemeral by the day. The lodge house at Coombe is home now, with its cosy rooms warmed by the stove, the roses that his mother planted growing along the fence.

He climbs the fence again and turns to face the nearest animal, balancing on the top rung, legs crouched. He reaches out, and brushes his hand over its broad back. The horse does not move. He leans a little further, and suddenly his weight is no longer in his feet, but over the horse, which continues to pull at the grass. Slowly, Wilf swings a short leg over each side, and sits up. He twists his hands through the mane, for there is nothing else to hold on to. He is not sure what to do, but he has heard his father urging other horses on. He clicks his tongue, and the animal suddenly sways forward, but his legs barely reach around its sides, and he loses his balance almost immediately, slipping to the ground and landing with a thud.

Shaken, he sits up, wipes the hair out of his eyes. As he searches for his cap, he hears quiet laughter. He gets to his feet, cheeks burning, brushing the mud and leaves from his knees, settling the cap back on his head. He looks around, and the herd of horses parts to reveal none other than the Earl of Hembury. Wilf bows his head, as he has seen others do, tugs his cap, waits for the admonishment.

But the earl is still laughing as he slaps the rump of one of the horses, and the animals move away. 'First time?' he asks.

Wilf shrugs defensively. 'I've sat on a pony.'

'With a saddle?'

'No, sir. Without.' Wilf keeps his head bowed, in expectation for the telling off, but still it does not come.

Freddie leans back against the fence. 'You know, I used to come out here when I was your age and do the same . . . though my father expressly forbade it.'

'My da don't like me coming here either,' says Wilf, relaxing enough to look up from beneath his cap. The master has a kind face, and the toy car that he allowed Wilf to keep has pride of place on his windowsill.

'I'm sorry to hear that. I suppose he is trying to protect you.' Freddie eyes him thoughtfully. 'They are powerful beasts, and it is easy to get hurt.' One of the horses starts to nibble Wilf's hair, and he pushes it away gently. Freddie laughs, 'But I can see they are at ease with you. And you with them.'

At last Wilf smiles. 'I feel good when I'm near them.'

'I understand that.' Freddie sighs suddenly, and frowns. 'I must go. But why don't you come up to the stables one of these days? I think you'd like it.'

* * *

144

Wilf slows as he draws near the lodge. He can see his father clearing the vegetable patch, turning the heavy soil so it is ready for the planting of the first potatoes. In the undergrowth, the delicate snowdrops are appearing in clumps, the faintest green painted on to their white heads. Victor looks up, eyes narrowed. 'Where have you come running from?'

Wilf waves an arm vaguely. 'Over yonder.'

'You better not have been near those horses again.'

Wilf reddens.

'You stay away. You hear?'

Wilf bites the side of a nail. 'Can I go and check the snares?'

'As long as you empty the earth closet first.'

Wilf wrinkles his nose, but collects the bucket. He lugs it down to the midden beyond the outhouse, the dogs Raven and Shadow scurrying around him, while his father watches. Sometimes it feels as if they are still strangers, just as they were when Victor arrived after the war and Wilf was expected to welcome him home and call him 'da'.

Wilf gladly takes up Freddie's offer, and is soon visiting the stables regularly, though of course he makes sure neither of his parents find out. Most evenings, as the shadows lengthen in the valley, and his da returns from the stables, Wilf heads out in the opposite direction on the pretext of walking the dogs or checking the traps. He lets the flatcoats race ahead, following the trails of woodland creatures that permeate their twitching wet noses. It would not matter if darkness fell: Wilf knows every field, every copse, every goyle better than he knows himself.

In rain, sun, wind, snow he would rather be out here than in the house, where sometimes the air grows so thick with things unsaid that it makes him want to shout out loud. He sees the way his parents dance around each other, senses there is something broken between them. The thought makes his chest tighten, as if someone is pressing on it. But out here, he is calm; the ancient trees are like friends watching over him; the thickets are full of promise.

Wilf looks around, surprised to find he has already reached the stables. He can see the master crossing the cobblestones. He glances guiltily over his shoulder, but there is no one following. He whistles to the dogs, and makes them sit in the shadow of a rhododendron. They will not move until he returns.

Unusually, Freddie doesn't greet Wilf. There are dark shadows beneath his eyes. Wilf follows him across the yard, passing Dan – one of the new stable lads – who is pushing a wheelbarrow, sweat spreading in great patches beneath his armpits, perspiration beading on his forehead. Wilf reaches the stable door, and Freddie glances down at him, then motions inside with a nod of his head. 'What do you think about this one?' he says.

Wilf grapples with his feet to get a purchase so he can lean his elbows next to Freddie's. He does not need to read the newly engraved nameplate to know that this is Total Eclipse. The three-year-old horse is special. Wilf has heard his father muttering that every sinew in the horse costs more than he could earn in a lifetime. He has heard it ever since Freddie returned from the Tattersalls auctions in London with the animal. He also knows that his father advised Freddie to return the animal as soon as possible. But Freddie did not listen – a master is a master, after all.

'How much longer must he rest?' asks Wilf, holding out his hand. But the horse remains in the far corner of the stable, rump turned in their direction, head down, just its ears flicking back and forth to show it is aware of their presence.

'Your father says at least six months.' Wilf can hear the exasperation in his voice. Freddie turns and rests his back against the door. 'But the horse has to be ready in three weeks. He's a special present, you see. An engagement present for my wife-to-be.' Freddie sighs, then calls to Dan, 'Bring him out. Let's have a proper look.'

Dan abandons the wheelbarrow and runs to fetch a halter. The stable boy knows better than to wait before carrying out Freddie's bidding, for his master has been lashing out at everyone recently.

Wilf and Freddie stand back as Dan leads the horse into the yard. It is a thoroughbred, all fine bone and bulging veins, with a coat the colour of molasses. Wilf watches, frowning, as Freddie runs his hands along the animal's withers, back, legs. He peers at its teeth and into the inky eyes beneath the long lashes.

'He looks good, don't you think?' says Freddie.

Wilf bites his lip. The horse's coat seems lacklustre, but perhaps it needs a brush, and he doesn't want to add to Freddie's problems. He knows there has been trouble with Freddie's mother, the woman who chased him out of the house. A stream of doctors have rolled up and down the drive, and Freddie's temper has grown worse with each visit, despite the master having a wedding to look forward to. Wilf tries to sound confident: 'Looks all right to me,' he says.

They are silent for a moment. Then Freddie turns away, his voice gruff. 'Tell your father that he must make sure the horse is ready by the end of the month. Or there will be a price to pay.'

Wilf does not want to tell him that Victor knows nothing of his visits here. It does not seem to be the right moment.

By the time Wilf returns to the lodge house, a light spring rain is beginning to sparkle in the air. His mother is pulling the laundry from the line in angry bursts, as if it has done her an injury. The dogs race in through the open door, and Aggie calls for Wilf to stop them, but it is too late. He is distracted by Freddie's words. He glances guiltily at Victor, who is feeding wood into the stove. How can he pass on Freddie's message without giving himself away?

Aggie bustles into the kitchen, arms full of half-dried clothes. Victor goes to help her but she scolds him angrily. 'Watch your hands on the clean sheets . . .' The dogs start to shake, their paws squarely on the floor, their bodies twisting from side to side as water spatters through the air. 'Victor! Send them out!' Her cry ends in a fit of coughing; her lungs are weak from the Spanish influenza that tore through their neighbourhood at the end of the war and stole so many of his mother's generation.

'It's my fault,' says Wilf.

She turns on him: 'And where've you been? You're soaked through.' She starts to tug at his jersey. 'This needs to dry by the fire.'

He pushes her away. 'I can do it.'

She turns back to Victor. 'Why can't you put them dogs in the kennels?' she says as she brings their dinner to the table, then returns to scrub at the stone sink, before bashing out the pastry for tomorrow's meal, and stirring the clothes in the copper.

'And why won't you stop your fretting and come and sit down?' asks Victor, but she gives no sign of having heard. 'What is it? What's bothering you?'

She stops, exhales. 'The dowager countess was down here again.'

'Did she come in?'

'No. She didn't have time before one of her women took her away. What if she catches him outside?'

'I'm not scared of her,' says Wilf. 'She's going to the mad-house.'

'Who told you that?' They both glare at him.

He shrugs, bites a nail. He can't tell them he overheard Freddie talking to his sister about it up at the stables. 'Must've been someone from school. Sam maybe.'

The adults ponder this for a moment then turn back to each other. 'Whatever happens you can't keep him shut up here. The diphtheria's passed. School's opening again next week.'

'I don't mind not going,' says Wilf.

148

'You don't want the attendance officer sniffing around,' says Victor.

'I just want him to be safe.'

'I'll walk him there myself tomorrow if it makes you feel better . . .'

She wipes her hands on her apron, made from old sacks boiled to softness. 'Would you?'

'Of course,' Victor holds out a hand to her, and she allows him to pull her on to his lap. When she smiles, the room appears to lighten.

Wilf knows his mother was the prettiest girl in Bedminster; he recalls people saying it in Bristol, and Victor still says it now, with her pale skin and the fine dark brush strokes of her eyebrows above the almond-shaped eyes. He sees Victor look at her as if she is the only person present, and he feels that same prick of jealousy as when Victor returned from France, elbowing his way into their lives.

With a jolt, Wilf suddenly remembers his uncle Robbo, who was more like a father to him back then. Robbo covered from head to toe in coal dust, just his tongue, pink as a newborn babe, and the whites of his eyes shining through as he climbed into the tin bath filled with steaming water from the copper, set in front of the fire.

Aggie is still seated on Victor's lap, relaxing into him, and Wilf feels the resentment rise. 'When will we go back to Bristol?' he blurts out. 'I'd like to see Uncle Robbo.'

'I didn't think you remembered any of it,' says his mother, looking at him in surprise.

'We're better off here,' says Victor, not relinquishing his hold on Aggie.

'Is he still a miner?' asks Wilf.

'Robbo will always be a miner. It's in his blood.'

'It's in your blood too . . .'

Victor snorts. 'I'm different to Robbo. I hated it down there. I had to get out.' His father has tensed up, and Aggie looks uncomfortable against the rigid body.

149

'To the army, you mean?' Wilf continues. 'Tell me about the artillery. Tell me how you won your medals.'

Wilf has only seen Victor wear them once: on Peace Day in Bristol, when there were street parties and brass bands, and his whole family smiling and laughing together.

'Devotion to duty under fire,' says Aggie, twisting her head to look at Victor with pride. 'Why don't you fetch them?'

But Victor will not be drawn. He shakes his head, and finally pushes Aggie from his lap. 'It's time for you to get up to bed, son,' he says to Wilf. 'I gave up fighting a long time ago, and you've got school tomorrow.'

The smoke trickles up the chimney, into the grey sky above. The world outside is a damp haze, as if they have been transported into a cloud. Wilf thinks about Total Eclipse, and whether the horse will be ready in time. He wonders why he should make the effort to pass on a message when his da won't talk to him. He watches Victor mending the holes in his boots so they will be ready for school, cutting a piece of leather to fit, and making it stick with melted candle wax before hammering the tacks in. Aggie is darning Wilf's socks as well as a hole in the elbow of his jersey. He remembers more than they think: he remembers Uncle Robbo, and he remembers the victory parade on Peace Day, the Union Jacks and the coloured bunting hung across the ramshackle buildings of their neighbourhood. But he also remembers the effigy of the Kaiser swinging above them, its stuffed head lolling among the red, white and blue that was slowly turning black with soot.

CHAPTER 21

It is early in the morning; the mice have not yet started to scratch in the attic. Wilf peers into the darkness, trying to make out the shape of his room. He is fretting about the horse again, wondering what Freddie meant by there being a price to pay. The month's end is already upon them, and he knows that the master plans to run the horse today, against his father's wishes. Thankfully neither man blames Wilf for any lack in communication. Instead each snipes about the other to Wilf, their previous friendship as precarious as a milking stool with a broken leg.

Victor calls and Wilf leaves the sleep-warmed bed reluctantly. Aggie left an hour ago to walk up to the hall. He heard the rustle of her clothes as she climbed into them, the glug of water from the ewer. He splashes water on his own face, gasping at the coldness of it. Then he remembers his plan for the day, and finishes dressing quickly. He lets the dogs out, completes his morning chores as the sky begins to lighten.

Victor doesn't walk Wilf to school any more, which means Wilf is free to do as he pleases, to search for birds' nests or grass snakes or to paddle in the river. Today he runs, arms outstretched to touch the plants that curl and droop from the sides of the lane. He stops to watch a noisy robin perched in a hawthorn tree, then carries on, skirting the edge of the village, where the cottages rise up, thatch heavy with dew; Wilf hears it crackle and pop as the water moves through it. Dogs race up to the gates to bark at him. Somewhere out of sight, a pig squeals, and a cockerel crows in answer. The school bell rings out, but instead of sloping through the school gates, Wilf pauses at the entrance to Sam Vellacott's farm, and waits for his friend.

He does not have to linger long. The boys slip through the fields unseen, drawing closer to the big house until they reach the cedar tree closest to the stable yard. Sam gives Wilf a leg-up, and then Wilf pulls him into the tree by his wrists. They climb into the higher branches, too full of adrenaline to notice the scraping of their knees and elbows.

Wilf positions himself so that he can see Freddie and Victor in the yard. Victor is shaking his head as the horse is led out.

'Looks all right to me,' whispers Sam.

Wilf shrugs. 'My da says it's not.'

'What's he say's wrong with it, then?'

'Something in its lungs.'

'Why don't his lordship think so?'

Wilf shrugs again. He can see that the two men are having a heated discussion. The authoritative tone of Freddie's voice reaches his ears, but Victor's gentler one does not.

Wilf sees Victor's shoulders slump. Dan is already waiting on a companion horse. Victor turns his back on them both. In two bounds Freddie is up on Total Eclipse's back. Both the horses are prancing now, and it takes a while for Freddie to slide his feet into the stirrups. Total Eclipse twists his head and Wilf recognises the movement of a horse coughing.

The boys pull their legs up into the tree as the horses pass within ten feet. Total Eclipse stretches his neck and coughs again. Wilf hears Freddie mutter, 'Cobwebs! He'll soon blow those away.' He urges the horse on, and it breaks into a fast trot, and then a canter, but there is something strange about the way it moves, and Wilf feels a cold dread claw at his chest.

The boys wait in the tree. Victor paces in the yard, busily pointing instructions to the lads left behind, carrying buckets of water, occasionally stopping to stare out in the direction

152

that the horses disappeared. Sam grumbles. He is hungry and bored.

'They'll be back any minute . . .' But before the words are out of Wilf's mouth, they hear shouting, and Dan appears, at a flat-out gallop until he reaches the yard. He dismounts, talks urgently to Victor, and soon the pair are running down towards Lower Meadow.

Wilf does not even think: he just slips and slides out of the tree and chases after them, ignoring Sam's cries to stop.

Wilf will never forget the sight of the horse on the ground. The sheer size of the animal brought down, helpless where it lies, struggling for breath, nostrils flared, a steady trickle of blood snaking down its muzzle.

Freddie is standing in front of it, trying to tug it to its feet, but the poor creature cannot even lift its head, and Freddie is shouting, 'What the hell is happening?'

'It's the horse's lungs . . .' Victor tries to stop Freddie pulling on the bridle.

'Why wasn't it ready, like I asked? Help me get it on its feet.'

'You can't! Leave it in peace!' Victor grapples with Freddie for control. The horse shudders, and then its whole body goes rigid with pain. Wilf lets out a cry and throws himself on to his knees beside it, hands on its sweat-drenched skin. It seems to him that he can feel its pain, like a million knives turning in his lungs, as if his heart is being squeezed in a fist. He loves these solid sensitive creatures that communicate more understanding than either of his parents ever have.

He strokes its cheek, trying to convey some kind of salve, some kind of peace. He feels Victor's hands trying to remove him, and he grips the horse around its neck. 'Do something, Da,' he says, twisting his head to look up, feeling the warm life still pulsing through the animal's hide. And all the time Dan is wringing his hands, and Freddie is tugging at the creature's head. 'Do something!' Wilf cries again.

Victor crouches next to him. 'There's nothing can be done.' He too starts to stroke the horse's neck as spasms rack its

153

body. He hums to calm it, breathing in through his nose, out through his mouth, the way Wilf knows he learnt in the pits. Wilf feels sick. He wants to scream, but all he can do is cling to the horse and listen to Victor's low murmur, and plead and beg with the grim-faced God they murmur prayers to every Sunday.

But like most adults, God does not care to listen to Wilf, and the horse sighs and lets out a long breath that finishes with the trace of a whimper, and it is the saddest sound that Wilf has ever heard.

There is a terrible silence. A black emptiness spreads through Wilf. The horse lies motionless, though still warm beneath his fingertips. The men stare. Victor sits back on his heels. Freddie starts to pace. 'Why didn't you call for the veterinarian?' he says. Wilf strains to listen to his words, to find some sense in what has just happened.

'There were nothing anyone could do,' Victor replies.

'You don't know that.'

'I knew as soon as Dan told me what had happened.'

'You should never have allowed him to be taken out.'

'But I told you . . .'

'Don't speak over me. You cannot remain in the stables after such an error of judgement.'

Wilf gasps as he jumps to his feet: he knows how much the horses mean to his father; he feels the same, cannot imagine not being allowed to spend another day in the yard. Victor stands too, and takes hold of Wilf's hand. He wills his father to argue back, to speak the truth. But instead Freddie carries on rewriting history. 'Do you know how much money that horse cost me? You should have advised against it. I should get rid of you altogether.'

'But that's not fair!' cries Wilf, for he knows that his father *did* advise against it.

'Control that child!' snarls Freddie, and Wilf boils at the insult. The master is meant to be his friend, but Victor is gripping his hand as if he might crush it, and glaring down at him

154

too. He looks back at Victor. How can he let Freddie treat them this way? He looks at Freddie. How can he say such things?

As their eyes lock, the master seems to give a little. His voice is calmer when he speaks, turning to look at Victor again: 'Look, I recognise that you are a diligent worker. I will give you another chance. You are useful outdoors. I would like you to concentrate on gamekeeping. We used to have four gamekeepers. Now we have none, and I have plans to revive the estate shoot.'

'I don't know how . . .'

Freddie stiffens again. 'It's common sense, Bolt. You're a practical man. You already do some trapping. I'm sure Lord Hampden's underkeeper will not mind answering any questions you have. Didn't you get those dogs from him?'

'But the horses . . .'

Freddie holds up his hand, anger creasing his forehead. 'It's my fault,' he says, and for a hopeful moment Wilf thinks he might apologise, but instead he says, 'We never needed another groom. We needed a keeper, and that's what you'll be if you want to remain in employment at Coombe. Now see to it that you get the hunt to collect the animal. I want it gone by the end of the day.'

Freddie turns and strides away. Wilf tugs at his father's arm, wills him to stand up for himself, to be the war hero that he's meant to be. But all Victor says is, 'Leave off, boy,' while shaking Wilf's hand loose.

Then Victor too turns and walks away, his shoulders hunched, his head bowed like a whipped dog. And Wilf can only watch in pain as he feels one of the delicate strings that binds them snap.

CHAPTER 22

They do not speak of that day again, though it hovers around them, as shadowy and choking as coal dust. Wilf feels a new emptiness, as if witnessing the death of the horse killed a part of him too. It's an emptiness heightened by the sense of betrayal that Freddie is not the kind master that Wilf thought he was. But what hurts most of all is that his own father pushed him away.

In fact, nowadays Victor seems to steer clear of Wilf altogether, leaving for his duties before Wilf rises in the morning, and returning when he is in bed, avoiding the boy's eyes when they meet on the stairs or in a doorway. Soon the memory of life as it was fades, and it is almost as if Victor has always been gamekeeper at Coombe.

One Saturday in mid-summer, Wilf makes sure he gets up early enough to help Victor, for the first pheasant chicks – reared from eggs swapped with other local keepers and hatched beneath the Hampden estate keeper's broody hens – have been released into the pens that Victor built.

Victor carries his shotgun, broken over his arm. Wilf touches the cold barrel and Victor slaps his hand away. 'It's not a toy,' he growls. There has been an increase in poaching in the area. It is a lucrative – and dangerous – business, since most men were taught how to use a gun in the war. Wilf knows that is where his father learnt to shoot too, for Victor told him so, but as usual he will not elucidate further, however much Wilf pushes.

The morning is already bright and warm, and the air carries the scent of the honeysuckle that has spread through the hedgerows. Victor seems to relax out here in the open, and Wilf's spirits lift. 'Do you think it's the men over the lane that's poaching?' he asks as they make their way through meadows heavy with dew. Shacks have sprung up in the small bit of woodland owned by the Cottams. The rumours about the men that gather there are many: they are tramps come to take all the work from the locals, or convicts hiding from the law, or gypsies grown bored of the travelling life.

Victor shakes his head. 'No. Those men do no harm, and don't let no one tell you otherwise.'

'David Tucker says they's cripples.'

'David Tucker should stop listening to his da.'

'Sam says cripples are a burden.'

Victor's demeanour suddenly darkens. 'Sam needs to keep his thoughts to himself.'

'But what use is a man who can't do nothing?'

Victor stops and looks down at Wilf. 'You don't remember?' he asks.

'Remember what?'

'You don't remember your grandad? My own da?'

A faint memory of a bear of a man, with a chest as broad as Victor's, and eyes as dark comes to Wilf. He can picture the man in the early morning, before dawn, collecting his snap from the kitchen with Uncle Robbo.

'How about the colliery? Deep Cut?' Victor frowns again.

Wilf closes his eyes. The name brings to mind the great wheel at the pithead, the vast square chimneys towering over the cramped houses of the neighbourhood, their tips hidden by the smog. But that is all. He opens his eyes and shakes his head.

'It's understandable,' Victor says, in a way that seems as if it isn't understandable at all.

'Tell me about them,' says Wilf. 'I want to remember.'

Victor sighs. 'Your grandad were injured bad in the mines. Real bad. He risked his life to help others down there . . .'

He shudders and lets go of Wilf as he straightens up. 'So don't you cast no judgements.' He pauses, and then takes a deep breath. 'We've got a new life now. So make yourself useful. Go and check there's nowhere for the stoats to get in.'

Wilf walks the perimeters of the pens while Victor feeds and checks the poults. The birds are still small and ungainly, strutting about in clumps, chirruping for food, mirroring his movements. The crows watch from the trees, hopping from branch to branch and calling angrily. Wilf throws a stone at them and they fly heavily into the air, wheeling and croaking at each other until they find a new vantage point.

From there father and son continue through the fields – Home Mead, Middle Brook, Lower Brook, Burrow Close – checking hedges and fences. It is already hot, and the sweat trickles down into Wilf's boots. He turns his face to the sun, enjoys the rays on his skin. So much better than the classroom. There is a sudden noise in the woodland beside them. A twig snapping, and the angry screech of a bird. The dogs are immediately alert, growling in low rumbles. Victor stops dead. Wilf cocks his head towards the wood. 'Poachers?' he whispers.

Victor pulls two cartridges from his belt and slips them into the barrel, clicks the shotgun ready. They stay still for a moment, listening, but all Wilf can hear is the rushing of blood in his ears.

'Stay back,' hisses Victor, indicating with outstretched palm. But Wilf follows in his shadow. The dogs forge ahead in hunting mode, ignoring the brambles that clutch at their coats, the nettles that rub at their bellies.

There is a sharp squeal, and Wilf's heart almost jumps out of his mouth. Victor whistles quietly and Shadow comes crashing out of the undergrowth, but there is no sign of Raven other than the dog's deep bark. They creep forward. Victor holds the shotgun ready to pull into his shoulder should he need to. Wilf briefly wonders if this is how Victor was in

158

France, searching for the enemy. Every inch of the man seems to focus on what lies ahead.

They emerge into a clearing, just in time to glimpse a fox trotting away. Wilf has never known a fox to escape a trap before, but then he catches sight of the reason why: there is someone standing over the sprung teeth, someone whose hair matches the russet pelt that has melted into the undergrowth.

Celia Cottam straightens guiltily as she spots Wilf and Victor. Fear swiftly turns to relief and her shoulders slacken. 'Thank goodness it's you,' she says. Then, looking down at the empty trap, she adds, 'I'm sorry. I was heading down to the river and I heard its cries.'

Wilf cannot hide his surprise: he has never heard of anyone releasing a live fox from a trap, but Victor stays silent, watching as her cheeks turn crimson.

'I know I shouldn't be here, but I couldn't leave it . . . it was in pain.'

'You shouldn't touch the traps,' Victor says at last. 'They're dangerous.'

'I know,' she answers. 'I've seen what they do to an animal.' She turns her hands outwards, and Wilf sees there is rust-coloured blood smeared across her palms. She crouches to wipe it on the grass.

'The fox is dangerous too,' Victor says. 'Could give a nasty bite.'

'It didn't. I think it would have thanked me if it could. They're so beautiful,' she adds sadly.

'They take the pheasants . . . the hens and geese too. Even lambs and piglets . . .'

'And they pay for it in the hunting season.' She comes nearer as she speaks; the conversation appearing to make her braver. 'I apologise. I know it's your job to deal with them.'

Victor shrugs, and Wilf is astonished to hear him say, 'Don't mean I don't agree with you.'

159

'That's an unusual position for a gamekeeper,' says Celia with a small smile. 'I wonder if you should have stayed working in the stables.'

'It weren't put to me as a choice.'

Celia raises an eyebrow, but Wilf is relieved that she doesn't delve further. Instead she puts a finger to her lips. 'Well, I won't tell anyone about the fox if you don't,' she says.

Wilf looks up at his father, and sees a smile breaking across Victor's face: it starts slowly and then deepens into his eyes. 'No. I won't be saying anything.'

Celia turns to Wilf. 'I won't say nothing,' he says, looking at his feet.

'That's good! Our secret. We city folk must stick together.'

They start to move away from the clearing, back through the wood and into the brightness of the fields. Wilf trails behind, listening. 'We were talking about Bristol,' say Victor. 'The boy don't really remember. I don't know if it's right that he should.'

'Oh – you mustn't forget where you came from. I don't. I never will.'

'I don't want it to be the marker by which everyone judges the lad as they do me.'

'It won't be. You've forged a new life for yourself, for your family. Look around! You should be proud to have made it this far.'

'What about the men you allow to live by the river? They are grateful for a place to rest, but how will life improve for them?'

Celia's voice grows quiet. 'For now I'm happy to offer them all I can: sanctuary and some kind of peace.' They come to a standstill. 'This is where I slope off back to my side of the lane,' she says, as she turns her attention to Wilf. 'Look at your boy. What a handsome lad! And how is school? What are they teaching you?'

Wilf shrugs. 'Woodwork, nature studies, arithmetic . . .'

'Well, make sure you keep it up: with an education you

will find anything is possible! You know, you and I have more in common than you realise. My ancestors were miners too.'

Wilf frowns at her. He cannot believe that this lady could ever have come from the same place as his own family.

'It's true. My family are living proof that you don't have to settle for your lot in life. And so is your da.' She laughs at his confused face. 'I can see it's a big leap to get from there to here. In my case, my great-grandfather worked his way up from miner to overman. His son – my grandfather – was a clerk who taught himself engineering and geology, and ended up on the board of Kingswell Colliery. He married my grandmother, whose father was also on the board, and by the time my father came along, he was able to buy his own colliery – with the help of a loan, of course.'

Wilf nods, not feeling much wiser.

Victor grunts. 'The only way I could get out was to fight in their war. And I were still expected to go back underground when I returned.'

'But you didn't give up, and your success will inspire others. We must encourage more to push back by whatever means necessary.'

Victor mulls this over. 'Even if those means are under-handed?' he asks.

She narrows her eyes, as if trying to read his mind. 'I think desperate men will do whatever they can.'

Victor bites his lip, looks at his hands. 'They will,' he says.

Celia tries to catch his eye again. 'I hope you understand you can come to us if you ever need help.'

Victor looks at her, and his slow smile breaks across his face again. 'Thank you, miss. It won't come to that.'

They stare at each other for a moment, and then Celia stretches out to catch a leaf that is twirling towards the ground. She grins with pleasure when she sees it nestled in the palm of her hand. 'You see, anything is possible!' she says, slipping it into her pocket. 'Now I must go.' She starts to move away, waving goodbye as she goes. 'Remember: our secret!' she calls before hurrying off towards the river.

Wilf turns to his father, and is surprised to see tears in his eyes.

'What's wrong?' he asks.

'Nothing, son. It's the heat. Come here . . .' He pulls Wilf into his chest, and Wilf breathes in the mix of woodsmoke and earth and laundry soap, and his father presses his face into Wilf's head, and he can feel Victor's hot breath in his hair, and it is strange to be hugged like this as if he was a small child again. Strange, but not unpleasant. After an age, Victor steps back and holds Wilf's face in his hands. 'You heard what she said,' he says. 'Anything is possible.'

He ruffles Wilf's hair.

'Come on. Let's get back to your ma.' And for a moment, the emptiness inside Wilf shrinks a little.

The kitchen window glows in the dimpsy light. Victor is still buoyant, but Aggie is distracted, twisting her hands in her apron. She has received a letter from Pam. 'Your Robbo's been arrested. On a strike.'

Victor pours some water from the jug, rinses his mouth. 'Not much I can do about that.'

'What if they find out up at the house?'

'They're too busy with wedding celebrations.'

She glances at Wilf, who is leaning against the dog, warming his toes at the stove.

'His lordship's already angry at you.'

'The business with the horse weren't my fault. He knows that. Please stop your worrying.'

'Why do you always think the best of people? After everything that's happened.'

'Because I believe no man is wholly bad.'

Aggie drops her voice. Wilf strains to hear. It seems they are either yelling at each other or whispering these days. He chews at his nails, feels the anxiety rise with his mother's voice. 'It were meant to be better here,' she is saying.

'It *is* better. You have only to read Pam's letters to see that.'

'It don't feel better to me. I'm still bone tired at the end of the day, and nothing to show for it.'

'We've a roof over our heads. Food on the table . . .'

'But couldn't we ask for more?'

'No. It's enough. Don't you put it in peril.' He glances at Wilf, then addresses Aggie again, his voice strained. 'Now go and sit.'

'I've got pies to finish,' she says.

'You need to eat first. And so do we.' Victor carries the pot of stew to the table, setting it down where the steam curls off it in mouth-watering waves. He ladles it into their bowls.

The food revives Wilf. 'What did Uncle Robbo get arrested for?' he asks. 'Is he a criminal now?'

'Never you mind,' says Victor, but not unkindly.

Wilf's face crumples. 'Why do you talk about our family one moment and not the next? Why is it only us here? Everyone at school has grandads and grandmas and cousins within a day's walk . . .'

Victor reaches out to put a hand on the boy's shoulder. 'One day we'll go to Bristol and visit, but for now, we're what you got, so make the most of it. Now tell your Ma what you learnt at school last week.'

163

CHAPTER 23

Passers-by come and go in the lane as regularly as the seasons. The stone-crackers hammer at their piles of rocks to lay the road; the steam-roller comes soon after to flatten them. There are butchers and bakers, even the onion sellers from France on their bicycles. They join the travellers and tinkers who call from door to door, hoping to sell one of the pots or pans hanging from their covered wagons.

One of these wanderers calls at the lodge during a summer deluge. It is the school holidays, and Victor and Wilf have taken shelter at home; visibility is so poor that there is nothing to be done outside. Wilf answers the door.

'Could I trouble you for some hot water?' The man holds his empty billycan up, but keeps his face turned away. The rain is streaming off his lank hair and his overcoat is soaked through.

Wilf stares, mistrustful. The man frightens him. He feels Victor's hand on his shoulder. 'Have some respect, son. Don't you recognise a man who's fought for king and country?'

Wilf cannot see how anyone could deduce this man was once a soldier, for his feet are bound in rags and they squelch as he moves from one to the other, and his clothes are stained and torn.

Victor takes the can. 'Nearest workhouse is Wellington,' he says. 'It's more than a three-hour walk. Why don't you shelter here a while?'

The side of the man's face twitches in a peculiar way, but he follows as father and son clamber into their boots and lead the way down to the toolshed next to the pigsty. The walls are lined with Victor's gardening and gamekeeping equipment: spades, traps, a poleaxe, rakes, pitchforks. The place is dark and smells of the pig, but there are no leaks in the roof, and there is clean straw on the floor. The man looks about him as if at a palace. The tremor runs down his arm and makes his whole side jerk and jump like a marionette. Victor holds out a hand as if it's perfectly normal. 'I'm Victor Bolt,' he says. 'That's my son, Wilf. You can stay the night if you like.'

The man shakes Victor's hand. 'John,' he says. 'John Harris. I'm looking for somewhere. I been told there are folk like me . . .'

Victor nods. 'I know the place. It's down by the river, on the Cottams' land. The men there sometimes help me with coppicing in exchange for meat. It's not far. But rest here until the rain stops.'

Wilf watches John Harris from the corner of his eye. He cannot understand how the Cottams can allow such people to stay on their land. He knows that the master would not.

As suddenly as the cloudburst passes, the sun comes out. The wooden slats on the shed steam as they dry. Victor and John sit in full sunlight, next to the mulberry tree that is dropping its sweet dark fruits on to the ground. Insects crawl and buzz. Wilf sits a distance away, inhaling the rich smell of grass after rain. He watches an ant climb over John's pale, bare feet. The toes are ruined, bent and misshapen, the skin white and puckered, and in the worst places yellow turning to black. They turn Wilf's stomach, but Victor is undaunted. 'Never thought I'd see that again,' he says.

John's muscles spasm, but there is more time between the convulsions. He sips the tea that Aggie has brought.

'Infantry?'

John nods.

'Artillery,' says Victor. 'Hard to believe it's five years ago now.'

165

John nods again. Silence envelops them, punctuated by the drone of the bumblebees and a song thrush in the mulberry tree. The men do not need to speak.

The following day Victor points John Harris in the direction of Miss Cottam's woods. Wilf watches the ragged man limp down the road, Victor's hand on his head. Victor sighs, a long, drawn-out sound. 'I'm going down to the smithy. Got a message for Alfred.'

'I'm coming.'

'You're not. You got plenty of things to be getting on with here.'

'Why don't you want me around no more?'

Victor's brow furrows and he looks down at Wilf as if seeing him for the first time. 'Is that what you believe? I'm sorry, for it's not true. It were our visitor. He threw me. Sometimes I fear I'll never escape the past.' He smiles sadly. 'But it shouldn't pain you too. Of course you can come.'

By the time they reach the forge, Victor's sadness seems to have dissolved, blown away on the breeze like the wildflower seeds. Alfred Hartnell is bent over, the great hoof of a plough horse resting against the leather apron that covers his knees as he rasps it into shape. Wilf watches the file move up and down. The blacksmith's swollen forearms are puckered from burns.

His apprentice pummels a horseshoe into shape on the anvil, orange sparks flying, sweat pouring down his narrow shoulders in dirty rivers. The air is filled with the smell of burning hoof and the clang of metal, and Wilf can feel the white heat of the fire on his skin. In the shadows, a fox terrier lies watching.

Alfred glances up, then sets the great horse's hoof down on the ground. The animal does not move, holding its head low by its knees. 'I suppose you're here to ask about the shoeing,' says the blacksmith.

Victor shakes his head. 'His lordship wants new catches for the gates, and the railings up by the house repaired. You'll need to come and take a look.' The apprentice plunges the shoe into a pail of water, sending up a cloud of noisy steam.

'At least he's settled his debts since he married Lady Elizabeth,' says the blacksmith. 'About time. He owed me for almost a year's work.'

'The master will of course honour his bills.'

Alfred harrumphs, and moves on, tapping the horse's next leg, and the animal lifts it gently. The conversation is over.

There is a crowd at the village hall, folk spilling out of the building, some craning their necks to see the speaker inside, some haranguing the crowd. Victor glances at Wilf. 'You stay here a moment,' he says.

Wilf settles down on the side of the road with the dogs, whose nut-brown eyes remain fixed on the last spot they saw their master. He sees Victor raise himself on tiptoes to get a better look, and the men behind shake their heads and click their tongues. Victor pushes his way further into the crowd. Whoever is speaking is doing so at the top of their voice, for Wilf can make out the odd word, about workers, about good men who fought for this country. The crowd murmurs in agreement, nodding their heads. One man raises his fist in the air, punches it upwards; others do the same. There is cheering and encouragement. Wilf sinks his hands into the shaggy coats of the dogs, feels the sun beat down.

Before long, the flatcoats rise, stretch their legs, and cross to Victor, who has reappeared. Wilf joins them. He hears a woman's voice calling from the emerging crowd. It is Miss Cottam from over the lane, smiling and waving as she quickens her step. 'Good afternoon, Mr Bolt,' she says. 'Hello, Wilf.'

Father and son remove their caps. 'Afternoon, ma'am.'

'How did you find the speech?'

'Couldn't hear much from where I were,' says Victor. 'It were a large crowd.'

'It was, wasn't it.' She looks at the people still milling around, grinning and chattering. 'Seems to have gone down well.'

Victor nods, as a tall man with Celia's red hair and blue-grey eyes, Celia's smile, approaches.

'George, this is Victor Bolt. He works for the Hemburys. But he comes from Bristol originally.'

'Always happy to meet a fellow Bristolian,' says George, shaking Victor's hand.

Wilf is surprised that these grandly dressed people with their smart words and their clean hands are happy to treat his father as if he is one of their own. It unsettles him, and it seems to unsettle Victor too: his father looks tense, tight-lipped suddenly.

'And let me introduce you to Raymond White,' says George, as a serious-looking man with round glasses joins them; he reminds Wilf of Mr Smithson the schoolteacher, except there is an air of fettered strength about the man, as if there is something simmering beneath the surface, waiting to burst out. 'Raymond was the man who spoke,' adds George. 'We've known each other a long time. In fact, we were at school together. Now we're working in government together.'

Victor removes his cap again. 'No need for that,' says Raymond, waving contemptuously, and Wilf thinks how strange for a man to dismiss such a common courtesy. 'What did you think?'

'Very good, sir,' says Victor.

'Victor couldn't hear much because of the crowd,' says Celia.

'You'll have to come again, then.'

Victor nods. 'Yes, sir.' Wilf notes his father's expression is still a mask, so different to how it was when they met Miss Cottam in the woods.

'Good. Good.' People are queuing, caps in hand, to speak to the two men, and they move on to acknowledge the next in line.

The atmosphere is suddenly awkward, as if the men sucked all the vigour out of the air when they left. Victor clasps his hands, thumbs working together. 'I sent another man your way, miss,' he says. 'Down to the river. By the name of John Harris.'

'There seem to be more arriving every day,' she replies. 'I'm taking Raymond down there later, to talk to them, to see what more could be done to help.'

'That sounds very good, miss.'

She leans forward a little, looking up at Victor, her brow furrowed. 'Have faith. Raymond is certain that change is coming for men like you, who deserve so much more . . .'

'It's kind of you to say so,' says Victor, and finally he seems to relax as his chest broadens and his back straightens.

'Celia!' The men are calling her on.

'I'd better go.' She smiles once more at Victor and Wilf, and then follows her brother and his friend to mingle with the people in the street.

CHAPTER 24

Summer slips almost imperceptibly towards autumn. The wheat, oats and barley heads sway heavily in the warm breeze. The yellowhammers add their bright colour to the darkening hedges, the sparrows chatter and fight in their dust baths. The schoolchildren have been given time off to help with the harvest. Wilf is meant to be making his way there now, but he has been sidetracked by an elusive jay. He covets its bright-blue striped feathers, hopes he might have the good fortune to find one on the ground if he follows it. He is watching it quietly when the bird suddenly screeches away in alarm, too fast for him to follow.

He turns to see Freddie riding along the track. The master looks ungainly as the track is narrow and the horse he is leading is resting its head awkwardly on his own mount's rump. Wilf shrinks back into the undergrowth, but Freddie pulls up when he is level with him. 'What luck to bump into you,' he says, smiling. 'We've missed you up at the stables.'

Wilf struggles to know what to say. He has not seen Freddie since the incident with Total Eclipse, still cannot understand the master's unkind behaviour, and its subsequent consequences for his father, though time has healed the hurt a little.

Freddie swallows, and speaks again into the silence. 'Terrible business with that horse. I'm sorry you witnessed it. I don't like to think of it . . . to see a creature like that . . .' He stops, as the horse he is leading nips the rump of the horse he is riding, which stamps irritably and tosses its head. 'But shall we put it behind us? How about you come with me now? You could ride Jasper. I think Tybalt would appreciate it. I know I certainly would.'

'Really?' The word bursts out as Wilf's heart leaps and the faded memory of that day is eclipsed by excitement: he's always dreamed of being able to ride one of the proper horses.

Freddie grins. 'I promised I'd let you one day. And Jasper is very easy. I would trust him with a toddler.'

Wilf steps on to the track, avoiding the shifting hooves of both the horses. He has ridden the trap pony Dandelion many times now, but Jasper is a horse, and a fine one at that. His reservations about Freddie recede: hasn't the master always been kind to him? Could it just be that Freddie and Victor rub each other up the wrong way? Sometimes people just don't get on together.

Wilf regards the height of the creature's back. Using the upward curve of the bank to lift himself higher, he grabs a handful of the animal's mane and pulls himself up, into the saddle. He adjusts the stirrups to their highest setting. They are still too long, but give some support to his feet.

'Quite the jockey,' laughs Freddie. 'Ready?'

Wilf nods, and Freddie kicks his horse on. Wilf feels Jasper surge forwards. It is intoxicating to be sitting so tall, with the power of such a creature beneath him. He cannot help grinning with joy. Freddie glances back. 'All right?'

'Yes,' says Wilf, his smile wide, his breath catching in his throat.

'Want to go faster?'

'Yes!'

They push on, and the wind is knocked from Wilf's mouth, and he hasn't felt this happy in so long, as if nothing else matters, as if it is just him and the horse without a care in the world: no whispered secrets or harsh words, no silent worries, no fear or lies.

Too soon they slow as they approach the edge of the wood,

and open land. Freddie grabs hold of Jasper's reins as the horse comes alongside. 'You're an absolute natural – on as well as off . . .'

'Like my da.'

Freddie looks strangely at him for a moment. 'Yes,' he says, before glancing away. 'Did you not have school today?'

'It's harvest. We're meant to be doing Miss Celia's fields.'

'Are you now?' Freddie looks back, one eyebrow raised.

'I'm going there now,' Wilf nods.

'How do you fancy earning a few pennies?'

Wilf leans forward and strokes the horse's neck. 'What must I do?'

'I want you to tell me if you hear that Miss Cottam's brother and his friend Mr White are going to speak in the village again.'

'Can't you ask Miss Cottam yourself?'

'I don't want to worry her. They are dangerous men.'

'They didn't seem so when my da saw them speak.'

'Those are the sort to be most afraid of.'

Wilf remembers the piercing look of Raymond White, and has an inkling that Freddie might be right. Perhaps he should keep an eye out for Miss Cottam.

'What do they do that's so bad?' he whispers.

'They want to change the way things are done, but we're all happy here, aren't we? And you certainly don't want your father mixed up in any trouble, do you?'

The clock in the bell tower chimes four o'clock, and Wilf realises that it is more likely that he will be in trouble, for his father will have long finished in the woods. 'I'd best go,' he says, sliding to the ground. He touches the horse's flank one last time before turning to race through the woods. He hears Freddie calling after him: 'Remember, there will be some money in it for you . . . and I might let you ride Jasper again.'

Wilf runs all the way to Littlecombe, the thrill of the ride bubbling in his chest. The sun is beginning to dip, but it is still warm, and voices drift across the valley. The fields are dotted with villagers. The hay wagons and the horses move patiently among them, the brasses on their harnesses shining as the men follow, stabbing their pitchforks into the stooks, and lifting them up to the loaders.

'Hey! Wilf! Your father's been looking for you.' It is the baker, whose daughters are in Wilf's class. He is carrying the wooden ladder for the loader to climb down. 'Al!' he shouts across at the man on the wagon behind, which is waiting to take the next load. 'Where's Bolt? His son's here.'

'He's gone to look for the lad in the hay barn. He'll be back dreckly.'

The baker whistles at the horse as it digs its hooves into the dry ground and the wheels creak into action. In the distance, the remaining stooks stand propped together like huddles of soldiers studying their field maps.

The women bring food, and the men stop for a while, mopping at their faces and pulling stray strands of hay from their hair, making themselves comfortable in little groups seated on the ground. Wilf sees Miss Cottam making her way towards them. She always brings refreshments for the labourers: cider, pies and a flask of tea; it is why she never has trouble finding help with the harvest. He spots Victor, striding to catch up with her, and then slowing so that they can converse.

When they reach Wilf, Miss Cottam offers the golden liquid to the men who gather around. It pours down the side of the clay flagons, dripping on to the ground as they gulp at it greedily, wiping it from their moustaches and nodding in satisfaction.

She sets her wicker basket on the dry stubble next to Wilf. The dust dances in air that is sweet with the smell of hay and horse and sunshine. Victor's sleeves are rolled up above the elbow, and his flat cap is crooked. 'Where have you been, son?' he asks, eyeing Wilf suspiciously.

'Here,' Wilf shrugs.

Victor narrows his eyes, but doesn't press in front of Miss Cottam.

'I've brought refreshments. Won't you stay and take some?' Celia addresses Victor, while handing Wilf a slice of cake. He eats messily as he listens, crumbs spilling among the chaff on to the red earth.

'Thank you for sending John Harris to the camp,' Celia says as Victor accepts a piece.

'How is he doing?'

'He's very handy. Like the others, he seems to find keeping busy takes his mind off his troubles. And they all find solace in the tranquillity of the place. But you understand. You fought too . . .'

Victor exhales hard and rubs his face. Wilf wants to warn her there is no point pressing him on stories of his time in the war, but she carries on as Victor crouches down to sit next to Wilf on the ground.

'There are not many who have been through as much as you,' she says, shielding her eyes from the lowering sun. 'I know the mines serve their own horrors, so to have worked there from such a young age – younger than your own lad here – and to have fought in the Great War too . . . well, you're a hero, Victor. Don't let anyone tell you differently.'

'If you say so, miss.' Victor rolls his eyes at Wilf, but Wilf can tell that his father is pleased by the compliment.

'You know, the world really is changing,' she says.

Victor grunts sceptically.

'You will come and listen to Raymond again, won't you? He's coming again with my brother. He is better at explaining things than I am.'

Wilf holds his breath, waiting for more information, but none is forthcoming.

'Let me know when he is next here,' says Victor, 'and I will listen.'

'I'll be sure to do that,' she says brightly. 'Now I'd better get rid of the rest of this food,' and she works her way across the stubble, bringing children running to see what she has.

The golden sun is setting, and the last wagon is being loaded.

In the distance, men balance on ladders as they make hats of thatch from last year's straw to keep the ricks safe from the autumn rain. Wilf glances at his father, at his square jaw, and his powerful arms. He has never considered the struggles Victor might have had, or that his father had a life before the war, was a boy like him once. He wonders what it was like to work in a pit, or to kill a German. He wonders if he should warn Celia of the dangers of Raymond White, but that would reveal that he has been talking to Freddie again. He will leave it up to the master to keep everyone safe.

CHAPTER 25

It is not long before Miss Cottam's brother and his friend return to Littlecombe. Aggie is making bread. Wilf is watching his father clean his shotgun on the kitchen table, taking note of how to take it apart, put it back together. He likes the smell of the oil, the spent gunpowder. Victor has managed to put on a few days of shooting for Freddie over the autumn, nothing grand, for they are both finding their feet. And his parents seem to be fighting less, and finding fewer excuses to spend time apart.

Wilf hears a voice calling from the lane and runs to the door. Aggie looks up, through the window. 'It's not for you,' she says, still kneading the dough. 'It's Miss Cottam.'

Celia is driving a pony and cart, her brother sitting up next to her. Raymond White is on one of the benches in the back. 'We're going down to the village to speak about the unions and the Labour party. Your father said to tell him,' calls Celia.

Victor turns to his wife. 'Aggie?'

She smiles and flicks a towel at him. 'Go on with you.'

Victor packs the gun away, and heads out, levering himself into the back of the cart easily. Raymond, his hazel eyes intense as always, nods a greeting. 'The general election's in less than a week. We're here to galvanise your people,' he says to Victor.

'Can I come?' asks Wilf, desperate to find out what is so dangerous about these two men, wondering if he should keep an eye on Miss Cottam's safety.

'Of course,' Celia calls over her shoulder. 'This is as much for you as for anyone.'

Wilf reaches out for someone to give him a hand, but his father shakes his head. 'No. He's too young. Besides, he's got chores to finish.'

Raymond shouts in amusement: 'We must never let socialism stand in the way of chores!'

The other adults laugh, and Wilf feels the colour rise in his cheeks, as much in anger as embarrassment. Celia calls to the pony, and Victor leans back opposite Raymond, his arms resting along the top of the trap, without a backwards glance. Wilf watches them roll away, their warm breath pluming into the chilly air, the Cottams' auburn hair glinting like buffed copper in the afternoon sun. Then he turns on his heels and runs up to the hall, still hot with anger, and ignoring the cries of his mother calling him back.

Freddie is not in the yard, but Wilf is determined that the master will want to hear what he has to say, and asks Dan to fetch him.

'They're here,' says Wilf breathlessly as soon as Freddie appears. 'Miss Cottam's brother and her friend. They've gone down to the village. My da with them.'

'Good chap,' says Freddie. 'Wait at the front of the house. I just need to make a couple of calls and then we'll go down.'

It doesn't take long before Freddie returns. Wilf is thrilled to travel in a motor car for the first time. The feel of leather and the sight of the world rushing past is almost as good as being on a horse. Almost.

By the time they reach the village, there is a small group of Freddie's friends – among them Lord Hampden and Sir Littleton, as well as other local landowners, and some of their men – waiting outside the village hall.

'What do you want to do?'

'Let's go in. See what's being said.'

Freddie talks to the man who is standing at the door. The

man shakes his head as Freddie raises his voice. 'There's no room, m'lord,' he insists.

Wilf takes matters into his own hands and ducks past; the men are too busy arguing to take any notice. The heat of the room hits the back of his throat, and he is faced with a forest of torsos. He starts to push his way through, ignoring the tutting, searching for Victor. The crowd know to whom he belongs, and somehow a corridor opens up that ends at Victor's side.

Victor is leaning against the wall. He glances down and frowns briefly before looking back towards the stage. Wilf stands on his tiptoes, but he cannot see over the shoulders of the men in front. There is a lady standing at a table next to them. Victor indicates her empty chair, and Wilf clambers on to it.

Over the tops of the heads, Wilf spots Miss Cottam at the front, her red hair showing beneath her hat. Her brother is seated next to her. Above them, Raymond White is a commanding figure on the platform, pacing up and down, burning with fervour. 'Let's show Baldwin what we think of his snap election. Let's show him that Labour is the vote of the people! Let's show him that now is our time, that the aristocrats and the capitalists must move over. The working man didn't just win the war in 1918, he won the right to vote! It is your duty to use that vote. Don't throw it away!'

'Why do you city people think you can speak for us?' shouts someone from the other side of the room.

'We don't want to speak for you. We want you to speak for yourselves. See over there. That's Becky Shillingford.' A hundred faces turn and look at the lady next to Wilf. 'She's ready to sign you up to the National Union of Agricultural Workers. Remember: we are stronger together.'

In his excitement, Wilf has forgotten about Freddie, but now there is a kerfuffle by the door. The crowd starts to mutter as Freddie pushes his way in. The mood changes, as people start cursing each other. Victor lifts Wilf to the ground and holds tight on to his hand. 'Stay close,' he warns, as the crowd starts to scatter, shoving each other out of the way as they fumble for the exit, hiding their faces behind their collars, beneath their caps. Now George Cottam calls out from the platform, where he has joined Raymond. 'Don't go. They don't own you . . .' A few of the crowd stand their ground, including Victor. 'Wait!' shouts George. 'This is how they rule with such ease. You must question their authority . . .'

But there are fewer and fewer people left in the room, and suddenly Wilf hears Freddie's voice above the commotion. 'You! Bolt!'

Silence. All remaining eyes swivel their way.

'What are you doing here?'

Victor tightens his grip on Wilf. But he does not speak.

From the platform George shouts, 'Why should he answer to you?'

'Like all these men, he works for us.' Now Wilf sees Miss Cottam join her brother on the stage and lay a hand on his arm, as if to temper him. And he sees that Freddie spots her too, and there is disappointment, anger, but also, Wilf fancies, sadness in the master's face.

'That doesn't mean he can't think for himself.'

'It does if he wants to keep a roof over his head.'

'You can't hold men to ransom.'

'We own their homes.'

'But not their lives.'

'Go back to the city or we'll send you back ourselves.' Lord Hampden's keeper puffs out his chest, looks ready to throw his fat fists. Next to him, one of the landowners' men taps a baton against his hand.

'You can't intimidate us.'

But the people are afraid, and more have sidled out already. There is barely a handful of them left. The air is charged, the static prickling at Wilf's skin. He has a sense he is floundering, out of his depth. He hears the master's voice again. 'Bolt, if you don't get out of here immediately, you won't have any work to go back to.'

Then George: 'Don't move, Bolt. He has no right to do that.'

Miss Cottam tugs at her brother as if begging him not to carry on. But Raymond takes a step forward, to the edge of the stage. 'Becky?' he calls to the union lady, but Miss Shillingford too has packed up her things, and is trying to shuffle out of the door.

Freddie shouts again, 'I'll give you one more minute . . .'

'You make it so that these men feel indebted to you,' Raymond says, his voice cold and hard. 'But it's you who should be indebted to them. They work your fields, cut your crops, look after your beasts.'

But Freddie fires straight back. 'And who do you think pays their wages, looks after them when they are old, gives them a roof over their heads, funds the school? Who do you think keeps the church roof from collapsing? Who do you think pays the taxes to keep everything going? Indeed, who do you think provides their jobs in the first place? What do you think these men would be doing if they didn't work for us? These men have served our families loyally for years, and there's a reason for that. We don't need you coming and stirring it all up.'

The people left behind start to mutter and nod their heads, and turn their hostile faces back to George. He has lost the upper hand, and before long, he has been booed from the stage. Victor remains silent throughout, though Wilf can tell by the strength of his grip, and the clenching of his jaw that he is cross.

They follow the dispersing crowd outside. Freddie says nothing as they pass, though he smiles at Wilf.

When they have gone a safe distance, Victor regards him with suspicious eyes. 'I thought I told you to stay behind,' he says.

180

Wilf does not know how to answer. He scuffs his boots in the dirt.

'You go on home.'

'What about you?'

'I need some time to myself.'

It is a still evening, and bitterly cold. The moon is already hanging in the sky, though the sun is still setting. There is sure to be a frost for the sky is clear. Wilf cuts across the fields rather than walking up the lane. A pale shape glides over him, a barn owl so silent that it could be a ghost. He hears the lowing of the cattle warm in the barn, the rustle of wood-mice in the undergrowth.

Aggie is at the kitchen table, head bowed over her sewing. She looks up and smiles as he enters, but her face soon drops when she realises he is alone. The dogs nudge at Wilf's hands. The kitchen is warm and cosy. 'I thought you'd gone to join your da?'

'I did . . . But he went for a walk.'

'At this time of night?'

Wilf tries to appear nonchalant, though it is hard to quell the guilt at his disloyalty, running to Freddie like a tittle-tattler. But there is something deeper than that: the words that George and Raymond expressed have lit a spark within him – as if they have given voice to something he almost understands.

Wilf sits down opposite his mother. She looks dejected, all the more so because recently she has been glowing. She leans across the table and stretches out her arms. He puts his hands in hers.

'You know I love you,' she says.

He nods, afraid of what is coming next: a sixth sense says it may not be good.

'I've got something to tell you and your da. Something very special.'

A sudden chill passes through him.

'I had hoped to tell him first, but since you're here now . . .'

'What?' he says. 'What's happened?'

She laughs and squeezes his hands tight. 'You're going to have a little brother or sister.'

He stares at her, uncomprehending.

'I'm having a baby.' She gazes at him, her eyes bright as she waits for him to . . . what? To be glad? It takes another few seconds for the news to sink in, and then he is on his feet and running up the stairs to his bedroom.

CHAPTER 26

By the time the daffodils have thrust their heads through the frosty ground, and the primroses lie sprinkled along the foot of the hedgerows, Victor has built a cot, and Aggie has made and hung new curtains in Wilf's room. The lodge house is full of their laughter, and each of their smiles makes Wilf more miserable. It seems that every time he comes into the kitchen, there is his father with his hand on his mother's belly, or stroking her hair, while she laughs and giggles like a child.

'There's no room for a baby,' insists Wilf.

'Hush, lad,' says his father. 'There's more than enough. You don't remember, there were nine of us living in a place barely half this size!'

Victor does not seem bothered by the endless spring drizzle, or the pervading mist that settles over the valley. He cheerfully repairs slates while the rain drives against his cheeks; he sleeps soundly, his arm draped across Aggie; he makes her sit and put her feet up whenever he can persuade her to rest. He never asks Wilf where he's been, or why he's late again. So Wilf slowly spends more time bunking off school, and back in the stable yard – where it seems he is wanted.

Besides, he has been banished from school for this last week for biting David Tucker. He hasn't told Victor or Aggie, because they haven't asked. Instead, he has spent a full, glorious week with the horses, and his reward has been that

183

Freddie has promised to let him sit on the stallion Remus while they lunge it.

By the time he reaches the stable yard, his cheeks are rosy and his lungs are bursting. The stable lads don't speak to him, just glance sidelong at each other with eyebrows raised, but he doesn't care. He knows he is better than all of them – otherwise the master wouldn't allow him this privilege. He grins when he spots the stallion, tossing its head impatiently while Freddie and the new head groom Reid stand beside it, deep in conversation.

Wilf walks straight up, reaching out to touch Remus's cheek. The animal's bones are sharp and fine; as Wilf's hand smoothes the skin, he can feel the grinding of its teeth, the pulsing of its blood.

Freddie looks down at him. 'No fear in this boy,' he says, and Wilf feels he might burst with pleasure.

Reid holds the end of the lunge rein as Freddie watches from the side. Wilf is absorbed in the feeling of being on top of the animal, using the lightest movement of his legs to guide it, just as Freddie suggests. He does not notice anything awry until the horse suddenly tenses and jerks sideways.

Wilf is skilful enough to remain seated, in fact gets a thrill from the sudden switch in power. He leans down to touch the horse's neck to calm it, and it is only then that he realises the horses in the fields along the drive are thundering along the fence, their hooves churning the ground, as a cart comes hurtling along the back drive, its driver standing up as he shouts to the pony to halt.

The stallion rears, and Wilf feels himself tumbling to the ground. The bump jars his bones, but he manages to roll out of the way of the plunging hooves, as Remus tries to break free of the lunge rein, and Reid hollers for the animal to stop. Out of the corner of his eye, Wilf can see the herd of horses trembling in the corner of the field, their sides blowing in and out, and he can tell that Remus is listening to each of them, communicating in some way that humans cannot understand. He pushes himself on to his knees, and then his feet, brushing the dust from his legs, spitting it from his mouth.

He hears his father's voice before he sees Victor striding towards them. 'What are you doing?' he yells. His large fists are clenched with rage.

But Freddie is just as furious, and blocks his path. 'What are *you* doing? You could have killed the boy . . .'

'Me? You put him on a two-year-old.'

'He's good.' Wilf's chest puffs with pride, but Victor ignores the compliment.

'He's a child.'

'He's a natural. And light enough to get the horses used to being ridden . . .'

'He shouldn't be here.'

'Why not? Plenty of boys would jump at the chance.'

Victor glares, and is about to say something, but instead grabs hold of Wilf's arm.

'Get off!' Wilf twists away, and moves to stand next to Freddie.

'You get on the cart,' Victor growls.

'No.' Wilf folds his arms, glances up at Freddie. 'I want to stay here.'

'Get on the cart.'

'No.' The word is forced abruptly from his mouth as Victor steps forward, pulling Wilf by the arm and at the same time catching him around the back of the head with a thwack. Pain shoots through Wilf's skull, and to his horror tears pool in his eyes. He breaks away from Victor and runs to the cart, his father following.

They set off down the drive, jerking to the rhythm of the pony's gait. Wilf watches the parkland roll by, his jaw clenched, his hands fists in his lap, for anger swiftly followed humiliation.

When they reach the lodge they both jump down, fulfilling their duties automatically. Wilf unhitches the pony, leading it around to the outbuildings, while Victor unloads a sack of flour. Wilf removes the pony's harness, hanging it on the peg on the wall, then pumps fresh water into a bucket. Victor carries it to the corner of the stall.

'I bumped into Mr Smithson in the village. He told me you bit David Tucker on the arm.'

Wilf grunts with indifference from between his gritted teeth.

'You must learn to control your temper.' Wilf closes the stable door. Victor sighs with frustration. 'Look at me when I'm talking to you,' he says.

Wilf looks.

'Then I went to Sam's. He said you haven't been there for months. Now I know where you have been. Didn't I tell you to keep away from the horses?'

Wilf can't help the words come tumbling out: 'I can't, Da. It's what I want to do. Like you did.'

'It's not the future we want for you.'

'I'm good with them. Didn't you hear the master? I'm a natural . . .'

'I told you to stay away from him.'

'You said to stay away because the master wouldn't like it. But he doesn't mind. He doesn't mind at all.'

'I don't care what you think. I don't want you going near him either.'

'Why not? Lord Hembury is nice to me. Nicer than you.'

'What's that supposed to mean?'

'You don't care what I do now you've got this new one on the way.'

Victor takes hold of Wilf's shoulders and gazes at him. In the gloaming Wilf can see his own face reflected in his father's eyes. 'You're wrong. Nothing will change when this new baby comes along.'

But Wilf knows that isn't true. Everything has already changed. He feels the spot where Victor clipped him around the cheek. It burns like poison.

* * *

186

Victor and Aggie's high spirits grate on Wilf's nerves. He almost prefers it when they are fighting. They giggle in the kitchen like children his own age. Victor grabs hold of Aggie and gently rests his calloused hand on her swollen belly. Wilf cannot bear to look.

'I'm going up to the lower paddocks,' he says. 'I want to see if the new foal has arrived.'

Victor scowls and his hand drops away from Aggie. 'I thought we talked about that.'

'You going to hit me again?'

Victor's mouth opens in shock at the impertinence. 'Count yourself lucky it were only the once. My da clipped me round the ear every day.'

Aggie looks at Victor. 'I've never known you to raise a finger to the boy.'

'He pushed me to it.'

'How?'

Wilf glares. 'It weren't nothing bad. I were just helping his lordship up at the yard.'

'I didn't know you'd been doing that,' says Aggie, staring at him.

'You going to tell me off an' all?' says Wilf. 'There's no danger from the dowager, if that's what you're worried about. She's been gone these last few months.'

His mother shakes her head, and then turns to Victor. 'Why is it so terrible?'

Victor frowns. 'You can't think it healthy.'

Wilf is surprised at his mother fighting his corner. He appeals to her immediately: 'His lordship says I can have a job there one day.'

'He does, does he?' growls Victor.

'That's good,' says Aggie. 'Maybe he wants to help.'

'I won't allow it.'

'Perhaps it's not up to you?'

Victor looks at her in rage. 'You can't ask me to be a father one minute, and not the next.'

He stops. She stops. They look at Wilf. He senses the world shifting.

A thundercloud settles on the lodge house. Over the days it thickens until like the weather one night it breaks into a wild storm. From his bedroom in the roof, Wilf can hear his parents arguing. The rain is hammering at the windows. No one hears him creak across the floorboards to the top of the stairs. He peers through the banisters.

Aggie is sitting at the table, the thin light from the flickering candle emphasising the deep hollows of her cheeks, the smudges of black beneath her eyes. Her stomach strains at the material of her dress, impossibly round and large compared to her slight frame.

Victor slams his fist on the table. 'We should never have come,' he says.

'You started it all, with your wish to get out. You asked me to speak to him. Why did you want to volunteer? You didn't have to. Mining were protected . . .'

'And you didn't have to . . . to . . .'

'What?' She gets her feet. 'Say it!' she shouts.

Victor puts his head in his hands. 'It weren't fair that he took advantage . . .'

She stamps her foot and turns away. 'No! Why does everyone assume I didn't like him? That I am innocent?' She turns back and leans forward. 'We spent a time talking. He were handsome. He were brave. Why wouldn't I have wanted him?' She pauses, and the anger seems to drain from her voice. 'I thought he liked me. That he might take me away from my life.'

'That's why it were taking advantage.'

'No. I know he liked me. There are things a man's body can't hide.'

'I don't want to hear that.'

Wilf sits back on his heels, shocked to discover that his mother was once in love with someone else. He had no idea.

He tries to think back to the time before Victor came back into their lives. But he cannot picture anyone. Unless . . . Uncle Robbo? But it couldn't be. His parents are talking of a time before Wilf existed . . .

The wind is whining in the woods behind the lodge house, and he creeps down a step to catch their words. His father is trying to calm her, but Aggie is pulling away, her face twisted in pain. Wilf strains to hear more about this life his mother once had, but they have started to argue about something else. Him.

'Why don't you want him working up there? Is it your jealousy?'

Victor's laugh is bitter. 'Of course not. I'm trying to protect him.'

'Let him do it. Maybe they'll accept him. Look out for him somehow.'

'You're still living in a dream world.'

'Why shouldn't I have dreams? Why is it wrong for someone like me?' She turns away. 'You used to tell me I was the most beautiful girl in the world. That I could have whoever I wanted. Why shouldn't it have been him?'

Victor turns her gently back, his hand on her shoulder. His voice is low. 'The world don't work like that. They're one type of person. You're another.'

'I don't want to be this person any more. I hate every day. I hate the work. I hate scrubbing their house and clearing their food. I hate coming back and doing the same here for you. I hate my hands. I hate my body. My face. I look like a woman twice my age. And I'm so tired . . .' Her forehead is creased in pain.

'I still think you're beautiful.' He tries to take her hands but she shrugs him away.

'Why didn't he come back for me?'

'I told you . . .'

Wilf shifts; one of his legs has gone to sleep. The movement alerts Raven. The dog raises his head from his paws, and his tail thuds slowly against the floor.

'Back to bed, Wilf.' Victor does not look up when he speaks. He is searching for Aggie in her dark eyes, but she is lost to him, lost in her memories, the hopes and dreams of her younger self.

'I can't sleep,' Wilf mumbles. Fear is whirling inside him. Now he understands why his parents used to seem so unhappy. But it is hardly his father's fault that his mother's first love died in the war. It happened all over the country, all that heartbreak, all those fathers and sons and brothers dead. It's even touched people like the Hemburys: the master's brother dead, and the countess driven mad.

'Come on, son.' Victor is helping him into bed, where he curls in a protective ball in the middle of the blankets, like a dormouse in its nest. Then they both hear the door slam, and Victor is running down the stairs, and Wilf is immediately after him, his stomach turning over. The kitchen is empty.

'Aggie?' Victor calls, stepping quickly into the parlour. She is not there either.

He runs back into the kitchen. 'Aggie?'

The dogs are on their feet, all thought of sleep and warmth gone: their dark eyes alert, their wet noses sniffing the air.

'Aggie!'

They both hear the latch catching on the open gate. Victor grabs his coat, thrusts his feet into his boots. 'Stay here,' he says.

Victor runs out into the night, the dogs alongside him. Wilf waits only to struggle into his own boots, and then he follows. The wind drives the rain through his nightclothes. Water is running in rivulets along the lane. Within seconds his hair is plastered to his head. The branches of the trees snap and crack above. He can just about make out the yellow ring of Victor's lamp, heading in the direction of the top lake, and then they are swallowed by the night.

Terror spreads through Wilf's body. He stumbles further into the night, but it is pitch black, and he is confused in which direction he is heading. He feels the grass under his feet and

190

knows he has come off the drive. The wind screams and the rain lashes at his face. He turns back to where he can see the dim light of home. He slips and slides in the mud. He sees another light, sweeping through the slanting rain. He must be near the road again.

The car stops just in time. Wilf blinks in the beam. He can hear the engine running, see wisps of steam rising into the night. A voice calls, 'I almost ran you over. What on earth are you doing out in this?' Freddie appears, a silhouette.

It is hard to find the right words. The water is running down his face, and his back, and his clothes are stuck to his skin. There is a chill in his bones, and his teeth are beginning to chatter.

Freddie bundles him into the car, grabbing a blanket from the back seat, rubbing it over his head, his neck. 'Where's your father?'

The rain drums on the roof. Wilf suddenly finds his voice. 'It's not him. It's my ma,' he says. 'She's gone.'

'What do you mean, "gone"?'

'There was a fight. She ran out into the night.'

'In which direction?'

Wilf starts to cry. 'I think it were the lake. I can't be sure.' He points to where he thinks he last saw Victor's lamp. Freddie starts to drive, bumping over the grass, peering out through the windscreen into the circle of light thrown by the head-lamps. Wilf watches the water run in lines across the windows, the little wiper going pointlessly backwards and forwards.

'There!' says Freddie, and Wilf sees a tiny patch of light in the dark: Victor's lamp. The car slides to a halt, wheels spin-ning in the mud. The headlamps light the dismal scene: Victor staring out across the black lake, the dogs up to their bellies, and, beyond them, a horrible shape on the water.

Freddie throws himself out of the door. Wilf is unable to move, his limbs are heavy as the buckets of water he some-times has to carry. He knows that Aggie cannot swim, and neither can Victor. Victor is wading unsteadily forwards as the

191

water sucks and pulls at his chest, his arms held high, the lamp dangling from one hand, and casting a pitiful light. Out of their depths, the dogs are unsure of what to do, whimpering as they paddle in circles before turning back. The rain slices through the headlights; it spatters on the tiny waves of the inky lake. The great darkness of it terrifies Wilf. He sees Freddie reach Victor, and then forge on, swimming now, towards the dark shape on the water. He has a hold of it, and he is pulling it, and Victor is helping, and together they are dragging Aggie to the bank, and Wilf knows he has lost his mother.

Through the raindrop-spattered windows Wilf sees the two men bent over the motionless bundle. He sees his father pull and push at it. Freddie tugs him away, but Victor shakes free and bends over her again. Freddie kneels in the mud next to Victor, and Wilf can hear snatches of words as they shout at each other. He catches something about the baby, an innocent, and the master's brother Edward, and war, and a promise, but none of it makes sense; every other word is drowned out by Wilf's sobs and the rain battering the car. The emptiness Wilf felt after the loss of the racehorse seems to swell inside him until the blackness is almost pressing against his lungs so that he cannot breathe. And the dogs stand on the edge of the circle of light, their heads down, their ears back, as the wind spits dark patches across the lake.

CHAPTER 27

Celia walks down the aisle as if in a dream. Her father and brother stride ahead, straight-backed beneath the fragile coffin, their shoulders bearing a wife, a mother, who in the end weighed no more than a child. She steps into the light. The earlier shower is over, and the sun has come out. Celia has worked with enough sorrow to know that her broken heart will mend around the scar. But still it is hard; no one can truly prepare for the final searing pain of losing someone they love.

Despite her frailty, Margaret Cottam made plenty of friends locally, and the service is packed. The procession follows the vicar, spreading out around the freshly dug hole. Celia's grieved mind processes snapshots: the sheep wandering among the gravestones, yellow teeth nibbling at tufts of wet grass, a mistle thrush singing in a holly bush, and somewhere far away a motorcycle backfiring. Her mother is lowered into her final resting place. Celia throws a posy of wildflowers on the coffin, her father and brother a handful of earth that breaks and scatters into crumbs. And then they are turning from the graveside, and people come to pay their respects to the diminished Cottam family.

The kind words and platitudes wash over Celia. She barely registers Freddie when he approaches. She does not catch what he says, but quietly notes that Elizabeth does not seem to have bothered to come. What does she care? She is too numb even to take any pleasure from the hurt that flashes across his face as she turns away from him.

She catches sight of Victor Bolt. He is standing near the boulder that the locals call the Devil's stone. The villagers are giving him a wide berth; it has been weeks since he lost his wife and unborn child, but the gossip is still fresh. Celia is touched that he has come when Aggie's own grave is still covered in fresh earth. He is stooped, slack-shouldered, holding his boy's hand. Above them, the jackdaws bicker on the crenellated parapet; the yew tree's dark branches twist into the sky.

She sees Freddie leave. He passes Victor without acknowledgement, though their bodies arch away from each other, as if repulsed. It must have been utterly devastating for Victor to lose his wife in such a way.

The child Wilf – usually a robust boy – is as pallid and apologetic as his father. She feels a stab of understanding, for she has lost her mother too. How different father and son are to the man and boy she sat with once during the harvest. She resolves to make an effort to check on the Bolts when she can.

She joins her own father and brother at the lychgate. The three of them have been drawn together in the last few months: bound to the nucleus of their mother, they have barely left the house. But now, with the sun on her face and the crisp spring air, Celia is minded to remain adrift for a while longer. She tells the men to drive on ahead. They protest that she should not be alone, but she insists she will walk home.

Once Celia is away from the village, the lane grows empty of people and motorcars, and the air is filled with birdsong. Clouds of butterflies hover along the banks where cow parsley nods delicately above upright purple orchids. As she rests at the mossy bridge to watch the water tumble below, she hears the sound of hooves trotting down the lane. She turns almost guiltily. The rider tips his head as he passes and wishes her good day, and Celia returns the greeting. The retreating silhouette transports her straight to the days she used to ride with Freddie and Ginny.

She shakes the image from her head. She was a different person then. She can see now it was a strange alliance. The Hemburys belong to an arcane world, where there is no place for her – and she is glad, because she has no desire to live in it. They can keep it all to themselves.

She moves on, passing the men's camp, which cannot be seen from the road, and the Littlecombe fields, dotted with their cattle, which have been let out now that the ground is drier. She is proud of the hard work that has seen the farm succeed, but there is something lacking from her life. She wants more. Like the fresh growth of feathery rowan and soft hazel in the hedges, it is time that new life sprang from old.

Celia smiles as she reaches the driveway to Littlecombe. In the years since they have been here the house and gardens have settled into each other. Maggie has long gone, but her knowledge helped create a successful farm, producing beef and dairy. They have built a prize-winning herd of Devon Ruby cattle, whose rich russet bodies grow fat on their lush grass, the same prime land that Freddie hankered after for his racecourse.

Two figures are reclining on the lawn. Raymond has arrived for the weekend, and he and George are already deep in conversation. George props himself up on his elbow when he sees her and waves. He has changed in the last couple of years: his suit is well-tailored, and his once-unruly hair has been smoothed back. This tentative victory of the Labour party forming the first Labour government has focused some of his bitterness.

Raymond stands and dusts down his trousers, fixing Celia with his unnerving stare. There is a robust self-confidence and a steeliness to him, a fire that can be catching. But recently she has noticed that when he is around her, he becomes a little gauche.

'Apologies for not making the funeral,' he says. 'I couldn't get out of London as fast as I'd hoped.'

She murmurs her understanding.

'It's a miracle you find time to do anything,' says George. 'You're more busy than ever.'

'That's because I have to work twice as hard trying to convince you to stay true to the socialist cause,' Raymond replies, winking at Celia. 'Why don't you come and sit?' Raymond asks, pointing at a spot on the grass. 'We were just discussing Ramsay's recent slip-up. I don't believe he will stay in power for much longer.'

She shakes her head. 'I must go and freshen up.'

'I would like to hear what you think. Your opinion is of great value to me,' Raymond adds, his eyes trying to search out hers.

'I'm sorry. Not now. Perhaps later?'

In the drawing room in the evening, she watches the sun splay across the fields, the scatterings of red cattle that dot the slanting fields. Her father puts his arm around her shoulders. She leans her head against him. 'We've had an enquiry from New Zealand: a farmer who wants to import one of our bulls. Your success has exceeded all expectations.'

'And to think the world expected nothing more for me than schoolmistress or wife.'

'I've only ever expected you to do your best, to question, and to keep an open mind.'

'You are a beacon of hope in a dark world.'

'Attitudes will keep on changing. Things will grow easier.'

'They couldn't grow worse. It was hard enough getting the men to take their orders from me rather than you, and what with the collapse of crop prices, the infestation of wild oats, the rain ruining our harvest, the insects spoiling our feed . . .'

'You've coped more than admirably. As I knew you would. I'm only sorry I haven't been around to help.'

'I sometimes wonder if you do that on purpose, to focus my mind.'

He smiles down at her. 'Would I behave in such a fashion?'

'Well Littlecombe is pretty much running itself now. I need a new challenge.'

'The Raddington colliery would do well with a woman on the board.'

She shakes her head. 'I don't want to sit on a board. I like to be in among people, getting my hands dirty.'

'That will change as you get older; it did for me.'

She squeezes his arm, then crosses to the mantelpiece to pick up an unframed painting propped up behind the carriage clock. 'After all that's happened, I'm glad we moved here, and I know mother was too. She had a good end.'

Joseph Cottam pulls a bright silk handkerchief from his pocket and dabs his head before pressing at his eyes. He nods. 'She's still here. In everything.' They look around the room, where her mother's paintings are scattered, on the furniture, the floor. They stand for a while, contemplating the canvases, remembering her mother in her chair, chewing the end of her paintbrush as she gazed out of the window.

They hear the heavy tread of men coming down the corridor. Mr Cottam clears his throat, wipes the corners of his eyes again before stuffing the handkerchief back into his breast pocket.

CHAPTER 28

Victor appears on Littlecombe's doorstep a week later. 'I been told to deal with the vermin in your South Paddock,' he mutters. 'Master says the east boundary is riddled with rabbits, and they're coming from your side.'

Celia wants to say that it's none of Freddie's business what happens on her side of the lane, but she knows Victor is simply following orders. Besides, she is shocked by the gamekeeper's appearance. Up close, she can see how very much altered he is: he has aged by a decade, his skin is dry and yellow, his eyes red-rimmed with exhaustion.

Before she can utter anything, there is a crash from the barns, the clanging of metal on metal, and Victor jumps a full yard away from her. His temples are wet with sweat, his pupils dilated. She understands grief can turn a man into a shell, but this . . . She puts out a hand to steady him, but he flinches from that too. 'Are you all right?' she asks. 'It was probably one of the cows kicking a pail.'

'It's nothing, miss,' he replies, wiping the back of his hand across his forehead.

'How long has it been going on?'

'I said it's nothing.'

Victor's anger dies as quickly as it flares, though his hands are still trembling.

'Is it since you lost your wife?' she tries again.

He rubs crossly at his eyes. 'If you please, miss. I've got a full day's work . . .'

'I'm sorry. Are the rabbits really that bad?'

He nods. 'They're taking a lot of our young crops. And his lordship's worried that one of the horses might break a leg riding over a warren.'

'Are you sure you can spare the time? I won't allow traps. Remember our secret?'

There is a whisper of a smile on his face. 'No point in trapping if you're going to release them, miss,' he says. Then he stares blackly at the ground. 'I'll use the gun.'

She watches him stamp away to inspect the Littlecombe fields, and an anger begins to bubble up inside her. She's fed up with Freddie behaving as if he's still the lord of Littlecombe. The farm belongs to her father now. He has no right to send a man over to take her rabbits. And can he not see that Victor is struggling? She thinks of how the Hemburys ride roughshod over people as well as land. In fact, the more she thinks about it, the more she realises something must be done. Why should he get away with such behaviour? He must be confronted. If she doesn't do it now, she never will. She knows where he will be.

Celia puts her shoulders back and sets off for Coombe. As she strides past the front gates, she notes that the lodge house is reverting to its previous state: the paint flaking while brambles reach out across the grubby windows, and the roses that Victor's wife tended have gone wild.

In contrast, when she reaches the stable yard it is a hive of activity, and swept to perfection. The stable doors and the metalwork have been painted. There are men busy working in the yard, leading horses, pushing wheelbarrows and carrying buckets.

She spots Freddie immediately. He is rubbing the back of his neck while talking to the head groom, Reid. She cannot help taking in the strength of his hands, the long fingers, the way his thick hair is so unruly that it cannot be tamed against his neck.

Reid catches sight of her and nods at Freddie, who turns, unsmiling. He crosses the yard to greet her.

Before he can speak, she blurts out, 'You sent Bolt over. Without even asking.'

He raises his eyebrows in languid amusement, which irks her further. 'Good morning to you, Miss Cottam. I see you are in fine fettle.'

'Bolt?'

'Those warrens on your land needed urgent attention. I apologise if perhaps you feel I should have addressed you first myself, but I didn't want to disturb you during your time of mourning.'

Celia flounders in the face of Freddie's behaviour. It's as if she is someone he's just been introduced to. As if they don't know each other at all. 'Bolt seemed to be in a bad way,' she says, hoping to regain the upper hand. 'He's still grieving for his wife.'

The smirk falls from Freddie's face, and his grey eyes darken. 'You know he blames my family for that,' he says.

'I don't understand. I thought you pulled her from the lake . . .'

'There's much you wouldn't understand,' he snaps, as the shutters come firmly down.

She tries to be more conciliatory; that night must have been a shock for Freddie too. 'I've seen men with similar symptoms,' she says calmly. 'With what he would have experienced on the Front, and now the death of his wife . . . I think you should talk to him.'

'Good lord! You can't be serious. He would be horrified. It's not the done thing.'

'Left untreated, it could get worse.'

'You seem to be taking an unhealthy interest in the man.'

'I take an interest in everyone.'

'Like those tramps you allow to camp by the river.'

'They do no harm.'

'It's only a matter of time.'

200

'You're entitled to your opinion.'

'It's not just me. You should hear what they're saying in the village.'

'I don't care what anyone says. It's no one's business but mine.'

'And Bolt is mine.'

'You make him sound like a horse!'

'I advise you to stay away from him. He's unpredictable. Possibly dangerous.'

'That's a bit strong,' she says, which riles Freddie all the more.

'What about his political leanings? He's been listening to your brother's claptrap, for one.'

'That's hardly a crime.'

'It is when they're insurgents.'

She is so appalled that she is speechless for a moment. A young stable lad walks up to the gate into the adjoining field leading a young horse. Celia watches as he removes the halter. He can barely reach, stretching up on the tip of his toes to lift the straps over the animal's ears. He catches sight of Freddie and Celia and tips his cap.

She recognises him immediately. 'But I see you still let his son work here?' she says. The boy seems brighter than when she saw him in the graveyard – more confident without his father gripping his hand.

'He helps out in the holidays, and at weekends.'

'So I assume you're not including him on your list of dangerous people?'

'I don't have to explain myself to you,' he snaps. 'You should be pleased I'm giving people opportunity.'

'Opportunity or exploitation?'

'I feel bad about the boy's mother, that's all. It must be tough for him . . .'

'But it must help to have another line of workers for your family to draw on.' Her bitterness at his behaviour adds a barb to her tongue.

Freddie's face darkens. 'I can't help being born into this family any more than you can help being born into yours.'

'I'm grateful for mine . . .'

'Who says I'm not?' he spits, as Reid hands him his horse, and he springs on to its back and rides away.

Against the shock of his nastiness all remaining bravery evaporates. A magpie starts to cackle at her from the oak tree. Tears prick at her eyes as she turns back the way she has come. She hurries away, the magpie's laughter ringing in her ears.

Celia meets Victor at the bottom of the drive. She forces her lips into a smile. Why should she listen to Freddie's warning? 'How did you get on?' she asks.

'It'll take a few weeks, but I'll get it done.'

He shifts from one foot to the other.

'Is there something else?'

'I think you've got a bigger problem than rats, miss.'

'What's that?'

'I seen fresh tyre marks leading from the back road and down the old drover's lane to Undercott. There's signs that men have been waiting there some time – plenty of cigarette ends and a torn part of a receipt for some Pratt's motor spirit. There's cattle tracks too. It's my belief that someone has driven off one or more of your herd. Have you noticed anything queer going on?'

'I thought something malicious was going on a long time ago. But I believed it had stopped. Surely my stockman would have said something?'

He shrugs. 'Just saying what I seen.'

'Could it be gypsies?'

'Unlikely, miss. Gypsies don't take no more than they need and they stick to the wild beasts, a rabbit or a pigeon. They haven't the means to get rid of a cow.'

'Will you do me a favour? Will you keep an eye out while you're trapping? I can't ask any of my workers. They're unlikely to betray each other.'

'You could put up the barbed wire like we have at Coombe.'

This proprietorial apportioning of land has been taking place across the countryside. Celia shakes her head. 'No. I dislike the stuff.'

Victor shudders. 'I'm none too keen on it myself.'

Celia is reminded of her former patients, and the everyday sights and sounds that trigger their fears, and she wonders if men who have suffered such horrors will ever find the peace they deserve.

CHAPTER 29

The starlings begin to gather in the skies over Devon, great clouds pulsing and shifting into apocalyptic patterns. The sweet chestnuts swell in their prickly casings, and the leaves wither and die, just like the Labour government. George and Raymond return to Littlecombe after the trouncing at the October election. George is disheartened, but Raymond is galvanised, convinced that a letter published by a right-wing newspaper linking the Russian Communists with the party was a forgery, designed to play on fears of revolution among middle-class voters. 'If they're stupid enough to believe the lies that snake publishes, then they deserve a Conservative government,' he says.

'I'm afraid it shows the power of the printed word,' says Mr Cottam. 'My wife knew that only too well.'

Celia thinks of the small stack of pamphlets that her mother kept, prized possessions that deserved a place next to her coveted paintbrushes and artwork. She makes her way to her mother's desk and slides open the top drawer.

Raymond's shoulders slump. 'It's so damn dispiriting. No one listens to the voice of the people.'

Celia lifts the leaflets out. Her mother kept every issue. The paper – one of the voices of the suffragette movement – had been slipped under doors and scattered throughout towns and cities. It was what her mother was eventually arrested for.

She smiles at the cartoons. A thought is tickling the back of her mind.

'What have you got there?' Raymond is at her shoulder. She finds comfort in his presence, and in his blatant regard for her. He always includes her in conversation. It reminds her she has a voice, an opinion, when she is feeling so wretched about Freddie.

She turns to him: 'What if you printed your beliefs in a newspaper?'

'No one would allow us. They're run by the very people we are trying to hold to account.'

Celia waves her mother's pamphlets: 'What if you set up your own?'

Raymond frowns but takes one.

'I'm sure there are old contacts who could help,' Celia adds, warming to her theme. She addresses her father: 'What about Miles?' Her mother's old friend had made a point of seeking her out at the funeral. 'He was co-editor with his wife. He must still know people who could write. Then all you'd need is a sympathetic printing press, and a network of distributors to hand them out. Once people realise there are others who share their views, who back their cause, it will be a way of gathering more support . . .' She stops.

They are all looking at her: her father smiling quietly, George with raised eyebrows, and Raymond, who is slowly breaking into a grin. 'This is the Celia I remember,' he says, as he too is transformed into the eager schoolboy who used to talk about revolution when they were children.

The men clink glasses, and let their mouths run away with the subject. Celia drifts to the window, warmed from the inside. She has a sudden connection back to the person she was before the hospital, before Littlecombe. It is fleeting, but nevertheless that person is still there, and it feels good to have found she still exists.

Outside, in the farm yard, the workers are busy preparing a wagon, rubbing at it with cloths, for it has not been used in a while. She recognises two of them as Harris and Strong, men who have lived by the river for more than a year, and longer than any of the others. She is getting to know them better now that they help out with odd jobs on the farm. She watches them work. Despite his strange twitches, Harris does the work of two men, and Strong is a perfectionist. She doesn't care what Freddie or the villagers think – she knows she's doing the right thing. The regular workers have warned her from employing vagrants, but Celia is not afraid of them: they are simply misfits as she is, outsiders who have made a home here – and today locals and outsiders are labouring together as they try to get everything ready. For the first time since seeing Freddie again, Celia feels her spirits lift. It is good to see everyone working in harmony.

Raymond reappears at her side, and they watch the men check over the wheels and fittings. The women are chattering and laughing as they help haul bales of straw on to the back of the wagon. 'Turn-out at rallies in areas like this is at an all-time low. Why do you think that is?'

'I think they're too busy trying to survive to spend time on politics.'

'Perhaps they aren't so hungry for change. They have space, fresh air . . . It's luxury compared to those in the city.'

'Have you not been down to the village? The families in the terraced cottages along the west side of Fore Street have to cross the road to share the privies on the east side. Half of the roofs are missing. I used to be guilty of thinking that people around here had it better – but it's not true. It's just as bad. They still struggle to stay warm, to eat, to work.'

'It sounds to me as if they need someone to fight their corner.'

'If only my mother was still alive. She had ideas . . .'

Raymond interlaces his hands awkwardly, rubbing his thumbs together. 'I want you to know I understand how difficult things must have been for you recently. I am so sorry that you lost such a source of light and inspiration. She was a rare person, unconventional and unafraid to question society's customs. But I see there is much of her in you.'

Celia is grateful for his thoughtfulness, and when George appears, and puts an arm around each of their shoulders, she feels something akin to happiness. Life has come so far since the war. Both she and George have made it in their own ways, and now she senses the three of them are a force of change. She feels the old buzz in her veins, the anticipation for the future. She thinks how perhaps she could write about these things – the things she knows so well – as her mother once did. Margaret Cottam had no journalistic background, just a determination to communicate why women must be afforded the right to vote. Celia could do the same for men like Victor Bolt, who still struggle with their memories of war, as well as for those others who struggle daily, who scratch a living while the few landowners like Freddie Hembury swan around dictating terms. There is power in sharing her knowledge, in sharing these people's stories.

George rests his head against hers for a moment. 'You're just like her, you know. And capable of as much.' She squeezes his hand with affection, and he steps away to look at them both. 'But tonight we have something new to focus on: the legendary burning tar barrels at Ottery St Mary. They say you're not a true local until you've been.'

CHAPTER 30

Celia regularly checks the stock books and finds that Victor is right: there are beasts unaccounted for, marked as lost to disease, though she recalls no illness in her herd. She resolves to keep a closer eye on the workers in the yard, while Victor remains vigilant in the fields.

Spring comes, followed swiftly by summer, and once again the young cattle fatten on the rich grass, standing in the cool of the river while around them the swifts dip and dart across the surface of the water like the bats that flit and swoop over the roofs at night.

She goes for a walk to clear her head. She has just finished writing an article on rural sanitation for Raymond's new communist party newspaper, and she wants to go through some more of the notebooks that Maggie left. If she is ever going to be able to get away, she needs to make sure there are comprehensive reference books. Besides, she wants to immerse herself in a different life. It is no good holding on to the past: it must be all or nothing.

It is muggy, with the threat of thunderstorms. She heads for the river, where she knows the air will be cooler. She cuts from the river back to the lane, past Half-Acre Wood, where the wanderers have made a home. Harris and Strong are there – as they always are – and there are others seated on logs they have dragged into a circle around a fire. The low murmur of the men's voices reaches her ears. They spot her and she waves, and they lift their hands in greeting. They have been useful laying hedges and clearing the river and ditches over the winter in exchange for food.

Their makeshift homes of tarpaulin and canvas are just visible strung between the trees. There are a couple of more permanent wooden shacks. Victor didn't need to confirm that they were ex-military: it is evident in the way they keep the camp so neat, the metal mugs hanging from the trees, their socks dangling from a line, and because she recognises expressions similar to those who came for treatment at the war hospital a lifetime ago.

Celia turns as she reaches the gate on to the lane. From here it is almost impossible to make out the individual men, for they have become part of the woodland. She knows they have found some kind of sanctuary here, and an idea has slowly been forming in her head. She is convinced that the countryside has some healing property – in its tranquillity, in the simple surroundings of bird and beast, in the quiet rush of the river. It has helped quieten her own mind of thoughts of Major Lewis. She wonders if it does the same for these men. She knows that Harris has all but lost the tremors and twitches that plagued him when he arrived. Could there be something in that for the future? The healing of the countryside has similarities to the healing work she practised with Dr Hayne.

She continues back up the lane to the house. A wren darts nervously into the hedge, a blur of chequered brown. She smiles to herself. She was nervous herself once, but no longer. The past cannot ruin her life.

In the distance, thunder rumbles like her father's new tractor engine. The air is close and perspiration is pooling in the small of her back. Victor is waiting at the cider barn.

'I know who it is,' he says, tipping his cap.

'How can you be sure?' asks Celia, leading him inside, away from the suspicious looks of the other men in the yard.

'I've seen him. I slept a week with the men at Half-Acre Wood. I followed him, saw him drive two youngsters across the river, into the truck of a man I know is a wrongdoer from the other side of Tiverton.'

'How could he do that to us?'

'Perhaps he had no choice.'

'We are all free to make choices.'

Victor gives a bitter bark. 'No disrespect, miss, but you're wrong. There's no freedom for the likes of us. There'll always be masters taking what they want from the lowborn.'

'But when we spoke . . .'

He cuts her short. 'No matter what you say, the truth of it is you've more in common with those at the top than us at the bottom. A mine owner is no different to a landowner: they both get rich off the back of others and discard us when they don't want us any more. That's not going to change. Not in my lifetime, anyway.' He averts his gaze, and she knows he is thinking of his dead wife, his unborn child.

She wants to list all the reasons why her family is different: how her father improved the lives of the men who worked for him, buying lamps instead of sending men underground with open flames, a proper system of checking in and out so that no one would be left behind in a collapse, a relief fund for the injured . . . but for now she reaches out to comfort him. He steps back, as if her hand is diseased.

'Don't give up,' she says. 'My father . . .'

'You can't use his story to compare all men. Your family had the luck that millions never will. I'm no overman. My boy's no clerk.'

'You've got to fight.'

'I were tired of fighting nine years ago. That's not changed.' His eyes are black as the coal pits they both came from.

'I'm sorry you feel that way.' She suddenly thinks of Freddie, and how he has slipped back beneath the veneer of the Hembury name, and it is hard to deny that they are all stereotypes, stuck in the roles that have been cast for them.

He shrugs. 'You got your own problems to deal with. Let me alone with mine.'

'Very well. I'll call a meeting.'

'I'll fetch help.'

'There's no need . . .' But Victor has already turned on his heel.

The workers arrive in dribs and drabs, the permanent, the temporary and the new: milkmaids, stockmen, ploughmen, as well as Harris and Strong, who are rebuilding the wall of one of the cow barns. They enter the cider barn, hats in hand, mumbling their good-days to Celia, who sits at the table where she distributes the wages every week. A second brood of fledgling swallows watches from their muddy nest in the rafters.

When everyone is present, Celia pushes herself to her feet. The workers shuffle uncomfortably from foot to foot and stare at the ground. She notes that the men from the camp stand apart from the regulars. She clears her throat. 'I've called you all here to get to the bottom of a problem,' she starts. 'It seems as if someone has been stealing from us . . .'

There is a collective intake of breath before the protestations start.

'You saying one of us is a thief?'

'Who are you accusing?'

'It weren't me.'

'It's they tramps from the river.'

'You should have moved they on.'

'Them'm stealing, all right. Them'm stealing our jobs.'

'There's scarce enough work for us.'

Celia holds up her hands to silence them, but the locals are rounding on the two outsiders, who start to edge towards the door.

'Stop,' she calls, but they ignore her, too busy jostling into a ring around the two frightened men. A fist sets a nose bleeding. The trickle of blood seems to incite the men further. The two men cower on the earthen floor, their arms held high to try to protect their bodies from the blows of hobnailed boots. Celia bangs on the table and calls out again. One of the milkmaids starts to cry. The men ignore them, and egg each other on. The room shrinks to the size of a prison cell.

A shadow falls across the door followed by a loud retort. The assailants fall back. The women fall silent. The spent cartridge falls to the floor, smoking. There is the tinkling of pellets raining down on the roof as the ringing in Celia's ears subsides.

'Step back!' says Freddie as he enters the barn in front of Victor, who has his shotgun cracked safely over his arm. 'What is the meaning of this?'

They hang their heads, eyes cast down, silent.

Celia walks in front of the desk. 'Thank you. I can handle this.' She holds her hands behind her back to hide their trembling: digging her nails into her palms.

Freddie folds his arms and leans against the doorframe. Old Tom's beard bristles. He appeals to Freddie. 'It's his fault,' he says, pointing at Victor. 'Him'm said how we've been stealing.'

'He's always had it in for us,' adds Ned Spiller.

Celia cuts them off. 'This is not a matter for Lord Hembury. Will you kindly address me.' All eyes swivel her way. Old Tom glares at the floor, mouth clamped shut.

'Right. Now I've got your attention,' says Celia. 'I will start again. It is not Bolt's fault. It is not the fault of the men by the river . . .'

'You know who it is?'

'I do, Tom. But I would like to give them a chance to come forward.'

The workers glance at each other uneasily.

'I assure you I will do all I can to help those who are honest, but there is no place for thieves here.'

The milkmaid Bronwen steps forward. 'I sometimes take a little cream,' she says nervously.

Celia smiles encouragement. 'I believe that is something that should be considered a perk of the job.'

The maid steps back, elbows her neighbour. Effie steps forward. 'I do too, ma'am.'

'I know you have young twins who must be in need of extra sustenance.' She addresses the rest of them: 'And I'm sure some of you take a little grain too. But animals are different.'

Silence falls again. Freddie shifts position.

'Will no one come forward?' says Celia again. 'I'm giving you a chance to tell the truth now, and I promise your punishment will not be severe.'

Still no one speaks.

'Perhaps you would rather see me in secret. I will give you twenty-four hours, and if no one comes forward, then you must suffer the consequences. Please leave.'

They file out until only Freddie remains. The cider barn suddenly seems enormous, a hollow shell ringing with her disappointment.

'You can't be a friend and a boss,' says Freddie, moving towards her.

'Let me deal with things my own way . . .'

'I'll eat my hat if anyone comes forward.'

Celia feels a prickle of irritation. 'Why did Victor fetch you?'

'He didn't. I saw him carrying his shotgun and asked where he was going. I thought you were going to steer clear of him.'

'I don't know why you think I should.'

'Because I asked you to.'

'You don't control us all. I'd like you to leave.'

For a moment, she thinks he is going to fight back, but then he looks miserably at his hands. 'I don't want it to be like this,' he says, but he goes, without glancing back.

Celia slumps backwards into the chair, drained – not just by the meeting, but by Freddie Hembury. It is clear she must get on with making something of her life – before her resolve falters.

The night is long. There is no moon, and the sky is as inky as the feathers of the rooks in the rookery. A cold north wind reminds Celia that autumn is almost here. She lies awake trying to convince herself that Frederick Hembury does not matter. She may not be not cut out to be a doctor or a countess, but there is a place for her out there somewhere. She feels a hardening in her heart. She has hidden away for too long.

The following day drags slowly to a close, and still no one has come forward. The workers avoid her gaze, carrying out their jobs with grim determination. There will be no second chances: she has had enough. She takes her findings to the parish constable. He arrives to remove Ned Spiller in the early evening, as he is preparing to return to the village with Frances. Frances gives a cry, to warn him, but it is too late. Ned hangs his head. He knows the game is up. The other workers stop to watch as he is taken away, their faces a mixture of relief, anger, resignation.

'You should have come to me if you were in trouble,' says Celia as the constable passes with Ned.

He spits on the ground in disgust, and Celia tries not to flinch. 'You don't understand. You're no better than that family next door.'

It is the second time in as many days that someone has levelled that accusation at her. She takes a deep breath. 'Stealing is wrong whoever you target.'

Ned glares at her. 'Don't tell me they noticed anything missing. You wouldn't have noticed either, if it hadn't been for that gossipmonger. But you can't trust someone if they're not from round here.'

'That's enough now,' says the constable, encouraging him into the car. When the door is safely closed, he turns to Celia. 'The man he's been selling to's a nasty piece of work. We'll have to keep him in custody until he appears in court. For his own safety.'

'His wife is expecting a baby.'

'He should have thought of that before he got tangled up with the likes of the Kerslakes.'

The tyres throw up loose stones as the car pulls away.

Frances takes a few steps after it, one hand over her mouth, the other on her belly.

'I'm sorry, Frances. I gave him a chance . . .'

The maid brushes at the dust that has settled on her clothes. 'Oh, you can pretend you're kind, that you care about the likes of us, but we know different.'

'I can't condone stealing. But Ned will have a job to return to when he's served his time.'

Frances laughs, a bitter bark. 'We're done with the lot of you,' she says. 'Soon as he gets out we're going to the city. Bristol or London.'

'You don't have to go.'

Frances sniffs, wiping her nose with her cuff. 'You don't know nothing about us. You don't know the treatment Ned's put up with. You've no interest as long as your clothes are pressed and your cows are fed. Ned's right. You're no different to the Hemburys.'

She turns and strides away, stopping briefly to rip off her white apron before throwing it to the ground, and once again Celia is reminded of Victor's comment that they are all stuck in their roles. But isn't she proof that people can get out if they try? Is she really that out of touch with those who work for her?

She watches Frances disappear into the lane, back straight, head held high.

Effie follows soon afterwards; she is a cousin of Ned's, and it won't do for her to stay. The apprentice stockman also fails to turn up one morning, afraid that he might be implicated in the misdemeanour.

'Would you like me to put the word out for two new stockmen?' says Old Tom.

Celia stares at him, taking in the leathery skin, the crinkled eyes. She wonders if he is younger than he appears. Beyond his stooped shoulder she can see Harris and Strong driving the weaned calves out to pasture. They are so different from the men who first offered their help in exchange for a few pennies. Once they were broken and apologetic and now they have a purpose and a spark in their eyes. It comes to her in a flash. She shakes her head at Old Tom, feels her soul toughen some more. 'There's no need. Their positions have already been filled.'

CHAPTER 31

Celia straightens her father's bow tie, smoothing her hand down his colourful waistcoat. He proffers his arm, and through it she winds her own. He pats her hand. 'Come, let's wassail!' he says in a cheerful voice, though laced with sorrow; these last few months have been hard for him.

They make their way to the front of the procession. It is hard to tell who is who beneath the lively line of flaming torches, for some men are dressed in women's clothing, and many of the people are wearing masks. The January air nips at their noses, and around them the fields are covered in a dusting of snow. The moon has turned the farm into a magical realm somewhere between night and day. They lead the way to the orchard, past the barn where the cattle huddle together, drawing heat from each other's shoulders.

Celia grips her father's arm tighter. When she heard that Freddie and Elizabeth were planning a Twelfth Night masquerade, she decided to throw her own celebration. Her guests came on foot and in carts – but she can still see the headlights of the motorcars in the lane as they swing the opposite way up the drive towards Coombe Hall, the length of which has been lined with Chinese lanterns. She imagines all the ladies in their finery, glittering up the steps, the men in their dinner jackets, the chauffeurs waiting in the dark below, blowing their cigarette smoke pale into the night air, the house festooned in lights. Well, she has lit her own lights: hundreds of candles decorate the cider barn at Littlecombe, and the walls are hung with sprigs of holly and evergreen left over from Christmas. She will rival anything the Hemburys can do.

They wind their way through the bare apple trees. The lamps she has hung in the branches glimmer and flicker like night sprites, picking out the crooked boughs, ghostly-green lichen growing on them like seaweed. They stop in front of the oldest tree in the orchard. Celia touches the knobbled bark, feels the sadness of the time passing. Old Tom – his face painted green, and ivy trailing from between antlers adorning his hat – steps forward. He is carrying a flask of heated cider. He pours it around the tree's roots. Its sharp, sweet smell mingles with the smell of leaf mould and earth. The people start to whistle and bang sticks together, the bells on their legs jangling. Someone fires a rifle, disturbing some roosting pigeons that crash flapping out of the ash tree beyond the orchard. Celia shivers. Her father squeezes her arm. 'Nothing like scaring away a few evil spirits,' he whispers.

Old Tom starts to sing a melody, and the song is passed along the line until everyone is singing, calling to the trees to wake up, wishing them health in the new year, and cajoling them into a bountiful harvest. Then they move to the next tree and the next, calling to the ancestors and hailing the future.

Afterwards they crowd into the cider barn. Last year's cider is stacked neatly in hogsheads along one wall. When Celia enters, there are cheers and toasts and someone offers her a mug. The amber liquid trickles down her throat, forcing a glow into her cheeks. There is plenty of laughter, and she is certain it is doing much to dispel the negative feelings that have been generated recently. It is warm, too: they have put a stove in the corner, and its glow seems to heat the entire space. A man starts to play the melodeon, and another the fiddle. The music is jaunty, upbeat, like the mood of the guests. Celia nods and smiles her way through the crowd. She joins George and Raymond and her father at a table, their cheeks as red and jolly as her own. The people seated around them change, coming and going with platefuls of food, or to fetch more drink. One minute she is sitting next to the milkmaid Bronwen, the next the baker.

She searches the faces for Harris and Strong, and spots them in a small group with some of the other men from the river camp. She is glad to see they have come, though they are not mixing with the other locals yet. Her father leans in. He looks happy, but he has lost weight. His cheeks are a little sunken, as if he does not fit his skin so well. The mines in Somerset have been foundering; the price of coal has fallen further, as has demand. To stave off wage cuts, the board tried to increase hours, but the unions are strong and miners will no longer take it. There have been hostile strikes and protests. She knows her father is doing his best. The mines mean more to him than simply profit; each of the workers is his grandfather, his great-grandfather.

'You should take more time off,' she says. 'You once told me there was nothing wrong with enjoying the fruits of your labours.'

He gives a short laugh. 'You know I'm no good at relaxing.'

'There won't be time for that while you're running the farm.'

'So you've definitely decided to join Raymond at the paper in London?' There is some of the old twinkle in his eyes.

'Perhaps.'

Her father reaches out to smooth a loose strand of hair away from her face, smiles. 'Don't squander opportunity. It comes only once in a blue moon.'

She glances across at Raymond, who is trying to explain to Old Tom what his brand of socialism is about. 'We believe all men – and women – should be treated as equal. It is the same as class: you can never truly be one of the people if one of you has more power than the other.'

Old Tom wipes the cider from his mouth and looks at his neighbour. The neighbour looks embarrassed, and excuses himself to dance. Raymond glances up, confused that he is not rousing people's spirits, and Celia laughs, remembering how hard it was to get the men – and the women – to accept her instruction. How they always deferred to her father – or to his lordship next door. Her smile fades. She watches Raymond. He is a straightforward man: a man who sticks to his own convictions. He would never give up on what he believed in for the sake of some unwritten code of family honour.

Bronwen's brother, who is apprentice to the blacksmith, slides into the empty chair. 'You've had your moment,' he says. 'It were supposed to be different with your lot, but we didn't notice no change down here.'

Old Tom nods in agreement. 'No one cares about the countryside apart from they that live in it,' he adds slowly. The whites of his eyes seem to glimmer ominously against the painted green of his face.

Raymond slams his fist on the table so that they all fall quiet. 'You've been indoctrinated by these people for so long you believe their lies,' he says.

'What would Labour do for us?'

George tries to calm them: 'We were hardly in power for long enough to do what we want: to help the unemployed, the poor, those who break their backs to keep people like the Hemburys in the manner they're accustomed.'

'It's families like the Hemburys that keep us employed!'

'It may seem so on the face of it, but have you ever stopped to think what rights you have? You're at the mercy of their whims.'

'What are ee going to do? Have a revolution?' The men laugh, and knock their mugs together so that the cider spills down the sides.

'Perhaps,' says Raymond quietly.

The men's faces drop. 'This isn't Russia, my friend.'

Raymond glances at Celia, who raises her eyebrows and smiles in encouragement. 'What about men like Harris and

Strong?' he asks. 'They fought for this country, and if it wasn't for the Cottams they'd have no roof over their heads.'

'It ain't only the poor who died in the war. The viscount was a good man.' A hush descends around the room.

Raymond pushes his glasses up his nose, leans forwards. 'The viscount treated you like slaves. Like the rest of his family still do.'

'The viscount gave his life for this country. We all know what you gave . . . or didn't . . .'

Raymond grows agitated, and pushes himself to his feet, eyes flashing. 'I stood up for what I believe in: that war is wrong. That a handful of the rich and powerful were sending men who had no quarrel to kill each other . . .'

'You hid at home while others went to fight.'

'Conchies,' mutters someone from the back of the barn.

'I went to prison for my beliefs.' Raymond is flushed now. 'And I'll fight any man who thinks I'm a coward.' He is seething with anger, and it is easy to see there is brute strength in his self-belief. 'I had my freedom taken . . . I had my vote taken . . .' He stops, and slumps back in his chair.

The men seize their chance, pointing at each other: 'So you're saying my uncle – and his father – and Bronwen there's oldest brother – all of them was wrong to fight?'

Celia cannot bear how Raymond looks beaten. She reaches across to lay a hand on his arm. She can feel the anger vibrating through him, but for once he seems lost for words. She addresses the men: 'What Mr White is saying is the war was *morally* wrong. He is not detracting from the bravery and sacrifice of any of the men who fought.'

'What about you, miss?'

'You all know very well that I was a VAD in Bristol. And my brother went to France.'

'He were against the war, though. He's told us.'

'It's no secret that I also believed it was morally wrong,' says George.

'But you still fought.'

'I didn't fight, but I was alongside you. I joined the Medical Corps, but did not bear arms. And I think we could have all done with my sister in our regiments,' adds George, toasting Celia, while Raymond mutters something under his breath that Celia doesn't catch.

The men laugh, and the situation is calmed. They look up as the crowd parts and a man approaches with a bundle of firewood. Old Tom stands, and takes the burning bundle, turning to offer it to Celia. 'What's this?' she asks.

'It's the ashen faggot, miss. You must pick a withy.'

Bronwen points at the strips of wood that bind the pile together. 'You must choose one of the bindings for your own. Then we'll know who it will be getting married next year . . .' Some of the other girls laugh as they nudge each other.

Celia shakes her head, indicating for them to pass it on.

Their faces fall. 'But it's tradition.'

'Possibly one that I won't be following . . .'

They look at each other, confused, and she sees there is still so much to do, so much to learn. These women's lives are the same as they've always been – and will remain so until they can see that other ways of being are open to them.

She points to a withy, and everyone immediately cheers up, and the others choose theirs, and the ash branches begin to smoke and catch with flames, and the girls giggle all the louder as Bronwen's burns through first. Their clapping and whooping is drowned out by a crackling and whistling and popping from outside. A collective murmur goes up, and the people begin to pour out of the cider barn, carrying Celia on a wave among them. Cries of delight fill the air. As if it wasn't enough to have to put up with another Hembury party, Coombe's fireworks are colouring the night sky with red and gold and blue, lighting the upturned faces of her guests as they stare open-mouthed at the show.

As soon as they are over, the people move back inside, and the music starts up again. Celia remains out in the cold, watching the moon, luminously pale, wreathed in the smoke. The branches of the trees are bare and cruel. She shudders. January is an unkind month. The sound of drinking and laughter spills from the cider barn. She senses someone approach, and Raymond appears at her side. 'Are you all right?' he says.

She nods and forces a smile.

'You know you're wasted out here,' he says.

'So you keep telling me.'

'The way you dealt with those problems with your workers earlier was admirable.'

'I am not sure the Spillers would agree.'

'They took advantage of you. There is a difference between the needy and deserving, and the plain criminal.'

He is trying to help, but his words remind her of Victor's belief of how a man can be discarded when he's no longer needed; it is how she feels: that Freddie no longer has a use for her.

Raymond puts his arm around her shoulder and she leans against him, and finds some comfort.

'And thank you for coming to my rescue in there. You are better at communicating things in gentler terms than I am. Have you given my proposal any more thought?'

'I have.'

He takes her hands, kneels as she tries to pull him back on to his feet, embarrassed. 'You'll come to London?' he asks, his voice thick with emotion. 'Join our fight?'

He's so different to men like Freddie, she thinks, and Major Lewis, men who hide their emotions beneath a veneer of propriety. Men who are impossible to read. Raymond wears his heart right there for all to see, on his rolled-up sleeve.

'If you're sure there's enough for me to do.'

'Enough? There's plenty to do! This is the struggle for liberation! A real war! An honest man's war!'

'I'm more of a pacifist than a fighter . . .'

'In addition to your writing, you can give speeches, talk to people – like you did in there. You can hand out leaflets, make cups of tea if you want. It all counts, Celia. All of it.'

The night spins. The music flows. She thinks of Freddie, feels the weight on her heart. She thinks of Elizabeth, vibrant and beautiful, an exotic, rare jewel. She thinks of herself in her drab clothes and her men's shoes. She thinks of Freddie's hands on her. She thinks of Victor, proud yet crushed. She thinks of how the old order still needs shaking up – for the poor, the women, the workers. She thinks of what her father said, and all she still has to offer. She takes a deep breath. 'I can't wait,' she says.

CHAPTER 32

France

The château is large, with a round turret and long shuttered windows. There are bullet holes in the masonry, and some of the tiles in the great roof are missing, but the building has withstood more than one bloody revolution. Madame Sauveur beams with pleasure as she alights. 'So Monsieur James,' she says, 'how do you feel now you are to see my home? After you and the girls so doubted me?'

'I never doubted you, madame,' he answers.

She laughs loudly, her large red mouth opening to the heavens, her lips blood red against the blue sky. 'Always the English gentleman,' she says. 'Though I wonder what secrets you are hiding.'

He hunkers down under his cap, does not answer, but it is impossible to stand before this facade and not let thoughts of Coombe crowd his mind. The mixture of grandeur and decay, the hills, lush and green behind. He has abandoned his home, his family, his name. Unshed tears needle at his eyes.

An old woman shuffles out to greet them on the steps, holding Madame Sauveur's face in her hands as she kisses her cheeks, then kisses them again. The children run away into the fields, down to the river, out into the woodland, a playground that could not be more different to the one they have come from. They have refused to go with the Red Cross; they have rejected the orphanages and the sanitoriums where

225

smartly dressed women offer a new life: these children do not want that life. They have known only the streets and one woman's kindness. They will stick to her as iron filings to a magnet.

Edward climbs the steps to the front door, which is propped open, a key the size of his forearm resting in the lock. The children return, and follow the adults inside, in silent awe at first, but soon they are racing from room to room, calling to each other from the spiral staircase up the turret, leaning out of the windows, opening and shutting doors.

Edward follows slowly. The house is sparse, the walls covered in blank spaces where pictures and tapestries once hung. There is no furniture, and the previous occupiers have graffitied the walls, shot holes in the panelling. Even the light fittings are gone.

Madame Sauveur walks next to him. 'I was not quick enough to hide my things as others did. I took only what I could fit on to my carts.' She reaches out to Aurélie, cups the child's cheek in her hand. 'But I have returned with so much more.'

Edward goes to help the other drivers unload the carts, ignoring the eyes running over the scars on the skin that he cannot hide, the involuntary retractions. At least men do not crumple to the ground with horror or pity as women have done. The children return from their exploration, breathless with questions, wondering if Madame Sauveur is a countess or a duchess. She fields their queries with laughter as she tries to calm them for the evening.

When the carts have been stored in one of the barns, and the men have gone, and the horses have been fed and bedded down, and straw mattresses laid out for the children in what once must have been a ballroom, only then does Edward collect his bowl of soup from Madame Sauveur. He sits with the children on the smooth floorboards in the hall, slurping food in the shadows, eyelids drooping. They cannot use the dining room, for the table is piled with things that the old lady must have saved – nothing of value, but at least some bed linen, curtains, practical things.

Madame Sauveur perches on a wooden trunk, watching Edward. 'You are the only one who does not question,' she says.

Edward wakes to the smell of bacon and coffee, and for a moment he is in the dining room at Coombe, where the breakfast steams on the hotplate, and his father rustles the morning papers. With relief he remembers he is in France. He scrabbles for his mask, fitting it in place before he dares turn from the wall and reveal himself to the room, but the children are already busy collecting their breakfast.

He finds Madame Sauveur in the kitchen where she is cooking with the old maid. 'Take!' she thrusts a plate of food at Edward. 'Today the real work starts.' She lays a hand on his arm and points through the door to the dining table, which she must have cleared in the night. 'And we eat as a family now.'

Reluctantly he takes his place at the head. He has not eaten in such an exposed manner since the hospital. There are things the mask cannot hide: the way he has to chew so slowly, the food churning around his mouth, sometimes spewing out of it, the way his coffee dribbles down his chin. He pushes the plate away, half of the food left uneaten.

Madame Sauveur leads them out into the surrounding fields. She shows them where the boundary lies, almost beyond where they can see. Nature is at last obliterating the horror of war: nettles and grass are growing over the mounds, leaves are sprouting on trees, and the horses are pulling not guns, but ploughs. Edward's eyes scan the ground. He searches for the familiar signs, the discoloured grass, the undulations that he can read like a map, but it seems this land has been cleared of death, and now it is time to reclaim the fields. The men from the village return to help. They hack at the undergrowth,

227

remove stones and weeds. Whenever they turn over a metal casing or a spent shell, Edward is called to check it is safe.

The hours pass quickly. The sweat drips down his back, exacerbates the angry scars on his face, tickles at his puckered skin. Soon they are ready for planting. Aurélie follows him, her small hands holding delicate seedlings. They sow and water, working from early in the morning until late in the evening when the crickets begin to make their music, and their muscles throb.

Edward chooses a room in the turret. He likes the curve of the walls; it can be nowhere else but here. He keeps it simple like before: a bed, a lamp, no looking glass. They eat food prepared by the old maid, rabbit stew and hunks of bread. Edward grows used to his place at the opposite end of the table to Madame Sauveur. The children sit between them, spooning food hungrily into their mouths. Edward pulls his cap low, keeps his head down. He swigs from his glass, tries to do it quietly, feels the familiar trickle down his chin. He wipes the glistening trail with the back of his sleeve.

'You should not wear a hat at the table,' says Madame Sauveur.

He does not reply, cannot contemplate sitting at the table in full view.

'I forbid it for *les enfants*. We set them an example.' She sighs when he still does not acknowledge her. 'You must answer me at least.'

'I'd rather not talk about it in front of the children.'

She laughs. 'You English are so – how do you say? *Refoulé . . .*'

'Repressed.'

'Exactly. This is why you do not understand the *maisons tolérées*, yet form the longest queues. You hide your true feelings from everyone. Your children. Yourselves.'

Edward senses Aurélie shrink away as he raises his voice, but he cannot help it; Madame Sauveur is infuriating sometimes. 'And what about these children? When will you find them homes? When will you invite their new families to meet them?'

Aurélie drops her fork. Madame Sauveur laughs her deep, throaty laugh. 'These children are not going anywhere.'

'What do you mean? I thought you were setting up an orphanage. Will someone not come for them?'

'They will not.'

'Why?'

'Take your pick. Some are certain their own will turn up to claim them one day. Some are refugees from Belgium, scared with whom they might end up. Others are what my countrymen call "Boche babies", the children of German soldiers. The products of violence and rape, shunned even by their own . . .'

He glances around the table, recognises the bowed heads of people who do not want to be looked at. His gaze returns to Aurélie, and he sees a tear fall like a raindrop into her lap.

He removes his cap at mealtimes. No one stares. They are too busy replenishing energy spent in the fields, heads bent over their bowls. Sometimes he forgets to put the cap back on.

Other children begin to arrive, finding their way like homing pigeons who have never had a home, unwanted, unloved until they come to Madame Sauveur with her garish make-up and her encompassing embrace. They come with nothing, their feet blistered from the road, their ribs showing, but they are all soon fattened by Madame's hospitality, their small hands eager to take on whatever jobs they can: feeding the chickens that scratch in the dirt; milking the goats; taking the pigs to forage for acorns.

One of the villagers teaches Edward how to work the plough, hooking it up to his own horses. The implement bucks and jumps as he forces it to find its furrow. It is strenuous work, and soon they stop to recover. The horses rest in the shade of a walnut tree. Edward cannot resist taking a moment to run his hand along their warm necks, stopping to examine a bare patch of skin where the fur has been rubbed away, bending to check for heat in the bumps of their knees.

'*Tu connais les chevaux,*' says the Frenchman.

Edward nods as he sits on the ground, taking the bread he is offered. The Frenchman is a rough sort with a dour expression, whose stained trousers are held up too short by their braces. Three of his teeth are missing. They eat their lunch and discuss the weather and the horses, admiring the work they have done so far. Somewhere high above them, a skylark is singing. Edward thinks how he would never have sat on the ground with a labourer at Coombe. And he remembers the war, where he learnt that the pulsing blood and spilt intestines of an officer look the same as those of a private. He regards the blistered skin of his burned arm, and shudders. It is only on the outside that they appear different.

He stands. He is ready to work again.

Madame Sauveur appears with another box of donations; they arrive from across the country weekly: crockery, glasses, board games, clothes. Edward helps to sort the clothes for the boys from those for the girls. 'You are surprised people will help after what I did in the war?'

He shrugs. He is rarely surprised by Madame Sauveur these days.

'We French understand there is no shame in matters of desire. There were boys who had no one to comfort them apart from my girls. There were men who had never touched a woman intimately. They died knowing some of the pleasures of life rather than only the horrors. And they did not steal that pleasure: it was freely given.' Madame Sauveur's teeth shine white between her ruby lips. 'And what about you? Did you know of the pleasures of life before the horror?'

He turns away from the flickering light thrown by the candles. He recalls the last times he slept with anyone. There was the odd fling on leave, creamy-skinned heiresses and fresh-faced debutantes. And there was that particularly pretty maidservant. But who would want to curry favour with him now?

Madame Sauveur claps her hands. 'But of course, a handsome officer must have had many lovers.' There is no irony in her voice. 'Perhaps he will again.'

He dips his head in shame, for even if he were less of a monster, he is unable to perform acts of either love or desire, another result of his injuries. 'I am not who I was.'

'There are many ways one can find pleasure.' She regards him coquettishly. 'We could have fun trying.' She touches his thigh.

He recoils. 'Don't you understand?' he snaps. 'I can't . . . physically, I mean . . .'

'You could give pleasure to others.'

'Who would want me near them? I'm disgusting.'

She sighs and retracts her hand. 'You must stop feeling sorry for yourself. You have been given a life where others have not.'

'I wish I had died.'

'Why? Because of the horrors you have witnessed? And yet these children have seen the same horrors – and worse – and they do not mope in the dark.'

'They do not look like I do.'

'Do not use your misfortune as an excuse.'

CHAPTER 33

England

Elizabeth has organised a lavish party at the Ritz to celebrate Ginny's wedding. In the hotel room Freddie watches her reapply her make-up. Her green eyes are startlingly bright against her skin. She smiles as she stands and turns, taking hold of both his hands. He bends to kiss her. 'My Lady Hembury,' he says.

'My earl,' she replies.

He catches sight of himself over her shoulder in the mirror on the dressing table, stiff and formal in the wingtip collar and white bow tie, hair smoothed. Shame floods his body: he feels so out of place, a fraudster. It should be Edward standing here, holding this elegant woman in his arms. He's just playing at being his brother, stealing his brother's life, stealing everything Edward will never experience – a wife, a family . . .

Freddie straightens, tries to compose his thoughts as he fiddles with his cufflinks. He must make the best job he can of it, for Edward, for his father. He will not let his mind drift to Celia, and the life they could have shared. He is no longer that boy with a head full of dreams.

Elizabeth touches his arm. 'Shall we go down?' she asks.

Freddie nods, forces his mouth to curve upwards.

'Don't worry,' she says, mistaking his worry for homesickness. 'We'll be back at Coombe soon.'

* * *

233

Downstairs, Freddie's cheeks ache from smiling at the endless stream of people. With relief, he spies Tom pushing his way towards him.

'Ginny looks so happy,' says Tom. 'And Elizabeth – I'm still struggling to understand how you bagged such a beauty.'

Freddie nods. Ginny certainly looks radiant. That happens when you marry someone you're truly sweet on, he thinks, stifling the vision of a woman with auburn hair and blue eyes. 'How's work?' he asks. 'I couldn't help noticing all the protestors out on the streets.' He is thinking not of the crowds of well-wishers on the steps of the church, but of the grim-faced men and women lining the pavements with their placards, unsmiling as the wedding procession rolled past.

'It's certainly hotting up. Did they give you any trouble?'

'Not much. They jeered and threw a few things. You?'

'The same. It's lucky you're staying here tonight. Things could get out of hand. All high jinx, of course. The miners have been full of it ever since their so-called Red Friday. They thought they'd won that battle.'

'It was a victory of sorts. The government agreed to their demand for subsidies.'

'No, no. That was just a stalling tactic. We can't afford to bail them out for ever. It's only a matter of time before we withdraw all we promised.'

'And then what?'

'We understand they plan for a full strike – across the nation! Miners, railway workers, buses, gas, electricity, docks, printers – you name it. But they won't be able to hold us to ransom. We're prepared, and the TUC have no idea! But here's one of the men who's primed and ready.'

'I certainly am,' says Nicholas, as he approaches with another man. 'And here's another. You've already met Clifford Montague, but I'd like to introduce him to Freddie.'

'Of course.' Tom gives a discreet bow, and turns to talk to someone else.

Nicholas introduces Freddie to a tall man with intense eyes

and a narrow nose above a thick moustache. 'Clifford is a very old friend of the family's.'

'I consider Elizabeth and Nicholas as my own,' says Clifford, shaking Freddie's hand firmly.

'We're training up some special constables to deal with this strike,' says Nicholas. 'I told Clifford you'd be perfect.'

'You know I wasn't in the army?'

'Don't worry about that. You're exactly the sort we're looking for, and you're handy on a horse.'

'Of course. If you need me . . .'

'We'll need you. I'm sure of it.'

An elderly cousin approaches. Freddie must bend to allow her to reach up and kiss him with her feathery lips. His nostrils fill with the rich scent of lavender. When he rights himself, Nicholas has moved on, and Ginny is at his side – a vision in ivory lace. She kisses him too. 'I'm so happy!' she says. 'I can't thank Elizabeth enough for all this. She is wonderful!'

'You look beautiful, sister dear – Hugh is a lucky man. And I like the new haircut,' he says, for she has had her long dark hair shorn off into a neat and glossy bob. They sip their drinks. Freddie begins to relax a little as they nod and smile at the guests. 'What news of Mama?'

'She's sad to miss the wedding, of course. But she isn't ready to leave the hospital. I fear she's becoming agoraphobic. You must go and see her.'

Freddie shudders. It is something he has been putting off. It is not just that he does not want to see her in the place she has gone to recover from her maudlin episodes. But how can he possibly explain that his mother may have been right, and seen her oldest son living on in his bastard child? He prefers to dismiss it as a lie. He cannot risk setting her recovery back by months.

'Don't look so glum. I've got a story that will cheer you up. Did you hear about Celia? She's run off to London with that friend of her brother's. They're somewhere in the East

End. Can you imagine the scandal back home? I would never have thought it of her.'

'Run off?'

'Apparently they're living together. In sin!'

Freddie feels a flutter of sadness tinged with longing, like watching the sun set. But it is too late for sentimentality. The Hembury line demands a future, and his next duty is to produce an heir – for his family, for his brother. He grabs another drink from a passing waiter.

Sybil joins them, picking up the last bit of the conversation adeptly. 'If we're talking about sin, I've got a good one for you,' she says. 'Remember Teddy Reith?'

'Of course.'

'It turns out he had a rendezvous or two with a girl when he was on leave. Said rendezvous led to the inevitable and the girl had a son.'

'But wasn't Teddy killed at the Somme?'

'He was. He never even knew about the child.'

'I'm sure it's very common,' says Freddie.

'How sad,' says Ginny. 'All those babies . . .'

Sybil raises her hand to hush them up. 'I haven't finished yet! The girl wrote to his parents. They only opened the letter after Teddy's stuff came back. She didn't want to keep the baby, and was giving them a chance to have it before she sent it off to the orphanage. Teddy's parents leapt at the chance, and they're bringing the poor little scrap up as their own.'

'No!'

Sybil grins, pleased that her story has had the desired effect. 'Teddy was an only child. With the recent adoption law, they can officially adopt the boy, and, I presume, pass on their estate.'

'Surely they can't accept such a child as an heir?' Freddie's throat constricts as his mind jumps to that night by the lake, and his promise to Victor in the heat of that awful moment.

'In all but title, of course . . . if it's what they want . . .'

'But he's a bastard!' Freddie drains his glass of champagne. It is filled immediately by one of the white-gloved attendants.

236

'Don't be so prudish!' says Sybil. 'The child belongs to Teddy. Just because they never married . . .'

Ginny frowns. 'I'm surprised at you, Freddie Hembury. I never thought you'd be so old-fashioned. I think it's a lovely ending to a sad story.'

'It just gives people the wrong idea. Before you know it everyone will be making claims against their so-called parents.' He grips his glass, wondering what on earth they would say if they had heard Victor's fervent assertion by the lake that Wilf really was Edward's child.

He feels his wife's delicate hand on his arm, as Ginny is swept away by her new husband.

Freddie allows the waiter to top up his drink again, while anxiety spreads like a virus through every inch of his body.

CHAPTER 34

Elizabeth and Freddie spend a few more weeks at the house in Cadogan Square, Elizabeth supervising the hanging of new curtains while Freddie tries to keep out of the way of the endless stream of tradesmen refurbishing the house. But Freddie cannot avoid Coombe for ever, and with the arrival of summer they return to Devon. As the top lake comes into view, Freddie is filled with the horror of the maid drowning. The scene often replays in his nightmares if he doesn't drink enough whisky to dull his senses before sleep. It vies for place with the broken horse, and his failure to have built Edward's racecourse, and his betrayal of Celia. And now there is a new anxiety to add to the list: Wilf.

Freddie desperately regrets his promise to Victor that terrible night when they knelt in the rain by the dead woman's body, and he agreed to keep an eye on the boy. He had been so caught in the moment, so horrified by events, by that sodden bundle of rags, by that blond head peering through the passenger window, that he would have agreed to anything. He may have grown fond of Wilf, but agreeing to employ the child is as good as accepting him. Could that mean Wilf had some claim one day? How would Elizabeth, and his own sons of the future feel if they ever found out? Or his mother? He must abandon this silly notion that he has some duty to look out for Wilf. How can he even be sure the boy is his nephew? His mind spins in circles. The only person he could have spoken to about it wants nothing to do with him any more.

There is some good news though. Matthew's reports still appear regularly, and the plantation is expanding. On top of that, Freddie managed to secure a deal to export their tea to Russia, with the help of some Russian aristocrat friends of Elizabeth's, who now live in relative poverty in London. It is best not to dwell on that – it is terrifying how quickly Russia was overrun by those Bolshies.

In his bid to avoid both Victor and Wilf, he follows Elizabeth around the house as she explains her plans for bringing hot water into the bathrooms, and redecorating his parents' room, now theirs, as well as updating the guest suites, and possibly even installing a lift.

'I'll barely recognise my own home when you're finished,' he says.

'I have some ideas for the outside of the house too. We must get rid of that man by the gates.'

'You mean Victor Bolt?'

'Yes. That house is in a frightful state, and it's the first thing visitors see. It does not give a good impression. Mrs F tells me that the keeper's cottage is on the other side of the estate anyway. If he moves, then we can rent out the lodge house privately. As a weekend cottage. Or even for Taunton races.'

'You are absolutely right as always,' says Freddie, kissing her on top of the head. It would be a relief to have the Bolts further away from the house.

'And then we need to advertise for a better gardener. The current man is useless. The hothouses must be restored. I am determined to grow pineapples!'

'You'll have us whipped into shape in no time.'

'No time like the present,' she says. 'Go and have a word with Bolt now. I'd like to get in there with an architect as soon as possible.'

'But can't we send Mulligan?'

'It's your job, not Mulligan's, to arrange estate staff. I'm going to see Mrs F about the cook. I know of a French chef looking for work, and I believe she would benefit from his experience.'

After the dust and crowds of London, it is a pleasure to be out in the Devon countryside. Freddie has Tybalt saddled and brought to the front of the house for him, so that he does not need to face the stable yard in case the boy is there. He feels the stiffness in his unused muscles, slack with fine dining. He dreads the thought of confronting Victor. He has barely looked at him since that night by the lake, does not want to face that pain, or remember the promise he made. He should never have been ruled by his heart. He was too soft. He must think like Edward now.

He procrastinates, and rides out towards the lane that affords the best view of the fields falling away to the woodland, the river, the village. The weather has been good, and the grass is growing long. Soon it will be ready for a first cut, the men with their scythes. He can picture the harmony in their move-ments, the swish of the blade, the blanket of cut stems that grows longer as they advance. He remembers the binder at work, the blades whirling, the rounded rumps of the Clydesdales gleaming. He remembers a time when he and Edward were still permitted to join the other children on their broad backs, legs dangling, listening to the crunch and crackle of sun-dried stubble beneath their hooves. But children grow up, and he cannot mix with those people any more.

He is interrupted by the sound of a tractor. He turns to see the machine bumping along the road towards him with none other than Joseph Cottam at its wheel. The man waves as he navigates past horse and rider, the tractor belching smoke and fumes into the air. Tybalt snorts and paws the ground. 'Good afternoon to you, neighbour!' shouts Mr Cottam. 'Come to spy on the future?'

Freddie nods curtly. Mr Cottam laughs and bounces on. The machine growls louder as it bumps through the gate and across the field, attracting the labourers who take a break

240

from their work to cluster around. Freddie feels a stab of jealousy. Those fields once belonged to Coombe. He has failed to keep the land together, but he will make sure that he holds on to what is left. He must do the best he can for his dead brother, and that does not mean allowing a bastard child to have a hold over him. It will be better for all if the Bolts were moved to the edge of the estate. It would be better if they could both be moved on completely.

He turns the horse, his insides churning. A thin trail of smoke trickles from the chimney of the lodge house. Freddie swings himself out of the saddle, loops Tybalt's reins over the horse's head and then over the fence. The horse is older, calmer. It bends its head to the ground, and, finding no resistance, is content to munch along the verge.

Freddie looks up at the house. From the ground it is easier to see how the place has deteriorated: how the brambles have spread their thorny tentacles and swallowed up the roses, and how the nettles have multiplied, creating dense, impassable thickets. The paint is peeling, and the gate stands ajar. It is by no means a lodge house fit for the seat of the Earl of Hembury.

Freddie hammers on the door, setting the dogs barking. As it opens, he is struck by the smell. Victor has aged; there are more creases around his eyes, his mouth. His hair is dishevelled and the stubble that darkens his face gives him the look of one abandoned. 'They didn't tell us you were returned,' he glowers.

'I can see that,' snaps Freddie. The worry that was twisting in his chest is turning to anger, for he has bent over backwards to accommodate this man. It is not his fault that the maid threw herself in the lake. Perhaps she threw herself at his brother. Why should he feel as if he owes these people something? There are bastards in the village rumoured to have been fathered by his grandfather, probably others belonging to his great-grandfather, and no doubt his father too. But none of them has special dispensation. He has allowed himself to be governed by some kind of sentiment for his brother, but Edward would say he was being weak, romantic. He must be strong.

'I thought you were going to look after things while I was gone,' says Freddie.

'I done my best, sir. Me and the boy been working hard. But without my wife . . .' Victor trails off.

Anger starts to needle under Freddie's collar. Over Victor's shoulder he glimpses filthy pots and pans cluttering the sink, a floor streaked with dirt, windows opaque with dust. Cold air passes over him like the breath of a dying man. Victor's eyes bore into his skin, and the anger turns to rage. Who is this man, who has taken a job and a home from him but still wants more? Who is he to have come here with his lies, to have taken advantage of their kindness? To have pushed his poor mother over the edge by dangling this spurious child before her? Look at Russia: that's what happens when you give an inch to such people.

He takes a deep breath. 'I've come to tell you that we need the lodge house back,' he says. 'We're moving you to the keeper's cottage in East Lane.'

'But this is our home.'

'Actually, it's not.'

Victor takes a step forward, his broad chest so close to Freddie's that they are almost touching. He can smell the man's stale breath. 'Is there nothing you wouldn't take from us?' he says.

Freddie steps back: it is unusual for Victor not to defer to him – further proof that he should never have acceded to anything. 'You've got until the end of the week.'

'And if I don't?'

'I will have the two of you removed. You will never set foot in Devon again.'

'On what grounds?'

'On the grounds of bribery, deceit, extortion. You took employment under false pretences. You were never a friend of my brother's, were you? How could you be, if what you claim is true? You must have despised him.'

Victor looks hard at him. Freddie can almost read the suppressed emotions: the desire to hit back, the reining in of his temper. Eventually Victor says quietly, 'I didn't despise him. I tried, but I couldn't.'

Freddie almost wants the other man to lash out, to hit him, so that he has the excuse to kick them both out of his life for ever. 'You're just a villain who tried to use my poor brother's death to your advantage,' he goads.

'I am giving up my life to raise the boy.' Victor's voice remains calm.

'Then you're as much of a fool as I am.'

Victor's face is ghostly white, the muscles in his jawbone working. 'But you promised to provide him with a position.'

'Well I regret that. I wasn't thinking straight. How can I make promises when I don't know whether you even speak the truth?'

'The truth? The truth is that your family is a curse. My wife dead. My baby dead. Destroyed by your brother.'

'You can't lay that at his feet! Tragic as it is, your wife decided to take her own life.'

'And why were that, do you think? Why?'

Freddie doesn't know how to respond. This isn't how he planned it to go. What right has Victor to speak to him like this?

Victor presses on: 'Your brother treated her no better than a piece of meat. Took what he wanted, no matter the consequences . . .'

'There's no proof of that.'

'All you have to do is look at the boy.'

'Looks prove nothing.'

Victor takes another step forward. 'Then let's find your brother, and ask him.'

'Don't be ridiculous. He's dead.'

'He weren't when I left him.'

243

Victor slams his fist against the door, so hard that Freddie feels the ground jump, and the blood runs from his own face. 'What the hell are you talking about?'

Victor's voice grows even quieter. 'I lied. The captain *did* get to the hospital. He were injured so bad that he wanted me to finish it before the ambulance took him, but I couldn't.'

Freddie runs both hands through his hair and starts to back away, eyes wide.

'He begged me to shoot him with his own pistol. He said he didn't want to live. He said to tell his people he were dead.' Freddie covers his ears, but Victor won't stop. 'I know he made it to the hospital. I saw him there. They don't bother to bandage the dead ones.'

Freddie's hands drop to his sides. 'But if Edward is alive, why didn't he come home?'

'You could never understand. No one could that hadn't been out there, that hadn't experienced it for themselves.'

Freddie shakes his head to try to clear it. 'Or perhaps it's all a fantasy cooked up by you. First you said he was dead. Now you say he's alive. Well, where is he then? It's more likely you murdered him so you could inveigle your way in here.'

'Sometimes I wish I had. It would have been kinder. But after what he did, maybe he deserved to live like that.'

One of the dogs pokes its muzzle into Victor's leg, but he remains immobile, blocking the doorway with his chest, staring at Freddie until he turns and stumbles away. At the gate he stops to gather Tybalt's reins from the fence. He looks to the right, to the house at the top of the drive, but he staggers to the left, leading the horse out of the gates and into the lane: he wants to get away from it all: Victor, Edward, Wilf . . . He hears the grumbling of the tractor engine again. He looks up, sees the machine almost upon him, a mishmash of red metal, exhaust pipes and wheels. For a moment, he thinks it would be a blessed release to be crushed by its weight. Tybalt rears, knocking him to the ground. The reins are pulled through his palms with searing heat, and Tybalt gallops away as the tractor judders to a halt. The engine splutters into silence. The sound of the horse's hooves fades away.

Freddie rises stiffly, cursing, but instead of Mr Cottam he sees Celia climbing down from the driver's seat, her face crinkled with concern. 'Are you all right? I'm so sorry. I almost ran you over. I was trying out the tractor. '

He feels her hand on his shoulder. 'Freddie?'

He cannot respond.

'Let me help you find Tybalt. Come . . .'

Freddie follows her down the lane, barely registering the pain in his hands.

The horse has not bolted far. There is a small cowshed a few hundred yards away, open-fronted and dilapidated, but a safe enough place for a distressed animal.

He watches as Celia approaches Tybalt, her hand out-stretched. She is dwarfed by the horse's shoulder, and has to reach up to take hold of its bridle. She turns to Freddie with a pleased yet worried look on her face, and Freddie is suddenly reminded of teaching her to ride all those years ago, and he is filled with sadness for the loss of those days of happiness and promise. If Edward had returned, perhaps they would have continued.

Celia leads the horse into the open, holding out the reins expectantly. Freddie tries to speak, but nothing comes out. Instead he feels as if he might vomit. He braces himself against the wall of the building, head between his hands. He pushes his sore palms against the stones so that they ground him in reality. If his brother really is still alive, then what does his life stand for? He thinks of all the dreams he's had, the hard work he's put in, he thinks of Ceylon, and his plantation, the bougainvillea spilling across the verandah of the bungalow, the tea leaves drying in the sun. He thinks of how he could have shared it all with Celia.

Celia touches his back. He turns, pressing his shoulders against the wall. He looks at her as if from a great distance. He hasn't seen her for almost a year. He is ashamed of how he has behaved. He wonders if she can ever forgive him. If only she knew what he truly felt for her. He thinks of how she would have loved to travel to another country, and then he thinks of Elizabeth, and of the maid in the lake, and the boy Wilf, and all the futures that are resting on a lie. His legs buckle, and he sinks to the ground. 'I can't do it,' he says. 'I can't go on. How can I? It's all a sham.'

'What is?' Celia crouches down next to him.

'All of it.' He looks into her eyes, the blue of a foreign sky. 'I shouldn't be here.'

'I thought things were going well? I hear the house and gardens are in good repair.'

'You don't understand.'

'Then tell me.'

He looks at her: Celia, with her grey-blue eyes and her rich auburn hair. She gazes back at him, every inch of her listening, interested. She is someone who takes him for who he is. Not the earl or the master or the younger brother – but Freddie. And he treated her no better than a common whore. He is more like his brother than he realised.

He feels tears welling. He wants her sympathy, wants to feel her hand on his arm, to see her forehead creased in concern. 'My brother may be alive,' he whispers.

'How?' The shock on her face is nothing compared to how he feels.

'And that's not all of it. That man's son . . . Wilf. You once questioned why he worked in the stables. He's my nephew. He's Edward's son.' As soon as he says it out loud, he knows that it is true, and he is so overwhelmed that he wants to lie down and be swallowed into the earth.

Celia kneels and puts her arms around him and holds him like a child, and he feels the tears inching their way from his eyes and down his face. He buries his head in her shoulder and cries as if he were a child again himself.

When he has finished, he sits back, ashamed, wiping his cheeks with his sleeve and turning away so she can't see. 'If

246

my brother is still alive, then I am not the earl. He is. And I could have gone away. I could have done whatever I wanted.' He looks at her, hoping she will understand that that includes being with her. It is almost too much to bear.

'Is there anything that proves what you've been told?'

'Nothing. Just the word of a gamekeeper who blames my family for his miserable life.'

'Yet you appear to believe him.'

'The boy . . . he's just like Edward in so many ways, not least that same peculiarity in his eye.'

'Your brother can't have vanished. If he is alive, perhaps you could find him . . .'

'Why should I? If he is alive I loathe him. How could he have abandoned us all? My father. My mother. Me?' He groans and rests his forehead on his knees. 'Why did he leave me to deal with it all? Why does he always have to control the game right until the end?'

'What will you do?'

'I have no idea. Lord knows, I already feel guilty enough for living someone else's life. A life I didn't want.'

'You're doing a good job.'

'Am I?'

She holds his face between her hands, forcing him to look at her, wiping the tears with her thumbs. 'Yes. You are.'

'Why are you being so kind after how I behaved?'

She lets go. He watches her. He could have followed a different path that led to a different life. But he chose duty over love, and he's a fool.

She does not answer his question. 'You will have to tell your mother,' she says. 'You can't hide such secrets. They will come out sooner or later.'

He shakes his head. 'I can't. She's almost recovered.'

'Then you must talk to your wife.'

'No! I couldn't possibly. If Edward were alive, where would that leave us? We wouldn't belong here. She would despise me for it.'

247

'Not if she loves you . . .'

He takes her hand, but she pulls away.

'And what about Wilf?' she asks. 'Doesn't he have some rights?'

'The illegitimate have no rights.'

'But he is your brother's son, despite what the law says.'

'I was nice to the boy because I liked him. And I knew deep down he was Edward's after I saw that eye. I felt some duty to the child, as if I should look out for him, perhaps I thought I could hold on to part of my brother. But it was stupid. We could never have a relationship. And now it turns out my brother might be alive. I can imagine what he would think about the whole situation . . .'

He tips his head back, watches a kestrel hover high in the sky. There are barely any clouds, and the stillness and warmth remind him of sitting in a field with Celia, the taste of cider on his lips, and hope in his heart.

'I miss this,' says Celia.

Freddie looks at her, and at the beech leaves she has picked that lie like velvet in her soft palm.

'Leaves?' he asks.

'Yes. And the space, the colours, the air, the trees . . .'

'You can come back any time.'

She scrunches the leaves up and drops them on the ground. 'For what? For you?'

He glances at her, notices that she has developed fine lines on her forehead, and creases around her eyes. He sighs, and rests his head back against the stone wall. 'It's all so messed up.'

'You know, if he is alive, your brother may not be thinking straight. Trauma does strange things to people.'

'You and your trauma . . .' He twists his head to face her, when they hear whistling and a large flat-coated retriever lopes around the corner of the lane, turning its almond eyes to look at them before looking back over its shoulder. Freddie looks at Celia, presses his finger to his lips, shrinking against the side of the barn. The dog lopes onward. Freddie hears the tread of boots on stone, and the person comes into view. His heart sinks. It is the last person he wants to see: Wilf.

The child has grown again. He must be around 11 years old, though he is as tall as a boy two or three years older. There is confidence in his stride – the same confidence that Edward possessed. He is whistling a tune and swinging a stick, occasionally swiping at the longer patches of grass on the side of the lane, and his gait and mannerisms are so similar to Edward's that Freddie is struck again by the horror of it all.

He pulls Celia even further down, so that she is lying against his shoulder. 'He mustn't see us,' he whispers. His heart is thumping. They lie still, listening to the breeze ruffling the leaves and the horse chewing the grass. He can smell her hair. He wants to bury his face in it, and never open his eyes again.

Wilf calls the dog, and then Celia starts to shake with laughter. 'What is it?' he hisses.

'The horse . . .'

'What's so funny about the horse?'

'We're trying to hide, but the horse is in plain sight. He must know you're here.'

Then Freddie starts to laugh too, and Freddie can feel her breath on his cheek, and her hair is the colour of autumn leaves and their mouths are so close.

Suddenly she is sitting up, agitated. 'Is that the time?' Very faintly he can hear the church bells ringing five, carried on the wind from the village. 'I have to go. Raymond is expecting me back.'

He pushes himself up on to an elbow. 'What is this about Raymond? Are you really living with him? And not married? Isn't he a communist?'

'Oh Freddie. The world doesn't revolve around you.' She crouches for a moment, finger on her lips, then on his, a light touch, but no less powerful for it. Then she is gone, and all he is left with is the imprint of her body against his, and his heart feels crushed as the blades of grass.

CHAPTER 35

Freddie cannot bring himself to say anything to Elizabeth over the next few days, even though he knows he ought to. Sharing the burden with Celia has given him some respite, though it has also reminded him how he has missed her. It is some relief that she seems to have forgiven him, and when news comes from the doctors who have been treating his mother, he seizes the opportunity to call on her for her advice.

Littlecombe's front door is standing open, and there is no sign of any servant. Freddie calls through the open door. After a few minutes, Joseph Cottam appears, wiping his hands on a towel. 'Good to see you, neighbour. I was assisting in the kitchen. I'm not very good at it.' He indicates the splashes on his waistcoat, shaking his head at himself and chuckling. 'How can I help?'

'They're talking about discharging my mother. I wondered whether I could talk to Celia about it.'

'Cee?' Mr Cottam strokes his moustache. 'I'm afraid she left yesterday.'

'Do you know when she'll be back?'

'No. I was lucky to have her here at all. She doesn't often get away.'

'Oh.' The disappointment bites more than it should; gone already – and without even letting him know. 'I'll let you get on then,' he says.

'You should look her up when you're in London. She's in the East End. 15 Ashworth Street, Whitechapel. It can't be far from where your tea auctions are? Mincing Lane, is it?'

Freddie nods, 'You are knowledgeable.'

Mr Cottam bows his head in thanks at the compliment. 'Next time you go, I'm sure she would like to see you. I do worry about her. Her life hasn't been . . . well . . . it hasn't exactly been straightforward. Going to London is brave . . .'

'Yes. She's a remarkable woman.' It is the first time he has said it out loud, and he realises how true it is. Joseph Cottam looks so glum that Freddie can't help adding, 'Next time I'll try.'

His neighbour's mouth widens into a grin. 'Would you, indeed? That would make an old man very happy.' He throws the damp tea towel over his shoulder. 'Now tell me, how are you getting on at Coombe? A place of that size must be a headache to keep going.'

Freddie blushes defensively. 'It is in hand,' he says.

'Your tea business should help. I believe it is only a matter of months before you will begin to see a decent return.'

'Do you really think so?' Freddie is surprised – although why should he be? The only other person who has seen the possibilities of his business is Cottam's daughter.

'Absolutely. I follow it in the newspapers with interest.'

'That is kind of you.'

'If you ever want to go over some figures or ideas, please ask. I have time on my hands. It gets lonely here without the children . . .'

Faced with the kindly Joseph Cottam, Freddie suddenly feels it might be a relief to talk about Coombe to someone other than a land manager. He remembers how he almost tried to go into business with Cottam before. He struggles to control the estate, never knowing if he is heading in the right direction. He cannot confide in Elizabeth; he would feel weak. He misses his father deeply, knows he would have guided him. 'Do you know, I think that I would like to do that,' he says.

'Splendid! Do you want me to come to you? Or you can come to my office?'

Freddie hears the sound of footsteps behind him, and the polite clearing of a throat. He glances over his shoulder and sees one of the Cottams' workers standing at a respectful distance. He suddenly feels embarrassed. Could he really confide in Joseph Cottam? What would Celia feel? He knows what Elizabeth would think. 'I'll let you know,' he mumbles. 'But now I really should be getting back.'

'Of course, of course.' Joseph Cottam nods and pats Freddie's shoulder. 'I'll be here whenever you need me.'

Elizabeth is bringing Coombe Hall back to life, as she did Cadogan Square. She has had the west wing recommissioned, flinging open the shutters herself to allow light to penetrate every room. She has cleared out the last of the shabby old furniture, replacing it with new – apart from in the earl's old study, where Freddie insists the tattered armchair remains.

Freddie stops to investigate the orchids that are growing in the hall when he almost bumps into one of the new maids carrying another vase of flowers. Elizabeth is right behind her. 'There you are,' she says. 'You haven't forgotten the Hetheringtons are coming for lunch? They'll be here any moment.'

'Would you like me to change?'

She shakes her head, adjusts his collar and reaches up to give him a quick peck on the cheek. 'No. You look perfect as you are.'

'Now, now, you two.' It is good to see James striding into the hall, as robust as ever. The two old friends greet each other vigorously, introducing their wives again, though Elizabeth met Annabelle at their wedding.

'Marriage clearly suits you,' says James.

'And you,' says Freddie, though he notes how James's hair is receding, the skin at his temples beginning to shine through.

Elizabeth rings one of the bells that brings a maid running. 'Please tell Mrs Foley we'll eat outside.'

They move around the front of the house, to the dining room, where the servants are already bringing chairs and a table on to the terrace. The men pull the chairs out for the women and they sit. Freddie has a couple of sips of wine before he spots Gibbs, the new gardener, standing at a discreet distance. He excuses himself for a moment.

'They've gone, m'lord,' says Gibbs. 'I seen they cart go down the lane.'

'Have you checked inside the house?'

'Empty, m'lord.'

'Thank you.' Relief rushes through him in a wave, and he cannot help grinning as Gibbs bows and disappears. With Joseph Cottam's optimistic words still ringing in his ears, and now the Bolts gone from the doorstep, things are looking up. Perhaps he can pretend none of the bad things ever happened: no illegitimate child; no hidden brother.

He returns to the table, bounding up the steps two at a time. Elizabeth is laughing. 'I'm surprised he didn't buy one of Lloyd George's peerages while he still could. Can you imagine, Sir Joseph of Littlecombe?'

'Little chance of that happening again,' says Freddie, feeling disloyal after the morning's conversation with the man.

James looks up at Freddie as he sits. 'Look at you, the cat that got the cream.'

Freddie pours a glass of wine. 'Who wouldn't be in my position? A beautiful day, a beautiful wife, and the Russians eating out of our palms . . . or rather, drinking our tea.'

Everyone laughs.

'And Coombe is looking magnificent,' says Annabelle.

'We'll give you a tour of the gardens after lunch. The renovations on the greenhouses start next week.'

Annabelle sips her lemonade. 'What are you planning on growing?'

'Peaches, oranges, nectarines . . .'

'Pineapples,' adds Freddie, reaching out for Elizabeth's hand. The wine is making him giddy.

'It's wonderful to see one of our gems being restored. So many of us are being ruined.'

'I don't know where she finds the energy. She's a marvel.'

Elizabeth's face suddenly turns serious. 'I thought I would never find happiness again when I lost Peter in the war. But then I met Freddie, and he brought me here, and well . . . I am the luckiest woman alive.'

Freddie blushes as James chants, 'Hear, hear.' A strand of guilt twists around his gut. He has married a wonderful woman, who is happy to devote herself and her money to restoring his family home. And yet his heart is always elsewhere, with another woman – and the wrong sort at that. Just like his brother, he thinks again. It must be in their blood, to take advantage of women below their standing, like their grandfather and, no doubt, a whole string of ancestors before them. He pours another drink. Suddenly he despises Edward: dead or alive, he is not the man everyone remembers. He is either a cad or a coward – and once again it is Freddie who is left to clean up his mess.

Elizabeth is staring at Freddie in a strange way. He finishes the wine and taps the glass with his knife to bring the maid. He holds up the empty bottle and she bobs away to fetch more. He tries to focus on the conversation.

'Did you hear the miners are going ahead with their strike, and all their little socialist friends are coming out in support?' says Elizabeth. 'We'll have to put up the barricades. You know, our neighbours consort with communists, though they claim to be merely left wing.'

'Labour supporters?' says Annabelle. 'Just as bad.'

'It's a little terrifying. They say that man who sometimes stays there – White, is it? – is right in the thick of it. Rather too close for comfort.'

'I'll keep you safe,' says Freddie, feeling gutless for not sticking up for the Cottams, and remembering why he could not involve Joseph Cottam in affairs of the estate.

'It will be chaos,' says James.

'Not if my brother-in-law has anything to do with it.' Freddie smiles at Elizabeth.

254

'Annabelle and I were going to motor up to London to lend a hand, but they'll need volunteers in Exeter too, so we're going to stick closer to home.'

They look at each other meaningfully, and Freddie realises that there is more to their lingering glances, the casual hand of hers on her stomach.

They are interrupted by Jennings. 'Nicholas Helstrom on the telephone for you, sir.'

'Speak of the Devil.' Freddie excuses himself and takes the call in the hall. The line buzzes and clicks in his ear, and then there is Nicholas's voice, excited, loud. 'It's happening!' he shouts, so that Freddie has to hold the receiver away from his ear. 'General strike! The printers have refused to print the *Daily Mail*. Something to do with them objecting to its editorial. The government's seizing all supplies of paper it can lay its hands on. They'll try and print their own newspaper – and take control of the BBC. We'll show these buggers what we think of their revolution. But we need men on the streets. Get down here. Quick as you can!'

CHAPTER 36

Freddie leaves Cadogan Square early. He plans to walk the two miles to headquarters at Earl's Court. It is the third day of the General Strike – a nationwide downing of tools, the cheap labour that keeps Britain going creaking to a halt. Freddie already knows what to expect. Some underground stations are closed until more volunteers can be trained, and there are limited bus and tram services. The taxi drivers have also come out on strike, so people are walking, hitching, begging a lift. Bicycles and pedestrians weave in and out of the stationary vehicles. Charabancs and lorries are crammed with passengers. Horns blare, drivers call across the gridlocked roads. Along Embankment, there are six lanes of cars heading towards the City, only two coming the other way; it will swap in the evening rush hour.

It is a far cry from the tranquil spaces of Coombe. Freddie's mind drifts to the behaviour of his own workers. He's glad he put a stop to the meetings of Celia's brother and his dreadful friend. The village hall would not dare put on another one. What do his workers have to moan about, anyway?

Earl's Court is bulging with volunteers, with more arriving daily. Men sit on their rolled bedding on the floor, fingers drumming on their suitcases as they smoke cigarettes and await instruction. Women dish out breakfast in the canteen. The air is thick with chatter. Nicholas is barking orders at people. He greets Freddie, then hustles him to collect his helmet and baton. Clifford Montague, to whose group he has been assigned, is already there.

Word comes that there's trouble at Elephant and Castle, and they set off. Freddie has still not got used to the clatter of hooves on the road, the buildings and the traffic pressing in. His horse is one of Clifford's best polo ponies, responsive to the slightest touch of the rein against its neck. The streets are clear of commuters, but now there are groups of men and women congregating around banners on the pavements. They stand with their hands pushed deep into their pockets, their expressions dark, and they watch the horsemen go by in silence.

Freddie's heart clenches with anxiety. But Clifford seems to take no notice. Even when the crowds thicken and start to jeer, Clifford rides straight-backed and proud, one hand guiding the horse, the other resting on his knee. He is a hero who fought at Passchendaele; nothing frightens him. He keeps the men in a formation of eight – four pairs behind each other – with himself and Freddie at the front. Freddie tries to emulate him. Even pretending to be brave seems to help.

'You handle Sorrel well,' says Clifford.

Freddie feels a genuine glow of pride. 'It's kind of you to lend her,' he replies.

'My club's given over all their ponies. Anything to stand up to industrial terrorism.'

They hear the men taunting the policemen before they see them. The mob has blocked the street at Elephant and Castle and is trying to press onward, through the police cordon. An officer walks backwards until he reaches Clifford and Freddie. He is frightened, the sweat shining on his top lip, his eyes wide. Freddie tries not to let the fear infect him too, sticking close to Clifford, hoping the bravado will rub off on him.

'Thank God you're here,' the policeman gabbles up at them. 'We're only just holding them off. Please do what you can to get them to disperse.'

Clifford nods, and reassembles the riders into a long row beside the police, facing the crowd of angry men. Freddie notices they all seem to draw strength from their leader, mimicking the grim expression, the chest out, mouths set in a thin line.

Black smoke billows from a smouldering bus, swirling around the protestors. A pungent smell fills the air. A brick smashes into no man's land, crumbling into smaller pieces that skitter across the ground, causing Sorrel to rear. A shiver of fear runs through Freddie. One of the mob runs forward and a policeman lifts his baton and runs to meet him. The man jinks away, back into the crowd for safety. Clifford remains unruffled. Freddie keeps his trembling hands low against the horse's neck. He must be brave for the horse too. It reminds him of hunting, this surge of adrenaline, this trying to convey calm confidence rather than excitement to his mount. He pretends he is at a meet: the hounds the policemen; the yobs their quarry.

The mob is chanting, goading the police officers, a mass of angry mouths and fists. It surges around the bus, pushing and pulling at it until it rocks over on its side. There is the sound of smashing glass and cheering. Freddie pictures the master of the hunt and the hounds on the lawn. They always have a good day. This is no different. Clifford turns his horse so that he is facing the other riders. 'You know what to do,' he says, raising his baton in the air, and pacing up and down in front of them like a general addressing his troops on a battlefield.

The special constables sit tight while their horses sidestep, the sweat shining on their rumps, foam beginning to fleck their mouths. 'These men,' shouts Clifford, his voice ringing with emotion, 'these anarchists would like to bring our fine country to its knees.'

The riders murmur and shake their heads, Freddie with them. Sorrel skips and jiggers backwards but he holds her steady. It will not do for the animal to sense his trepidation. He steadies his breath, wills himself to calm, to focus. He is unbeatable on a horse, just as he is on the hunting field. Always at the front. Never afraid to tackle the biggest hedges. Hunting, he thinks. It's no different to hunting.

'They want to bring down the government! They want to trample over our democracy! A democracy that we fought for! That our brothers and fathers and sons died for!'

Freddie glances at the other riders. They are captivated, their eyes following their leader. He knows they are thinking of people they know, lost or maimed in the Great War. Fathers and brothers – like Edward. He steels himself. The policemen draw their truncheons, feeling braver now they have this army of horsemen at their sides. Freddie allows the words to goad him towards courage.

'But we're not going to let them do that. We're going to show them what democracy looks like. We're going to show them that we won't let it be trampled on and lost to some socialist claptrap.' Clifford is snarling, the words spitting from his mouth with rage. He turns his horse as if they are the cavalry facing down the enemy. 'You are either with democracy or against it,' he shouts, and he points his baton and lets out a great cry. 'We are at war!'

The men do the same, and suddenly they are charging down the road, the horses flat out, necks outstretched, manes flying, and Freddie feels the heat in his veins, and he is hunting, and he is certain that this is how Edward must have felt in the war, the blood pumping in his ears, the hooves thundering. The crowd parts, and the smug face of a striker changes to fear as Sorrel bears down upon him, and now that Freddie is committed and sees Clifford bring his baton down into the crowd, he does the same, and feels the satisfying thump as it connects with something solid, and he barely hears the cry of pain as the man beneath him stumbles to the ground before picking himself up and running for cover. It's either democracy or anarchy, he thinks; it's either them or me. He pushes further forward, into the crowd, the horse's chest clearing a path, and he brings his arm up again, and again flings it down into the crowd, and again it connects with something, and he swings it down to his right, and then across the saddle to his left, until the street is clear and he is swiping at thin air. And they have won.

The crowd is dispersing, clutching at arms and heads, scuttling to safety through twisting back alleys and passages. And suddenly the road is empty, and the clamour of attack is replaced by the sound of the riders and horses breathing fast, their sides heaving as they fill their lungs, their eyes shining.

Clifford rides closer to Freddie, not a hair out of place. 'You did well, son. An honour to your brother's name. I'd be proud to have you in my regiment.'

Freddie's heart swells. He is as good as Edward. No, better, because he is here, in the thick of it, and the house is still a Hembury house, and he is making it work, really making it work. Clifford's magic is catching: he feels invincible, like the horse that is arching its neck and shaking its mane beneath him. He suddenly has a purpose, power – no longer the weak younger brother, but a man to be reckoned with.

'Where have they all gone?' he asks. He is disappointed that the action is over. He has more to give.

'Scuttled back under their stones in the East End,' says Clifford. 'Whitechapel and beyond.'

Whitechapel. Where Joseph Cottam said Celia was living now. Freddie imagines the surprise on her face if she saw him riding down the road on a horse.

Clifford examines him. 'Adrenaline still flowing? You want to do a victory parade? Make sure they know we're still here? We could go back north of the river. Cross at London Bridge. It's not much of a detour, and the more of these people that see us, the better.'

Freddie grins. 'Why not?' He knows those streets a little, for not only are they near the auction rooms, but also St Katharine Docks, where his tea is stored.

In his euphoria he feels light as a feather as he jogs next to Clifford. This suddenly feels like *his* city, *his* country. The streets are eerily quiet, people are making themselves scarce. He catches a glimpse of himself in a window, and sits up straighter, pushes his chest out. The few people they pass don't dare look up. They glance away from the oncoming riders, or turn their backs and pretend to busy themselves, as if too frightened to look at their conquerors.

They reach the Thames that twists like a dirty scar on through the city. The air smells putrid, and Freddie senses the atmosphere change, as if the brisk breeze is blowing their success away. He can see the barges and ships queuing to be unloaded, coal smoke belching into the air, dusky red sails flapping. Only a few of the derricks are moving. The tide is out and there are children picking their way through the sticky mud. They glance up as the horses cross the skyline, then turn back, uninterested.

From his elevated position, Freddie can see beyond the grand facades of the main thoroughfares to the labyrinth of the East End. A group of young men glower and elbow each other at the other end of the bridge, recalcitrant gatekeepers. Freddie is struck by how similar they are to the villagers in Hembury: they wear the clothes of the poor, flat caps and grubby trousers, scuffed boots, that same stubborn look. He hears a whistle, a warning to another group further up the road. A woman scowls. Two men stand, arms folded, their eyes following the horsemen. The feeling of power starts to ebb from Freddie's body. His arms and legs are aching. He had not realised how tired he was. The horse too is flagging. He can sense the tiredness in her bones, like after a day's hunting.

Someone pulls up a window, and starts to heckle them, and then another and another.

'Piss off!'

'You're not welcome here.'

There are more people coming on the street. 'Dirty bunch,' says Clifford. 'Can you imagine living here, among all this squalor? It's what happens when immigrants and Jews are allowed to reside among us.'

Freddie stays silent. This is the place that Celia chooses to live, and it strikes him firmly between the eyes how very different they are. He is an imbecile. Elizabeth is a better match than he could have ever hoped for.

'Come on, Hembury!' Clifford's voice cuts through his daydreaming. 'Let's show them how we have more decency and honour in one little finger than they do in the whole of one of their squalid streets. *Non ducor, duco!*' And he kicks his horse forward with Freddie at his side, and once more they are cantering.

Word reaches them that strikers are stopping supplies leaving the docks. 'Damned picket line holding food to ransom,' says Clifford. 'There's a military convoy going to assist, but they need us to help keep the louts off . . .'

'Dockers, is it?'

'Dockers shored up by the Communist party, apparently. Those Reds seem to have more backbone than the trades unions.'

Freddie dwells on this, is sure that vagabond Raymond White, who has somehow managed to pull the wool over Celia's eyes, will be caught up in it. His name often comes up in police reports and newspaper articles. Freddie burns with the fire of the righteous: how he would love to show that ex-convict what true grit is. Raymond may be good at smooth talking, at riling a crowd, but how would he fare in the face of Clifford's special constables?

The traffic is once again at a standstill.

Freddie settles back into the saddle, his tired muscles remoulding to the horse, enjoying thinking about what he might do to Raymond if he gets hold of him. His initial rush of fear has been replaced by adrenaline, and all that remains is the thrill of power. He barely flinches at the furious blaring of a police whistle as a young boy is caught defacing a poster. Policeman and boy zigzag away down the street; the Emergency Powers Act is in full force, and anyone considered a danger can be detained – even a small boy.

A few yards further, a line of people waits patiently at a bus stop. The queue snakes so far that it is hard to see where it ends. A crowd of strikers is goading the waiting passengers. The bus pulls in as they approach, and Freddie sees the roll of barbed wire around the cab, the policeman sitting with the driver, but it is the passengers who are in danger now. The strikers raise their voices as they chant, 'Not a penny off the pay; not a second on the day.'

Someone throws a missile at the bus window. The glass cracks, and the passengers cry out in alarm. Freddie and Clifford kick their horses closer, and the men back away as they see what is coming. The passengers cheer. Freddie suppresses a smile, though he acknowledges their gratitude with a quick tilt of the head. Just wait until he catches hold of Raymond White.

They pass beyond Whitechapel, and then on, further east to reach Victoria Docks. The atmosphere crackles under the glare of unfriendly eyes. On reaching the dockyard, they find the gate is blocked by an angry mob. Missiles and curses cut through the air as they muscle their way through. Freddie can sense Clifford's anger. As the crowd grows, so too does Clifford, sitting taller, his chest out, his medals glinting in the light. The men press in against their legs, closing around the horses. Freddie glimpses arms thickened by heavy loads, hands blackened by coal, faces etched with grime, and among the posters calling for the workers of the world to unite, there are the banners of the Communist party: the stars, and the hammer and sickle.

'Strike or starve! Strike or starve!'

'Blacklegs!'

'Scum!'

Freddie searches the faces for the bullish, bespectacled Raymond White, but the crowd is so feverish that it is hard to make out any particular person within its undulating waves. Clifford lashes out with his baton, catching a man's temple. This crowd will not be cowed, and their shouts of protest turn to howls of anger as they press in on the riders, but the military are on hand at the gates, and they let the special constables through as they hold the dockers back. When they are safely inside, Clifford spits on the ground. 'If Churchill had let us be armed, this would have been over a lot more quickly,' he says, 'but that idiot Baldwin said no.'

This side of the gate, the docks are eerily quiet; only a few of the cranes are working, creaking with cargo from the ships. Freddie and Clifford are directed to the officer in charge, Captain Rivers. He is standing by a long line of armoured vehicles, machine guns poking out from beneath their canvas, while the soldiers hang around in groups watching some students unload the hold of a ship. The boys, dressed in their Oxford cricket sweaters, are heaving sacks on to wooden trolleys.

The man overseeing their work is chewing tobacco. 'Don't look old enough to be out of the nursery,' he sniffs. 'Still wet behind the ears.'

'They're doing a grand job,' says a soldier.

The man grumbles to himself, shaking his head. 'They're being paid the same as my dockers, but they're shifting a quarter of the load.'

'That sounds like revolutionary talk to me,' snaps Freddie.

The man glares at him but doesn't reply. No one wants to be arrested as a Communist.

The fresh-faced undergraduates joke among themselves as the mountain of food sacks on the side of the wharf slowly disappears into the waiting lorries. The din of the crowd outside the gates rises.

Captain Rivers walks up and down the convoy, inspecting the vehicles, checking straps and chatting to his men. At his signal, the soldiers clamber up on to their allotted trucks – some sitting on top of the cabs, others manning the armoured vehicles. An overcast sky is reflected in their solid helmets, their polished boots.

The captain gives the command and the lorries start their engines. As the convoy rolls forwards, the men on the ground slowly open the gates again. The crowd roars, and the horses start to prance. Clifford and Freddie ride to the front, batons raised. The soldiers on the ground pull their rifles from their shoulders.

'Scab! Scab! Scab!' yells the crowd.

They are a mob that do not know how to conduct themselves, thinks Freddie. They unnerve, but also disgust him: how can people behave in this way? Have they no respect?

The first armoured truck is level with the gate. The crowd will not part. The driver revs his engine and inches forward. The soldiers and the policemen start to shout. Freddie urges Sorrel on. A man from the crowd reaches out and grabs at his leg. Freddie turns and tries to hit the man with his baton, but he is too close, and has a good grip. And then there he is – a few feet away – Raymond White, with his false look of learning, his treasonous beliefs. Freddie knows the truth: the man is a thug, a criminal. He feels his blood boil as he tries to propel Sorrel closer, but the other man still has hold of his leg, and Raymond is moving away, raising his placard high as he slips into the crowd.

'Get off!' shouts Freddie.

'Fascist!' the man shouts back.

'This is food. So that people can eat.'

'We're people! We need to eat!'

'You've only got yourselves to blame.'

'We're watching our children starve . . .'

Clifford comes to the rescue, barging the man out of the way with his horse. Freddie hears the sharp inhaling of breath, and then the man is gone, and Raymond White is gone too, but replaced by hundreds of other hands, reaching out, touching, grabbing. Someone knocks Freddie's stirrup away. The horse is frightened and starts to dance. Freddie wraps the hand with the reins into the mare's mane. He doesn't want to fall into the crowd. More hands pull at him. He tries to swing his baton, but there isn't room, and he feels himself slipping, slipping. And with the fear now anger pulses, and he feels the crunch as at last he connects with someone, and the hands retract, and he has some space to haul himself back in the saddle. The mob is screaming, baying for blood, but he is strangely calm. He sees people grasping at each other, tearing at each other's hair, he sees mouths snarling with rage, fear. And there are women and children too, and a woman whose hat has been torn from her head and her hair is falling in thick strands of auburn down her back: Celia! Of course she would be here with Raymond . . . and he calls out to her, but too late, as she is knocked sideways by a horse, and into the path of a truck. Freddie kicks Sorrel sharply in the sides, and the horse bursts from a standing into a gallop. The truck rolls forwards, and Celia is within reach of its wheels, and Clifford is shouting at Freddie to leave her, it's her own damn fault, but Freddie is leaning down out of the saddle and somehow he manages to grab hold of her and swing her up in front of him, and they are still on a collision course with the truck, but the polo pony is used to sharp turns and it spins on the spot, as Freddie hauls it to a standstill.

The woman pushes away from him and on to the ground. She looks up, and he sees that it is only her red hair that is like Celia's. Her skin is grey as off-milk, untouched by the Devon sun, and her pale eyes are dull. 'Get your hands off me, fascist,' she spits. 'What sort of men are you that you would run down a defenceless woman?'

'I was trying to help . . .'

'Help? Look at you. You think you're so brave, so manly, with your trucks and your guns and your horses. You probably call yourself a gentleman, but you're not. You're just a bully.'

He has no time to respond as Clifford jostles through. 'Move!' he shouts, and thrusts towards the woman, who gives Freddie one last triumphant look before she is swallowed up into the crowd.

'That was inspiring horsemanship,' says Clifford, 'but next time don't put yourself or my horse in such danger.'

'I couldn't let her be run over . . .'

'Try not to think of them as people. They are animals infected with the communist disease.'

Freddie does not reply, but he is as shocked by Clifford's outburst as he is by the woman's. Then he pictures the woman's furious face, her vitriolic words, and he can see that perhaps Clifford is right. There is no hope for some people. Celia and he are bound to different paths now.

Hyde Park has been closed to all but volunteers. Along the black iron railings, the Navy man heavy artillery. Children gaze in awe at the guns, calling to the sailors through the bars. Freddie's convoy passes through the gates, and is signalled on to an unloading slot. They are given time off to find refreshments, and Freddie searches for his sister, who he knows is feeding volunteers somewhere. He rides along the lines of bell tents, past rows of battered milk churns stacked the length of the road that cuts through the park. He catches snippets of information as he passes.

'Did you hear they derailed a train? Chained lorries to the tracks, and the train just went . . .'

'They've been surrounding fuel depots, stopping buses filling up.'

But it is clear from the cheerful atmosphere that it is the government and not the strikers who are in control.

Freddie finds Ginny peeling potatoes into an enamel bowl perched on a wooden trestle table. She laughs with delight when she sees him, drying her hands on her apron before coming up to stroke Sorrel's neck. Freddie jumps down, his knees giving way slightly; it has been a long day in the saddle. 'You must be starving,' she says. 'I'll get you something to eat. I'm sure you count as a volunteer driver.'

Freddie removes his hat. His hair is plastered to his head with sweat. He roughs it up a bit, then smoothes it back down, noticing that his riding breeches are also filthy – a mixture of dust and grubby hand prints. Sorrel nudges him in the back, and he reaches out to stroke her soft muzzle. 'I need to find something for the horse first,' he says. Ginny points, and Freddie takes the mare to join a line of other horses being fed. The smell of horse sweat and sweet hay reminds him of home.

'Looks like you've had quite a day?' Ginny sounds concerned. Her jolly face, her hair neatly pinned in place, her starched apron seem such a far cry from the wild and filthy women on the street that he feels a sudden rush of love for his faithful sibling, and for the other people working hard to keep everything going. It disappoints him that Celia will be doing the opposite: stoking the disorder rather than trying to make sense of it. But it highlights the fact that he is right to try to forget her, to look to his own.

Ginny waves her hand in front of his eyes. 'Are you all right?'

Suddenly he has an urge to tell her about Wilf and Edward, because he sees now that surely she is the one person in the world he can trust: who understands the importance of Coombe and the family. 'What if I told you something extraordinary?' he says.

'Such as?' She smiles at him, tilts her head to the side.

He opens his mouth, closes it again. How can he tell her that their brother may be alive? That there is a child? It is a betrayal he has carried for too long to divulge now.

'Have you had a knock to the head?'

He tries again, but he does not know where to start.

'Goodness, what have you done?'

He glances down and sees that blood has seeped through his sleeve, drying in a dark patch along his arm. 'It's nothing. I'll go and wash it off in the Serpentine before I leave.'

'Listen to you! You're quite the hero! Why don't you join us for drinks later? Hugh would love to see you. And Libby Montague-Watson is here, and so are Daphne and Sybil. Masses of people you know.'

'I need to get back to Elizabeth. She's at the house. She's been wondering what she can do to help.'

'Tell her to come here tomorrow. It would be a hoot.'

'I'll ask. Though she's been feeling a bit unwell recently.'

'Maybe I'll see you later?'

'I'll see what she says.'

'I absolutely understand. She'd be a brave woman to leave you on the loose looking so dashing.'

He grins at her. 'I must say, a crisis seems to suit you too.'

'It's good to feel useful. And to be surrounded by friends. But I'd better get back. Look at the queue!'

Ginny joins the other women doling out the food. She nudges her neighbours, and they look across at Clifford and the other men, who are making their way towards Freddie on revived horses. The women smile self-consciously. Freddie retrieves Sorrel, and filled with renewed energy he bounces into the saddle, jogging to take his place among the men, tipping his hat like the others at the ladies as they pass by.

CHAPTER 37

Volunteers continue to come forward while the strikers crumble in disarray, and after only a few more days, the Trades Union Congress calls off the General Strike. The largest industrial dispute in Britain's history is over, a damp squib, ruined by the government's ability to rely on those who stepped up to the mark. 'Men like you,' says Elizabeth, smiling at him across the back seat as they are driven home to Coombe.

'And women like you,' Freddie agrees, taking her hand. But he cannot help feeling a little bereft, without a purpose, as the weeks slip by with games of tennis and picnics by the top lake. He keeps away from the stables, ordering Reid to bring their horses to the front of the house when they want to ride. He has managed to avoid Victor and Wilf for the whole summer; it is easy now they are not living on the front drive. It becomes clear that he must find a way to get rid of them entirely. He is surprised that he did not see it before: it is an untenable situation.

He steps out of the way of another workman. They are everywhere: up on the roof, at the windows, inside the house. Electric cables have been wound throughout the rooms, and hot water plumbed into the upstairs bathrooms. The leaks in the ceilings have been traced to source, and there is no further need for the cracked chamber pots. 'And come and see what Gibbs has done.' Elizabeth leads him into the garden, around the house, avoiding the ladders and the buckets.

The new gardener has cut a design into the top of the yew

hedge. Freddie stands back to admire it. 'I can't tell what it's meant to be,' he says, wrinkling his nose.

'It's a fox, being chased by hounds. Obviously.' Elizabeth laughs and leads him on, past the ornamental pond which has been cleared of weeds, leaving only heart-shaped lily pads with crisp white flowers floating on the surface, and on through the rediscovered maze, where once he bumped into Celia. Like her, there is no trace of that garden, that time now; instead there are new benches, and old statues have been uncovered.

'It's astonishing,' he says when they get back to the morning room. He remembers the grubbiness of the East End, and the violence of its people, and is flooded with happiness to be back at Coombe. Everything he needs is right here.

Elizabeth claps with delight. 'The glass in the greenhouses is being replaced next week.'

'I don't know what to say. You're brilliant.' He kisses her, then pulls away as a bell rings.

Along the corridor, he briefly hears the clatter of pots from the kitchen before the baize door that separates the servants' quarters closes gently again. Recently they have been filled with the aroma of new spices from abroad.

'We need to talk about the stables,' Elizabeth says gravely.

Freddie's heart plummets.

'We haven't had much success breeding a winner.'

'We've been close.'

'I know.' She pats his hand to show she understands. 'It's just that if breeding and owning racehorses isn't our thing – and I fear, with the best will in the world, that it might not be – then it would be better to cut our losses now. Sell the stock we have . . .'

'But horses are my thing . . .'

'You say the same about the tea.'

'That is breaking even now . . . it's only a matter of time.' But his promises that his business will one day take off ring more empty in his ears than anyone else's.

271

'So you keep declaring.'

'I have the projections . . .'

'It just seems you are not so adept with money.'

The statement cuts deep, and he is glad more than ever that she does not know it was a loan from Celia that kept the plantation afloat. 'I can show you the figures.'

'No, no. It's not my place. But the horses I do have an interest in . . .'

'I won't give them up. They're part of Coombe . . .'

For a moment, he thinks she might push back, but she draws closer to him, and slides a finger down his chest. 'You seem to have found your calling, Freddie Hembury. Being a special constable suits you: you've become very forceful. But how about you slim them down?' She presses her body against his. 'They are expensive, and there's a limit . . .'

He steps away, feeling trapped. He knows he can't insist; she is right: they are expensive, and they have yet to make their fortune. 'I suppose we could lose some,' he says.

'Why don't you keep the hunters? Those seem to be doing well, though they're never going to provide us with more than pin money.'

'I'll find buyers for the racehorses.'

'Good,' she says, reaching out to take his hand, 'because I'd like to divert some money into the stock market.'

'That's not something I know much about.'

She lets a small laugh escape. 'I wouldn't expect you to take charge of it. Nicholas can advise us. He's making masses at the moment. It's simply a matter of choosing the right thing. And it is my money we're using now, after all. Not that I mind, of course.' She pats his arm. 'What's mine is yours and vice versa.'

He does not know if she means her comments to wound him, but they do. He is a charlatan, just playing at being a firstborn; he will never succeed. He steps away. 'If it makes you happy,' he says.

'You make me happy,' she says, refusing to let him go. 'And

you make Clifford happy. I get quite fed up with him telling me what a good egg you are. As if I didn't know already.' She takes his face in her hands and kisses him, giggling as he pulls her close once more.

Elizabeth has invited her brother and Ginny and Hugh for the weekend. 'All the siblings,' she says. Not all, thinks Freddie for a second. Ginny gasps in amazement as they walk arm in arm around the garden. 'Papa would be so proud.' Freddie glows. She glances at him. 'It sounds disloyal to say it, but I don't think that Edward could have done any better.'

Freddie swallows the guilt. 'Thank you.'

They join Sybil and James at the tennis court. Annabelle sits on the grass, her pregnancy more obvious. Sybil has dug out the rackets and Ginny joins her with a handful of balls. Freddie sits at the wooden table with Nicholas, Hugh and James. Their discussion turns to Clifford, who Nicholas is working closely with. 'He talks about you often, old chap.'

'Just as I said,' adds Elizabeth, rolling her eyes.

'You know he's actually going to start this new party?'

'I'm not surprised. He's got real magnetism.'

'He's in Germany right now, meeting this new leader of theirs. He's hoping to get some funding. They could join forces. A European movement.'

James clears his throat. 'I haven't heard the nicest things about this new chap.'

'Clifford says he's wonderful,' replies Elizabeth. 'And I feel sorry for the Germans. Did you hear they have to take a wheelbarrow of money just to buy a coffee? The French are really making them pay.'

'Not just the French . . .' says Freddie.

'Well I think they deserve it,' says Nicholas.

'Surely it's time to put all that behind us,' says Hugh.

'Have you read about how popular the chap is?'

'What's he called?'

'Adolf Hitler.'

'Camilla had tea with him once. She said he was rather sweet.'

'He's certainly got a lot of support. The Germans are fed up with being kept under our thumb.'

They all clap as Sybil wins the game with an ace down the line, and the women come to join them, pouring glasses of Pimm's from a jug that has been brought out by one of the kitchen maids.

'I don't think you should face fire with fire,' says Ginny. 'It sounds as if this Hitler's getting everyone so riled up.'

'Nothing wrong with a strong leader.'

'I just don't think it's safe. We've all seen what happens when a crowd becomes a mob.'

'You'll be telling us you're joining one of these women's peace marches next!'

Freddie suddenly notices Elizabeth is missing. 'Where's my wife?' he says.

Ginny looks around in surprise. No one had noticed her going. 'Please excuse me.'

Elizabeth is not in the drawing room or at the dressing table in their bedroom. He notices that the new electric lights are burning in the staircase up to the nursery.

She is standing at the far end, staring at a teddy bear that she has removed from the shelf.

He crosses to her, and asks, 'What are you doing up here?'

She shows him the bear, then holds it to her chest, smiling.

'You know, my mother forbade anyone to come up here in the years after the war,' he says. 'Though she often sat in here alone.'

'Why?'

'She didn't want anyone to touch anything, as if moving it might rub out Edward's fingerprints.'

'Well' – Elizabeth draws the word out to attract his attention – 'we're going to need to prepare it. For our own child.'

His heart leaps at the thought he may provide Coombe with a legitimate heir. 'Really? That's wonderful news.'

'Do you think so?'

'Of course.' Inside he feels a strange mixture of elation and terror.

'I don't feel responsible enough to be a mother.'

'We'll have to find a nanny.'

'But first we'll have to redecorate . . . Do you mind?'

Freddie glances around the nursery. A thick layer of dust coats everything. His gaze settles on the doorframe where they marked their heights. The thought that his own child will soon be here, playing with the wooden trains, riding the old rocking horse, setting up the tin soldiers, brings so many memories flooding back, and instead of sadness, he feels anger again that Edward has abandoned them, leaving them to clean up his mess. Why should they keep anything in his memory if he has erased them from his?

'I don't mind one little bit. Do what you want.' He will tell Mrs Foley that she must do whatever Elizabeth demands. Make the nursery splendid. And change Edward's room. Throw out the things that won't be needed. They could have an enormous bonfire, make way for the next generation of Hemburys, who need not inherit another man's mess. He flings open the window and calls across the lawn: 'We're going to have a baby!'

'You are wonderful.' Elizabeth puts her arms around him, placing his hand on her belly. 'I know it must be hard for you. It's the same for me. But my ex-husband . . . and your brother – they would understand.'

'Would they?' Freddie cannot help the bitterness souring his tone. He glances away, cannot hold her gaze. He feels his cheeks begin to burn.

Elizabeth's smile slips from her face. 'What is it? What's happened?'

He runs his hands through his hair and down over his face. He would like to keep them there, to hide his face from her. But she deserves to know the truth, and anger at his brother strengthens his resolve. 'It was something Bolt said.'

275

'Why would you care what a gamekeeper said?'

'I never told you how he came to be employed here. He was my brother's batman during the war. He told us that Edward had always promised to give him a position here, to repay his loyalty, and their friendship.' Freddie bows his head. Elizabeth rubs the back of his neck. Where does he start? He takes her hands. 'I don't know how he could have held this from us all these years, but he told me that when he left the battlefield Edward was still alive . . .'

'Alive?' Her reaction reminds him how deeply shocked he still is by the thought of it. 'I don't understand. Why would he say such a thing?'

She starts to tremble and her hand flutters at her stomach. He dare not tell her the rest – about Wilf – it could be too much for her in her current state.

'I don't understand it myself. Maybe he thought we'd be more likely to give him a position if we thought Edward was dead.'

'Which implies he is lying about it all.'

'Perhaps. He said Edward was badly injured and wanted Bolt to finish him off. Bolt couldn't do it. He says he saw him later. In a field hospital.'

'But not afterwards?'

'No.'

'So he could be dead.'

'But he could also be alive.'

'How will we ever know?'

'Shouldn't I try and find him?'

Elizabeth grips his arm, turns him to face her. Her eyes have gone hard, pale green like ice on the pond in winter. 'Why would you want to stir things up? If you find him, what happens to us? Surely he is still the earl . . . we would lose our titles . . . our position . . . it would be embarrassing . . .'

'But he's my brother . . . I have to know.'

'We can't rely on the word of a gamekeeper. It is most likely a lie.'

'Then what do we do?' He is relieved to pass the burden to her.

She frowns, takes a turn around the room. Finally she says, 'Don't tell anyone else. We could lose everything, and I am not prepared for that to happen. God knows, we all suffered in the war. When I think about what I had with Peter. The pain of losing the person you love most in the world. The person you were going to share everything with . . .' She has a faraway look in her eyes, and he reaches out to touch her arm, to bring her back. She glances at him. 'You know I am happy with you now. I didn't believe I could ever enjoy life again.'

'I know.' He reaches out to take her hand, but she turns to grip the tops of his arms.

'You must forget your brother,' she says, iron in her voice. 'It's been what? Eight years? Either he is dead, or he never wants to be found. We should respect that.' Freddie nods, but Edward's behaviour is still a betrayal. 'Promise me?'

'I promise.'

Elizabeth turns and stares out of the window. 'And what about Bolt?'

'I hope to find a way to get rid of him.'

'Don't do that. He would be more likely to say something if he has cause to dislike us.'

Freddie nods, though he cannot bear the thought of having the Bolts in his life for ever. 'Very well.'

'And he is the only other person who knows about this?'

'Yes,' he lies. He trusts Celia enough to know she would never betray a confidence.

He lets Elizabeth take his hands again. She holds them against her stomach. 'Don't worry about Bolt,' she says. 'Leave him to me. It is always best to keep one's enemies close. It's about us now. Nobody else.'

CHAPTER 38

Celia takes a deep breath and straightens her shoulders, thrusting a leaflet towards a woman walking briskly towards the platforms, child in tow. The woman is the kind of person she knows they must appeal to: neat as a pin though her shoes are scuffed. She has the briskness of intelligence and hard work, not the arrogance of someone to whom life is handed on a plate. But the woman pushes the leaflet away. 'I don't want none of your trouble.'

'It's some information about a new newspaper from the Communist party of Great . . .'

'Ain't no party that can help me.' Celia recognises the accent of the East End.

'If I could explain. It will only take a moment.'

The woman stops and glares at Celia. 'You really don't get it, do you?' She grabs the leaflet and throws it on the ground, trampling it underfoot. 'You're all as bad as each other. We all know the Tories won't fight for us. We was told a Labour government would, but we got them again, and our lives ain't got no better. We don't need politics. We need food. We need work.' She pulls the child between them, tilts her chin up to show Celia. 'You see my girl here? You see how pale she is? I gave her my breakfast and she's still hungry because she ain't had a proper meal in weeks. That's what you and your politics does for us.'

She releases the child, who stares glumly at her shoes.

A small crowd has gathered, attracted by the rumpus. Celia tries to stick up for herself: 'We are a party for the people . . . We want to help . . .'

'And you think you can do that by standing here, all sweet and pretty, handing out bits of paper?'

The people who have stopped to stare at the altercation mutter in agreement. 'Didn't you hear the lady?' says one man.

'Go on. Sling yer 'ook,' says another.

'You're all the same.'

'Can't you see we don't want you here?'

Celia is surrounded, and to her horror she feels tears spill out and escape down her face. Perhaps Raymond is right, after all. Her wish to raise awareness of what they can do is a waste of time: they should be being more pro-active, causing trouble. Words are not helping these people, but action might.

'All right, all right,' says the woman who stamped on the leaflet, addressing the small crowd. 'You've had your sport. Off you go . . .' She takes Celia's hand, her voice suddenly kindness. 'I'm sorry, love. It's been a bad week. Come outside, into the fresh air.' She begins to steer Celia towards the entrance of the station.

'Won't you be late for your appointment?'

The woman looks up at the clock. 'Ellie, you run along to platform five. See if you can't collect your dad. We'll be outside.'

They find a bench. The woman gives her a handkerchief. Celia pats at her face, then hands it back. The woman smiles, pushes it away. 'Keep it,' she says.

A pigeon waddles at their feet, searching for scraps. Like the people who pass by, it is tattered and thin, nothing like the shining plump birds that sat heavily in the beech trees at Littlecombe. Across the road a rag and bone man lets his horse suck water from the trough, bending his own head over the drinking fountain next to it. It is warm on the streets, and they take their time before moving wearily on. A group of children replaces them, splashing the water at each other, grinning as the droplets catch the light. Celia feels the sting of failure again. Is she unnatural that she does not want to have a child? She tells herself – tells Raymond – it is because there is too much stigma to having a child out of wedlock, when there are already too many pressures for a child in the world. But deep down, she knows she could not give time to a child when she still yearns to make something of her *own* life. She sniffs again, as the tears spring back.

'A man, I take it?' says the woman when Celia has finished blowing her nose. 'Whether they're in your bed, or in charge of the country, they generally make a mess of it.'

Celia cannot help smiling.

'That's better. Now I'm Iris Roper, and I'm sorry. I know I have a harsh tongue.' She sticks out a hand for Celia to shake.

'Celia Cottam. And I'm sorry too. I don't make a habit of crying in front of strangers. And I don't enjoy handing out these leaflets.'

'Why'd you do it, then?'

Celia shrugs. 'I'm helping to spread the word about a party that can effect real change,' she says half-heartedly.

'That don't seem to be going so well for you.'

'No. But I'm not comfortable with the alternative.'

'Which is?'

'More direct action . . .'

Iris laughs. 'Men!' she says. 'They always think with their fists first.' She stands as she spots her daughter returning. 'Now there's my man. The source of my own mess. Not his fault, though, poor love.'

Ellie is almost upon them, her thin face lit with pleasure. Her father is swinging her by the hand and she is laughing. When he reaches them he pulls Iris to him, and gives her a long kiss, Ellie sandwiched between their tangled arms. Celia pretends to focus on a passing tram, though she cannot quell the flash of jealousy; Iris Roper may be poor, but she has something Celia lacks.

'Sea air done you a world of good,' says Iris, stepping back.

'I hope so, my love. For all our sakes.'

Iris stands aside. 'This is' – she glances at Celia's ring finger – '*Miss* Celia Cottam?'

Celia nods, and the man shakes her by the hand. 'Matthew Roper,' he says. 'Pleased to meet you, Miss Cottam.'

A man riding a tricycle stops a few yards along the pavement. He is almost immediately encircled by the children who were at the trough.

'Ice cream,' says Ellie. 'Can we?'

The two parents look at each other, and before they can answer, Celia is digging in her purse. 'Here,' she says, crouching down and handing her some pennies. 'Let me. To thank you for assisting me in there . . .'

The child takes the money, and joins the queue with her father.

'Thank you,' says Iris as she watches her husband talking to the ice-cream seller over the bobbing heads of the children. 'You wouldn't believe it to look at him, but there are days he can't get out of bed. It's like having another child. I have to wash him, dress him . . .' She stops, looks at her hands. 'It don't seem real, but I know it'll be back. Tomorrow, or next week . . . People say it ain't normal, but he can't help it. He's no shirker, but it means he can't even hold down a job, however hard he tries.'

'That must be hard for you and Ellie . . . and for Matthew.' Celia cannot help admire this woman, with her no nonsense, and her determination to look after her husband and daughter.

'It is. He's not lost a leg or an arm, so folk don't understand. But I'm telling you he's a different man to the one what went to war. He's been injured bad.'

Celia nods. 'Just because you can't see it doesn't mean it isn't there.'

'Your man had experience of the same?'

She shakes her head. 'I used to work with such cases . . . A long time ago . . .'

282

'Well, I wish they had people like you at the Ministry of Pensions. They don't see it that way. Nothing to do with the war, they say. No evidence it was responsible. But I know it was. It sounds cruel, but I'm glad he lost his toes, else we'd get nothing at all. They got a chart, see. You got to stand in front of a committee, and they decide what you're owed for your sacrifice. They pay you according to how many limbs you've lost, but they can't measure spirits, can they?'

Iris stands to take the ice cream from her returning husband.

'If you knew what he'd suffered in treatment . . . And then the committee has the right to say he don't deserve no more money.' She shakes her head and falls silent as she takes a lick.

'Tell me more about this committee,' says Celia.

Matthew glances at his wife. Iris reaches out to pat his arm. 'There's no shame on you, love. It's them that needs to be brought to account.'

'I'm long past shame,' he says, as he rubs his Adam's apple unconsciously, and with a flash Celia remembers the inhumane treatment of early neurasthenia patients, before she joined Dr Hayne's ward.

'Please know that I understand. I worked in a hospital . . .' she stops as he takes a step back, and she can picture the electrode applied to the pharynx, the buzz and the jolt, the eyes rolling. 'But we were progressive. We did not agree with the prescribed treatments . . .'

Matthew's hand falls away from his neck. Iris takes hold of it. 'I wish there was someone could explain to them what it's like,' he says. 'I ain't got the words. When I'm sitting in front of them, and they're telling me that the war was long ago, and any effects now must be something to do with my poor character—'

Iris butts in. 'If you knew what a sunny character Matthew had.'

He touches her face. 'We pay for our own treatment when we can.'

283

'That's where he's come from today.'

'But it always comes back, worse than before.'

'There are more bad days than there was ten years ago.'

Celia nods. 'It is unlikely to improve unless you get the right treatment for a length of time . . .'

'You understand that, but the board don't.'

'Then they need to be made to.'

'Well he's up in front of them again soon.' Iris cocks her head to one side. 'If only he had someone to go with him that could explain . . . I don't have the right words for those sorts of people.' She fixes Celia with a beady eye. 'But perhaps you do?'

On her way home, Celia's spirits are lifted for the first time in ages, and she finds she is smiling at everyone she passes. It strikes her that this is something she can do – in a sense a physical fight – and really make a difference. There is a happy parallel with the veterans by the river at Coombe, as well as with the work she used to do all those years ago in Bristol. She can discuss it with Raymond tonight . . . Which reminds her she must stop at the market on her way home. She needs to find something to cook for the editor, Miles, who is coming to dinner.

The market is still busy with trade. Two men lean against a shop front as they spoon jellied eels from teacups into their mouths; a small boy, his knobbly knees covered in scabs, offers to carry her basket. In the alleyways, girls in crumpled dresses play hopscotch on the cobbles, bare feet scuffed in chalk dust.

At the edge of the market, where the crowds start to thin, Celia almost stumbles against a cage set up in the middle of the pavement. Inside it a small puppy is pressing itself against the ground. Celia cannot help bending down to touch the rough fur. 'Only one left. Perfect little lady's companion, madam.' The man steps out of the shadows. He has a jovial demeanour, but something more threatening lies beneath. 'Better breeding in a fox terrier you won't find nowhere.' The puppy shrinks away into a corner, eyes large, tail between its legs. A puddle of urine spreads from underneath it, and he kicks the cage in anger.

'How much?'

'Two shillings to a pretty little thing like you.'

She avoids his lingering eyes as she drops the coin into the sweaty palm, swapping it for the puppy, which she places carefully in her basket.

Another half-hour walk and she is at the gate to their terraced home. She glances up, one hand on the latch. It is a far cry from Littlecombe: the neat little windows and front door are replicated along the whole street, each low fence with matching gate enclosing the scrap of front garden with its feeble wisps of grass. But, as Raymond points out, it does them good to live like the people they represent.

Raymond is working on a piece, banging away on his typewriter. He is surrounded by stacks of books and papers, on his desk, on the shelves, across the floor. 'Miles wants more on Gandhi and the Indian fight for independence,' he says as she enters the room. 'He said my last piece went down well with the unions as well as with the party.' He takes off his glasses and rubs his nose, looking up at her, eyes gleaming. 'We're reaching more people every day, gathering strength. Soon the country will have to take us seriously.'

She lays a hand on his shoulder. 'Well done. You deserve it after all your hard work.' The newspaper has already graduated from its early days in a candlelit corner of a grimy warehouse to a proper office in Shoreditch.

Raymond pushes the chair out from the desk and reaches for her. 'Did you manage to get rid of all your leaflets?'

She nods, smiling again at the memory of her day, feeling some of the old excitement of her own building.

He pulls her on to his lap. 'Imagine a world without class, without poverty, where all men and women are equal . . . and all dogs?' The timbre of his voice rises at the end of the sentence as the basket she placed on the floor falls over, spilling its contents, including the puppy. Celia slides off him to pick up the timid creature. 'I couldn't leave her. You should have seen the conditions . . .'

'If only it was so easy to rescue people,' he says, smiling as the dog licks his fingers with its small pink tongue. 'Let's call her Hope.'

Celia takes the basket into the kitchen where she unpacks, opening the door to the yard to let Hope explore. As she prepares the evening's food, she can't stop thinking about Matthew and Iris, and whether his depression has already started to seep back. She looks out of the back door, along the rows of houses, wonders how many more people there are out there trapped in their lives, like the jellied eels at the market.

The editor of the *Workers' Week*, Miles Hartman, still bristles with the energy of the young man who once worked along-side Celia's mother and her best friend, who later became his wife. His combination of charm and grit reminds her of both her parents, particularly in his enthusiasm for everything that she does: how she has made the house homely, the food she serves, always asking for her opinions.

Miles takes a sip of his drink, congratulates Celia on the meal. 'It does get lonely eating on one's own,' he says.

'You're welcome here whenever you want,' she replies.

'I fear I would expand further if I ate like this every day.' He pats his stomach as he leans back in his chair. 'I trust your father has grown similarly in stature? I remember he enjoys his food.'

'Sadly we don't see him much.'

Miles's eyes narrow. 'You must get there for the occasional weekend?'

She glances at Raymond. 'Littlecombe is a long way,' he says, 'and there is much to do here.'

Celia nods in agreement, though she wishes they could visit more often. She worries that her father is alone, and she misses the countryside.

'It makes me laugh to think of your father farming. It's a far cry from the old days.'

'He appears to enjoy it.'

'He has an aptitude for throwing himself into anything. Like his daughter, it seems.'

'And I am indebted to Joseph for introducing us, Miles,' adds Raymond. 'I'm so glad you agreed to be editor.'

Miles raises his glass in a toast. 'It gives an old widower much happiness to emulate his late wife – and Celia's dear mother. They worked so hard on their own newspaper. And it was the start of a long career for me. It seems fitting to return to the coalface, to give something back.'

'Suffragettes and Marxists have always had close ties,' Raymond replies. 'There are many old activists joining our cause.'

'I'm sure. How did today's interview go?'

'It didn't happen. MacDonald wouldn't speak to us, the fool. Labour will never be re-elected if they refuse to see the value in courting the press. But then, perhaps they don't deserve to be.'

'That's unfair,' says Celia. 'They've been working hard—'

'You're biased because of your brother.' There is a bite of anger in Raymond's voice. He and George have grown apart once more as Labour consider rejecting Communists as members of the party.

'They're not all ogres,' says Miles. 'Dear George. He's put up with some rough treatment. I am glad he has found his niche.'

'Hardly rough,' says Raymond, scowling. 'Compared to many.'

Celia takes a deep breath: now is a good time for distraction. 'Speaking of cruelty . . . I met a man today. Matthew. He's a disabled ex-serviceman, though the more severe of his disabilities is a mental rather than a physical one.'

'You have been busy collecting waifs and strays,' says Raymond, glancing at Hope.

Celia stretches a hand below her chair, feeling for the puppy's warm head. 'His wife is an inspiration. She works hard too, but they barely scrape a living. And now the government is cutting war pensions again, so they're reassessing the men in front of a board, much like the tribunals that both you and George faced during the war. Men like Matthew are struggling to prove their less obvious problems stem from all that time ago. I thought I could go to Matthew's meeting, help him speak, and then report on what I find for the newspaper. I have an extensive knowledge of such conditions, as you both know.'

Miles watches her with interest. 'Yes. I remember that excellent piece you wrote on neurasthenia.'

Celia blushes. 'It was only a paragraph. You needed something on shell shock, and Raymond remembered I used to work with Dr Hayne, who is now recognised as one of the forefathers in the field.'

'Short pieces are the most difficult to write. And yours was full of compassion without being patronising.' He strokes his moustache. 'I'm interested in these medical boards. Ex-servicemen have been treated badly, and there is always much public sympathy for them.'

Raymond pours himself some water. 'The entire war was an abuse of the ordinary man. Anything we can do to prove it is worth doing.' His jaw is clenched, and Celia reaches out to touch his hand across the table. She knows how hard those memories are for him.

She is gentle in her retort. 'They don't see it like that. They fought and were injured in our defence. That's honourable. Pity is the last thing they want.'

'So it's not just rehabilitation that's the key, but the public's perception?' asks Miles.

'Exactly. Which is where the *Workers' Week* comes in. If we help to raise public awareness, then the government will have to listen.'

Miles inclines his head, pleased.

'And at the same time we can show them up to be the callous brutes they are,' adds Raymond, equally pleased, and clasping Celia's hand tightly.

Miles nods. 'You two make quite a team. And I believe our readers would love to hear from Celia more regularly. What do you say, Raymond? I know she is already working hard running the household, and handing out leaflets, but surely you can find someone to help with the latter. We can't let her go to seed. Let's get her into the office for a few hours a week.'

'Of course,' says Raymond. 'If that's what she would like.' He squeezes her hand again. 'We need everyone working together on this. One last push.'

Later that evening – the same as most evenings, Raymond rolls on top of Celia, and they have perfunctory sex. It is not his fault. She is not scared or even disgusted; she is simply not excited by him. She knows that she should be: he is attractive, and she sees the way other women look at him, but it seems she is not a natural woman – she has no desire to have children, no desire to lie with a man. Yet sometimes – when she remembers the warmth of Freddie's skin against hers – then sometimes her body responds, and she wonders if things could have been different.

CHAPTER 39

In Devon each year passes much the same as the one before for every man and beast, bar Wilf. For him, the loss of his mother seems to have opened a chasm in his soul that cannot be closed. It is as if he has been knocked off his feet and cannot now find a solid footing to settle on. His spirits rise and fall as relentlessly as the seasons. The countryside is awash with colour: the yellow leaves beneath the field maple; the blood-red rosehips and the fat purple sloes in the hedges. Pale seagulls circle hopefully over the plough while glossy pheasants strut around the coverts. But the keeper's cottage does not feel like home to Wilf. Although he keeps the fire in the stove going, it never feels warm. Without Aggie, everything is emptier and colder, including his father. They move around each other as quietly and painlessly as they can, a dance of avoidance and survival.

Victor cooks, something he learnt to do in the army. Wilf earns extra pennies catching meat: rabbits and pigeons are always easy to sell in the village. There is a woman called Sarah who helps with the laundry.

It is Friday night, and there is a shoot to look forward to instead of school in the morning. Victor is checking his equipment, laying his best boots, breeches and flat cap on the kitchen table, something Aggie would never have allowed.

Wilf is finishing cleaning the dishes. He tries to keep his voice light and carefree: 'Can I take charge of the dogs tomorrow?' he asks, without turning from the sink.

Victor does not even pause: 'No. You're beating.'

Wilf screws the dishcloth in his hand. 'But I'm ready for it.'

'Don't get above yourself, boy. You're too young.'

Wilf throws down the cloth and turns. 'I'm not. I've left school!'

'It's hardly leaving if you weren't never there, the amount of times you played truant.'

'Let me prove it.'

Shadow nudges his leg. The dogs hate the raised voices, the silent fuming.

The anger drops from Victor's voice; he sounds tired: 'Maybe next time. I need tomorrow to go as best it can.'

'Why wouldn't it?'

Victor sighs. 'His lordship is still off with me.'

'Why do you let them treat you so? You never even fought back when he told us to leave our home.'

Victor's rage flares. 'You mind your lip, boy. And do as you're told. You're still a child to me.'

Wilf's own fury sticks in his throat. Sometimes he can't believe Victor is his dad. They don't even look like each other. He remembers well how he felt when Victor suddenly appeared, though he can't have been more than four years old. He resented the way he lost his mother's attention then. Perhaps if Victor had never come back, then she would still be alive. Perhaps she would have married this man she loved before Victor. Perhaps if she had then he could have had a different father . . .

He shoves a chair out of the way, enjoying the noisy scrape of it across the floor.

'Where are you going?' asks Victor.

'Bed. It's an early start, isn't it?'

He sits in his room, staring at Aggie's locket, which Victor gave him as a memento – the only possession it seems that his mother owned, apart from her clothes. At times like this he misses Aggie more than ever, her sudden smile, her singing, her rare giggle, her fierce protectiveness. It galls him that this trinket is all that's left, as if her life was worthless. But it was precious to him, and he will not to let her fade from his mind. It seems to be the opposite for his father: whenever Wilf mentions her, Victor clams up.

He shoves the locket under his pillow at the sound of Victor's voice: 'I'm sorry, son. It's just . . .' The loss of Aggie hangs silently between them. Victor continues, gripping the doorframe like a man on a stormy sea: 'Let me explain: I need tomorrow to go well because Lord Hampden's going to be there, and I want to put myself forward for the head keeper's job. Larry Johnson is retiring.'

Wilf is at a loss what to say: it was bad enough to have to move from the lodge house, but to leave the whole estate – the fields and the woods, the stables and the river – it is his home. 'But you're head keeper here.'

Victor's voice bursts out with such anger that Wilf is taken aback. 'I can't work here any longer. Not for them . . . it's a disservice to your ma.' His voice peters out, and he looks miserably at his hands, takes a breath, returns to his usual controlled state. 'Look, son. I'm the *only* keeper here, and I need a change. Everywhere I turn, it's too much of a reminder . . .' He tries again: 'You have left school and now you'll be finding your own work, but there's a cottage, with room for you.'

The resentment that started all those years ago still simmers in Wilf's heart. 'I'll be staying here,' he says. 'Her ladyship wants me to find a pony for Miss Dilly. She's asked that I take personal responsibility for her own horses.'

'You watch her. She's not one for people like us. I know she don't like me . . .'

Wilf shrugs, as if he doesn't care. 'She likes me well enough,' he says. Inside he feels the last rickety foundation of his world crumble away.

Saturday's shoot begins at the Hall. It is a crisp, but overcast morning, with the promise of rain in the dark clouds that sit low on the brows of the hills. It is the first time Wilf has seen

Freddie in many weeks, for these days the master spends most of his time in London. Since marrying, it seems that Freddie has distanced himself from the stables, and from the staff. It is well known that it is Lady Hembury who holds the purse strings now, and the menfolk whistle and shake their heads, for never in the history of Coombe has a woman been in charge, and a woman who doesn't understand the ways of the countryside at that. But it is another kind of freedom for Wilf, for whatever the truth, her ladyship certainly holds little interest in the stable yard or the estate beyond the formal gardens, particularly since the arrival of her first child, a girl, followed by another only a year later.

Freddie does not even glance in Wilf's direction. Age seems to be catching up with him, and he has lost the natural ease he once had. He is ill-tempered and curt, and Wilf cannot believe he ever felt close to the man. A sadness at the way Freddie ignores him is turning to anger, and he is ashamed at his father loitering meekly and tugging his forelock while he waits for the aristocrats to finish their braying conversations.

There are eight guns altogether, young men growing into the images of their fathers, dressed in their tweed suits, plus fours pinching in below the knee, shotguns resting in the crooks of their elbows. Their loaders hang back, weighed down with spare shotguns and cartridge bags full to the brim, gaiters not yet muddy.

Wilf stands with the other beaters at a respectable distance. They mumble quietly among themselves, admiring each other's dogs, until the guns start to move, and the rest of them fall to their duties, like cogs in a timepiece. Wilf hears Lord Hampden call for his loader to follow. He glances at his father, can see by Victor's body language that he is tense as a set gin trap.

The first birds are to be driven up from the lower woods. Victor confers with the beaters, mainly local boys from the village, as well as some older men who remember the shoot in its heyday twenty years ago, when Coombe had a keeper and two under keepers, and once entertained King Edward and Queen Alexandra, as they so often remind him. The blacksmith's two lads are here, as well as David and Sam. They congregate around Wilf, follow his lead, because it is his patch, and because he is popular among them. Wilf scowls at Victor; he knows it all: that they must not allow their spaniels to flush birds meant for a later drive; that they must keep in line. They move into the trees, and soon the wood is filled with the sound of men and boys calling and whistling, tapping the trunks and the branches with their sticks while the dogs leap through the undergrowth, their ears becoming matted with burrs, their rumps endlessly wagging.

Along the edge of the wood, the guns stand at their pegs, the cold air steaming from their mouths, their loaders at their elbows. Wilf can tell that Freddie is as anxious as Victor: the master's eyes flicker along the line – a good day will show his guests that he is capable of running Coombe as well as any of his ancestors.

Elizabeth and the other wives, including Ginny and her friend Sybil, watch from behind, cosy in their long tweed skirts, hats pulled low over their cold ears as they sip cherry brandy. There is no sign of either of the children. Wilf tips his hat at Elizabeth, and she acknowledges him with a small smile. He is learning that charm can go a long way, and she seems as susceptible as the girls in the village.

A flurry of pheasants rises up from the wood with a grating call. The sky darkens. There is a volley of gunfire. The men swap their guns, and the barrels steam. The smell of gunpowder fills his nostrils as the pellets rain down. The empty cartridges fall to the ground smoking as the loaders slide two more into the barrel, back and forth.

Wilf can see Raven away to the right and Shadow already returning to Victor, a dead cock bird hanging from his mouth. Victor takes the bird. He is on the edge of the wood, in plain view of the guns. A rabbit gets up and then another, pale streaks tearing across the ground. The guns fire again and one by one the bodies slide lifelessly to a halt. The dogs race to pick them up, returning to Victor, who seems slow to send them away again. Wilf clenches his teeth. It's so frustrating that his father won't allow him to take one of the dogs: he could do as good a job, if not better. And he knows that Victor should be blowing the horn to finish the drive, but he seems confused about which dog to handle, and Wilf is about to whistle to attract his attention, when he sees Victor stagger, and steady himself against a tree. His irritation quickly dissipates: something is not right. He walks as quickly as he can without raising suspicion. 'Da? Are you all right?' he hisses.

His father does not seem to hear him. He slides to his knees, still gripping the trunk, his forehead touching the bark, his breath coming in ragged bursts. Songbirds call to each other in the hawthorn. 'Da? Get up!'

Raven is standing waiting for Wilf to remove a hen pheasant from his mouth. Shadow is crashing through the undergrowth, on the scent of a runner. Wilf takes the horn and blows it to signal the end of the drive. The noise brings Victor to his senses. He tries to stand. Wilf can see that his hands are shaking and there is a sheen over his skin, as if he is sweating a fever. 'Can you take them on, son?'

Wilf frowns. 'To the next pegs?'

Victor nods, still taking short, desperate breaths. 'It's Middle Brook. I'll join you. On Three Acres.'

Wilf hesitates. It is a sudden handing over of responsibility. He looks at Victor, who is still using the tree to steady himself. He nods. 'I know what to do.'

The last drive is over. The watery light is leaching from the grey sky. Wilf helps tie the birds into braces, for Victor's fingers are still trembling too much. They hang the birds in the back of the cart. They bind the dead rabbits too, by their hind legs. The pony strains to drag the heavy load back to the game larder, where the Hemburys are gathered with their guests. Wilf notices Lady Hembury glancing Victor's way more than once while she talks to Lord Hampden. Her face is serious, even when she catches sight of Wilf. The guns press tips into Victor's hand before turning for the warmth of the house. The loaders repair to the gun room: the shotguns must be stripped down, cleaned, oiled and put away carefully in their boxes. The beaters rub their hands together to keep warm. They are waiting for their money. Victor pays them. 'You go on too, son,' he says to Wilf.

'No. I'll stay and help.'

Victor nods and smiles sadly. 'I'm sorry, son,' he says. 'You were right: you are ready. Thank you for today.' He glances at his hands. 'I don't know what came over me . . . the guns . . . the smoke . . . it brought something back I thought I'd forgotten . . .'

Wilf understands his father is talking of the war, and that is something he finds difficult. He nods, enjoys the feeling of pride for once, swallows the guilt for thinking such bad thoughts about his da.

True darkness has fallen. There is still the cart to clean out and the pony to rub down. The pheasants will hang for a day or two before the butcher comes to collect the ones that the cook does not want. Wilf takes the lamp, hangs it on the ring on the outside wall. It lights the long row of dead birds swinging in the dark.

He begins to unhitch the pony, unclipping the harness and sliding it free. He will hang it in the tack room ready to clean tomorrow. He steps out into the black night that presses in around the weak lamplight. There is an eeriness now that so many of the stalls lie empty.

He hears a crash and the sound of cursing. On the other side of the yard he sees Victor lift the lamp from the wall and peer into the shadows. 'Who's there?'

Wilf is surprised to see Freddie step into the circle of light. 'Sorry. Didn't see the handcart.' He lingers awkwardly. Wilf remains hidden, sensing that Freddie would clam up if he saw him.

'I think the guns went for tea and scones, m'lord,' says Victor, replacing the lamp and tugging the pony on a stride.

'Yes. I know. They're all having baths.'

They regard each other in silence.

'I didn't realise anyone would still be here.' Freddie rubs a hand over his face.

'The pony needs bedding down.' Wilf can tell that Victor is straining to keep calm, controlled.

'I don't mind. You're not banished from the stables completely . . .' He reaches out to touch it. 'I miss the horses, you know. When I'm in London.'

The pony stamps its feet and moves to nip Victor. 'Can't understand why,' he says wryly as he leads it into its stable.

Freddie follows with the light, hanging it on the hook inside the door. He seems loath to leave, leaning against the doorframe instead, watching as Victor begins to rub the pony down. 'Not a bad bag today,' he says.

'Thank you, m'lord.'

'Rather, I thank you. You gave us a good day. Lord Hampden was singularly impressed.'

'There were some fine shooting.'

'He mentioned something about his keeper leaving. That you had expressed an interest in the job?'

Victor does not respond, but Wilf can imagine the clenched jaw, the steely expression.

'I won't stand in your way . . .'

Still Victor says nothing, and Wilf can see that Freddie is nervous, abstractly rearranging the pony's mane. 'How is the boy?'

'He's well, m'lord. No thanks to you.'

'Does he wish to follow you?' Wilf's shock at his father's insubordination turns to surprise – and a little gratification – as he realises Freddie is talking about him.

'I think he'd rather stay here. He prefers the horse to the gun.' And now Wilf sees Victor step up to Freddie, and face him squarely. 'Is your promise restored?'

Freddie is silent again for a moment. Something deep inside Wilf clings on to the notion that the master *does* care for him, *is* interested in his wellbeing. Perhaps their previous understanding was not all in his imagination.

Freddie takes a step backwards, and Wilf hears him say, 'You know, my brother was an ace shot . . .' He knows that Freddie's brother and Victor fought together in the war, but he has never heard either man speak of him before. He strains to catch more. 'Actually, he taught me to shoot.' Freddie gives a bark of laughter. 'Imagine! He probably taught you too.'

'He did, sir,' says Victor, impassive. 'Your promise . . . ?'

But Freddie is deep in reminiscing: 'We used to come out and practise on pigeons.' He sounds sad, but then Wilf hears him smile. 'Shot the vicar once. It was an accident, of course. We used to conceal ourselves on the edge of Mount Pleasant. We'd been waiting there for hours, when the vicar came wandering past, and put up some birds. I aimed, missed, peppered the man. I hadn't realised he was quite so close . . . It sounds awful, but he was fine. He never knew it was us. We ran all the way home. I've never laughed so much.'

One of the dogs whines. Wilf tries to silence it, but too late, Freddie holds the lamp high, spilling its light across the yard. He catches sight of Wilf and pales. 'I didn't realise you were here,' he says.

'Good evening, sir.' Wilf steps forward, expecting to join in the friendly conversation.

But Freddie is suddenly in a hurry, and there is an awkward moment where they almost trip over each other in Freddie's rush to get on. 'Anyway,' he says, his voice brisk again. 'Good job. See you tomorrow. If you'll excuse me. Goodnight.' He slips past Wilf, and bolts into the darkness. Victor does not look up.

CHAPTER 40

The shooting season draws to a close, and the guns fall silent. To Wilf's relief, Victor has no word from Lord Hampden about the keeper's job. Spring returns, and so do the gypsies, setting up camp near the village. Wilf sees the men sliding in and out of the hedgerows like wraiths, their lurchers skulking at their heels. His father turns a blind eye. Men need to feed their families. Their womenfolk come knocking, babies swaddled on their hips, along with clothes pegs and rolls of lace. There are horses too, among them a small pony that Wilf believes is perfect for Freddie and Elizabeth's oldest daughter, Dilly.

He persuades Elizabeth to allow Victor to check the animal over in the stable yard, telling the truth that his father has better knowledge than anyone of such things. The animal is docile, if a little scruffy, with a kind eye, blowing warm air over the back of Victor's neck as he reaches beneath its rounded belly. Wilf watches, feeling the same soporific calm as his father works. It is like observing the Victor of old, composed and confident rather than anxious and unsure.

Elizabeth has brought Dilly with her. Nanny Stirling has the afternoon off and Elizabeth is flustered, unused to entertaining the toddler on her own. Dilly keeps tugging at her skirt, as her mother pushes her away. Freddie is back in London. There is a rumour that they lost much of their money in the stock market crash. Wilf wonders if that is why Elizabeth seems so angry. Or perhaps his father is right, and she simply doesn't like Victor, does not want him near the house.

Victor keeps his eyes averted from the countess, which begins to grate on Wilf's nerves. Such deference belongs in the past: if you act meekly, you will be treated in kind. He heaves two sacks of feed on to his shoulder. He is stronger than Victor these days, his muscles honed from physical labour. He covers the work of two men, and he is not yet 16. He is as relaxed in her ladyship's presence as he is in everyone else's. It pays dividends: you only have to look at the different way she treats him. He sets the bags down outside the tack room, then ambles over to join them.

Elizabeth swats Dilly's hand away again, and the child starts to gripe. Wilf crouches next to her. 'Would Miss Dilly like to sit on the new pony?' he says. He does not wait for an answer, but takes the small fat hand in his and walks the child to the pony, her feet wobbling unsteadily on the cobbles.

'You understand it has to be perfect,' says the countess.

Wilf shoots his father a look over the pony's neck, then lifts the child up. Her legs do not even come down over the sides of its broad back. Dilly giggles and bounces up and down, pats the animal's warm fur, presses her face into its thick mane.

'You're dismissed.'

'Yes, m'lady.'

'Oh – and I had Lord Hampden asking for your references the other day. I'm afraid I had to tell him we couldn't possibly let you go now that the shoot is doing so well.'

When the shadows begin to lengthen in the clocktower, Wilf heads home. The keeper's cottage is further away, on the far south boundary of the estate, quite close to the village. The house is smaller than the lodge, but big enough for two men who need a roof over their heads.

He stops on the way to check his traps. Three rabbits for the pot. He resets each, placing the animals in his bag. He needs more if he is to sell any in the village. Snatches of song and men's voices lace the breeze; the labourers have returned to help with the planting, the old footpaths once again cleared by their tread.

Sarah is hanging out the washing. Wilf stops to watch her for a moment. He has a sudden image of his mother in the same pose, pegs in mouth, arms aloft, sheets flapping. The pain radiates deep in his gut. Sarah waves in greeting. He does not wave back. He dare not admit how much he misses his ma. It is a weakness: plenty of folk have dead parents. Besides, who would he talk to about it? Victor, who never speaks of such things? Sarah? He reaches down to touch the grey-muzzled dog that has come to greet him. He tells them. Nobody else.

He lays the dead rabbits on the table when he enters the kitchen, Sarah close behind him. 'There you go. How about a nice fat pheasant tomorrow night?'

'You be careful. If you get caught taking one of they . . .'

He shrugs off Sarah's words. She is always worried about what might happen. 'Season's over,' he says. 'Besides, Lady Hembury isn't going to do nothing to me. I can't do no wrong. Isn't that right, Da?'

Victor shakes his head slowly. 'You watch it, boy. They take it as quick as they give it.'

Wilf pulls a sharp blade from the bag that was strung across his chest. He grabs one of the rabbits, and the dogs push their noses at the table. The innards of all Wilf's skinned and gutted creatures belong to them.

'Not in the kitchen!'

Sarah's rebuke smarts, despite him knowing Aggie would have said the same. 'You're not my mother.'

'Wilf!' growls Victor.

'It's more my house than hers.'

'It's nobody but Lord Hembury's house,' says Sarah, and they both stare at her.

Wilf sits down and starts to unlace his boots.

302

Sarah places the stew pot between them, lifts the lid. Steam curls into the air, bringing with it the aroma of the kitchen garden, of carrot and potato, parsley, the goodness of the earth. Victor pours them both some of the white ale he ferments in earthenware jars on the windowsills. Then he pushes a letter into the middle of the table. 'How'd you like to come to Bristol?' he asks.

Wilf stops chewing and looks at him. 'When?'

Victor shrugs. 'Day after tomorrow?'

'Why?'

'Your grandma wrote. Seems your grand-da has taken a turn for the worse. I'd like to see him one last time.'

They catch the train from Hemyock. Wilf is excited by the prospect of adventure: he has never travelled further than these hills since they moved here. He watches the world flicker past the window. The train stops to let some cattle cross the track. Some of the passengers alight to pick flowers, until the conductor calls them back.

They change on to a larger train at Tiverton. Outside the window fields and hedges turn into flood plain and back into fields before the houses start to grow into a forest of brick and concrete.

The great city of Bristol lies beneath its blanket of smog. Wilf walks open-mouthed, turning around to take in the train station, its tower and turrets as grand as Exeter Cathedral – he knows because a drawing of the cathedral used to hang on the wall at school. They cross the Avon at Bedminster Bridge, the water in the New Cut oozes with effluent from the saw mills and smelting works, the glue factories and tanneries. The smell takes him back, to memories he thought lost: to playing in the streets, to walking with his mother, his small hand held tightly in hers. He knows this place: you cannot erase what is in your bones.

A woman tries to sell them some wood. The meagre bundle makes Wilf smile, for he could collect twice as much in half

303

an hour. But his smile soon fades. The houses grow closer together, leaning and buckling against each other, rows so identical that he worries they will get lost. They overtake a girl with eyes too old for her young face pushing a cart of coal. The soles of her bare feet are thick-skinned and cracked, the toes spread, the nails blackened by the lumps of coke she scrabbles for in the slag heaps. The adults are no better: their clothes ragged and worn, their skin as pale as if they had never seen the sunlight. The acrid air tickles at his throat.

Victor slows to check the street names. The back-to-back houses are long walls lined with identical windows and doors, cracks and fissures splitting the bricks like scars on skin. 'It's been that long, I've almost forgotten my way,' he says, before hurrying on.

Wilf catches a glimpse of an alleyway, redolent with the scent of overflowing privies. He hears women talking, voices rising and falling with gossip as washing flaps above their heads, and he is filled with the memory of children of all sizes and ages clambering over the slag heaps while the wheels whirred in the headstock. And he can hear again the grinding of the belts, the slamming of the pistons in the engine house, the sawing of timber. They were the sounds of his life: the ones he knew as well as the boiling of the copper and the clucking of the chickens that scratched in the shared courtyard.

Along the street there is a commotion, a crowd gathered around the front of one of the tiny houses. The gaggle of children who are following them breaks away, to surround the stand-off.

The crowd is confronting two grim-faced men. A woman shakes her broom. 'Go on,' she says. 'You ain't welcome here.'

The unwelcome visitors are wearing matching overcoats and hats. 'Move aside, madam,' says the taller one, 'or we'll have to move you ourselves.'

A man steps between them, folds his arms. The crowd starts to jeer again. 'Leave them alone! Go on!'

Wilf feels Victor's hand on his shoulder.

An old lady, stooped and shaky, stands in the open door, its crooked lintel bent beneath the weight of the house. It is clear she is blocking the entrance. But when she catches sight of Wilf and Victor, she gasps and points. 'My Victor!' she cries. 'Is it you? Is it really you?'

The crowd turns to look at the pair of them. Wilf stands shoulder to shoulder with Victor. He is almost as tall as him. Victor moves forward. 'Ma?' he says, both a question and a statement. And suddenly she is shuffling forwards, through the parting sea of people, past the men in overcoats, and she is taking Victor's face in her hands, covering him with kisses.

When she has stopped, Victor nods at the crowd. 'What's this?' he asks.

'The usual,' she says. 'Bailiffs . . .'

All of a sudden another person bursts from the shadows of the house. A man almost identical to Victor pulls Victor into a backslapping embrace.

'Robbo!' The brothers stare at each other, laughing, and Wilf recognises this man's face as a part of a childhood he thought he'd forgotten, and he experiences a sudden stab of loneliness, for it makes him think of the sibling he could have had, and in turn of his mother, and the time they lived here and were happiest.

'Can someone explain what's going on?' says Victor. And then they are all talking at once.

'Landlord put up his rent to try and get us out.'

'If it's not the coppers, then it's this lot,' says Robbo. 'Harassing us every day.'

'You owe money,' says the bailiff. 'You can't claim harassment when you're in the wrong.'

'Stuff and nonsense,' says his mother.

'If you can't pay, maybe a night in the clink'll sort you out.'

'And how do you think you'll get me there?' bristles Robbo.

'I'm sure the constabulary would be interested to know how much you owe . . .'

The crowd watch in expectant silence.

'How much is it?' says Victor, and his mother grabs his hand: 'Oh Victor, can you help?'

'Ten bob,' says the bailiff.

'And you come and make a commotion outside for all these people to see for ten bob? You come and frighten these children for ten bob?' says Victor, turning on the bailiffs with quiet disdain, and Wilf feels a flash of pride for his father.

Victor shakes his head in disappointment. 'No one's outside the law,' the bailiff replies, looking embarrassed.

'And to think we fought in the war to keep young men like you in jobs like these.'

The crowd mutters. The two men look nervously at each other.

Victor sighs as he rifles through his pockets. 'No matter. I'll pay it.'

Robbo stills his hand. 'You don't need to do that.'

'I want to.' He fixes the bailiffs with a stare. 'Long as it means you'll leave these good people alone?'

The bailiffs nod.

After the bailiffs have left and the crowd scattered, Victor's mother gathers her son to her bosom. 'Come in, come in. Oh son, it's so good to see you.'

'We've missed you,' says Robbo.

'Uncle Victor! Cousin Wilf!'

Victor's mother and brother, and a whole load of Robbo's children as well as his wife Pam are crying out their greetings as they pull Wilf into the house that is like the imprint of a dream. His eyes take a while to adjust to the interior. Barely any light penetrates the windows, which have no glass and are boarded up. There are scorch marks on the walls from the spluttering stubs of candles. There is no air, no ventilation, no oxygen. Wilf's chest feels as if it is being crushed.

The children stare at Wilf, reaching out to touch his blond hair, his arms, as if he is a mythical creature. The rest of the room slowly comes into view: the sacking and blankets that must be beds at one end of the floor, and then the fire – unlit, but with the same small grate, the same tiled surround that give him a jolt as he remembers.

'Sit! Sit!' cries Wilf's grandmother, pushing the cups on the table along to clear a space, but they are all tripping over each other.

'Thanks for bailing me out, brother.' Robbo coughs, and it jogs Wilf's memory again: the tin bath, the clothes hanging to dry.

Victor smiles, and again Wilf feels jealous of that brotherly bond that passes between them. 'You always did steal everyone's thunder,' says Victor. 'Now where's the big man himself? The reason we're here?'

Wilf's eyes wander to a shape in the corner. His breath catches in his throat, and an unfamiliar feeling of panic hammers at his ribs.

His grand-da is a bundle of bones, his skin hanging off him in folds. Victor crosses the floor in a couple of strides and crouches to take his father's hands. The skin looks soft and papery, the knuckles protruding. Wilf remains where he is. He does not want to draw near this creature, who is nothing like the grandad of his memories.

'Hello, Da.' The old man's lips draw back to reveal stained teeth, a smile so thin that it could be a grimace. His eyes are half-closed, his legs are shrivelled. Wilf feels his grandma's hand on his shoulder. 'He is near the end now,' she says, 'but he'll be so happy you're here.'

Wilf shudders, presses back against the hand on his back that encourages him closer.

'Haven't you grown into a strapping lad.' Robbo examines Wilf closely. 'Must be all them vegetables your da grows.'

Wilf studies his uncle's face, remembers how his uncle allowed Wilf to trail around after him, and dandled him on his knee in place of the father who was away fighting. He sees the way Robbo welcomes Victor, and how Victor's face lights up, and he has a sudden understanding that Victor has given up more than he realised to live and work at Coombe.

'Gracie and Jim wanted to come,' says his grandmother, 'but Gracie couldn't get no time off from the factory, and Jim's carrying luggage at the hotel.'

'We didn't want a fuss,' says Victor, standing awkwardly in a corner. Wilf retreats until his back is against the wall. Two of Robbo's small children are still staring up at him, sucking their thumbs. It is difficult to find a place without being in someone's way. He edges towards the table next to his grandfather's chair, and settles on to the bench. His grandmother quickly turns her attention to him. 'What a handsome boy! It's hard to believe you're one of ours. Look at those cheekbones. Strong, too.' She squeezes his muscles as if he were a prize racehorse. 'We were so sorry to hear about your ma. And the wee one . . .' Wilf swallows, and Victor looks away.

'Losing a baby never leaves you,' says Pam, gathering one of her children in her arms.

Wilf's grandmother nods. 'I remember mine every year, all their birthdays. Your uncles and aunts, lad.'

Victor clears his throat. 'We're not doing so bad,' he says. Wilf glances up, to where the ceiling is falling in. 'Ma, you could still come and live with us . . . after?'

'I couldn't leave Bristol now. Pam needs me.'

Pam shifts the child on to her other hip. 'We'll be moving into a new house soon anyway. A bigger one. One of them council ones. Isn't that right, Robbo?'

Robbo bumps Victor along the bench. 'We're on a list,' he says, his voice gruff.

'They're knocking these down. Going to clear the whole lot out.'

'Good riddance.'

'Sally says they're coming for our things next week. Going to take all our stuff and clean it first. Don't want it soiling the new houses.'

'New places have got electric lights.'

'And a bathroom.'

'We'll even have our own privy by the back door. We won't have to share!'

'And two bedrooms upstairs . . .'

'Then I don't have to sleep with you any more . . .'

The older children start to push each other around. Robbo snarls, 'Out, you lot. Go and play.'

The children slip out into the street, barefoot as the others that are still standing outside, trying to peer in through the cracks in the boarded windows. Wilf longs to go with them, but he is too old. The room presses in on him. Sounds come from everywhere: a neighbour arguing, someone crying, a dog barking, children playing.

The family listens while Victor fills them in on life in Devon. Wilf's grandfather's chest gently rises and falls. Wilf drinks his tea, but even that has a layer of greasy grime floating on the surface. Robbo starts to cough again, and has to stand to clear his chest. Victor goes to help, and the room bends and tilts at the sound of Wilf's uncle choking on his own lungs while Victor rubs his chest, and their mother offers soothing words. Wilf realises he could never ask them about his mother's past: they have greater issues to deal with than who she might once have lost her heart to, and they are held together by some family bond that he senses he could never break – especially as he yearns to join the safety of its embrace.

Finally, Robbo is breathing easily again. 'How about the Miner's Arms for a drink?' he says.

'Can I come?' Wilf is already up on his feet.

Robbo shrugs. 'Of course. You're a man now.'

The fetid air of Bristol is welcome after the stale air of the house. They make their way through St Philip's, across roads busy with traffic, past the grocers selling off the last of the vegetables before Sunday. The cobbled streets grow narrower, and the sky seems darker beneath the swinging signs. Wilf follows along behind, his head turning this way and that as he takes in the rubbish swirling in the corners, the faces pressed against the grubby windows.

On the way, the brothers banter, Robbo getting Victor in a headlock, Victor pulling away. After a while they settle into fraternal companionship. 'It's worse than you think,' says Robbo. 'I haven't the heart to tell them we're not moving.'

'What do you mean?' says Victor. 'I thought you said it were sorted.'

Robbo shakes his head. 'Soldiers who fought in the war get priority over miners, and there's still more of them without homes . . .'

'Can you find somewhere else?'

'We haven't the money. Even if there were work to be had, I couldn't get it. I been blacklisted. Haven't worked since I were arrested. They hit us hard after the General Strike, to make an example. No work. No accommodation.'

'You always were good at getting into trouble.'

'I weren't the only one.'

'I were mostly trying to sort out your mess . . .'

They laugh ruefully, and Wilf is eager to hear more, but Robbo is serious again. 'No one can sort this one out for me,' he says. 'How am I meant to find work? There's only one working pit left in the city.'

'Can't you claim from poor relief?'

'Perhaps for now. The councils are taking over from the Guardians. There's talk of a means test. I don't want no one coming to our house. It's shaming how we live.'

'There's no shame. You're doing your best.'

'That's right, brother.' Wilf sees fire in his eyes, like sparks from the blacksmith's hammer. 'And I'm not going to let them win. You'll see.'

They have reached a small public house. Robbo pushes the door open and they are immediately hit by a blast of warm air, on it the scent of ale and sawdust.

The tables are busy with men escaping squealing children and hungry wives. They nurse their drinks, mumbling low over their glasses, or staring at the reflections of light in the dark liquid. There are more men leaning at the bar. A couple of them nod hello as Robbo passes, before turning back to their conversations.

The barman is already pouring Robbo's ale before he reaches the bar. 'We'll take them out the back,' says Robbo, and the barman nods and starts to pour another.

They follow Robbo into a small room furnished with one large table and ten chairs. 'Your own private bar, eh?' says Victor.

'There'll be others along in a while. Sit.'

The barman brings their drinks. Robbo nods and takes one of the glasses in his hand, raising it up so that the light shines through, turning the ale amber. 'To family,' he says, and his eyes linger on Wilf's face for a moment. Victor grabs his drink and also holds it aloft. Wilf hesitates. He has tried beer and cider before, of course, but never a pint in the pub. 'Go on. No one here minds your age. You look a man, or near enough. Besides, who's going to tell my nephew to leave?' Robbo grins.

Wilf glows with pleasure as he lifts his glass and echoes, 'To family,' and the three of them drink.

'And to you, my brother. Thank you,' Robbo adds, and once again Wilf sees what Victor has given up – a bond that Wilf will never feel, for he will never have a brother.

'You said others?' says Victor.

'That's right.' Robbo puts his beer glass on the table and looks into Victor's eyes. 'We've got much to discuss.'

'Such as?'

'News travels far, brother. We heard about the discontent your way. Some unhappy employees sent away after years of loyal service . . .'

Victor seems to fold into himself. 'They were wrong to steal from Miss Cottam,' he says slowly. 'She's a good lady.'

'It's not her we're interested in. It's their previous employers. The very same that you work for now: the Thorneycoombes and their kind are the root of our problems. Maurice Thorney-coombe owns most of the land the collieries were on. He was putting up his rates even while good men were losing their jobs . . . and their lives. Deep Cut and the rest were only following where he led. But you already know it's not only the men underground that suffer. Think of your Aggie. She worked for that man, and she were treated no better than . . .'

Victor raises his hands to stop his brother; it is almost as if he is shielding Wilf from Robbo's words. 'How can anything we do change that?' asks Victor.

'We want you to strike them from the inside,' says Robbo, and Wilf just manages to stop himself gasping: the Thorney-coombes are the Hemburys, and getting back at the Hemburys is something he often mulls over. If ever he felt an affinity with his uncle, it is now.

'I don't want nothing to do with it,' says Victor in his level, quiet way.

'You'd turn your back on your own?'

'I'd keep a roof over mine and my boy's head. I haven't got no one to bail me out.'

Robbo looks downcast for a moment. 'That's not fair.'

'I'm leaving soon anyhow. Soon as another job comes up locally . . .'

'All the more reason to strike before you leave.'

'And then no one would employ me. And what about the boy?' Wilf wants to say he doesn't care, but the look in his father's eyes keeps his mouth shut.

'But it would be a blow at the heart of those that will trample us.'

'No. I won't sacrifice anything more.'

'Your loyalties have always been misguided.' Robbo's eyes flicker again to Wilf.

'What in hell do you mean?'

312

The two brothers have scrambled to their feet at the same time, and are standing chest to chest.

'You've always had a notion you're better than the rest of us,' hisses Robbo.

'I never thought I were better than you,' says Victor. 'I've always looked up to you. You're my big brother.' His voice is thick with emotion.

'Then why did you leave for the war? Why did you want to get away so soon after you returned?'

'You know I always hated it down there. The darkness. The heat. And after what happened with Da . . .'

'You helped get him out.'

'And I were weak with fear every second of that rescue. To go back when we should have been going up.' Victor slumps back in the chair, his head in his hands. 'I could never set foot in the cage again.'

'Da wouldn't have survived without you.'

'It's not been much of a life for him since.'

'So isn't it time we stopped men like the Thorneycoombes destroying more men's lives?'

'You're my brother, and I'll always love and admire you above all else, but I won't let you ruin my life or the boy's. Or be the cause of ruining someone else's. Taking another man down is not going to help you or our family or our kind.'

Robbo sits with a thud, the fight gone. Victor watches Robbo carefully, as if ready to strike back if needed. They both seem to have forgotten that Wilf is in the room.

Robbo sighs. 'It is hard to know my little brother has made a better go of life than I have. You were right to get out. But it's too late for me. I must run with my chosen path. I'll fight for the men here, for the miners. But I'll not expect you to get involved.'

'I'm sorry things are so tough,' says Victor, and Wilf can sense a new sadness between them, as if they are being pulled further apart.

313

There is a sharp bark of laughter as a man walks in, followed by another, and another. Victor looks uneasy, but Robbo cheers up immediately, opening his arms to welcome them.

'Martin! Sidney! This is my brother, Victor. And his boy Wilf.'

'Any brother of Robbo's is a brother of mine,' says Martin, pumping Victor's hand, and then Wilf's.

'What news?' asks Robbo.

'The hunger march in Wales is on. We've got a contact in Rhondda. They'll join with us and finish outside the TUC office.'

'The TUC won't listen,' snorts Sidney. 'They're as bad as the government. Look how they ruined the strike of '26. Only the Communist party fought hard. We must turn to them.'

There is a new charge in the atmosphere, and Wilf can almost see Robbo's spirits rise. His uncle turns to Victor. 'You see! We *can* fight back; there are others. The movement grows every day. Are you sure you won't join us?'

Wilf pleads silently that his father will see the light, but Victor is shaking his head.

'There'll be marches coming from Plymouth, Exeter,' adds Martin.

'Come on!' says Sidney. 'You can't turn down Robbo Bolt!'

They are all speaking over each other, with breathless excitement. Wilf feels a small spark in his own soul. No more talk of foot rot and milk prices. This is real life. This is the stuff that matters.

'Your uncle always gets the men behind him,' says Sidney, addressing Wilf.

'It's true. The union is now a force to be reckoned with,' adds Martin with a grin.

Wilf can believe it: he sees the steel in his uncle's mouth, and in the slant of his shoulders.

Martin lights a cigarette, and smiles as he blows out the match. 'And what about you, boy?' he asks. 'You ready to fight for change?'

'Just tell me what I should do,' says Wilf, and he means it with all his heart.

But Victor stands, and lays a large hand on Wilf's shoulder. 'Not this time, son,' he says. 'We don't want to miss the last train home.'

'But Da . . .'

'You'll come now.' Wilf resists for a moment, then follows him out on to the street. His head is bowed, but his eyes are gleaming. It is dawning on him that he is not only Wilf who knows the call of the nightjar, or where the kingfisher nests; he is Wilf whose family was forged in the mines, men like his father, his uncle, and his grandfather.

CHAPTER 41

Wilf strides up the lane. A new energy has fizzed and popped in his veins since their trip to Bristol. It is as if a missing piece of a puzzle has been locked into place. At last he knows who he is.

The change Miss Cottam and Robbo talked of is here: the success of the agricultural union in Dorset is already spreading into Somerset and Devon, and recently there have been union marches as close as Taunton. All Victor has done is swapped smuts for mud, but Wilf can choose his own path, and he is not the only disgruntled worker in the village. He enjoys stoking their fervour as he does his rounds with the meat.

Wilf's empty bag bangs against his back, and the money jingles in his pocket. Along with his confidence grows his disdain for the Hemburys – all apart from the children, who will only turn into their parents if nothing is done to stop the relentless cycle. He understands how the girls yearn for their mother, who never displays affection, and for their father who is all but absent. Above all, he understands he is best placed to smash them from the inside: he will take care not to squander that privilege.

He pauses when the little stone cottage comes into view. He is relieved to see that Sarah's bicycle isn't propped against the fence, which means his father will be alone. He will avenge his mother's loss before he can accept anyone trying to take her place: the Hemburys destroyed her by working her too hard when she was so fragile. He sees how they still treat

Victor: moved from home to home, job to job at their whim. His own father, who won a medal in the Great War, and who rescued his grandad from the mines. A true hero. He grits his teeth when he thinks of how Freddie used him: to spy on Miss Cottam's people, to run hither and thither. Well, the Hemburys have broken his parents, but they won't break him: he can give as good as he gets.

He hangs his coat and bag on the peg and crouches down to rub the chests of the dogs that come to greet him. He laughs as they push their cold noses, grey muzzles into his face. He deposits the money on the table in front of Victor. There is more than double the usual.

Victor eyes it suspiciously. 'Where'd you get all that?'

'Sold some meat.'

'What sort?'

'Venison.'

'Venison? You can't touch their deer.'

'Why not? They've got plenty.'

Victor frowns. 'It's stealing.'

'It's not stealing. They're wild animals, and that family is rich enough.'

'I don't know what's happened to you,' says Victor with a small sigh. 'There were a time you liked his lordship.'

'That were before I realised what he was doing to us.'

'You seem happy to bow and scrape to her ladyship.'

'It's useful. Means she don't notice what else I'm up to.'

'And what is that?'

'A bit of fun. Tipping the balance. Nothing you need to worry yourself with.'

'It ain't no game,' says Victor angrily, pushing back his chair and getting to his feet. 'You need to learn your place.'

'No,' says Wilf, squaring his chest at his father. 'They need to learn theirs.'

His father searches deep in his eyes, and Wilf has to look away. There is still room for a tiny bit of guilt, but he does not want his father to see that. He does not want to weaken his resolve. He folds the top of his bag over, and starts to move upstairs. Victor puts a hand on his arm, but Wilf pulls himself free. He can see the anguish in his father's eyes and suddenly feels ashamed. He isn't sure where his anger comes from. Sometimes it's as if the despair in the aching hole his mother left has festered into rage so tightly packed that there is no room for compassion.

He breaks Victor's gaze and pulls free, but he does not continue up the stairs. 'There's a new world on the horizon, Da,' he says, forcing his voice to sound calm. 'A world that will be better for the likes of us.'

'Can't you be grateful for what you've got? Food in your belly, a roof over your head?'

'Same as them skunks from the Americas they're breeding up on Dartmoor? A roof and food, but we'll both be flayed. Think of Ma . . .'

Victor runs his hands through his hair and closes his eyes. 'I think of her often.'

'Even with Sarah . . .'

'Having Sarah visit doesn't mean I love your ma any less . . . but life can be lonely, without family, without comfort. Now let's eat. I'm starving.'

They have finished eating when they hear the sound of hooves in the lane: the gypsies are on the move. Victor rises from the table to join Wilf at the threshold. The first riders are in view, young men riding bareback, with only a rope to guide their horses. Behind them comes the herd, snorting and stamping, eyes rolling. A passing motorcar has to pull in to the side, the driver angrily winding up the window as they pass in a swirl of dust. The front riders halt when they see Victor and Wilf at the door, leaning back to slow down.

Elijah cuts his way through, as Victor helps pump the water, refreshing their animals, and filling containers for their journey on to the horse fair at Bridgwater. 'How's that pony faring?'

the gypsy asks, wrinkled and brown as a walnut beneath his bowler hat.

'It's a cracker,' says Wilf. 'As I knew it would be.'

'You got a gift with the horses, like your pa. Must be Romany blood in there somewhere.'

'Then won't you join me when we march to London?'

Elijah laughs and shakes his head. 'You tried that already, and my answer's the same. We don't march for no one.'

The gypsy turns as the covered wagons transporting the families bring colour to the lane. They pause briefly for Elijah to take his place, and then the children wave, the lurchers bark, and the wagon horses take up the strain once more.

Wilf watches as they go, yearns to follow them north, but instead he turns for Hembury. Ahead of him, the impatient motor car honks its horn as it screeches off down the lane.

'Where are you going?' Victor calls. 'You only just got back . . .'

'There's a meeting in the village. I said I'd be there.'

Wilf does not catch Victor's eye. Instead, he slings his jacket over his shoulder, and follows the trail of exhaust fumes.

Autumn brings bouts of heavy rain. The fallow deer stags stop bellowing, and the russet squirrels hunker down in their dreys. Victor repairs his boots, hammering new leather soles on to them with tacks. He sits back to admire his handiwork.

'Are you coming?' asks Wilf, worried that the answer might be no, since they seem to argue more often than not these days.

His father glances up with a tired smile. 'I'm looking forward to it,' he says.

Together they walk down the darkening lane while around them the trees sigh and the hedges whisper. It is easy to believe that ghosts of the Monmouth Rebellion still hide in these hills. They reach the outskirts of the village as the church bells begin to ring, their sharp peals splintering the twilight. Victor's steps seem to slow. 'Come on,' Wilf urges.

Victor coughs to clear his chest. 'It don't seem so long ago that we were walking to school and I were saying the same to you,' he says.

The villagers have gathered in the churchyard around the enormous stone that lies beneath a stunted oak tree. It is said that the stone fell from the Devil's pocket as he was banished howling to Hell, and because of its evil it must be turned each year or else bad luck will spread through their homes, and their crops will fail.

Wilf is one of six strong lads from the parish to be chosen this year. He takes his place next to Sam, and they dig the ends of their crowbars under the stone while the crowd spurs them on. The vicar starts to chant a prayer, and Wilf grunts as they take up the strain. The flickering lanterns illuminate the white mist that puffs from their mouths into the black night. Wilf feels the stone shift as it begins to roll on to its side. It is a vast boulder, the size of a table and weighing more than a tonne. The boys groan and bare their teeth, and the stone moves again and finally it flips, the weight sending it crashing over into its new position. The thud of its landing shakes the ground beneath the soles of his feet, and he feels stronger than he ever has.

The crowd whoops and hollers, and the boys slap each other on the back and grin at the group of girls who are laughing shyly at them. Victor smiles at Wilf as he claps, and Wilf remembers when they were close, and all he wanted to do was follow his father through the fields, and he wonders at how parents change.

'You coming to the Plough?' asks Dan. 'We're discussing Thomas Quicke.'

'I can't tonight. I want to walk back with my da. But I'll be at the next meeting.'

'See you on Friday, then.'

'See you.'

Wilf is surprised to see Victor talking to Celia Cottam; their neighbour has barely returned home since moving to London.

She smiles at Wilf as he approaches. 'You're at least a foot taller than last time I saw you,' she says.

'He's no boy any more,' says Victor.

'How is your brother, ma'am?' asks Wilf. 'Do he still talk around the country?'

His father sighs. 'Miss Cottam don't want to get into that.'

'It's all right,' she says. 'He's very well, thank you. Working all hours in Parliament, so he rarely has time for the hustings. It's a shame; he loved that part of it.'

'You can tell him some of us is still trying to spread the word.'

'I'm so glad to hear that. Do you remember Raymond?'

'Of course – who could forget such a man? I should dearly like to hear him speak again.'

'And I'm sure you will. Did you know he has set up a newspaper? It might interest you. It's more like a pamphlet at the moment, but we are confident it will grow as it finds a place among the workers.'

'I'd be very interested to see it.'

'I have a copy at Littlecombe. Come over tomorrow. I'll give it to you.'

'That would be most kind.'

She smiles. 'I have a feeling you will go far, Wilf Bolt. Keep speaking out. If you are ever in London, I will introduce you to our editor, Miles Hartman. There might even be work if you want it, handing out leaflets, perhaps something at the printers. We're always grateful for spare hands. I'll write down the address for you tomorrow. I'd better go. That's my father calling.'

Celia takes her leave, joining Joseph Cottam, who has been waving his walking stick from the gate.

Wilf turns to Victor with a grin. 'Did you hear? She thinks I'll go far.' His father does not seem to share his enthusiasm, but he cannot dampen Wilf's spirits. He sees doors opening, paths branching into new lives. He breathes the night air deep into his lungs; he has left school, he imagines London, the whole world at his fingertips . . .

'What meeting were you talking about to the lad before?' asks Victor.

'Dan? We're working out how to help the Quicke family. Thomas couldn't pay the rent again, so the Hemburys' man Webster told him he'd have to go, and sold his cattle to pay his debts. That herd can be traced back to his grandfather. Thomas was found by his children swinging in the shippen two days later.'

'I'm truly sorry to hear it. I know he struggled with drink.'

'That was his da. Died of it a while back. Thomas took over, and made more of a success of the place, but with prices falling, it's been impossible. While they look for a new tenant, there are three workers out of a job too. One of them is Dan. His four-year-old's already bird-scaring to earn pennies.'

Victor whistles. 'Times are bad, and set to grow worse.'

Wilf lets out an exasperated sigh. 'That's why you must join us.'

'Join who?'

'There's a group in the village . . .'

'I thought you were going to step back from causing trouble.'

'I never agreed to that.'

'What do you hope to achieve?'

'We will make them ask who will do their ploughing if they cut our wages? Who will cut their corn if they make us work longer hours?'

'Why kick a nest of hornets? You got good prospects, but if his lordship finds out you're meddling with unions, you'll be out.'

Wilf snorts. 'Remember what Uncle Robbo said . . .'

The anger flashes in Victor's eyes. 'Your Uncle Robbo's been fighting for twelve year and got nowhere. We're bottom of the order, boy. Whether it be the mines or the army, the stables or the woods, the village or the town. There ain't no way out. Believe me, I've tried.'

'Sometimes I wonder whose side you're on. You know, Dan

told me what happened to his brother, Ned Spiller. The same man that Robbo spoke of. It was you that grassed him up.'

'As I said to Robbo, he were wrong to cross Miss Celia.'

'He were desperate. What the Hemburys did to his family turned him sour, and he had a baby on the way. Don't you remember what that was like?'

Victor falls silent. The stones crunch beneath their feet. The sound of revelry drifts up from the village.

'I suppose you know you took Ned's job, and all?' says Wilf.

'I don't want to talk about this.'

'His dad were head groom before him, and his grandad before that. His dad went to war with Viscount Damerel and never came back. Died in his second week in France.'

'I missed him. I went out a while later,' says Victor quietly.

'I know. His death left the opening for you.'

'I told you I don't want to talk about it.'

'It's not the war I'm talking about, it's before then . . .' But Victor is striding on ahead. Wilf calls after him: 'Did you know they never even paid his last wage? The family lost the lodge house – where we used to live. They were split up: their mother had to take a better paid job the other side of Honiton. The older brother took apprenticeship with a wheelwright in Ottery. Two of the girls went into service in Exeter. Only Ned and Dan stayed in the village, with an aunt, so Ned could keep on at the stables. It was always promised he would be head groom like his father. Then we came along, and the Hemburys change a man's fate just like that.'

Victor has reached the gate. He turns to look at Wilf. 'You can't change what's past.'

But Wilf cannot stop. All the injustice is boiling inside him; he wants Victor to understand. 'But that ain't the worst of it. Did you know there's more than a handful of families in the village whose womenfolk were used by the Hemburys for their own pleasure, treated like chattels over the years? It's said Ned's grandad was the fifth earl's bastard.'

'Stop now!'

'Even the fact they were blood kin meant nothing to those people . . .'

'I said stop . . .'

'What happened to you? Other folk say you were once a hero. But you're not. You even let my mother walk all over you. How could you live with it, when you knew her heart belonged to someone else?'

'Don't you ever mention that again,' says Victor, slamming the gate between them. 'Or . . .'

'What?'

'I'll not live under the same roof as you a moment longer.'

CHAPTER 42

Celia is meeting the Ropers at the Royal Hospital in Chelsea. When it is time to go in, Iris and Ellie wait on a bench outside while Matthew and Celia enter the room. Matthew is nervous in a suit and tie. Celia introduces herself as his nurse, a white lie that is necessary to hide her journalistic bent, and somehow serves to dissolve her own apprehensions.

They sit down opposite the two men from the Ministry of Pensions, who are shuffling their papers and peering over their glasses. One has curly hair, the other is bald; both are tight-lipped. They run their fingers down the chart. 'Four missing toes, two on each foot?'

Matthew nods.

'Have you found yourself regular employment?'

'That's the thing . . .'

'Because there must be plenty you can do. You have a more fortunate injury than many.'

'But . . .'

'Your payments will be reduced in line with all disability payments. We do not want to encourage you *not* to work.' The two men look at each other, and nod.

Celia clears her throat. 'With respect,' she says, 'Mr Roper is unable to work because he suffers from more than the loss of his toes. He suffers from a terrible depression brought on by the things he saw during the war.'

'Such an injury is not prohibitive to work.'

'No. But being so ill that you cannot get out of bed is.'

The men stare. She encourages Matthew. He swallows, touches his neck. The bald man taps his pen on the table. 'The war was over twelve years ago. It cannot be said to still be affecting men's minds.'

'Why not? Would you not consider a disability such as that in a man with no legs, who is confined to a chair and so develops heart disease, one which is having a secondary effect on him? The heart disease is still caused by the war.'

'We have had this man assessed by one of our panel doctors—'

'This kind of illness requires a certain type of understanding that a regular doctor may not be party to—'

'How do we know that he was not like this before the war?'

'We cannot provide physical evidence, apart from that offered by his wife and family, who surely are best placed . . .'

'We cannot provide physical mention in his war records.'

'Because the illness did not manifest itself until now.'

'Then what is this illness you keep talking about? Explain how it manifests itself.'

Celia looks at Matthew. 'You must explain.'

Matthew blinks once, then begins. 'I want to work, sirs. But when it comes, it's as if a pool of black oil leaks into my brain so that all my thoughts are covered in it. Sometimes I believe the only way I can get away is if I . . .' He pauses for a moment. There is shame in suicide. '. . . end my own life.'

'Then perhaps you have a disorder of the character, and should be sent to an asylum.'

The men start to scribble on their papers.

'No!' Celia bangs the table to get their attention. Even Matthew looks startled. 'You are not allowed to do that any more. Do you know what an asylum is like? Would you really be content to send a man like this, who gave his mental health for this country, to languish in his own mess in a cell . . . These are men who are proud. They don't want charity; they want to work, but many of them can't, or at least can't do

326

the things they used to be able to do. The government *must* step in to help. It is the state's responsibility.'

'Are you denying that men like this can be cured?'

'I am not denying that. But in many cases, if psychological problems aren't dealt with in the correct and humane way, then they become more violent, and more ingrained. That is why you are seeing the effects of the war only just beginning to manifest themselves in men like Matthew. You must come to see that these men are almost braver than those with evident injuries, because they have to face ignorance and abuse and a lack of understanding every day from myopic, parochial, entrenched bigots like yourselves.'

She leans back, her face flushed, her heart racing, slightly taken aback to rediscover the fire she had when she was eighteen. The bald man puts down his pen. 'Thank you for your passionate and eloquent explanation. We will be in touch.' He smiles, and it is not unkind.

Outside, Iris has chewed her nails down to the quick. She crosses the neat courtyard as soon as they appear.

'She was good,' says Matthew. 'Really good.'

Iris takes Celia's hands in hers. 'I knew you would be. I knew it when we first met.' She links her arm through Celia's while Matthew and Ellie walk ahead. 'Will you come back to Limehouse with us? There's someone I want you to meet. She's called Daphne. She runs the pub with her husband. He can cope in the quiet, but when it gets busy he has to hide away, else he becomes violent. He's up in front of a committee tomorrow. Do you think you can help them?'

'I can try my best.'

Celia's first piece about the treatment of Matthew Roper is picked up by newspapers around the country. The flush of excitement, the buzz of adrenaline that something she has done is commanding such attention, leaves her glowing for days.

She is sitting at her desk in the Shoreditch office, Hope's head warm on her foot as she types, when the receptionist calls over again: 'It's another one for you.' Celia nods and takes the call. They are coming in daily from veterans in lodging houses and hostels, church homes and on park benches across the nation. But this time she recognises the voice at the other end. 'Celia, I want to congratulate you. And to offer myself as a witness if you need me.'

'Alan Haynes! I thought you were retired.'

'No, no. Can't put me out to pasture quite yet.' Her mind is filled with memories of the anguish of those days waiting for him to write. She smiles to herself. Her pride in her current achievements is all the better because she did not rely on nepotism like those privileged men in their clubs.

'I'm so very proud of you, young lady. I'd like to help if I can. The sooner the public understands that mental health is as important as physical health, then our work will gain support . . . and funding.'

The doctor is right: already the newspaper is receiving letters from angry members of the public who are shocked by the way ex-servicemen are being treated.

Days later, Celia is surprised to hear Miles calling for everyone to stop what they're doing. She blushes as he asks them to gather around her desk. He smiles down at her. 'I want to congratulate you,' he says. 'Though we don't pretend it is solely down to Celia, this campaign to help ex-servicemen has certainly brought us more readers, and of course more staff. While others struggle with unemployment, and cuts in wages, we are able to expand to another four pages.'

Celia notes that Raymond has remained at his desk at the end of the room. She makes her way over to deliver her latest article, which he takes and puts to one side.

'Are you not happy with the work I'm doing?' she asks.

'I'll read it later,' he says.

'I mean in general.'

He looks up at her. 'You're doing great things. Didn't Miles just tell everybody?'

'Somehow that sounds as if you don't agree.'

He sighs, and pushes his chair back from the desk, stretching his legs out in front of him and pressing his fingers into his nose, beneath where his glasses bite. 'Of course I do. But even this expansion is still not enough. We need more members to make a significant impact.'

'Give it time.'

'The Comintern says we don't have time.'

He looks at her, and for the first time she sees something frightening in the fixed determination in his eyes. There is a loyalty among Raymond and these men she has yet to meet that she could never come between. But she doesn't like the way they lean on him. Sometimes he has the look of a hunted animal, like the foxes at Coombe – beautiful, clever but always wary. She recollects the fear in the eyes of the creature she once released, her hands sticky with blood, and shivers. 'So what are they asking you to do?' she says.

He doesn't answer, just shuffles some papers awkwardly.

She reaches out, but he shrugs off her hand. 'If it makes you uncomfortable . . .' she starts.

'Revolution isn't meant to be comfortable,' he snaps. Then runs a hand through his hair. 'I'm sorry. There's a lot of pressure.' He glances around the room, as if to make sure no one is listening.

'What's going on, Raymond? You used to talk to me about everything.'

'That was before you got so busy with the committees . . .'

'I'm listening now.'

He stands and takes a deep breath, indicating for her to step towards the window. The sound of traffic three floors below drifts upwards. Raymond leans closer. 'The party wants Miles to take a stronger line,' he says. 'They cannot understand why he is so conciliatory.'

'He doesn't want to put readers off. They need to be eased into a change in thinking. Do it too swiftly and it scares them.'

'Do it slowly, and there won't be change for decades. The time to fight is now, and the party wants him gone.'

'But he's doing a good job. Our readers like him.'

'Life is not a popularity contest.' He draws himself upright, taking her hand, and as she so often does, she wishes she felt truer passion, for him and for the party. He smoothes her hair away from her face, as Miles makes his way over to them. 'Look. Forget I said anything.'

Raymond sits at his desk again.

Miles smiles as he reaches them, but his eyes are weary.

'Did you think about what we discussed?' asks Raymond.

'That we should stop printing sport?' Miles shakes his head. 'I think that would be a mistake.'

'We believe it is a capitalist construction.'

'But it is popular with our readers.'

'We are meant to be a mouthpiece of the party.'

'I thought we were meant to be a mouthpiece for the workers . . .'

'You will regret going against them.'

The threat hangs heavy in the air, but their exchange is cut short by the sound of angry voices. Celia turns to see four policemen muscling their way in through the door. The journalists stand to block them. The police order them to move aside. Raymond clenches his fists. Celia puts a hand on his arm to calm him but he shakes it off.

'You've got no right,' says Raymond.

'We've got every right, Mr White,' says the oldest policeman, who is evidently in charge of the others. 'These are dark days, and the government takes a dim view of all seditious material.'

'You'll find nothing here,' says Miles.

'Then you won't mind us looking. Now step aside.' He indicates to the others to start their search.

Celia's mouth is dry. 'What exactly is it you're looking for?'

'We've had a tip-off,' says the policeman. 'Incendiary paper-work of a Bolshevik nature.'

'Tip-off from who?'

'We have people everywhere,' he says ominously.

The constables rifle through drawers, opening and shutting them, knocking over stacks of paper. Raymond mutters under his breath. 'Fascists.'

'What did you say?' The constable returns, folding his arms and staring back into Raymond's eyes.

'Cup of tea anyone?' asks Celia.

'Good idea,' says Miles.

The cross-armed policeman shakes his head, but his attitude seems to soften a little. Then he spots Hope and his mouth curves upwards into a smile. He crouches down, reaches out to scratch her belly as she rolls over. 'What a lovely dog,' he says.

'Are you sure you wouldn't like a drink? It's a cold day out there.'

'How about it, lads?'

The other police officers stop. 'That would be grand, madam.'

Once they have finished their tea and said their goodbyes, and stroked Hope one more time, the policemen finally leave. The door closes behind them, and the entire office breathes a sigh of relief.

Raymond helps to tidy the desks. 'Time to fight fire with fire. They won't stop now. They'll grow worse.'

Celia glares at him. 'Why were they here? What are you hiding?'

'Try and remember whose side you're on,' he says.

CHAPTER 43

France

Every morning Edward lifts the mask out of its box. The enamel paint is chipped in places, but the face is still there, his past staring back at him: Edward Damerel, viscount, brave captain, eldest son and heir, preserved for ever, but dead to the world for ever. He fixes it in place, knows the cold metal will soon be too warm, abrasive against his puckered skin.

Today is market day, and they have four horses to sell. He looks forward to these days; they are something to work towards. He smiles to himself, briefly wonders what Spiller would have made of it all, and is surprised that instead of the grim and painful memory of the loyal old groom's death, he recalls the man in life, standing stiffly to attention, buttons shining, chest puffed out, as they left to serve king and country all those years ago. He wonders how Spiller's son is faring, whether he is cut from the same cloth as the father: proud of his association with the Hemburys, proud to continue the tradition.

Edward flicks the reins to urge the horses on. Aurélie sits beside him, as she always does. She has blossomed into a long-limbed girl with a shy smile. With their blonde hair, they could almost be father and daughter. Behind the cart Jonah and Louis ride two of their horses, and lead another one each. Jonah's mount is a dappled grey, and reminds Edward of his own horse of that name. He is glad that the markets are no longer full of the horses and mules that were left by the army when they returned home. He bought every one he could, nursing them back to health with Aurélie, and breeding from the best. It has given him a purpose, keeping those fine old cavalry and heavy horses going for future generations.

In the marketplace, people still stop to stare. It took him a while to realise they were not looking at him, but at the children, these brazen Hun orphans who are not shy, because Madame Sauveur has taught them they do not need to hide away. Aurélie tilts her chin like a visiting queen, and Edward feels a surge of pride for the way she focuses ahead, ignoring the nudges and whispers.

The boys slide to the ground, Aurélie too. She nods greetings to the onlookers. She has a quick smile, and Edward knows that many of the regulars that gather around are not necessarily here only for the horses. The farmers admire the beasts, shooting sideways glances at Edward, at the English soldier who decided to stay, and who strikes as hard a bargain as any Frenchman.

Jonah talks to one man, walking him around, pointing out the animal's strong legs, muscle, its healthy teeth, its powerful shoulders. The farmer nods and mutters. Jonah looks at Edward, who encourages him to continue. Louis, the more confident of the boys, joins in, and before long the man is leading the horse away, while the two boys count the money in their palms. Their heads are almost touching, the blond and the dark, and with a lurch Edward suddenly remembers conspiring with his brother Freddie, their own heads bent together as they dangled their arms in the pond looking for newts. He blinks and the memories disappear. He has a new family, of sorts.

Edward hands Madame Sauveur the money from the market. 'Another success,' she says. 'Congratulations. Your reputation is growing. Soon you will not have to go to market. People will come to you.'

This does not fill Edward with the horror he would expect, rather he feels his chest expand with something like pleasure. They watch as Jonah and Louis wheel the cart under cover, and prepare to put the horses out. They are in high spirits, acting the fool, vying for Aurélie's attention. She smiles, the dimples in her cheeks deepening. She is a different child to the one that sat next to him on the journey here all those years ago: she is proof that people can change.

He glances at Madame Sauveur. The natural light shows up the wrinkles and creases beneath the make-up. She is older than he first suspected.

'Why does she still not speak?' says Edward.

'We are all still hiding things.'

He ignores the barb. 'You never told me how she came to you.'

'She didn't. I found her *abandonnée*. She had been locked inside a cellar. I had to shave her head for her hair was so matted. She had scratched herself raw. She was surviving on rainwater and insects that came through a drain.'

'Does she remember any of it?'

Madame Sauveur snorts. 'I am sure. She was six when I found her. One day she will tell her story, as I'm sure will you. But until then we can only return the love she has shown us.'

'I don't deserve it.'

'Perhaps not. But you have it.'

In the evenings he helps the children to read and write. The atmosphere is relaxed in the flickering candlelight, so different from lessons at boarding school. He watches Aurélie trace the words with her fingers. She looks up, and his heart melts: her smile is like the sun rising. She sits alone. Further down the table from Aurélie, some younger children are practising their handwriting. On one side of the room, one of the older girls is reading aloud to a group. Edward walks closer to listen. As the girl's voice rises and falls, he thinks of his sister, Ginny.

335

When he last saw her, she must have been this age. She will surely be married by now. Did he really teach her to stalk grasshoppers in the long grass and count the time on dandelion clocks? That boy is a child he no longer recognises.

He is broken from his reverie by the sound of fighting. He turns and sees a crowd has gathered at the far end of the table. Jonah is dragging Louis from his chair, and pummelling him at the same time. Edward runs to split them up. It is not as easy as it once was: they are almost as tall as him, and he is always astonished at the speed and ferocity of anger in these young people.

The ring of children grows quiet. Edward holds the boys apart. 'What is all this about?'

Jonah and Louis do not look at each other, but glare at invisible spots on the floor. The other children peel guiltily away. Edward feels the fight leave the boys, and he lets each of them loose. They stand, heads hanging, reduced to being children again. A purple bruise is beginning to bloom around Jonah's eye.

'If you won't tell me . . .'

The boys glance at each other, but remain tight-lipped.

'Then I will have to tell Madame, and she will ask you to leave. We cannot have violence here.'

Louis starts to cry. 'No, please. I will be good.'

'Well?' Edward crosses his arms.

'He called me *bâtard*.'

'A loaf of bread?'

The boys look at each other and laugh.

'*Non. Bâtard*.'

'And was that a reason to hurt him? Because he called you a name?'

Louis shrugs.

'Bread or bastard, it's only a word.'

Jonah chews his lip.

'Then how can we resolve this problem?'

Louis sniffs. 'I am sorry,' he says.

Jonah nods. 'I am sorry too.'

They shake hands, and within minutes are working quietly side by side again. Edward leaves to go and help Madame Sauveur in the kitchen. 'You are good with the children,' she says.

'It is no harder than dealing with squabbles between my men.'

'Then you must have had their respect too, for it is respect that commands their attention.'

He nods. He was a good officer. He can see that now. But he knows it was not always the case. 'Would you understand if I said war had been good for me?'

'But of course. You could allow the war to ruin the rest of your life. Or you could embrace it for the lessons it has taught you. Humility. Understanding . . . You cannot change your past, but you can choose your future.'

He looks around the table. She is right. He is learning that simple things make him happy. The taste of a good wine, fresh food. The smell of cut hay. The sound of a child's laughter. The sun on his back, the rain on his skin. There is satisfaction, fulfilment in the end of the day, settled around the dining-room table, as the children dig into the food they have grown. Sometimes it puts him in mind of the dining room at Coombe. He imagines walking from there into the panelled Great Hall next door, where the list of ancestors waits for the next in line to be added. But he does not want to go back to being who he was. He does not believe in that way of life any more. He thinks of the man Bolt, who saved him that day, and, instead of cursing him as he usually does, he silently thanks him.

After dinner the mask is rubbing painfully. He goes into the hall and settles on a window seat. The children are busy getting ready for bed, running up and down the stairs, looking for nightclothes and towels, water is coursing through the creaky pipes. His face is so sore. He thinks he is alone. He reaches up to remove the mask. He pulls it away from the skin, feels the air like a soothing balm. But suddenly Aurélie is there. He reaches to put the mask back on, but Aurélie stops his arm. 'No,' she says. 'No more.' He freezes. It is the first time he has heard her speak.

Aurélie sits next to him on the window seat. The shutters are closed, and the only light comes from further along the corridor, where it spills out of the dining room. She makes herself more comfortable. She begins to talk in stilted sentences, as if her tongue is still trying to remember how to work. 'My father was killed fighting the Germans when they first came to our town. My mother was part of a network. She helped people escape from occupation so they could fight. She had a friend who helped too. He became more than a friend. He tried to replace my father. But it was a lie. One day the Germans came for her. Michel had told them what she was doing. The soldiers were all smiles and kind words at first. The same as Michel. But my mother knew what was going to happen. She locked me in the cellar so that I would be safe. I hear the soldiers do what they want while Michel was there. She did not scream. She did not cry. She did not beg. When they finished with her, I hear the shot. Then no more.

'The soldiers tried to break the door down, but the door was too strong. And then there was noise and fighting and they went away. I could not get out. I could hear the bombs. The guns. Sometimes I cried out to people in the street, but no one heard me. There was some food stored in boxes. There was water when it rained. I was there for so many days, in the dark, with my mother dead on the other side of the door. No one came for her, apart from the dogs.'

She looks up at him, and he sees a kind of relief that she has given voice to the demons. 'Those men . . .' She drops her eyes. 'It is worse to be ugly on the inside.'

Edward looks again at the mask in his hand, at the cracked paint, the threadbare eyelashes, the splash of colour on the cheekbone, faded now. His old self, the handsome arrogant young viscount, is slowly being eradicated. He stands and walks along the corridor to the looking glass in the hall. He has avoided his reflection for more than twelve years. He raises his head and meets his own gaze. He sees a stranger with his blue eyes, a stranger who is not nearly as terrible as the creature of his imagination.

CHAPTER 44

Celia greets Iris and Matthew warmly outside the Houses of Parliament. Iris adjusts her hat. 'I can't believe we're here,' she says, tilting her head to look up at the gothic building, majestically peaceful in the midst of the London traffic.

'I can't believe we're here, either,' says Celia. 'It's a long way from collapsing in tears at the railway station.'

'I've brought a handkerchief,' Iris smiles.

As Celia watches the other families she has chosen as they support and encourage their fathers and sons, she realises this is as much about them as it is about the men. She gathers the little group together and they make their way inside. In the central lobby, the sounds of the motorcars, the policeman directing traffic, the rattle of the streetcars, are dulled. Footsteps echo on the tiled floor, and the group shuffles closer together, gazing up at the arches and statues in awe.

Celia searches for George among the men who hurry this way and that, but instead of her brother, she is stunned to see Freddie Hembury watching her with amused grey eyes.

The years fall away, and it is as if she only saw him yesterday. She cannot help smiling back, and he immediately makes his way over, adeptly avoiding bumping into the stream of people.

'Miss Celia Cottam,' he says. 'It is still Miss, isn't it?'

He takes her hand and kisses it, and the touch sends a jolt of electricity along her arm. She is flooded with a mixture of guilt at the betrayal of Raymond, but relief that she is not made of ice, as she was beginning to suspect. She is sure

341

Freddie holds on to her for a beat longer than he should. 'How long has it been?' she says, keeping her voice steady.

'Almost five years.' He does not hesitate.

'Can it be really? You don't seem to have changed.' Even as she says it, she realises it isn't true: he does look older, there are deep frown lines in his forehead, and around his eyes.

'I'm a little greyer . . . but you' – he stands back – 'you seem to have grown younger.'

'How is Coombe?'

'I don't go much . . .'

He hesitates, and she suddenly pines for the way they used to be so easy in each other's company. She has never experienced the same with Raymond. 'The last time I saw you,' she says, 'you'd been talking to Victor Bolt—'

He holds up his hand, and bends closer, speaking urgently. 'Don't ever mention that again. Please.'

'But you told your wife?'

'In a manner of speaking.'

'But . . .'

'Please, Celia. Never.' He steps away and draws himself up to his full height, raising his voice. 'And who are these fine people?'

She turns to introduce her group. 'Ex-servicemen, here to talk about the shoddy way they've been treated by successive governments.'

Matthew gives a little bow, and the others take off their hats. She wishes they wouldn't.

Freddie smiles his greeting before turning back to her. 'I'm glad you are still fighting the good fight. Your constancy is one of your greatest attributes.'

'How about you? You're a politician now?'

'Oh no,' he laughs. 'Not that you'd approve, but I like to take up my seat in the upper house occasionally. Today I thought I'd pop over to have lunch with a friend.' He points, and it is only now that she notices a tall man with fierce eyes and a neat moustache. Her heart sinks as she recognises Clifford Montague, who is often under attack in the *Workers' Week* for the fascist views of his party.

She is surprised when Clifford advances and shakes her warmly by the hand. 'Veterans, I hear? Well done you.' He continues to the little group behind her. He moves easily among them, shaking their hands and thanking them for their service, taking no notice of the missing limbs, the scarred faces, the twitches and tics. She wants to hate the man, but she can see how he charms, listening to each individual story, looking the men in the eye, treating them as equals. It makes her uneasy, this blatant difference between inside and out; one can never truly know what is going on in another person's mind.

'They remind me of those men you had on the farm,' says Freddie. He is so close that their arms are touching. 'You should take this lot there. It might help them too.'

She glances at him in astonishment, for he has given voice to something that she knew but has been unable to express until now: that Littlecombe is a sanctuary with the power to heal.

At last George appears. He nods a perfunctory hello to Freddie, who reciprocates before taking his leave. He holds Celia's hand in his again and bows. 'A real pleasure,' he says, and his fingers burn an impression on hers. 'I pray our next meeting is sooner than our last.' Her heart leaps and her head castigates it as a fraud: here she is, longing to spend a few more minutes with a man who has never wanted to commit to her, never seen her as an equal, and who now consorts with fascists. It is no different to how successive governments have treated her veterans. She tears her eyes away from his departing back.

George ushers their group up the stone steps and along corridors until they reach another vast room. Celia's battle for the servicemen has become so high profile that he has arranged this meeting with politicians from all parties – including the opposition. A long table is set with glasses of water, and pieces of paper. The opulent surroundings – patterned carpets, elaborate wallpaper, gilt-framed paintings, panelling – remind her of Coombe Hall, no doubt because she has just seen Freddie. She pushes him from her mind, watches George as he makes introductions. He is filling out into the image of their father – but not only in stature; once he would not have considered working with men from the other side of the House, but he has learnt the art of compromise.

When everyone is seated, George begins by addressing Celia, but she retorts, 'Don't ask me. Ask them. This is their moment.'

George nods, and turns to direct his questions to the men. Matthew is the first to talk. He starts tentatively, but soon gets into the swing of it with George's encouragement. Celia settles into her seat, happy to watch each family take up their cause. They discuss how the government should deal with Armistice Day, and how there are too few places of rehabilitation. They discuss their fear of the return of war, and its hidden effects on a man.

When it is over, and the politicians and servicemen and their families have shaken hands, beaming as if they have been friends for years, they make their way back down to the lobby. It seems there is a bottleneck of people trying to leave, and George goes ahead to talk to the men at the door. The sound of jeering and shouting drifts to Celia's ears; there is some kind of kerfuffle outside.

The veterans look worried as the waves of sound come and go: singing, chanting, a policeman's whistle, a woman's scream, more shouting, growing louder and seemingly closer. Iris grips Matthew's hand as he clearly starts to panic, his eyes flickering to the doorway and around the room, as if searching for alternative ways out.

More policemen arrive. Celia glimpses the flash of a drawn sword as they run out into the daylight. She tries to see what

344

is going on, but the men guarding the door yell at her to stay back.

She turns to join her group, but she finds herself blocked by the chest of Clifford Montague. She feels insignificant in the shadow of his towering frame. He looks down. 'Tell me, how does it feel to be a traitor to your country?' he asks in his polite drawl, as if he is simply asking about the weather. 'I honestly don't know how you lot can sleep at night.'

She frowns, leaning away to put some distance between them. 'What are you talking about?'

'That lot of scum out there with their socialist banners, protesting about capitalism under the guise of unemployment, and trying to muscle their way in. There's more than one poster with the name of the *Workers' Week* scrawled across it. Isn't that your rag?'

'You must be mistaken . . .' She feels fear prickle on the back of her neck, and she tries not to show it.

'It seems your little plan didn't work.'

'What plan?'

'It's evident that you are here as a decoy, Miss Cottam. What were you hoping? That you could distract everyone inside with your pretty little innocent face while the rest of them stormed the Bastille?'

Her heart is pulsing in her neck and her hands are growing clammy. She digs her nails into her palms and takes a deep breath. 'If you're frightened of a peaceful demonstration,' she says so loudly that some of the others glance their way, 'then your reputation has been blown out of all proportion . . .'

'Peaceful!' he snorts. 'There are three policemen out there who will need hospital treatment.'

To her relief, George appears at her side. 'What's going on?'

'I think the question should be why has your sister been allowed to come inside. She is clearly a threat to us. To democracy.'

'Oh nonsense. It's nothing to do with her.'

Clifford raises his eyebrows. 'I'm not sure that's how

everyone else will see it.' Then he spins on his heel, saluting as he passes the servicemen, and jogs away up the stairs.

'Are you all right?' asks George.

Celia nods. 'I promise I knew nothing about any demonstration. I would never have jeopardised their day.'

They both look at the group of veterans, who are still huddled in an anxious knot.

'Less of a demonstration, more of a riot, by all accounts. You're going to have to ask some serious questions. Why don't we take everyone back upstairs? It might be quieter up there.'

It is early evening by the time it is safe for them to leave. The police escort them over trampled posters, broken bottles, bits of torn clothing – all the signs of a brawl. There have been at least eleven arrests, including two journalists from the *Workers' Week*, charged with breach of the peace. Another is jailed for writing the article that told activists to come to the House of Commons in support of the veterans – something that Celia had missed on publication.

When she finally walks through her own front door, feet aching, head throbbing, she finds Raymond banging away at his typewriter, cheeks red with excitement, hair dishevelled. He pauses to look up at her. She notes there is a rip in his jacket.

'How could you have done that?' she asks. 'How could you have hijacked their day?'

He stops to look at her, and she sees a new intent in his eyes. 'It was too good an opportunity to miss.'

'And you've been planning this all along . . . and not said anything to me?' She is not sure which is more painful.

He sighs and tries to take one of her hands. 'The public is really behind those veterans,' he says. 'I knew we'd get a lot of support.'

'Need it have been so violent?'

'It's no different to how the government treats its enemies. Think how they behaved during the General Strike . . .'

'And now you've given them the moral high ground. And you used my men to do it.'

'"My men"? You sound just like them.'

'You embarrassed George too. Everyone knows you used to work together.'

'I don't care about George,' he says, thrusting his chair backwards as he stands to face her. 'His government might as well be Tories. I've seen how the prime minister fawns over aristocrats and wealthy women. He even proposes cuts in public spending and wages! And of course your brother is sticking by MacDonald. Doesn't even have the guts to go against him.' He juts out his chin. 'The Comintern don't want you seeing him for now.'

'They can't dictate that. He's my brother!'

'They believe Labour are as bad as the fascists.'

'They're mad. Please see that.'

'How can you say that, after Labour refused to allow us to affiliate with them? They cut us off. They're traitors to the working man and to the socialist cause. But they won't survive this. The end of the Labour party is coming. And then you can see George as much as you want. The Conservatives will be gone too: they tried to frighten voters with talk of a revolution, but they didn't expect it to actually happen. Well, those capitalist dogs had better watch out, because it's coming.' He pauses, eyes glittering maliciously, then delivers a mean blow. 'Perhaps it is too difficult for you to see, because your own family are capitalists. People who have money are all the same.'

'You can't always blame everything on money,' she counters.

'As spoken by someone for whom money is no issue.'

'Money that you seem happy to live off. I can't help where I come from any more than you can. And you didn't exactly come from the gutter. Your father owned a shoe shop.'

Now his face darkens, and that look comes into his eyes. He clenches his jaw. 'The father that disowned me? In the same way as did my friends, my mother – my country?'

She strengthens her resolve. She must challenge him now, or it will be never. 'Why is it that you're happy to take my money, to live off it, yet you deny me a status, an opinion?'

'Don't be so fatuous,' he says, his nostrils flaring. 'You know that I believe in fair distribution. What's mine is yours, and what's yours is mine.' He suddenly sounds contrite as he takes her hands. 'And I'm very grateful for it. And I'm very grateful for you. I'm sorry if you felt I used you . . . and "your men". I didn't want to tell you in case you talked me out of it. The party is calling for direct action.'

'Ah yes. The party. Why do you let it push you around? You seem to love it more than you ever loved me – *if* you ever did love me,' she adds pulling away from him, her bravery growing with every word.

'For me the party will always come first. It's greater than love. Why can't you understand that?'

'I do understand,' she says. 'And I hope it makes you happy, because I'm leaving.'

He stares at her, his mouth falling open. 'You can't.'

Her gaze does not waver. 'I can. I'm going back to Littlecombe tomorrow.' She feels a rush of relief as she says it. She can already feel the weight lifting from her shoulders, taste the fresh air of freedom, feel the spring rain on her cheek. And Freddie's words still echo within her: Littlecombe is a haven that holds solace not only for her, but for others too. The answer to a productive life was within reach all along.

CHAPTER 45

Freddie searches the room for Elizabeth, spotting her through the haze of cigarette smoke. The lighting has turned everything blood red, as if they are dancing in a womb. His wife is dressed from head to toe in a scarlet evening dress that clings to her slender frame. Her skin is white as hoar frost against the velvet material, a white silk sash around her waist. She is dancing with a man who has the poise and bearing of the military, the straight back, the determined angle of his shoulders, by his height and build he could be Edward.

Freddie exhales sharply. Ever since Victor told him that Edward could be alive, the conviction has grown inside him, so that he catches sight of Edward everywhere: at the end of the street, in the shadows of the theatre, staring out of a passing motor car. It always takes him by surprise, the bitter cocktail of hope, anxiety, and finally despair. He fears he is becoming unhinged like his mother.

Elizabeth beckons, and, as he approaches, Cecil Fortescue turns; Edward is gone.

'Hembury!' cries Cecil. 'Come to reclaim your countess?'

Freddie nods, the guilt vying with the alcohol to take hold. These are Edward's old friends, this is Edward's life. What a sham! But even worse: it didn't have to be like this. Edward is out there somewhere, and Freddie is still living in his brother's shadow, unable to be his own man and follow his own dreams.

Elizabeth reaches out, her hand trailing down his chest. 'I told you you'd love it once you got here,' she shouts into his ear. Her hand crawls around his back and she pulls him close. Around them the smiling faces and swaying feathers and glittering jewels flash and float like phosphorescence in the sea. He pushes her away, into the arms of another man, this one with a garland of flowers around his neck. He was annoyed that she did not support his wish to look for Edward, cannot help flashes of wondering where his brother might be, what he might be doing. Yet perhaps she was right: what good would it do to look for him anyway? If his brother is alive, he does not want to come home: whatever he is doing, wherever he may be, he is happy enough to forget his family. Freddie finds an empty spot on a sofa between a couple who are entwined in each other's arms, and a young man with an impressive moustache. Somewhere someone is playing a church hymn on an organ. He takes the powder from his pocket, inhales, feels the rush begin to rise in his veins. He likes this moment best, the transition from sluggish confusion to steady conviction. He pushes himself to his feet, places the glass back among the remnants of the earlier feast on the table: the lobster shells and salmon, the red caviar smeared across a plate, the crushed meringue. A man in a white ski suit with fur trim is feeding strawberries to a woman in a red toga. The juice drips down her chin. Freddie is ready to face them all.

The Hemburys have filled their time with an endless stream of parties like this, each one bigger and more lavish than the last. While the rest of the world is swallowed up by a financial crisis, the harder they party. Since their catastrophic loss of money in the stock market crash, Freddie has relied entirely on Elizabeth's funds. She cannot really complain, since it was she who was desperate to invest it. It irks him that so much is gone. If only they'd something to show for it.

Then he reminds himself of how he behaved with Celia's money – frittering it away on the tea business. Still, he is glad he never used that money on the horses: though both projects have failed, at least the tea business isn't quite finished – yet. The latest problem has been with the workers – even in Ceylon there are trades unions, but Matthew is positive this is the last hurdle. Freddie is nonplussed. He cannot believe it will ever come to fruition, and Elizabeth seems happy to keep spending her money. Her only stipulation remains that Freddie must never mention Edward again. He dreads what she would say if he told her about Wilf. He fears how she might react to his dishonesty; he has left it so long now, he knows she would not forgive him – especially as she has taken a shine to the boy.

The sun is up when they leave. Freddie turns to admire the magnificent house. Elizabeth finds the car among the countless parked willy-nilly across the parkland. All around them people are stumbling and clambering into their cars, sounding their horns as they call to each other. The roof of the vehicle in front is down, the passengers standing on their seats. He can hear them singing opera as they bounce down the drive and away from Regent's Park.

They roll past the early-morning city, the men who sweep and mend the roads; the newspaper sellers and the market traders who watch the revellers pass with impassive faces; they have seen it all before. By the time they reach Cadogan Square, the bowler-hatted men are already stepping smartly out of their front doors, disapproval clear in their downturned mouths, their neatly oiled moustaches. Freddie waves and Elizabeth laughs, dragging her husband towards the front door as she blows kisses to their neighbours.

The maid bobs at the door. 'Sir Nicholas is in the sitting room,' she says, as Elizabeth puts her hand to her mouth.

'I'd forgotten you were coming,' she says as she rushes to greet her brother.

'Where on earth have you been?'

'Having fun.'

Elizabeth calls for the butler Ward, her voice echoing in the cavernous hall. The house is bright and airy, the windows in the sitting room stretch from ceiling to floor, overlooking the leafy garden square. Today's newspapers are strewn across the table and sofas. 'I've been here for hours,' says Nicholas. 'I've read them from cover to cover.'

'I'm so sorry,' says Elizabeth. 'What can I do to make it up to you?'

'A Scotch would go down a treat.'

Ward comes with a coffee and she waves it away. 'Scotch for the men and a brandy for me,' she says. Ward moves to the cabinet in the corner, pours the drinks and places them on the side tables.

'So tell us what's going on in the world, then,' says Elizabeth. 'Have they printed any photographs of the fantastic party we've just been at?'

'No. I'm happy to report Lord R has gone right off you lot. Thinks you should all be knuckling down rather than spending so much time partying.'

'Oh really. He's such a grouch. What does he want us to do? Mope about feeling sorry for ourselves? What else cheers readers up in a recession but seeing pictures of people having a grand old time? It's what sells his papers in the first place.'

Nicholas looks serious. 'He's right, you know. It doesn't look good. We should be setting a different example. We need to lead this country back to glory.'

'Don't be such an old stick-in-the-mud.' Elizabeth laughs and pours herself another glass of brandy. 'Freddie, talk some sense into my brother.' Elizabeth stretches out her legs and eases off her shoes, leaning her head back against the chair and looking at Freddie with one eyebrow raised.

But Freddie's mind is beginning to fill with anxieties as the drug wears off. He moves to the drinks cabinet, removes a small pot from the cupboard.

Nicholas sighs. 'I do wish you'd stop that. It's not good for the grey cells.'

Elizabeth rolls her head sideways to look at her brother. 'Everyone's doing it. You should try. It might lighten you up a bit.'

Nicholas frowns, then addresses Freddie again. 'Clifford was asking about you,' he says.

Freddie pours another drink and turns to Nicholas. He feels quite normal again. 'Sounds like his new party is gaining support.'

Nicholas nods. 'He's been abroad, talking to the Italians. He's impressed with the way they're handling things on the continent. He wants to coordinate some kind of defence strategy in case there's a war.'

'What sort of war?'

Nicholas raises an eyebrow. 'We've had enough of the chaotic pandering of government which has allowed the Bolsheviks and the Zionists to water down our country. The nation needs to be taken in hand. If it isn't, then men like your brother died for nothing.'

Freddie grips his glass and knocks back another slug of whisky. It is never long before the golden-haloed hero is dangled before him.

'You should stand for PM, darling brother,' says Elizabeth. 'You could rally anyone to the cause.'

'We've got Clifford for that,' says Nicholas.

There is only a small dusting of powder left in Freddie's pot. He inhales it, then wipes his finger around the inside of the casing, sucking the dust from his fingertips, feeling his gums and the tip of his tongue go numb. 'Clifford's a great man,' he says.

'I know you think that. It's why I came to see you. I was hoping you two would let him use Coombe for a while. He needs somewhere to train his men. Coombe would be perfect . . .'

'Absolutely!' says Freddie. An idea suddenly dawns on him. 'We could rent it out to him.'

'Freddie!' says Elizabeth. 'We could not . . .'

'Why not?'

'He's almost family.'

Freddie bites his tongue. He won't argue with his wife in front of her brother. He wants to say that they cannot keep spending money the way they do, but the Helstroms seem to have bottomless cash reserves: all they were lacking was a British title, but of course that is no longer the case.

Nicholas steps in. 'Perhaps he could use it as a base at first. While he canvasses support in the South West . . . I say, are you all right?'

Freddie's heart is beginning to spin. He feels the sweat prickle at his skin. His head aches. Nicholas is pointing but Freddie can't hear what he is saying, the rush of blood in his ears is too loud. Nicholas's face crumples into a frown, and now Freddie can feel the drip of warm liquid, and he puts his hand up to his face, and when he looks at his palm it is sticky with blood.

'Damn it,' he says, covering his nose and turning back to the cabinet. He uses the sleeve of his jacket to wipe at the sticky trickle. Red on red. He holds his finger against his nostril, willing it to coagulate. The room tilts, then rights.

'Here you go.' Nicholas is holding out a handkerchief.

Elizabeth shakes her head. 'Perhaps Nicholas is right and you should stop. This seems to be happening rather a lot . . .' Freddie feels the heat of shame engulf him. He does not dare remove the handkerchief from his nostrils for the moment. 'I mean, it can't be good, can it, darling?' He peers at her over his hand. 'Don't look like that. I'm not criticising. Just worried. You do tend to take things to the extreme.' She may be right. Sometimes he can't remember how the evening has gone. There are flashes and images, but no coherent narrative. She is disloyal to say this in front of Nicholas, but then they have always been close siblings. He feels a flash of irritation, takes the handkerchief away. The blood has dried.

Nicholas clears his throat. 'You should both slow down. You're not getting any younger.'

'I'm fine,' says Elizabeth. 'I don't touch that stuff. Champagne and brandy cocktails are enough for me.'

There is an awkward silence, before Nicholas addresses Freddie again. 'How about it, Freddie? We could go down today. It looks as if you could do with a break anyway. As long as you're happy for us to use the house.'

'Of course he's happy,' says Elizabeth. 'Aren't you? I'll join you next week. After Lydia's wedding. I can't miss that. I'm matron of honour.'

Freddie's heart sinks. He dreads returning to Coombe, the thought of that other part of his brother roaming free. He can't bear to look at Wilf, with that eye like Edward's, those same mannerisms. The last time he went home, he noticed a swagger about the boy that was Edward to a tee. He cannot understand why no one else sees it. But then, Ginny hardly ever visits now, and his mother . . . well . . . he dealt with that. And of course Elizabeth never met Edward. No doubt she would have preferred him if she had.

His answer has been to avoid the place as much as he can. Of course they pay the occasional visits to the children, but with a governess teaching the oldest, and Nanny Stirling in charge, Elizabeth and Freddie have been free to enjoy themselves as if there were no responsibilities, no dark secrets, no children. His thoughts turn blacker. There might as well be no children, for they have produced only girls – no sons. No heir for the family. He can't even do that right.

Elizabeth stands, and walks towards him. 'Nicholas is right. I have been worried about you for a while, darling. This is as good an opportunity as any to clear out the system.'

'There's no need . . .' He shrugs her hands off. If only she understood it helps him through the days, stops him thinking of Edward and Wilf at every turn.

'You're not yourself.'

'I don't want to be at Coombe alone.'

'You won't be alone. Nicholas will be there. And Clifford. And the children. You're never alone at Coombe.'

355

Nicholas's voice is calm, authoritative. 'You'd be doing us a huge favour.'

Freddie feels the fight leave him. He can see his reflection in Nicholas's dark eyes, small and insignificant and dreadfully tired.

By the time they reach Coombe, the car is spattered in mud. The light has leached from the sky, and the surroundings Freddie knows so well are only a blend of shadows. A new housemaid is still sweeping the steps up to the house, a dark shape crouched in the twilight. Another is laying a fire in the hall. Jennings limps past with some flowers. Mrs Foley has a face like thunder.

'You've not given us enough notice to have the house ready.'

'It will be fine, Mrs F.'

'There's no food. Only some cold cuts.'

'We don't need anything, really.' The housekeeper seems to have shrunk, her back more stooped, her hair more grey than he remembers.

'Nothing for me,' agrees Nicholas. 'I'm for my bed.'

'Won't I bring the children down to say goodnight, m'lord?'

'They're still up?' asks Freddie.

'Oh yes.'

'No. Don't disturb them. I'll see them in the morning.'

'Very well. I'll tell Nanny Stirling to put them to bed.'

'Could you show Mr Helstrom to his room on the way?'

'But . . .'

'I'd like to be alone, Mrs Foley.'

He heads to the study, where he knows the decanters of gin and whisky will be lined up like old friends. He switches on the light on the desk and it casts a warm glow around the room. He has a clear image of his father sitting here, downy head resting in the armchair by the fire. But his father is gone and there is only a dusting of ash left in the hearth. He pours himself a whisky, taking comfort from the feel of the cut glass,

356

the weight of the tumbler, and then he drinks, savouring the heat that flows down his throat.

He sits there for a while, his jumbled thoughts clattering in his head. What would happen if Edward suddenly came back? If Edward walked in through the door, older, greyer, but with his cocky smile, and those piercing blue eyes. What would Elizabeth think of him if she was faced with the blinding brilliance of Edward? Would she still want Hembury's Other Son? What would Edward do differently if he were sitting at this desk? Freddie pours himself another whisky, thinks bitterly how he will never know, yet will always be kept wondering – particularly with Wilf under his nose.

The clocks in the hall begin to chime midnight, cutting over each other in sad harmony. He must go to bed. He climbs the stairs slowly, the tumbler still in one hand. Each step is ingrained in his memory: he knows how many there are, how wide they are, and where they flatten out near the top to spread into the landing. How many times has he ascended and descended them since he was a child? He can even remember having to slide down backwards, trying to keep up with Edward who tottered unsteadily below.

He reaches the top, glances backwards down into the hall. The moonlight penetrates the dark only a few feet in from the windows. He shudders, drains the glass and leaves it on a small wooden table on the landing. He has a sudden urge to see the children. He continues up to the top floor.

Outside their bedroom, a spotty dog and a battered tin man in a battered tin motorcar have been abandoned in the middle of the carpet. The dog sits on its haunches, mournfully regarding the fallen motorcar, as if waiting for it to right itself so their game can begin again. Freddie stoops and picks it up, lifts it to his face, breathes in a smell that takes him back to his own nursery days, for this was his dog, which he used to take everywhere until Edward threw it out of the nursery window. He had thought it was lost. Could his brother have remained hidden all these years too?

He pushes open the bedroom door. The girls share Freddie and Edward's old room, joined to Nanny Stirling's, which in turn is off the nursery. Here they will live, sleep, eat, everything that Edward and Freddie did before them, until they are young women. His eyes adjust to the dark. There is a night light on in the corner of the room, a glowing ballerina whose pink skirt fills the room with a soft light. Freddie's eyes adjust and he sees the beds jutting out from the wall. He advances quietly until he is standing between the two. The girls are fast asleep, their deep breaths regular, the mounds of their bodies visible beneath the eiderdowns. He places the dog on the pillow of the oldest child, Dilly. The room smells of toys and nursery food, of youth and promise. How ironic, he thinks, when this is it: the end of the line. Serves Edward right.

Dilly moves and her eyes flicker open, taking him in sleepily at first, and then she jolts upright, fear in her eyes. 'Shh,' he says. 'It's me. Daddy.' But she cries out and Nanny Stirling comes tripping in, rubbing her eyes. She too jumps when she spies Freddie, and lays her hand over her heart. 'I'm sorry, m'lord. Mrs Foley said you weren't to see the children tonight.' She bustles past him to enclose Dilly in the safety of her large arms.

He steps backwards. 'I didn't . . . I . . .'

'It's only your father, dear.' Nanny Stirling smooths Dilly's hair, but the girl does not take her eyes from the stranger. Anne, the youngest, sleeps on, oblivious.

'May I suggest that you do something in the morning with the children rather than disturb them now, m'lord? How about an early ride? Before lessons?'

Freddie nods as if he too is a child again. He leaves the room, cheeks burning with humiliation as piercing as his despair.

CHAPTER 46

Nicholas is already at the breakfast table, shaking out the newspaper while a full plate of bacon and eggs steams in front of him. He looks surprised to see Freddie up so early. Freddie rings the bell. Mrs Foley appears at the door. 'Coffee,' he says. 'Strong . . .'

She clicks her teeth. 'There are eggs on the side.'

He dismisses her with a hand.

'You'll need energy for your ride,' says Nanny Stirling as she ushers in the children in their matching riding outfits. 'Kiss your father good morning.'

Anne is happy to advance, planting a kiss on Freddie's cheek and smiling up at him with the trust of an innocent, but Dilly refuses. Nicholas watches with amusement, one eye keeping watch over the newspaper.

'Actually, I'm not sure I have time for a ride. There's a lot of paperwork . . .'

'The girls will be disappointed . . .'

'I have to help Nicholas.'

Nicholas shakes his head. 'I'll be busy on the phone this morning, old chap. Clifford won't be here for a week. You go and enjoy some time with your girls.'

The children sit at their places, Anne chattering about all the things they have been up to, while Dilly remains silent, the green eyes of her mother giving nothing away until Nanny Stirling claps her hands. 'You'd better get going if you're going to ride, or you'll be late for lessons with Miss Newham.'

The two ponies are ready and waiting in the stable yard, their fat bellies straining at the girths, their hooves shiny with oil. And there, of course, is Wilf, checking the buckles. Cold dread creeps down the back of Freddie's neck. This is what he has been avoiding, but there is no escape. He wishes Elizabeth had not grown fond of the boy; he wishes he had had the courage to tell her the truth when he told her about Edward. How could he broach the subject now?

Wilf glances over, doffs his cap in a way that somehow seems insolent. But surely Freddie is being paranoid? He holds Wilf's gaze for too long. The boy is now an adult, and as tall as Freddie. His hair is darker than it was, though the tips are still blond, and his eyes are still Edward's blue. The cut of his cheekbones, and the confident air bring Edward back, as if he really is standing there, face to face. Freddie feels sick to the stomach. He will never escape from his brother's shadow while the boy is under his nose. He simply has to get rid of him. He may have promised Bolt he would always make sure the boy had employment, but he is not the only one who breaks promises – and there was no one there to witness it.

Wilf doubles over as the girls rush up and tug at him, and the gaze is broken. 'Where are we going today, Wilf?' asks Dilly. 'Can we go around the lakes?'

'Can we go to the village?'

'Can we jump the fallen tree?'

Wilf laughs, and Freddie feels a stab of jealousy at his easy manner with the children, at their small hands pulling at his arms and legs. He wonders how they would feel if they knew the boy was their cousin. He strengthens his resolve: all the more reason to find a way to move him on.

'Thank you, Bolt,' he says. 'I'll take it from here. In fact, the girls won't need you for at least a couple of weeks . . . until I go back to London.'

Dilly cries out and clings to Wilf's leg. 'No!' she says, stamping her foot. 'I won't go if Wilf's not allowed.'

Wilf tries to prise her hands from his trousers.

Freddie clears his throat, fixes her with a look, forces a smile. 'I thought it would be nice if it was just us.'

'No!' She starts to scream, a piercing sound that makes Freddie want to cover his ears. Anne starts to cry, and the ponies lay back their ears.

Dilly only stops when Wilf holds up a hand. 'You must listen to your father, Miss Dilly. I'll stay right here. Cleaning out the stables ready for your return.'

'Promise?'

'Of course.' He addresses Freddie. 'Would you like me to bring a horse?'

'Tybalt will do me very well, thank you.'

'You have to watch him with the water. He's none too keen—'

Freddie cuts him off. 'Yes, I know that.'

Wilf leads Tybalt into the yard, and Freddie realises the horse must have been ready for the boy to ride, which irks him further. Dilly mounts her pony herself from the mounting block. She sits po-faced while Anne looks to Wilf for help, her trusting face breaking into a smile when he puts out his clasped hands to give her a boost.

Freddie has to use the mounting block too; his legs are not as supple as they once were. He tightens the girth as the horse starts to move forward, and his muscles clench and screech into action. It has been a while since he has ridden.

'Would you like me to hold him for you, m'lord? He's an impatient sort.'

'I think I can manage,' Freddie snaps. For a moment, he is sure a look of disgust crosses the boy's face, but it is quickly replaced by cool deference. He is a different boy to the one who was once so keen to help in the yard. But then Freddie is different too. If he is to pretend to be the Earl of Hembury, he must act like him, and take no more of this nonsense. The Bolts must go.

361

At last the buckles slot into place, and Freddie is ready. He twists in the saddle, addresses Dilly. 'Where's this fallen tree you were going on about, then?'

'I'd rather wait until we go with Wilf.'

'Where would you like to go instead?'

'You choose.' Her green eyes remain cool.

'The river?'

She shrugs and pushes her pony into a gallop, and he wonders if he and his daughter are more alike than he realised.

It is soothing to be out in the fields, back on a horse. It seems to calm Dilly too. The edges of the fields are a patchwork of colours, where stitchwort and red campion romp around clumps of bluebells. 'Have you seen the ice house?' he asks.

Dilly eyes him suspiciously. 'How do you know about that?'

'I grew up here.'

'What else do you know?'

'I know where there will be snow.'

Dilly rolls her eyes. 'That's silly. It hasn't snowed for weeks.'

'Follow me.' He leads them through the woods until they reach the ancient crab apple tree. He dismounts, and the girls follow, leaving their ponies to tear at the grass. The tree is crooked and majestic. He stands underneath it, the light flickering on his face. He lifts Dilly into the lower branches, sees Anne watching her, remembers following Edward up, knees grazed, small hands gripping the gnarled wood.

'Where's the snow, then?' says Dilly.

Freddie shakes the trunk and the delicate white spring blossom falls around them like snowflakes.

Anne laughs and tries to catch it, and even Dilly smiles as she rocks in the branches. He helps them climb, two sisters in the footsteps of two brothers.

A pair of blue damselflies flitter and dart towards the river. Anne jumps down, starts to collect the daisies that are sprinkled around their feet like fallen stars, linking them together

362

until they are long enough to loop around Tybalt's neck. Freddie feels the tension slip from his shoulders.

On the way home, Dilly points out the fallen tree, a Scots pine that has landed across one of the paths leading into the wood. Dilly turns her horse towards it. 'Wait!' shouts Freddie, but she kicks her pony on, and Freddie follows close behind, too breathless to shout, his heart in his mouth as he watches her race towards the jump. As she draws closer, she briefly looks over her shoulder, and he remembers Edward once shouting at him to stop, and he sails over it just after her, landing with a grin almost as wide.

Nanny Stirling is waiting, arms folded, on their return. 'You're late! Miss Newham has been waiting for the girls, and Mr Webster is in the hall for his lordship.' Freddie rolls his eyes behind her back, and Dilly covers a smile with her small hand.

Elizabeth has replaced Arthur Mulligan as estate manager with Mr Webster, a humourless man in a sombre suit. He is tapping his umbrella on the floor of the hall.

'I'm sorry,' says Freddie. 'It's such a fine morning. I got carried away.'

The man does not smile, just places the umbrella in the stand and turns to follow Freddie to the library. He places his leather case on the table, and adjusts his tie, waving away the offer of tea. He wants to get straight down to business, for he has other landowners to visit.

'It is almost impossible to run a place such as this when there is no one to sign off paperwork,' he says, pushing some papers towards Freddie. 'And we must talk about your houses in the village. I told your wife. You have to sell them. They're nothing but a drain. I'm advising all my clients the same. There is no point in keeping tied cottages. You don't have workers to live in them, and you couldn't let them without spending a significant amount getting them up to standard. That's if you could find any tenants. The farmers are struggling to survive with prices so low and costs so high. They can't afford to pay labourers. Labourers can't afford to live. They're heading to the towns and cities to find work. And empty houses help no one.'

'Let me think about it.'

'There's one last thing.' Mr Webster shifts, looks uncomfortable. 'You should know that your gamekeeper's boy has been stirring up trouble in the village. There have been complaints from some of the other landowners . . .'

'Should I go and talk to them?' Here is the excuse he's been looking for: get rid of the boy for being a troublemaker.

'Talk to Joseph Cottam first. He has been trying to keep the peace.'

'My neighbour?'

Mr Webster nods. 'He's a godsend, that man. He's put in a decent offer for your cottages. I urge you to take him up on it.'

'That's really not necessary.'

'I don't think you understand the situation. I've brought along the most recent balance sheets.'

'Don't we pay you to come up with solutions?'

Mr Webster straightens the knot in his tie in irritation. 'And I have. Selling those cottages would be a start. But in the long term . . . Well.' He pauses, won't meet Freddie's eye. 'The best advice I can give is to sell the entire estate.'

'That will never happen.' Even as he says it, Freddie knows it's something he may have to consider. So many friends have had to sell their homes, while others have pulled down entire wings to make their houses more financially viable.

At that moment Wilf saunters past the window, catching Freddie's eye, and he is reminded of the fact Coombe is not necessarily his to sell. 'We will not be moving,' he says. 'And my sister has two healthy boys, not that it's any of your business.'

'If you intend to keep running the estate as it stands, then

I am out of suggestions, and you will be out of funds within five years.'

Freddie feels like flinging his pen at the man, with his tasteless suit and his provincial accent. He does not mention the tea plantation. Negotiations to sell the business are in the balance and he isn't sure they will find a buyer. He knows Elizabeth holds Mr Webster in high regard, but neither she nor the land manager has ever shown an interest in the plantation. Like everyone else, they always thought it was a waste of time and money. Everyone else apart from Celia and her father, of course. He stands, and indicates the door. 'Good day, Mr Webster. You can see yourself out.'

Freddie feels the country air cleanse his soul, the strength return to his legs and arms. The thought of having to sell Coombe makes him appreciate every little thing that he has missed: the cry of a startled pheasant; the splash of a thrown stone; the creak of the trees in the woods; the thunder of racing hooves; Dilly's lips curled into a smile when she races him up the hill towards home, her eyes flashing with pleasure when she wins. The girls start to seek Freddie out for a game or a ride. He takes them swimming in the top lake and hears the sharp intake of breath when they jump into the icy water from the swing. Dilly's bravery – foolishness others called it when he behaved the same way as a youngster – makes him laugh. She can stand on her pony's back. She can climb higher than he ever could. And though Anne is more conservative, even at her young age she is quick to notice where the fields are poorly drained, or where the fencing is down.

Wilf keeps his distance. It is as if he senses that Freddie is going to take him in hand. It is only a matter of time before the right moment will present itself. In the meantime, Freddie is so tired at night that he has time only to eat ravenously whatever is placed in front of him, and then collapse into a bath and bed. He avoids alcohol, finding he wakes more refreshed without it. Nicholas does not seem to mind. He is busy finalising travel arrangements and booking halls across the South West.

At last Clifford Montague arrives. Freddie watches his car sweep up the drive like a visiting statesman's. He is surprised to feel Dilly's small hand take hold of his as Clifford climbs the steps.

'Why is he wearing all black?' she whispers as they follow Nicholas and Clifford into the hall.

Freddie shrugs. 'Some kind of uniform.'

'I don't like it.'

But later, when the girls have had their tea in the nursery, and been scrubbed and dressed for bed, they are brought to entertain the adults in the drawing room, and Clifford works his charm. Anne is already in awe of his celebrity – he is as famous as Judy Garland, and they have all seen him in the newspapers. But he is more charismatic in the flesh. He listens to the girls sing, his stern face softening, and then he tells stories about evil Russians while the fire crackles in the grate.

Freddie sits with the girls as Clifford's eyes grow wild above his moustache. 'We must be ready to fight them off at the gates . . .'

'I'll set Teasel on them,' says Dilly, reaching for the old greyhound that is curled next to her on the sofa.

'That's the ticket!' says Clifford.

But Anne's bottom lip is beginning to quiver. Freddie shifts to reach out and stroke her hair. 'Mr Montague is joking,' he says as Anne clambers into his lap.

'Of course I'm only joking, girls,' says Clifford, jumping up, 'because we won't let any Bolshies on to our island.' He laughs, a loud sound that resonates around the room, and then he pretends to fence his shadow in the panelled wall. As the atmosphere dissolves into something benign, he suddenly stops, his eyes blazing. 'But we do need to mobilise ourselves.'

'With the money coming in from Italy, we can afford uniforms and kit for hundreds of men,' says Nicholas.

Freddie chivvies the girls. 'Bedtime,' he says. 'Go and give Uncle Nicholas a kiss goodnight.'

The children move reluctantly as Nicholas adds, 'The first lot are arriving tomorrow.'

'Did you say hundreds?' says Freddie. 'I didn't realise there would be that many . . .'

'Not here,' Nicholas laughs.

'Not yet,' adds Clifford, turning to the girls. 'But you see, Uncle Clifford will do whatever it takes to keep you safe.'

Freddie stands with one hand on the open door of the motor car, distracted momentarily by the leaves of the copper beech spreading beetroot colour in the sunlight, remembering a time many moons ago when he stood here, and a telegram boy put an end to the life he had hoped for. He would like to be going riding with the girls, but Clifford has suggested he watch the recruitment drive in the village.

He leaves the car near the church. It has been a while since he has walked through Hembury. After the wide, leafy streets of Chelsea, it seems more squalid than ever. The air is fetid; effluent streams down the open sewer in a side street. The houses have deteriorated, their walls crumbling, their roofs caving in. Many lie vacant, the weeds scrambling across the gardens, the gates lying open. He remembers what Webster said. The old labouring families who worked for his grandparents and great-grandparents have gone. He feels a stab of shame that this has happened on his watch, but he cannot halt the march of time.

He pauses at the bench where he sat with Celia and Ginny while they ate sweets all those years ago. Some of the slats have rotted. The shelves in the village shop are empty, for there are not enough residents to shop there. The blacksmith's anvil is silent now that the Cottams are not the only people turning to machines. The silence is broken by the sound of motor cars as they arrive bearing young men dressed in black like Clifford. They trickle on to the streets, calling to the locals who eye them suspiciously. They stop at the bakery, and at the Plough, encouraging men and women to come and listen. A few people dribble after them towards the hall, where Clifford is busy dragging a table outside.

The crowd grows, people stepping tentatively out of their homes, drawn by the din of Clifford's men, for there are quite a few of them now, lining up in rows before their leader. When he is ready, Clifford steps on to the table, assisted by two of his men. The crowd starts to clap. Freddie's chest tightens with excitement. He had forgotten how impressive Clifford can be, how he can swing a crowd behind him. Clifford stands straight-backed and solemn. Slowly he raises his arm, and the crowd quietens. He begins to speak.

'Thank you for welcoming me to your beautiful village,' he says, his voice ringing out across the sea of upturned faces. 'I am here to tell you about a new movement. A new party. With new agricultural policies.'

Someone on the ground shouts out, 'What makes you different to all the others? This lot promised to help, but we're barely surviving . . .'

There are murmurs of agreement in the audience. Clifford's men look around disapprovingly.

Clifford raises his arms, calls for silence. 'I hear your pain. That is why I want to help. That is why I bring you something new.'

Freddie glances around: he recognises many of the people in the crowd, some of whom are beginning to nod in agreement. Clifford will soon have them in his palm. Clifford's voice rises. 'Britain has become a dumping ground because the rest of Europe have closed their doors, and are feeding themselves. Why can't we do the same? Why are we allowing all this cheap foreign rubbish to infiltrate our shops? By feeding ourselves, we'll be creating more work . . .'

'You don't truly care about the workers . . .'

Along with the rest of the crowd, Freddie looks around angrily at the rude interjection. There is something that he recognises about the voice, but the speaker is hidden among the caps. Clifford is undaunted. 'You're wrong! I do care. About you and your families. I want to see cheap foreign imports banned. I want to protect the food we – you – grow. I want to protect British interests, and the farmers who feed those interests. "Britain First" is my call!'

There is cheering and whistling, Freddie feels his spirits buoyed, his patriotism lit.

'Our countryside needs to be protected: after all, what is Great Britain but a sum of her parts – each of which we will make greater?'

Fists are raised in the air.

'Don't be bullied by the parties of government that you have grown used to. Let them drag each other down. When we're in power, you farmers won't be worrying about taxes. You'll be doing what you do best: farming, and feeding the nation.'

One man near the front nods, and calls out, 'I urge you to sign up today. These lads are on our side.'

Invigorated, Freddie spots the ploughman who is now farming Home Farm. 'Come on, Albert,' he says. 'Why don't you go first?' he indicates a way through the crowd. Clifford pulls Albert up on to the table, so their clenched hands can be seen by all.

'What about the tithe?' Freddie recognises Walter Prescott's grandson – the son of his boy Michael who was reduced to a child himself during the war. The boy must be eighteen or nineteen now.

Clifford confers for a moment with one of his advisers, then stands, reinvigorated: 'We stand with you on that too,' he says. 'Why should a farmer give his hard-earned money to the Church?'

'Specially when he's a Quaker,' shouts another.

'But the collectors is sending the bailiffs out to those who won't pay,' says the Prescott boy.

Clifford holds up both his hands. 'We will help defend you against those bailiffs. We will help you fight them all: the politicians who don't understand you. The Church who wants their pound of flesh. We'll make sure there's more work, more money, and a healthier nation . . . Let's put the great back into Britain. It's what our boys died for . . . Do not let their deaths be in vain.'

The crowd grows rowdy, but Clifford's men handle it deftly, funnelling people towards the tables in the hall where they can sign up, even the ones who try to scarper when asked for money. Freddie watches it all, recalling the previous rousing speeches from Clifford, when they quelled the unrest in London. But he is suddenly distracted by the sight of Wilf, and he realises who it was who spoke up against Clifford.

'Hey, Bolt!' he calls.

Wilf glances briefly at him before turning to leave, and Freddie feels the lurch of recognition in the disdainful curl of his lip. It could so easily be Edward shouldering his way through the crowd. Freddie pushes after him, breaking into a jog when Wilf crosses to the other side of the road. But Wilf has reached the Plough. He stops at the door and looks back once more, and Freddie sees Edward's arrogant smile before Wilf disappears inside, where he knows Freddie will not follow. Freddie kicks the ground in frustration, for it would have been the perfect time to throw the boy out on his ear.

CHAPTER 47

Elizabeth returns as Clifford's men begin to turn up in droves. Coombe is suddenly bursting with life. There are tents in neat rows across the lawn, and the air rings with male voices. Elizabeth organises inside the house; Clifford orders outside. There is rarely a sign of the children. Freddie's heart aches for them.

Clifford and Nicholas discuss the lack of new recruits in the area at the dining-room table. 'It's always been hard to get people in agricultural areas to change their minds.'

'Can't we capitalise on this tithe situation?' says Clifford. 'It seems to get them riled up. Someone explain it to me again.'

Freddie explains: 'It's an ancient tax that landowners are meant to pay to the Church,' he says. 'The farmers are refusing to pay it, since land has tumbled in value and produces only a fraction of what it did. The Church is sending bailiffs to collect goods in kind – sheep or grain or whatever they can find.'

Clifford nods as he takes it in.

'They're calling it the tithe war in the South East,' adds Nicholas. 'We've got men on the ground there keeping the bailiffs out. We've had success painting "stolen" on livestock at the markets so that no one bids for them. Haulage companies are refusing to help seize animals in some areas.'

'The Tories back the Church, of course,' says Nicholas.

'Good. Full steam ahead, then.'

'Thought you'd say that. We've been busy setting up a

network of men to liaise with farmers in the South West, so things should start hotting up.'

'And what's the word in your village?' Clifford asks Freddie. 'I am aware your neighbour has links to that Russian pamphlet the *Workers' Week*. You understand that we need to be seen to be surrounded by friends in the place I have chosen as my stronghold . . .'

Freddie picks at a flake of paint on the window. 'You don't need to worry about her. She'll be in London.'

'No other nasty surprises?'

Freddie shakes his head; he will not credit Wilf with any power. 'You won't find any dissent among the locals. You have my word.'

'Sounds like a military campaign,' says Elizabeth.

'That's exactly what it is,' says her brother. 'We've also got chaps helping out at marches across the country. Deliberately targeting picket lines. Just like the General Strike. Remember that, Freddie? We'll need you out there before long . . .'

They are interrupted by one of the eager young recruits, who bursts in without waiting for his knocks to be answered. 'I've had reports from Tiverton that the bailiffs' trucks are heading here now.'

'Have you the addresses?' asks Nicholas.

'Only that they will be visiting the remaining debtors in the Hembury area.'

'We've got men at each of our estate farms,' says Freddie.

'What about the other farms?'

'There are men at Hampden's as well . . . So that leaves Yondercott on the far side of the village, and Littlecombe on this side.'

'Do you know if they pay tithe or not?'

'No idea.'

'Joseph Cottam is away in Bristol,' says Elizabeth. 'I only know because he almost ran me over driving another one of his ridiculous vehicles.'

'Is that the farm opposite?' asks Nicholas.

Freddie nods.

'We must take a group of men over there now then. The bailiffs evidently plan to take advantage of his absence.' Nicholas calls for William, one of the men at the top of the pecking order.

'It might be better to leave it,' says Freddie, not wanting a confrontation so close to home.

Clifford stands. 'I have to leave for the Honiton rally, but you can't risk bailiffs on your doorstep. You gave me your word that we would have local support.'

'Very well,' says Freddie, though it crosses his mind that Clifford demands quite a lot for someone who is taking advantage of his hospitality. 'But let me come with you, Nicholas, in case Cottam returns. He doesn't know you.'

William gathers a party together, and they make their way down the drive, a small procession of a motorcar and a couple of old carts. Nicholas hoists a Union Jack.

The Cottams' farmhouse is shut up, the windows and doors shuttered.

A labourer appears as they enter the courtyard of barns. 'What do ee want?'

'We've come to assist Mr Cottam,' says Nicholas. 'The bailiffs are on their way.'

'The master's in Bristol . . .'

'They won't wait for you to send a telegram.'

'But . . .'

'Move aside. We need to set up.'

The farmworker stands open-mouthed, unsure what to do. These men are trespassers, but they are trespassers of a class he must defer to. He watches them roll the logs off the back of a cart. 'Aren't you going to lend a hand?' barks Nicholas, but the man turns and runs out of the yard.

They wind barbed wire around the gate, taking care not to lacerate their hands. They drag the last barricade into place. Freddie perches on the edge of one of the carts and lights a cigarette. It is a satisfying feeling to be ready for the assault.

Suddenly there is a voice calling out to them and a woman in a long skirt striding across the grass from the direction of the fields. 'What on earth are you doing?' she calls.

Freddie jumps to his feet, throwing the cigarette on to the ground and crushing it beneath his boot. He glances at Nicholas and William, his heart leaping and bounding. Celia! He had no idea she had returned. He takes her in: her thick hair tied loosely, her blue eyes flashing. He moves to greet her, but she is in no mood for civilities. 'Open that gate!' she says. 'And take that wire off. I won't have that anywhere near my animals.'

The men do not move. 'Where's the landowner?' asks William.

'I am able to speak for him.'

William snorts derisively.

'Celia,' says Freddie. 'I didn't realise you were home.'

'Now you can see that I am. I didn't give you or your men permission to come on to our land.'

For a moment Freddie is wrongfooted by her abrupt manner, then his anger begins to rise too. He only came to make sure that Joseph Cottam wasn't surprised if he returned to find strangers guarding his farm. And now he's being humiliated in front of the men. 'The bailiffs are in the area,' he says tightly. 'Collecting unpaid tithes. They could arrive at any moment.'

'And what if we've paid?'

'Have you?'

'I don't see that's any of your business.'

Celia keeps her chin raised, her gaze on his. She was always strong, but there is a renewed steeliness about her – he is reminded of when he first laid eyes on her all those years ago at the auction. William's eyes flicker between them. Freddie grits his teeth. 'I'm making it my damn business,' he says. 'This is my area. These are my people. We've lived here for generations . . .'

She laughs, a deliberate snub. 'Not content with owning half the land around here, you have to act as if you're in charge

374

of everyone else's? Don't you think those of us who are fortunate enough to own land should pay tax on it? Or are you above the law as well as the labourers now, Lord Hembury?'

Nicholas raises an eyebrow. 'That's rich coming from you,' snaps Freddie. 'I remember your little show at Westminster. A shocking attack on democracy.'

'That was nothing to do with me.'

'That's not what everyone else believes.'

Nicholas and William grunt in agreement, and he feels a stab of regret at the hurt that flits across her face. But she gathers herself quickly: 'I've asked you politely to remove yourselves. The next time I won't be so polite.'

The farmworker who greeted them minutes ago appears again, armed with a pitchfork. He stands next to Celia like a Roman sentry.

Nicholas nods at the men, and some of them begin to dismantle the barricade. 'You know tithe is a Jewish tax,' he mutters as he passes between Celia and Freddie.

'Do you want me to fetch a shotgun?' she answers.

'It's true. Look it up. "Tithe" – it means a tenth in Hebrew.'

'I don't care if it's a Jewish word, an English word or a Russian word, I just want you to leave.'

The men have finished flinging their things on to the carts, but Freddie feels he must have one last go at asserting authority. 'I'd have thought you of all people would be pleased that we're standing up for those who are treated unfairly,' he says.

Celia laughs, a short, sharp burst of disbelief. 'More likely you're trying to gain local support for your particular brand of politics, but you won't find it here. You never will with that lot.' She points at the men in their uniforms, boots shining, arms crossed, pale faces above black polo necks. 'So please stop playing at soldiers, get off my land, and take your thugs with you.'

She folds her arms. Freddie clenches his fists as rage bubbles to the surface. To be treated like this by a woman, and a

375

socialist to boot. 'Clifford Montague won't be happy when he hears about this,' he says. 'He knows exactly who you are.'

'I remember his unique charm at Westminster.'

'You should remember too that these are dangerous times for Communists . . .'

'Are you threatening me, Lord Hembury?'

There is a noise in the lane, the sound of men singing. Celia's arms fall to her sides. The men turn. Freddie sees another group of men at the Littlecombe gate, young labourers carrying the red flag.

'Friends of yours?' snarls Nicholas. 'It seems Lord Hembury is right to be concerned about your connections . . .'

'I don't know who they are,' says Celia, her face falling. 'Maybe you should wait here while I go and talk to them.'

She starts to move, but Nicholas and William immediately block her. 'And let you incite your friends further? No. You've asked us to leave. We're going.' They start to move off, the motorcar first, the carts behind, the rolls of wire bouncing, the men hanging off the back, bristling with righteousness. Freddie jumps on to the back of the last cart, and watches Celia as they roll away. It is impossible to deny that part of him wants to jump back down and go to her – to apologise for turning up unannounced, for bringing these men here. But he knows his regrets are too late; his shame unwelcome.

His little group makes it to the Littlecombe entrance. The labourers stand in the road, blocking their exit, the open gate an invisible line between the two groups. The men in the road sing and jab their flags in the air. Clifford's men are easily outnumbered, by about four to one. But not for long. Freddie hears more men calling, and sees a stream of black-shirted and black-booted supporters is snaking down the drive from Coombe. They are singing one of their patriotic songs, and as they meet the group of labourers in the lane, they raise their arms in a salute.

William orders the men to climb down from the carts, and the men in the lane cannot now move forward.

'All power to the people!' someone shouts.

Clifford's men shift on their feet.

'Fascists go home!'

Nicholas gets out of the motorcar and shouts, 'This is a tithe war. Nothing to do with you.'

And now the speaker for the labourers steps forward, and Freddie's heart begins to pound as he sees that it is Wilf, tall, proud, blue eyes burning. 'This is our country. We don't want your wars,' he calls.

'Yet you're happy to bring one from Russia,' spits Nicholas.

'If their cause lies with ours, then we're happy for their support. All we want is freedom from the capitalist oppressors.'

Freddie is speechless for a moment. First Celia, now Wilf. Is everyone out to get him? All he's tried to do is help. Around him, the men are restless, snarling and needling at each other. Freddie's bewilderment turns swiftly to resentment. And then suddenly one of Clifford's men launches himself into the crowd, and there is blood and the crunch of fist on bone, and there are weapons, a crowbar, a poker, and spittle flying, split skin and the crack of bone.

Someone crashes into his side, and Freddie elbows the man hard in the ribs. He hears the heavy thud of fist and boot on flesh. He briefly wonders whether Celia knew these people were coming to her defence, whether she and Wilf are in cahoots. Did she send Wilf some kind of signal? He feels outrage course through his body, and he remembers the General Strike, and how it felt to control the rabble from a horse. Well, he may not have a horse, but he is still on the side of the righteous: isn't he Lord Hembury? Isn't this his patch, his home, his village, to protect as did his father, his grandfather, his great-grandfather before him?

He spins around and lands a fist on the side of a man's head. Someone yanks him by the shoulder, but he lashes out again, before the person can get a strong hold. He whirls around to face another attacker. Out of the corner of his eye, Freddie can see one of Clifford's men pummelling a man on the ground, and then there is Wilf, eyes misted with anger, and they have a hold on each other's collars, and they are looking into each other's eyes, and there is Edward, and for a moment Freddie is paralysed, unsure what to do, and he sees Wilf draw back his arm, and readies himself for the punch. The blow to his cheek is hard, but does not knock him down. Instead it serves as clarity that now at last he can engineer the boy's dismissal, and take Coombe forward as is his right, and his duty. The blood sings in his ears, along with the howls of men and the whistles of the constables as they arrive with their truncheons raised.

CHAPTER 48

Elizabeth and the girls meet Freddie on the steps. The girls reach up to him with small hands. 'Are you all right? You're hurt. There's blood.'

Freddie wipes his face, and crouches down. 'I'm fine. Nothing serious.' He ruffles Dilly's hair, and lifts Anne as he straightens himself.

Elizabeth is pale. 'What happened? We heard the din from here.'

'A mob from the village . . .'

'How did they know you'd be there?'

He shrugs. 'There's no shortage of prying eyes.'

'No doubt the Cottams were something to do with it.'

'The thought crossed my mind too. But they were led by Wilf Bolt.'

Elizabeth's mouth falls open. 'And to think I trusted him with the girls.'

'Don't you worry. It's being dealt with. The police want to charge the ringleaders with affray and assault: at least one man had his arm broken. Clifford is talking to them now. He'll get us off the hook, but I've told the constables where they can find Bolt.'

Anne gasps, and releases her arms so that she slides to the ground. Dilly takes a step back. Freddie is irked and calls for Nanny Stirling to remove them. 'Keep them up in the nursery for now. They'll be safer until this has died down,' he says.

Dilly shoots him an angry look. 'If you harm Wilf, I'll never speak to you again.'

'Don't talk to your father like that, young lady!' snaps Elizabeth.

'But Wilf's nicer than all of you put together!'

'It appears that his rudeness has rubbed off on you,' retorts Freddie. 'You're as uncouth as he is.' But he cannot catch her eye.

'You see that she washes her mouth out with soap,' adds Elizabeth as Nanny Stirling drags Dilly away by the hand, and the child's feet scrabble and claw at the ground.

Elizabeth touches Freddie's cheek, where the blood is slowly dripping. 'Thank goodness the police turned up when they did.'

'Who called them?'

A familiar figure steps forward. 'I did.'

Freddie gasps. 'Uncle Maurice!' His uncle is silver-haired but still spry, the dark eyes lively in the wrinkled face.

'Indeed. Now tell me, what the devil has been going on here?'

In the study Maurice picks up the whisky decanter.

'Not for me,' says Freddie.

'Just one to settle the nerves. Looks like you've been in the wars.'

He is right. Freddie is shaking, and a little breathless. He takes the glass, reluctantly at first. He has not touched a drop in weeks, and does not want to muddle his thoughts. It all seemed so clear: now is the time to put the past firmly in its place and gather the reins of the future. But then . . . the sting of his cheek, and his confusion about Wilf – and about Celia's behaviour – make the movement of glass to mouth automatic. He had forgotten the heat of the liquid. It makes him wince at first, then he relaxes with the pleasing warmth, the dulling of the senses. He faces his uncle. He feels a stab of sadness; for the first time he sees how his uncle looks so like his father, and it brings back all his old insecurities – he suddenly feels as if he is twenty again.

Maurice does not sit down. He rests his hands on the back of the old earl's chair. 'Now. I arrive to find my nephew caught up in a street brawl. I can't get into my old room because some fascist has commandeered it. There are men trampling all over my childhood home pretending to be soldiers . . . And as for the gardens, they're practically ruined. Your mother will be furious when she gets back. You do remember she's coming back, don't you?'

'What do you care? You've always made things hard for her.' As Freddie's thoughts calm, he cannot help the bitterness rising. Of course he remembered his mother was returning – it is another thing that plays on his mind constantly, that he has still not told her about the existence of the child. But how can he?

'I care. Of course I do. I might have cocked up in the past. I might be useless at running my own affairs. But I cared deeply about my brother, and I care about Coombe, and all who are part of it: you, your sister, your mother, and all who follow.'

Freddie gives a bitter bark. 'Perhaps there won't be anyone to follow. In case it's slipped your notice: I've been unable to produce an heir.'

Maurice tuts. 'Yes. That is rotten luck. It seems to be the downfall of us second sons. But it's not the end of the world. Your girls seem robust enough. You'll just need to make sure you select good marriages for both.'

'But the Hembury name.'

'There are things that can be done legally. You can insist that whoever marries Dilly retains our name. A double-barrel is very common these days.'

Freddie bites down on his frustration. Producing only girls is as bad as being infertile in some circles.

'I know better than anyone that there are plenty of worse things than not producing sons,' says Maurice. 'My girls have been a blessing to me – as yours will be to you. And I'm sorry I haven't been here for a while, but I wanted you to stand on your own two feet. And it seems you've been doing that rather well.'

'Have I?'

'Well . . . apart from these men who appear to be running around the place as if they own it.'

'They're acquaintances of an old family friend of Elizabeth and Nicholas's . . .'

'Clifford Montague?' Maurice grimaces.

Freddie nods. 'I'd have thought you'd approve.'

'Why? I'm no fascist. And neither are you. Stop trying to be someone you're not.'

'Who am I meant to be?'

'Yourself!'

Freddie pours himself another drink. The familiar smell, the warmth – it is like an old friend with a calm touch. His shoulders slump. Even his brother wanted no part in this life, or he would be here now. 'I don't know who I am.'

'You're the Earl of Hembury.'

'Perhaps I don't want to be. Perhaps I don't deserve to be.'

'Whatever you feel about it, you are. So buck up, and stop blaming everyone else for your woes.'

Freddie feels self-pity well in his eyes. What would his uncle think if he knew of Edward's existence? Would he still think Freddie had done well? Or would he be desperate to trace his older, better, favourite nephew?

'Aren't you even going to ask why I'm here?' asks Maurice.

Freddie shrugs.

'I came to congratulate you.'

'About what?'

'Ceylon.' Maurice looks at him in a strange way. 'Do you ever open your post? Or read the newspapers? Your plantation is one of the success stories of these dark times. Carrington and Thorneycoombe has just been listed on the stock exchange. Matthew must have written to you.'

Freddie thinks of all the unopened telegrams lying in the drawer in his desk. 'It was dragging on so long I started to think it would never come to fruition . . .'

Maurice laughs. 'Well it's fruited, old chap. It really has!'

He thrusts the *Financial Times* at Freddie.

Freddie can barely take it in. His thoughts are tumbling and whirling, pounding against his skull. 'It's a good start, but won't be enough to save this place.'

'It will be if you sell off those houses in the village as Webster suggests. Cottam is there, waiting.'

'How do you know about that?'

'I'm still a trustee; Webster keeps me updated.'

Freddie pours himself another whisky. 'Ah. And now I realise why you're really here. How much are you hoping to squeeze out of me?'

Maurice shakes his head. 'Nothing. I'm genuinely pleased for you. I know it's been tough.'

'Or perhaps you've somehow syphoned something off like you did when you sold Littlecombe?' Saying the name reminds him of his altercation with Celia, which burns as bitterly as the wound on his cheek: and now the irony that it was her generosity that kept the whole business going.

'I have done no such thing. I have learnt from the mistakes of my youth. As must you. Let me help. Things need to be taken in hand. Your father will be turning in his grave to see these men having the run of the house. It is time to stop burying your head in the sand as the debts pile up. No doubt you have a mound of unopened letters somewhere. I know what it's like. I've been there. But it's time to face the music – to be man of the house!'

But the drink has ignited a furnace in Freddie that is beginning to roar. He has had enough of being told what to do by Maurice, by Elizabeth, by Nicholas, by Celia, by his father, by everyone. 'Hang you and hang my father, and hang Edward too.' He grabs a new bottle of whisky from beneath the table, left there for filling the decanter. 'Hang the lot of you!' He steps out on to the terrace for peace and quiet, but even out here, there are people shouting and drilling and milling around, and his head is throbbing, so he heads to the lakes, where he knows he can sit in peace.

He walks fast; he wants to get as far away from the house as possible. His trousers are muddy, his shoes ruined, but he doesn't care. He walks all the way to the far lake, where the bridge crosses the weir. Birds scatter across the water and up into the trees, calling out in alarm as he appears. He finds a space on the bank and sits miserably in the dappled light, watching as life returns to the water: a dark coot given away by its white stripe, and a couple of moorhens that stretch ungainly yellow legs into the tangled roots on the opposite bank. The sound of the water rushing away beneath him is comforting, and he watches himself reflected in the alternative world as he used to do when he was younger.

He is not sure how long he has been there when he becomes aware of another presence. Celia gives a half-wave. In the afternoon light she seems tired, diminished. There is none of the earlier fire.

She walks slowly towards him. 'I came to make sure you were all right,' she says. 'Your uncle told me he had seen you heading in this direction. It wasn't hard to follow your footsteps.' She points at his filthy shoes. 'How's your cheek? It looks painful.'

He covers the wound protectively. 'You must be satisfied.'

'Don't be silly. I don't like any of this violence.'

'So you didn't tell the boy I was there?'

'Wilf? Of course not. I didn't tell anyone anything. I had no idea what either of you was up to.'

The relief is instantaneous. His anger subsides. To know that Celia isn't involved with Wilf. To know that she still cares for him. He removes his hand from his cheek.

'I'm sorry I was rude earlier,' she says.

'You certainly were.'

'Your men were winding me up. But that doesn't excuse my behaviour.'

384

They are silent for a moment, listening to the churning water, Celia standing awkwardly next to him. He wants to reach out to her. 'Thank you for checking,' he says eventually, 'but as you can see, I'm fine.' He holds up the bottle.

She glances down at it nervously. 'I should probably go.'

He does not want her to leave. He wants her to laugh like she used to. He wants her to look at him the way she used to. 'Stay for a while,' he says quietly. 'Please? I promise to be nice.' He pats the ground next to him.

She sits down, frowning. He takes a swig of whisky. The world sways a little. He offers her the bottle, but she pushes it away. He remembers sharing a drink from his hunting flask with her years ago, after she'd had a fall.

'Where's Old Red?' he asks.

'Raymond is in London. How's Elizabeth?'

'Probably wondering how to get over the disappointment of who she's married to . . .'

'I'm sure that's not true.'

A reed warbler darts into the bulrushes. Freddie wishes he could disappear into the vegetation too. He drinks again from the bottle.

Celia sighs. 'How did she take the news about your brother?' she asks. 'And what about Wilf? Has anyone spoken to him of it?'

Freddie snorts dismissively. He glances at her. She is thinner than he remembers, and the splash of freckles across her gaunt cheeks highlight the pale skin beneath, but her eyes are the same: the colour of harebells; lighter and clearer than his family's cornflower blue. 'We sat here once,' he says. 'On one of our walks. I thought you were the strangest woman I'd ever met . . .'

'Don't . . .'

'All those years ago, but it feels like yesterday.'

'A lot has happened.'

'What exactly is Old Red doing in London while you're here alone?'

'I don't want to talk about it.'

She pushes herself to her feet, and he does the same, so they are standing looking at each other. The leaves shiver above them. She pushes the hair from her face. He watches the skin pulse gently in the hollow of her neck. She's no longer the girl he first met, but she's still so beautiful.

'Things could have been so different,' he says.

'You got married!'

'I knew I'd made a mistake. But I *had* to marry her.'

'Let's not . . .'

He takes one more gulp from the bottle, places it on the ground. 'Did you hear? My plantation. In Ceylon. It worked out better than I ever imagined.'

'My father told me. I'm pleased for you. You deserve it.'

'It's all thanks to you . . .'

'That's not true.'

'If you hadn't lent me that money in the early days . . . And now I can pay you back. Double.'

'There's more to a good business than money . . .'

'If I'd known it was going to end up like this, then we could have married. I wouldn't have needed Elizabeth.'

'You didn't need her anyway. You were always too worried what other people would think.'

'I had to keep this place going somehow. It was my duty.'

'Well congratulations. You did it.'

'It's not too late for us.'

'It is, Freddie.'

'I know you still have feelings for me.' She doesn't deny it. He reaches out and touches the skin on her face. It is as soft as he remembers. He wants to be near her. He has always wanted to be with her. He cups his hand behind her head, leans forward to plant a kiss on her warm forehead. The smell of her invades his senses. She steps away, but her protest is only mild; he knows she doesn't mean it. They are meant to be together. She is the only one he can talk to, the only one who understands, and he wants to understand her. He can feel how very fragile she is, how delicate, and he wants to protect her, and he can feel her body against his, the softness of her chest, the hardness of her ribs, his thigh against hers. He wants to consume her, to own her. And now she is calling out, and someone has his hands on Freddie, and is yanking him off, away from Celia, and for the second time that day he is staring into his brother's blue eyes.

'Go!' Wilf shouts at Celia, as she stumbles backwards, her hair loose, her eyes afraid.

But she stops for a moment and stares at Freddie. 'What happened to you?' she cries. 'When did you turn into one of them?' Freddie fights against Wilf's grip, but he cannot escape; he cannot avoid her distress. 'I thought you were different. But in the end you're all the same. You take what you want, by force if you have to. You bully and manipulate. You're monsters. All of you.' Then she turns and hastens away, tripping back along the path and into the woods, tearful, dishevelled, leaving Freddie burning with humiliation.

At last Wilf releases his grip and Freddie retreats to a safe place, rubbing his neck. He can barely look at the boy, at the loathing etched into his face, at the revulsion in those eyes. He just wants him gone. 'You can't hide out here for ever,' he snaps. 'I'll tell the police. They'll hunt you out.'

'They won't find me. I know these woods better than anyone.'

'You don't know them better than me. They are my woods, after all.'

'And what will you have them arrest me for?'

'Threats, bodily harm, breach of the peace . . . you choose. But you'll be put away for a long time. I'll see to that.'

'You're the one they should be talking to. Assaulting a woman!'

Freddie feels the bile rise in his mouth. 'You watch your tongue . . .'

'You've no right to tell me what to do. I'm no child. I'm my own man.'

'You work for me!'

Wilf draws himself up. He is taller than Freddie now, and he looks down with contempt, so painfully similar in manner to Edward that Freddie has to glance away. 'I wouldn't work for the likes of you,' he spits. 'Not if you were the last man alive.' And he shoves Freddie hard. Freddie staggers backwards and lands in the mud. He lies there in the dirt, as Wilf disappears into the woodland, from the back so like Edward in height and posture that it makes him wince. The wound on his cheek has opened up again, and blood is oozing down his face. His clothes are wet and filthy. The bottle of whisky has fallen on its side. He watches it drip, like the last drops of his dignity, into the lake. He wonders how he could ever have sunk this low. And he starts to cry. He cries for Celia, for his father, for Edward, and most of all, he cries for himself, for the boy who had such a dream of escape, a decent and good child, who somehow died without anyone noticing at all.

Freddie hears voices calling for him in the wood. He pulls himself on to his knees. His limbs are stiff and his teeth are chattering, but he doesn't feel the cold, only the biting numbness at the mess he has made of his life.

Someone shines a torch in his face. He blinks, recognises William's voice. 'What the hell happened?'

'I slipped,' says Freddie. 'Must have hit my head.'

Nicholas picks up the bottle. 'Or something . . .' he says.

Freddie has never noticed the contempt in his brother-in-law's voice before. He gets to his feet. His legs are shaking, but he bats away the offer of help. They usher him back to the house, past the men clustered around fires, the men queuing for food. There are men standing at the front door, guarding it like gatekeepers. There are men lounging in the drawing room, their feet on the sofas, there are men sitting at his mother's desk in the morning room, men bent over the snooker table, there is even a man sitting in his father's chair by the fire in the study, and when they stop, it is Nicholas who makes his way to sit at the old earl's desk.

Elizabeth comes running to the study. 'I've been so worried.'

Freddie shakes her off. He does not want anyone to touch him. He does not deserve anyone to care. He is a monster. 'Your cheek's bleeding again. It was him, wasn't it? Bolt.'

Freddie shakes his head, but no one takes any notice.

'We've been searching for you for hours,' says Nicholas. 'We'll send William and Dan off to that young toerag's cottage.'

Elizabeth nods, and the men grin, and Freddie sees that Dan has a metal bar in his hand, while William is tapping his baton against his leg. Freddie knows how it goes: a knock on the door, a crowbar in the face. And then what? Retaliation. Over and over. Does he want this? Can he condone this for any man, let alone one who shares his own brother's blood?

'You want to come?' says William. 'Should be fun.'

Freddie shakes his head. He sees it all as if for the first time. Through the window, the tents cover the lawn. The grass court is ruined. The roses are trampled.

William sneers again. 'And after that, we could go and have a quiet word with that bitch from next door.'

Freddie swallows. 'No,' he says quietly. 'I don't want you to do anything but leave. Everyone. I want you all to go.'

'You're not thinking straight,' says Nicholas.

'I am.' Freddie tries to stand tall, despite his torn and muddied clothing, his bloodstained shirt. 'You've been here long enough. I want everyone gone by the end of the week. The men out there. All of you in here . . .'

Nicholas appeals to Elizabeth. She advances, places a hand on his arm. 'Freddie, darling, how about we run you a bath? You'll feel so much better.'

'I don't want a bath. I want everyone to leave.'

'You must have hit your head harder than you realised,' says Nicholas.

'Quicker we move, the more likely we'll catch the little bugger before he does a runner . . .'

'No!' shouts Freddie, shaking off Elizabeth's arm as he bangs his fist on the desk. 'There'll be no more fighting. And there'll be no more training. This is my house. And I want it back. I want you to tell the men to pack up and be ready to move out tomorrow.'

'We should wait for Clifford . . .' says Nicholas.

'No. This is my home. My decision.'

'You've never exactly taken control before.'

'Well now I am.' Freddie stands with his arms folded. He's sobered up, and he sees them for the bullies they are, and he is repulsed. How could he ever have let himself become part of their movement?

A shadow falls across the door, and to Freddie's relief, Maurice crosses the study to stand at Freddie's shoulder. He surveys the room. 'You heard the man. Go and spread the word!'

William and Dan glance uneasily at Nicholas, who nods. The three men start to move, slowly, towards the door.

Freddie turns to his uncle once they have left. 'I need to ask you something,' he says. 'Was there a situation with a maid and Edward at Parkfield?'

Maurice laughs. 'There were plenty of dalliances in the good old days . . .'

'It's not a joke, uncle. It would have been in 1914. Around the time Edward left.'

Maurice rubs his chin. 'I wasn't ever party to housekeeping rules. Your aunt might know.'

Freddie nods. 'Can you ask her to come and stay? I want to talk to her about it. There's been too much lying, too much secrecy. As you said, it is time to stop blaming everyone else for our woes. And can you arrange a meeting with Joseph Cottam?'

CHAPTER 49

Wilf takes the stairs two at a time, his father close behind and out of breath. 'Where have you been?' gasps Victor. 'The police . . .'

'I know. I have to leave.'

'No! Stay. Whatever it is can be sorted.'

'Not this time,' Wilf laughs bitterly. 'This time that bastard's got it well and truly in for me.'

He starts to pull clothes from his drawers.

'Can't you just lay low for a while?'

'No. They're on their way, Da, with your master urging them on. If it's not the police, it'll be the rest of those fascists from the house.' More than ever he is swamped by that feeling that his own father doesn't understand him, of being adrift since his mother died. He scrunches the clothes angrily into his bag. 'It's time for me to go. I *want* to go!' He knows there are people out there who *do* understand him, people like his uncle, like Celia Cottam, people who are ready to take a stand.

'Go where?'

'London.' The idea has been circling in his head for a while.

'London! What know you of London?'

'There are friends there. People like me.' He will find Miss Cottam when she returns there. He still has the copy of her newspaper. He has not forgotten her suggestion that he might one day find work there. He is willing to do anything, however small, to have a part in it. And after what's just happened, he is certain she won't turn him away.

The anguish is plain on Victor's face: 'Won't you at least let me see you there safely?'

Wilf pulls the buckles tight on the bag and swings it over his shoulder. He strides towards the door, stopping when he reaches his father. The irony that Victor fought in the war, and never since; no wonder he is too ashamed to wear his medals. 'I don't want you to come,' he says. 'You'll hold me back.'

He barges past before Victor can reply. He feels a flicker of remorse, but it is lost in the maelstrom of other emotions. It is clear to him now: a gamekeeper is no different to a groom; a stable lad is no better than a miner. Their family has come nowhere; manacled to the same life as those who came before. Well not him. He is going to get out. Like Miss Cottam and her family.

He hears Victor's steps following him down into the kitchen. He does not turn around; he does not want to see the hurt on his father's face. He bends to pat Shadow's grey-flecked head one last time before he leaves, his meagre possessions bundled on his back. The village sleeps. He leaves Victor sitting at the table, his head in his hands, the old dog lying at his feet, its tail between its legs. He heads east, to where the pale dawn is beginning to break.

For the first few days, Wilf keeps away from the roads, out of sight, sleeping in ditches and under hedges. It is late summer, the nights are warm, and the ground is dry, but he jumps at every sound: the cough of a sheep; the snap of a twig; the screech of an angry blackbird. He never stays long in one place, wary that the police are on his tail.

He is amazed to discover the worlds just beyond Coombe. The Blackdown Hills are full of secret pockets where a man could hide for ever: among forests of twisted oaks and thick bracken, or down low in the clumps of boggy reeds and swampy mires. He washes in a small stream that meanders through a deep coombe, submerging his body in the ice-cold water, rinsing his clothes and leaving them to dry in the spindly willow branches, while he enjoys the weakening sun on his skin. The bruises on his knuckles turn deep purple, then blue, then yellow as they fade. He forages for food, for nettles and mushrooms, for cobnuts that have not been pilfered by the squirrels. His stomach gripes and twists as it grows used to the river water, and the acid of the berries that weep in strands from the hedgerows. Sometimes he feels as if he is being followed, but when he looks over his shoulder, there is no one there. He pushes on. He cannot be caught. He knows Freddie will not give up; he saw the loathing in his eyes. He has crossed a line.

Once he reaches the east side of the hills, Wilf becomes braver, following better-trod footpaths, and even the quiet lanes. He remains on high alert, always aware of where next he could slip into the shelter of the undergrowth. He is not sure whether he is in Somerset or Devon or Dorset; all he knows is that he is heading for London.

The further he walks, the hungrier he becomes. He stumbles across a vegetable patch, well-tended, but out of sight of its homestead, a tumbledown farmhouse of chert with dairy cattle milling around its courtyard. He unearths some fat potatoes and muddy carrots. As he is shaking the soil from the roots, someone emerges from the lane. Wilf drops the food and darts away, but the man holds up his hands in a peaceful gesture. 'I don't mean no harm,' he calls. 'I'm just a fellow traveller. How about sharing they teddies?'

Wilf eyes him from a safe distance. The man is certainly no policeman: cut from the earth with a wizened face weathered by outdoor work, he would not be out of place among the gypsies. He nods a greeting; he is tired of his own company. What harm could one meal do?

Benjamin is a shepherd by trade, though he has no flock of his own, since his farmer went under. He has left the south coast to find a new position tending sheep, but work is scarce, and so he has turned his hand to whatever he can. 'But I'm near-sixty. Been with that flock for more'n forty years. It hurt me bad to see they sold. Almost as hard as leaving the sea behind. What about you, son? Where's your people?'

'Over near Wellington.' Wilf gestures vaguely.

Benjamin nods slowly. 'Did you see any of they troubles that way? They was talking about it as far as Honiton. Don't often get rioting around these parts. They're generally peaceful folk in Devon.'

Wilf bites his nails. 'First I've heard of it,' he says. 'Did they arrest anyone?'

Benjamin's watery blue eyes twinkle. 'A couple of men. It's said they're still looking for the ones what started it. But I'm sure they'll give up when winter sets in.'

Wilf busies himself lighting a small fire. Benjamin collects some dried wood, and they sit together as the smoke starts to rise. Benjamin rubs his hands and holds them out to the flame. 'Fancy sticking together for a while? Seems we're walking in the same direction, and it's been a while since I had company.'

Wilf shrugs his acceptance. Benjamin removes something from his coat, plops it into the bubbling water and stirs. 'You want some?' he asks.

'What is it?'

'Dog's bone.'

'You eating dog?'

Benjamin shakes his head and laughs. 'The dog were chewing it.'

Wilf shakes his head. 'Not for me,' he says.

Wilf enjoys his time on the road with Benjamin. The old man is knowledgeable on living off the land, being used to spending the days and nights with his flock. Wilf begins to feel as if he has been on the road all his life. As the danger of being caught recedes, he congratulates himself on how he has survived. The knuckles on the hand he used to split Freddie's cheek have healed, and now there is no proof of what occurred.

The mild weather is on the turn. Benjamin points to the gathering clouds. 'We'll find work now,' he says. 'Farmers'll want to finish double quick.'

But Wilf wants to press on. The men part as autumn begins to blow in, making the leaves fall in showers of red, gold and brown.

Early afternoon, in a ditch on the outskirts of Reading, Wilf wakes with a start. 'Come on, son. Up you get.' He catches sight of the policeman's uniform and scrambles to his feet, heart racing. How stupid to have been caught when he was so nearly there. But lately he has managed only short bursts of walking before his body demands he rest. He bends to gather his things, fear making him clumsy.

Out on the open road, the constable looks him up and down, taking in the torn trousers, the ragged shirt. 'Follow me,' he says, not unkindly.

Wilf grips the strap of his bag. He contemplates making a run for it, but his legs are too tired.

'No need to look like that. It might not be legal to sleep outside, but there are places you can go if you have nowhere.'

Wilf follows suspiciously, unsure whether the constable is tricking him or not. He keeps expecting more men to arrive, perhaps Freddie Hembury at their head, pointing an accusing finger, but no one appears. They travel some way along the road. The passing traffic pays them no heed, and the policeman keeps chattering. It reminds Wilf for a moment of Victor, soothing the horses as he brushes them down. 'Not far to go now. I know he's here somewhere. Saw him this morning. There!'

The policeman calls out to a short, stocky man with white hair, who is sitting on the side of the road, picking his teeth. 'Harry! I've got another new one. Could you make sure he's fed and watered tonight?'

The tramp stands, shaking out his legs, before shuffling gingerly forward, as if each step is painful. 'Pleasure to meet you,' he says, sticking out a hand rough with calluses. He looks Wilf up and down. 'Green as fresh grass.' He turns to the policeman, straightens and salutes. 'Thank you, Sergeant Neary. I'll take it from here.'

The policeman smiles and salutes back. 'Make sure he gets cleaned up too, or he'll start to frighten folk.'

Wilf watches the old man. 'I'm not going to no workhouse.' He feels braver now that the constable has gone. He can return to his journey. He does not want to befriend more strangers.

'Hush.' The tramp puts a finger to his lips. 'It's not called the "workhouse" no more. It's an "institution". And those of us that are in the know calls it a "spike".' He scratches the side of his neck. 'Course, they can change the name, but the place is still the same.'

'It doesn't matter. I'm not going.'

'Got somewhere important to be, have you?'

'London.'

'I've seen enough of the world to know you won't get there without a decent meal and a sleep.'

Wilf shrugs. 'I think I can make up my own mind.'

All of a sudden Harry grabs hold of Wilf's collar. The old tramp is stronger than he appears. 'Look,' he says, 'you might be a big shot where you come from, but out here you ain't nothing but a child. There's people on these streets would eat you for their breakfast. You mind your Ps and Qs, stick with me, and you might learn something that will save your life.'

Their destination is a large, grim Victorian building that once was the workhouse, and is still regarded as such by the locals. Most of the building is turned over to an infirmary, full of the mad and the sick, but one wing is a casual ward for vagrants passing through.

They join the queue of men stamping their feet at the door. The government's new means test has stripped more families of their benefits, and there are men here who have only recently lost their jobs, and are still in the habit of looking respectable in suit and tie. An agitated young man walks in circles on the spot, occasionally cursing loudly and then covering his mouth as if to keep the words in. Another, with a sticky dribble of spit dangling from his chin, is humming loudly to himself, the same short burst of music, over and over again. They all seem to know Harry.

The door is unlocked, and a thickset man calls for quiet: 'I won't let any of yous in if you don't keep it down.'

'Stick close,' whispers Harry as the queue shuffles forward.

Wilf scratches at the bites on his head. An official scribbles in a ledger as the doorman asks the same three questions: 'Where are you from? Where are you going? Occupation?'

'Yeovil,' says Wilf. 'London. Agricultural labourer.'

The man looks at him. 'What's an agricultural labourer going to do in London?' he asks.

'Lad's going to visit family,' says Harry over Wilf's shoulder.

The doorman turns to the tramp. 'Ah. Harry Prendergast. Can't keep away?'

'Something like that, sir.'

The doorman shakes his head. 'Why don't you stop? Go to the infirmary. You're not getting younger . . .'

But Harry rubs his hands together and laughs. 'I ain't dead yet.'

Once they have been admitted, Harry nudges Wilf, nodding towards the next official, who is standing at a table. 'Tramp major, checking for money and knives,' he says. 'Every spike's got one. Long-term tenant. Born here in the workhouse. This one thinks he's a cut above the rest.'

The official taps an inner doorframe with his stick, indicates for Harry to empty his pockets, then strip. Harry hands over his clothes. The man wrinkles his nose. 'Come for your annual wash, Harry?' he asks. 'Next.'

Wilf hesitates.

The man fixes him with a stare. 'Got a clever one here, have we? There's always the clink if you'd rather.'

Wilf is aware of everyone watching. He takes a deep breath, and starts to remove his clothes. He hands them and his bag to the man, who immediately bundles them away, leaving Wilf stripped of all he had in the world.

'Next!'

Naked, Wilf follows Harry to the bathroom. The tramp does not seem to regard his nudity as anything unusual as he elbows through the sea of exposed flesh to one of only two bathtubs. Bright pink bodies contrast with arms and faces blackened by sunshine and dirt. 'In you get.' Harry points at the other tub as he clambers into the water and starts to swill the rags from his feet. Wilf cannot bring himself to do the same. Unrecognisable things bob around in the filthy liquid. He is pushed aside by another man, who has no such compunction.

'You say you're to London, lad?' says a voice in his ear, and Wilf turns to see a man with a neat little moustache standing closer than is comfortable. As other bodies press in around them, Wilf loses sight of the baths and of Harry. His mouth goes dry, and he tries to move away, but the man clings to him like a burr.

'No offence, but a country boy in the city sticks out like a bullock in a tea shop.'

Wilf pretends to ignore him, but the man is so close, their flesh almost touching, skin against skin. He shudders, feels the fear creep up his spine. He realises how right Harry is: he's nobody here. He has no friends, no family among the men milling about. He's just another youngster without a home.

The man raises his eyebrows: 'There's talk of people looking for a young lad from out west. I heard there's a reward . . .' He holds his hand out and cups Wilf's chin. 'I didn't realise he'd be so pretty.' The man runs a finger down his chest, and Wilf wishes he was brave enough to lash out, but he is frozen with dread.

'Leave the lad alone,' growls Harry quietly, appearing from nowhere. 'Or I'll break your arm.' There is not an inch of fat on the tramp's compact frame; he is all wiry muscle.

'All right, all right.' The man steps away. 'We can talk in the morning. None of us is going anywhere tonight.' He sniggers to himself, and moves on.

Harry shakes his head. 'I believe it's time for me to share what I've picked up in the years I been on the road. A little bit of guidance. Rules, if you like.' He marches off, Wilf trying to stick close. 'So here goes. One: don't be cocky, but don't be meek neither. You stick up for yourself when the time is right.'

Wilf fights the lump in his throat as he follows the tramp. He thought he was stronger than this. If Freddie is offering a reward for his capture, then there is no way back; only forward. He must learn what he can. Harry dries himself on a tatty cloth attached to the wall by a roller, as if it is the most luxurious towel in the world and not sodden with the residue of God knows how many men. 'Two: steer clear of danger. No matter who you are, there's always someone bigger, or more dangerous, round the corner.'

Wilf copies Harry as he collects a large shirt to sleep in; once white, the cotton is now stained grey and stinks of disinfectant, but at least it is warm and dry.

Harry keeps talking as they move. 'Three: best to be friendly as you can.' He pauses here and looks at Wilf. 'But not too friendly, if you know what I mean.' Then he carries on. 'Four: keep your business to yourself. And don't get involved in no one else's. You never know who they've upset further up the ladder.'

Wilf jogs after Harry into a corridor, where they enter a cell. Immediately the door clangs shut behind them. A key turns in the lock. 'Five,' says Harry, 'trust your instincts.' Wilf looks at the bars on the windows. There is no bed, not even a shelf. There is an old pail, yellow droplets still clinging to its insides. His instincts tell him this is not where he wants to be.

A while later, some watery tea and bread with oily margarine is slid through the door. Harry eats it with a look of bliss on his face. 'Six: make the most of whatever you get, because who knows where your next meal is coming from.' He licks his fingers. 'And seven. This is the most important one.' He wags his finger at Wilf. 'Don't see your life for its failures. See it for its successes. Here you are. Alive and fed. You've survived this far. That's an achievement.'

He wiggles his toes, stretches his legs, before reclining on the blanket on the floor as if it is a bed fit for a lord. Wilf cannot help smiling. 'That's better, sonny. Ain't nothing that can't be fixed by a hearty meal and a good night's sleep.'

He pats the space next to him, and Wilf lies down. The blankets are rough and itchy. The floor is hard, but Harry is soon snoring loudly. Wilf lies awake in the half-light, ashamed of his weakness. He might have been almost a man around Coombe, but among these men, Harry was right to say he is a child. It is that child who misses his father, and yearns for his mother. And it is that same child who – though he hates to admit it – misses Freddie, and cannot understand the change in Freddie's attitude towards him. Wilf pushes those thoughts from his mind. The master sees him as nothing more than a chattel. As he does any of his workers. And Wilf is no longer that naive child. That child is gone.

He stares at the bars on the window. He longs for open skies, for a cold ditch, for the stars above and the earth below. He dozes fitfully, listening to Harry's deep snores. He thinks of how the dogs had a better place to lie than this. And with the memory of those kind-hearted dumb beasts, inevitably come the memories of his father and mother, the three of them sitting around the table in the kitchen, the dogs drying by the stove, and he allows a couple of warm tears to spill down his face and on to the cold floor.

In the morning they are made to peel potatoes in the yard before they can collect their things and go. 'Better than breaking stones,' says Harry. 'Them's the spikes to avoid.' Wilf's eyes wander across the rest of the old workhouse: the infirmary, still separated by a wall that once divided male paupers from female, or children from adults. He stares at the great brick barrier and wills his hands to work faster. He wants to get out of here as soon as possible.

Harry gives him a nudge, almost causing him to cut his numb fingers. 'If you're worried about that chancer, there's no need,' he says. 'I had a little word with the tramp major, and they found he's not done any of his potatoes this morning. He'll be here for at least another day.' He grins his toothless grin as he chucks another spud on to the pile.

They clamber into their old clothes, which appear to have been cleaned, or at least dried, for no amount of cleaning can erase an itinerant life. Then Harry accompanies Wilf back to where they first met. The old tramp pumps Wilf's hand as they say goodbye, and Wilf does not want to let go of the strong, gnarled fingers. Harry has saved him from himself, shown him how to survive in a world far bigger than that of his youth. 'Thank you,' says Wilf. 'For everything.'

'A pleasure,' says Harry, beaming broadly.

'One last thing,' says Wilf. 'How do you keep so cheerful?'

'What's to be sad about? Look at me. I've had my monthly wash. Got someone to clean me clothes for me. Now I can take to the road, and go wherever I want. I'd be happy for some company if you fancy it . . .'

Wilf shakes his head. 'I want to make it to London.'

'Don't suppose you know of a place down your way, helping folk – ex-soldiers and the like?'

Wilf nods, tries to stop his voice breaking. 'I could tell you how to get there.'

Harry peers at him, beady eyes narrowed. 'You want me to deliver a message?'

Wilf pictures his father at the kitchen table, his head in his hands. Then he remembers Freddie, and the cut on his cheek, the men on his tail. 'No,' he says.

'Then there's nowt left to say but happy travels.' Harry salutes, before he shuffles back the way Wilf has come.

Wilf turns for London, leaving his childhood self in Reading spike. It is time to embrace the man he has become.

CHAPTER 50

The streets grow busier as London rises from the roadside. A motor car blares its horn, startling Wilf. He is not used to such a maelstrom of people, buses, bicycles, buildings. Soon he comes across a large river, and it reminds him of Bristol, the stink of the Avon oozing its way through the city the same as this, though the houses here are grander, more prolific, the roads wider, the traffic more chaotic. In fact, everything about London is bigger.

This time he has no Victor to follow, no Victor to shield him. He feels a lump rise in his throat and a flash of pride that he has made it here at last. It has been four days since Reading; he has avoided the busier roads, seeking shelter in the byways. He is so tired and hungry that sometimes it feels as if he is walking through a dream. He marvels at how his legs seem to keep marching while his mind wants to sleep. A taxi cab splashes muddy water on his trousers, but they are already so dirty that it makes no difference. The streets seem to go on forever. His feet are throbbing; his boots have holes. He wonders how much further he must walk to reach the right part of the sprawling city.

He pulls a crumpled piece of paper from his pocket. It holds the address of the *Workers' Week*, which Celia gave him all those years ago. The name of the street means nothing to him. He glances at the people on the pavement, busy walking this way and that. No one will catch his eye. He spots a matronly-looking woman standing at a bus stop. She turns away as he approaches. He edges towards another woman in the queue. She too turns her back without looking at him.

'No one's got no change, mate,' says a young man, taking charge.

Wilf blushes. 'It's not money I'm after. I'm only trying to find an address.'

'Come here, then. Let's have a butcher's.'

Gratefully, Wilf hands him the paper.

The man whistles and shakes his head. 'That's right the other side of town, that is. Must be seven, eight mile at least.'

'Can I follow the river there?'

'It'd be quicker to take this bus, though it'll cost ya.' The women glance nervously in his direction.

'I'll walk,' says Wilf.

He walks for another four hours, learning who he can and who he can't ask for guidance. Surrounded by all these people, he is embarrassed by the way he looks, with his frayed cuffs and his unruly hair and beard, but after a while it seems he is invisible anyway. After the quiet country lanes, where every passer-by wants to stop and pass the time of day, he sees how useful the anonymity of the street is, where even a passing policeman doesn't give him a second glance. He is melting away. He does not need his father to protect him: the city will do that.

He knows he must be close to his destination. The road has grown quiet, apart from a rag-and-bone man walking his cart slowly, stopping every so often as children come out of their houses to see the horse, and feed it carrots. Wilf cannot help being drawn to the animal. The children's mothers call them back inside, but the man, dressed in an ill-fitting suit, is happy to converse.

Bess is a pretty skewbald, a patchwork of brown and white. Wilf feels the warm fur, the muscle beneath. He places his face against the horse's neck, breathes in the smell of grass and rain, freedom and light.

The rag-and-bone man laughs. 'Never tire of that smell,' he says. 'Where are you headed, lad?'

'I'm looking for a newspaper called the *Workers' Week*.'

'I'm going that way now. Can't be more than a mile. Hop on.'

Wilf senses he can trust this man, whose horse is as well fed and content as any beast at Coombe. He has seen others on this journey, their ribs clear beneath shabby fur, their knees scarred and swollen, their eyes dull. He clambers on to the cart and the horse takes up the strain. Wilf leans back against the pile of old clothes and junk that nobody wants. The movement reminds him of home, and within seconds, he is fast asleep, dreaming of his mother rolling pastry, his father stoking the fire.

He is woken by a dig in the ribs.

'There you go.' He rubs his tired eyes. The building has no distinguishing features, only a small plaque on the door.

'But I'd clean myself up before going in,' says the man. 'Not being rude, like . . .' He wrinkles his nose. 'But if I can smell it, it must be bad.'

Wilf feels in his pocket for the last of his money. 'Do you know a respectable lodging house near here?' he asks.

'Do I look respectable?' the man laughs. 'But I might know a place.'

Evening is falling. The cart trundles down another street. Here, beggars block the doorways, and women stand in the street, surrounded by their belongings and children with empty stares. He calls to the horse to halt. 'This is your stop. Number 17. It's a madhouse, but it's got a reputation for being safe. Tell them Charlie sent you. And hang on.' The man rifles through the pile of rags in the cart until he finds something. He holds up the trousers and jacket. He adds a shirt. 'Those should see you right.'

There is such a din coming from behind the door to number 17 that Wilf is sure he will be turned away. He fights his way inside, past men and women, sailors with kitbags, vagrants with bandaged hands and feet, people from all corners of the earth, with hazelnut coloured skin and hair as black as an oiled hoof. Wilf searches for someone who might be in charge, settling on a Chinese man holding court in the kitchen. The man looks him up and down.

'Charlie sent me,' says Wilf.

'He did, did he? Well you're in luck. One bed left in a men's room. Cash first.' He holds out a hand.

Wilf is not sure how much to pay. He pulls a couple of coins from his pocket and the man snatches them up, biting them as if they were gold coins. He beckons to an enormous bald man with pasty skin and hands the size of hams. 'It's yours for a week. Lofty'll show you up. And no funny business or Lofty'll show you out again.'

The room is a dormitory of beds, no more than wooden boards, raised at a slight angle so that the head is higher than the foot. The window is sealed shut, the glass – smashed long ago – has been replaced by wooden boards, reminding him of his family's home in Bristol. Perhaps he has not come as far as he imagined. He clenches his jaw: it simply means he has further to climb – but he is young and strong and he has got this far on his own. Lofty indicates the spare board, and Wilf drops his bundle on to it. The man on the next-door bed grins, and his teeth are as yellow as the thin and greasy sheet.

Wilf finds the nearest public washhouse, and cleans himself properly for the first time in weeks. It has the magical effect of restoring his confidence. He has survived his journey to London. He is not the naive boy he used to be. The clothes that Charlie gave him are an odd match, but at least they are clean and they fit – and in London it seems anything goes. People wear all manner of eccentric outfits, just as all manner of classes rub shoulders: the poor and the middle class, the married and the not married, all of life, bright-eyed, searching for the next break. The only ones missing from this part of London are of the Hembury ilk, which suits Wilf fine.

The following day he returns to the offices of the *Workers' Week*. He climbs the narrow stairs to the third floor, and knocks on the door. Like everything else in the city, the office is a whirlwind of noise and people, walking in different directions, tapping at typewriters, shouting down telephones, and all in a haze of cigarette smoke.

'Can I help?' a woman asks, squeezed behind a desk by the door.

Wilf removes his cap and holds it in his hands, turning it round and round nervously. 'I'm looking for . . . Miles Hartman,' he says.

She looks at him in confusion. 'Mr Hartman hasn't worked here for quite a while.'

'Miss Cottam, then?'

The woman raises an eyebrow. Then she shouts, 'Raymond! Think this one's for you!' without taking her eyes off Wilf. 'Go on, then. No one will bite,' she adds, motioning him inside.

A man is making his way past the desks. Wilf recognises Raymond's earnest face from his boyhood. There are more lines around his eyes, but they are no less piercing. Wilf explains himself again.

Raymond looks him up and down, narrows his eyes. 'And it was Miss Cottam recommended you come here?'

Wilf thinks of her that afternoon by the lake, frightened yet proud, defiant, an inspiration. 'She mentioned it a few years back. It stuck in my mind. She'll vouch for me,' he adds.

Raymond frowns. 'You know she's not here? We're not together any more.'

'I saw her in Devon . . .'

'Well, she's landed gentry now. I understand she has no plans to return to London. It seems she is unable to relinquish her lavish country lifestyle.'

Wilf detects the insinuation in his voice, and suddenly another image pops into his head – of Celia and Freddie together years ago, by the cowshed in the lane near Littlecombe.

407

Back then, Wilf had seen no evidence of a struggle, just lovers in a secret tryst, unaware that they had been detected. He pushes the picture from his mind. It is confusing, and he is glad to have left it all behind. 'That suits me,' he says. 'I don't want people back there finding out where I'm to. In fact, I'd be grateful if you didn't tell anyone I'm here.'

This seems to satisfy Raymond somewhat. 'And what exactly is it you've come to do?' he asks, folding his arms.

'Anything, sir. I'm happy to help hand out leaflets, carry papers, or make tea. I don't mind.'

Raymond finally smiles. 'Well, you've come at the right time. We could certainly do with some help. Things have never been so busy. We don't pay that well, I'm afraid. Not at the moment. Perhaps one day.'

'I don't mind about that. So long as I can be useful.'

'Come and meet Molly Browning. She's my right-hand man, so to speak. We'll see what she thinks.'

Wilf follows Raymond across the busy room, until they stop in front of a woman who is typing fast, a cigarette dangling from her mouth. She glances up; she does not look pleased to be disturbed. She raises an eyebrow at Raymond, who repeats what Wilf has said.

'Sent by Celia?' asks Molly.

'In a manner of speaking.'

'How do we know he's not a spy?'

'A spy?' asks Wilf. 'For who?'

'Ain't she close to those toffs she lives next to? The fascists? How do we know you don't work for them too?'

Wilf squares his chin. 'They're the reason I left, miss. I led a march against Mr Montague's men.'

'That was you?' Molly raises her eyebrows in genuine surprise.

Wilf hesitates, unsure for a moment whether to admit to his behaviour, but Molly is rummaging through drawers, and across the top of the desk. 'We covered it,' she says. 'Here!' She holds up an old newspaper. 'Fascists repelled by villagers!

There's hardly ever stories like that from out in the country. Did you hear Clifford Montague's men turned tail after that, and scattered back to wherever they was from?'

'All of them?' Wilf asks in surprise.

Molly grins and nods. 'You must have frightened them off. Shows what we can do when we unite against an enemy.'

Wilf flushes with pleasure. 'I'm glad they took us seriously.'

Raymond grins and slaps him on the back. 'Why didn't you say?' he asks. 'You can be sure we won't be giving away your whereabouts to anyone. We don't want to lose such an asset.'

'A true hero to the cause,' adds Molly. 'If only all youngsters were as brave. Now let me sign this off: it's our comment on the death of our beloved monarch. What d'you think of that, country boy?'

Wilf takes a deep breath. Here at last people care for his opinion. 'I think the king's no different to the landowner, and they'd both best watch out, for villagers everywhere are rising.'

Raymond bursts out laughing, and so does Molly. She pulls the paper from her typewriter with one hand and stubs the cigarette out with the other. 'I'm done,' she says, standing. 'It's all there; pretty much the same as our new hero's take on things.' She leans forward and offers Wilf her hand, then grabs the coat from the back of her chair. 'Come on, then. Let's get some food into you. We pay badly, but we eat well. And you look half-starved.'

CHAPTER 51

Wilf treads every inch of the East End, running errands for the newspaper. He talks to the droves of feral children running past men carrying towers of boxes, the women selling matches. He chalks graffiti on the walls. He learns the area's secrets: the places that even the police do not dare patrol, where the homeless can sleep peacefully, and the crooks can plan. He gets to know the gangs of refugees trickling in from Germany and from the rest of Europe. With the encouragement of Raymond and Molly, he feels his confidence grow.

Though he finds he is popular with women of his age, Wilf dabbles only in brief liaisons. Women perplex him: his mother's face is fading from his mind, but he remembers well the night she died, when he crouched at the top of the stairs and overheard his parents arguing. He remembers that she had loved someone other than his father, but that Victor loved her anyway. Then he remembers Freddie and Celia in a tender embrace that transformed into an angry assault years later. He remembers Elizabeth and her overfamiliarity too, her lingering touch. And he concludes that it is easier to focus his energy on the fight, the party, rather than get entangled with a woman.

Before long he is journeying back and forth between the newspaper and the local party headquarters, passing messages, carrying boxes of leaflets. Spain is now the cause that takes up most of their time. Since the military coup in the summer they have watched in horror as Spain descends into civil war, and the nationalists try to crush the people.

Molly speaks at rallies and demonstrations. The newspaper is raising funds to help the Spanish Republicans fight back after the Nationalists tried to overthrow the government. 'We must help the Spanish people,' she cries. 'Their fight is our fight. The unions, the communists, the workers stand in solidarity against all forms of fascism: the army, the landlords, the upper classes.'

Wilf pumps his fist in the air, imitating Molly as his bitterness grows. He watches her in awe: how she is happy to stand on stage in front of hundreds of people, how she commands attention despite her diminutive size, how all defer to her, the old suffragettes as well as the middle-aged union men. He studies it carefully, sees how he has much to learn, how the quiet encouragement needed to raise support in the Plough is different to the sheer force of enthusiasm required to raise the spirit of a crowd.

But it seems that Clifford Montague's popularity is increasing too: as fast as the workers band together, so too do the fascists. Molly and Raymond call a meeting at the office. Raymond stares angrily out of the window across the city, while Molly perches on the desk to address the staff. 'We've heard that Clifford Montague's men plan to march through the East End,' she says. 'Thousands of them.'

'Won't a march like that be banned?' asks one of the reporters.

'*We* wouldn't be allowed to do it,' says another. The other members of staff mumble in agreement.

'Of course we wouldn't,' says Molly. 'But the police have approved it.' Molly holds up her hand to quieten the angry mutterings. 'And so we must see that we give them the welcome they deserve.'

Wilf grasps her meaning immediately. It's the moment he's been waiting for. 'I'll do whatever you need,' he says, stepping forward.

Molly turns to him. 'We were hoping you'd say that. You already have experience confronting them.'

411

Wilf nods. 'I remember it like it was yesterday.' He recalls the look on Freddie's face, too. 'They might look organised, but they fight dirty.'

The meeting ends, and people return to their desks. Molly calls for Wilf to stay. 'We had an idea,' she says, as Raymond joins her. 'You've got certain attributes – confidence and youth – that we'd like to capture in a poster. What do you say?'

Wilf stands proudly in his new shirt, bought with money he has saved. Molly watches as he is painted, her intelligent eyes travelling over his motionless body. He shifts: it is awkward keeping his fist raised and clenched in the forced gesture, and he is not used to such blatant scrutiny by a pretty woman. He lets his tired arm drop.

Molly immediately tells him to raise it again. 'Don't you get all self-conscious now,' she says, reading his thoughts. 'All the Republicans are doing it out in Spain. It's a symbol we can unite behind. A way to show our solidarity. A fist is strength and unity. It's the opposite of that open-handed fascist salute.'

Wilf curls his fingers into his palm again.

'I could add a rifle into the fist afterwards, if you want,' says the artist, cocking his head to one side, then beginning to add colour.

'I think it's all right as it is,' says Molly. 'Look at those cheekbones. I'd follow him, wouldn't you?'

'Will you be coming out there to fight?' asks Wilf, trying not to move.

'I would if I wasn't needed here.'

'Would you not be afraid?'

'All revolution is dangerous, but without danger there'd be no change. Besides, what do our little lives matter when there is a higher cause?'

Wilf nods, suddenly remembering that Victor fought in another war, though he did not like to talk about it. He wishes he could tell his father he was taking up arms, wonders if

412

Victor would be proud of his son now. He wonders too what his ma would make of it, regrets that she never had a chance to choose a different path like Molly. Sorrow passes through him like a wave. He must not dwell on the past.

'What about Raymond?' he asks. 'Will he come?'

'Oh, Raymond is desperate to go, but he's getting old.' Molly says this in a stage whisper, laughing. Then she raises her voice. 'Make sure you capture those blue eyes,' she instructs the artist. 'We want more women to sign up.' She flashes Wilf a smile. 'We must encourage Communists everywhere to fight. The other political parties will never support intervention over there. Neither will the TUC. It's all down to us.'

The artist stands back from his easel. Molly turns it so that Wilf can see. The image is hyper-real, almost as if he is built from straight lines. He is relieved: it is barely a likeness, which means no one will recognise him – friend or foe.

'I could add the red flag instead of the rifle,' says the artist. 'It would make for an even stronger message.'

'What do you think?' Molly asks Wilf.

'I think we'll deliver a strong enough message next weekend,' he answers.

Wilf cannot wait to face Clifford Montague and his men: it gives him a peculiar thrill to think of coming face to face with someone he loathes. Sometimes when he closes his eyes, he juxtaposes Clifford Montague with Freddie Hembury. He won that fight; he will win this one. He has helped spread the word around the city, gathering information on the kinds of numbers to expect. If they think he's good enough, then Molly will help him get to Spain to fight the fascists there.

Most of the lodgers at number 17 stay for only a few nights, though there are some permanent residents, like Lofty and Zhao. The high turnover means there are always new people to encourage to join the cause. Wilf likes to hold court in the kitchen, loves to hear the hubbub die down to a whisper when he speaks.

413

The morning of the march finally dawns. Wilf stands with his back to the fire, the flames leaping and burning like the fervour in his chest. He watches the faces in the crowd glowing back at him: such a mixture of people – old and young, men and women, local and foreign – united against the enemy. He conjures up Freddie Hembury in his mind's eye: Freddie Hembury attacking him in the lane at Littlecombe. Freddie Hembury with his hands all over Miss Cottam. Freddie Hembury working his mother and father to the bone. His stomach churns and his heart races with excitement.

'They cannot be allowed to spread their hate,' he says. 'To intimidate us. To fill our children's ears with their poison, to keep their jackboots pressed against our necks. We'll stop Montague's men, just as we'll stop the aggressors from destroying Spain. We'll show this government that the working class will not take it any more! We're asking everyone to donate an hour's pay to the Communist party – that's all. An hour's pay to fund a lifetime of freedom.' He hands his cap around, hears the pennies dropping into it.

Even Lofty is animated, carrying a placard in his large hands. 'Are you ready?'

The people nod and cheer as they start to spill out into the street, until only Zhao is left, unmoved as he sweeps out the grate. He is bare-chested, dressed only in loose-fitting trousers.

'What about you?' says Wilf. 'Will you join us?'

Zhao shakes his head. 'Why do you white men always insist on passing one man's war for another's?' he says.

Outside the air crackles with energy. Gangs of men on street corners chatter excitedly. Women grin at each other and roll up their sleeves. Wilf feels the fight rise in his blood. Housewives offer weapons to passers-by: brooms, mops, frying pans. A lorry is parked sideways on. The crowds thicken, slowing his progress. A woman calls out, cheeks glowing with a smile, dark eyes shining, hair as black as coal, and he thinks, that could have been my ma, if only she'd held on, for this is what hope does. He thinks, maybe I will go to Victor when this is over; he just needs to see what hope looks like – like the men, women and children with their clenched fists raised from bended elbow. This is how to make a stand.

Wilf helps a man drag part of a wooden fence into place, then a woman rolling a barrel. People are gathering whatever they can: drums, doors, tables, crates, ladders, chairs, anything to block the street. Banners hang above them, written in Hebrew and English. They greet Wilf as part of their extended family. He knows so many of them now. He clambers up on to the barricade, and turns to address the crowd. 'They're trying to drive us apart,' he shouts. 'But it won't work.' The people look up, nodding and murmuring in agreement. He looks down, sees Victor and Aggie in their hopeful faces. 'They think they can whip up anger and hatred among you. But they can't. They want to make you believe that foreigners are the cause of all our troubles. But they aren't.'

Some men raise their fists. 'It's not us!' they say.

'They want you to set upon your friends and neighbours.'

'Never!' says the crowd.

'They want you to hate!'

'No!'

'They want you to fear!'

'We don't!'

'They shall not pass!'

'We'll stop them!'

Wilf hears it before he sees it. The clamour from the City as the stream of thousands of fascists stamp relentlessly towards the East End, buttons and boots shining, blood-red armband against black uniform, straight arms raised in salute to their leader, Clifford Montague. Ahead of them and around them come the police, marching boots tramping, followed by horses. And behind them come their own crowd, women and men carrying Union Jacks, stepping smartly along, proud to stand up to the socialist threat; to express their desire to rid their country of the immigrants.

Wilf remembers marching up from Hembury village, his people around him, making a stand against these same fascists that Freddie had invited into his home. Wilf remembers the brawl, and his blood surges. He will send more men home with bloodied cheeks today.

The religious leaders and the politicians have told them not to fight, but the East End is ready, galvanised by left leaders of all kinds. Wilf and his comrades, man and woman, adult and child, Labour and Communist, immigrant and native, they stand side by side. They link arms, they raise their own banners and chants against the fascists. Their voices fill the air.

Suddenly, the mounted policemen charge the crowd. Wilf catches sight of the marchers waiting to be let through as the policemen strike at the people on the ground with their batons. For a moment Wilf tastes childish fear in his mouth, but then he remembers that he is one of these people now. Fascists be damned. He pushes forward to meet them. He hears the angry roar of the crowd; the crack of baton on flesh; the thud of fist against muscle. People are knocked to the ground, trampled, screaming, bloody. He sees a large docker, sleeves rolled up, lunge at a fascist, his massive fist catching the man a blow on the temple, but the fascist comes back, and slashes at the man's face. The docker staggers back, and when he takes his hand away, a red line in the skin gushes blood. He sees a child crouched in fear beneath boots that kick and stamp, and anger surges through his body.

The fascists are on the move again. In the running battle alongside, fists become weapons. Brick smashes down on flesh, knuckledusters crunch on bone, stockings filled with glass slice the air. One horse is screaming as it stumbles, throwing its rider. The policeman hits the ground hard and is dragged into the crowd until more policemen, their helmets bobbing, manage to surge forward and retrieve their man.

The angry mass plunges forward again, trying to thwart the marchers. Wilf allows himself to be swept along as the crowd moves and countermoves, parts and reforms like a stormy sea. He reaches down to drag an injured man to the safety of one of the first-aid posts stationed at intervals along the street. The numbers of unconscious and injured are growing, but their places are quickly filled by more people.

There are faces at the windows, and all along the street. As the fascists push on, the police hold the East Enders back, but now women are leaning out of their top floors, tipping pails of rotting refuse and the contents of their chamber pots on to the heads below, calling and caterwauling their encouragement. The cries pass from house to house. Children throw marbles, adults throw bottles. Wilf hears the tinkle of broken glass. He tries to race ahead of the march. He bumps into someone, and spins sideways, tripping on some debris on the road. A horse barges past, and when Wilf looks up, he is suddenly face to face with Clifford Montague. Time stands still as all the hurt and pain pulses through Wilf's body. He is staring directly into Clifford's eyes. He remembers Clifford standing on the table outside the village hall, trying to garner support. He remembers speaking out against him that day. But now, as Clifford looks back with a sneer, Wilf knows the man doesn't remember him at all. Why would he? Wilf is insignificant, unworthy of remembering.

His hands grip the metal bar he has been carrying. He does not care about repercussions. He will strike a blow against the heart of this evil. He raises his arm. He sees for a split second the doubt in Clifford's eyes. He brings his arm down, but instead of Clifford, he makes contact with a horse that has come between them.

The sounds and heat and smell of the battle return all at once. Wilf sidesteps the flailing hooves. He sees the animal is in pain: in its flared nostrils, its rolling eye. His heart sinks in horror as he realises he inflicted the weeping red gash in its rump. He reaches out to grab hold of its cheek strap.

The horse rears. Its rider loses his stirrup and begins to slip, not good enough a horseman to control it. Wilf sees the fear in the young policeman's eye as he grapples to hold on to the animal's mane. Wilf hums like Victor used to, to calm the animal. He runs his hands along its neck. Soon the horse is shuddering beneath his fingers, still blowing hard. Wilf can sense everything it feels, as it jumps at each loud shout, clash, and he wonders how he got to this moment, where he is injuring and frightening animals. And he remembers Total Eclipse's last, shuddering breath, and how cruel men can be.

The policeman has managed to get his foot back into the stirrup. His hand is on his baton, but Wilf knows he will not use it. For a moment, something passes between them. Then there is a cry as someone comes from behind with a weapon, and Wilf lets go of the bridle, and stills the newcomer's arm. The horse jogs forward, and he is confronted once again by Clifford.

Wilf takes a step backwards. Not sure what to do with this feeling, sensing the futility of this violence. Is he weak? Is there something wrong with him?

But the young policeman on the horse is backing between them again, bending out of his saddle as he tries to catch Clifford's attention. The other officers too are shouting at the marchers. It seems they are trying to persuade the fascists to turn back. And then a great cheer goes up from the crowd: the fascists *are* turning. And Clifford frowns, and then Wilf is laughing and jeering at his haughty back. It is a victory, though a disorienting one.

CHAPTER 52

The streets and pubs are full of revellers. The publicans are handing out free beer, but Wilf is still high on adrenaline. The lodging house is empty apart from Zhao, who is boiling potatoes in the kitchen. Wilf greets him, cannot wait to fill him in on the day. He is a giant. 'I wish you'd seen it. Clifford Montague was there at the front. He used to stay where I worked. Can you believe that? I would have taken him down but I couldn't get close enough. They call us scum, but they're the true scum. I almost got arrested, but the cells are full.'

Zhao is unimpressed, polishing a mug with a tea towel. He indicates the chair by the fire. 'There's a man . . .'

Wilf's first thought is the police, but then he sees a face he knows as well as his own, and he freezes. Victor is sitting there, somehow dwarfed by the chair, as if he has shrunk to half his size in the last year. Time has softened Wilf's anger at his father, and he realises how much he has missed him. He is shocked that the broad man is now this bag of bones, but worst of all are Victor's eyes, devoid of hope and expression – like his mother's before she died.

'How . . . how did you find me?'

'It weren't easy. A tramp called Harry brought word of a Devon lad a long while back,' he pauses as coughs rack his body. 'I always asked the newcomers at the camp. They see things others don't on their travels. He told me not to worry. Had a feeling you'd be all right. Said he'd pass on a message if he ever saw you in London. I've been up and down every month since. Then I saw the poster last week . . . I were in no doubt it were you.'

Another cough bursts from Victor's chest, and with it the last remnants of Wilf's anger disperse. He crosses the room in two strides to crouch at Victor's knee. He takes his father's hand. 'It's good to see you, Da. I'm sorry I left how I did. I had to get out before the police . . .' A thought occurs to him: 'You still have a job? There were no repercussions?'

'No. No repercussions.'

'But his lordship set the police after me . . . I heard there was a reward.'

Victor shakes his head. 'No. We were both looking for you. But not to punish you.' Victor reaches out. 'It's why I'm here. There's something I have to tell you.' He covers his mouth as he coughs again, and this time he can't hide the speckled blood that catches on the sleeve.

Wilf grabs hold of it. 'What's this? I must fetch a doctor.'

'No. It's too late. There's nothing can be done.' He takes hold of Wilf's hands. 'I don't have much time left. That's why I had to find you. To tell you the truth about your family.' Again, that rattle deep in his chest.

'I know my family: Robbo, Jim, Gracie, you . . .'

Victor winces. 'You have another family. Your father's family.'

The smile falls from Wilf's face like snow slipping from the roof in the thaw, as icy as the blood is turning in his veins. 'You're my father.'

Victor swallows hard. 'We should have told you a long time ago. Your real father . . . He never came back from the war.'

Wilf sits back on his heels, his face hardening. 'I don't want to hear.' He tries to close his mind to the truth he knows is coming, the truth that will sharpen all the images and worries that have hovered in his mind over the years, of not being good enough, of not being sure where he belongs.

Victor's voice grows stronger. 'First, you must know that I wish I was your father. You are my son. My only child. But we are not of the same flesh and blood.'

Wilf stands, takes a step backwards. In a flash he knows that his mother's lover was his father. But what does it matter now? The man is dead. 'I'm happy that I can call you my father. Let's leave it at that.'

'I must tell you.' Victor gasps for breath, as if the words are sticking in his throat.

'Why must you?' Wilf turns and takes a pace to the door, but he cannot stop Victor's words from entering his ears.

'You know, you look so like him . . . and so unlike me or your ma. You must have wondered. The blond hair, the blue eyes, the mark . . .' Memories of childhood taunts fill Wilf's head – of being touched by the Devil, his mother tending his hurt soul, Victor gruffly telling him to ignore the insults.

'I don't need to know.'

'You do. I can't go to my grave knowing others hold the secret that you don't. It has to come from me.'

Wilf senses he cannot prevent what is coming. He rests his head against the doorframe.

'Wilf, your father were the captain, the viscount,' says Victor. 'The brother of Master Frederick.'

The room pitches like a ship. Of all the people . . . it can't be true. He won't believe it. 'Why are you saying this?' he asks, gripping the doorframe.

'Because it's the truth, and you must hear it from me. Because there's more . . .'

Wilf is torn between running now, along the corridor and out on to the streets, where he could lose himself for ever, or turning to his father, who is not his father any more. The pain is akin to when his mother died, a wrenching that takes the ground from beneath his feet, the darkness of something beyond his control.

He hears the air gurgle in Victor's chest, and he knows he must face that darkness. His hand falls from the door and he turns slowly to face Victor, bracing himself as Victor begins to speak:

'I met your ma when she was eight, on the slag heaps, the same ones where you used to play. She were looking for bits of coal to sell. She were born in the workhouse at Eastville. Never knew her mother or her father, but she had a spark, and she were beautiful, the most beautiful girl I've ever known. I always joked I'd found my diamond in the coal.' He stops for a breath, and Wilf can picture his mother with her long dark hair and her coal-black eyes. 'She used to sing while she was working. She had a voice that could make a dead plant flower. All the boys from Bedminster were in love with her.'

Tears blur Wilf's vision. He sees his mother singing as she makes his favourite biscuits, and while she dresses his knees when he falls, and as she dances around the kitchen while Victor drums on the table. When he opens his eyes, he sees the muscles in the arms that used to hold him high in the air have wasted away to nothing; the big hands that showed him how to lace his boots are scarred and crooked. The chasm is almost too wide to cross, but he has to try. He squats down at Victor's feet. 'But you won her heart,' he says.

Victor smiles, his thin lips stretching over his teeth. 'There was a boy, Arnold Richards. She were a scrap of an orphan, but he were trying to steal her coal. She were scratching like a cat, but he were a big lad. Twice the size of me. I punched him. Must have got lucky. He ran away, crying like a baby. We were never parted after that. I promised I'd take her away from there. She said she always knew she'd marry a hero . . .' He pauses again, and his lungs whistle with effort. 'In the workhouse she were trained for domestic service. She managed to get a job in a big place on the edge of Bristol. A place called Parkfield, where the old earl's brother lived.'

'Maurice Thorneycoombe? I remember him. He disliked the horses. Ma never said she knew him . . .'

'She were good at keeping her own counsel,' Victor says it

422

without bitterness. 'And he would never have recognised her. We're all the same to them.'

Wilf clenches his teeth, thinks of Clifford, but says nothing. He waits for Victor to carry on.

'In them days I still hoped to find a better life for both of us. I didn't want to be a miner. I saw what it does to men like my own da, my older brother. I saw what it does to those ponies, forced to live underground. I thought volunteering in the war would be a start. I'd heard of men making careers out of it. One day your ma heard the viscount talking about his servant who'd been killed. The viscount were a cavalry man, and he were having trouble finding someone in Bristol who were good with horses. Your ma put me forward. Explained how I worked with the ponies. She pushed hard to get me an introduction, went out of her way to speak to him whenever she could, more than any maid should. But she fell in love with him. And what girl wouldn't fall for a handsome rich captain instead of a poor miner? And she still only seventeen. Impressionable. She didn't stand a chance.

'She found out she were with child not long after. She thought that the captain would come for her. Of course he never even wrote. As soon as she started to show she were asked by the housekeeper to leave Parkfield. It were a regular thing, apparently; they went through young maids in that house as fast as firewood on a winter's day. I found out when I were next on leave. I persuaded her to marry me, and she moved in with my family. We told them you were mine. I didn't care about you. I married her because I'd always loved her. I hoped she would love me too one day. But Wilf, I grew to love you as my own. You're my son, whatever blood says.'

Wilf doesn't speak for a while, just lets the horror sink in, until eventually he asks, 'And what about the war? Did you hurt him then? To avenge my mother?'

Victor shakes his head. 'No. I saved him. Those damn medals you and your uncle were always on about . . .'

'You saved him? After what he'd done?'

'I can't abide suffering, and after those years of war I'd seen enough to last for this life and the next. And he were your father, Wilf. He gave you life.'

'But ma thought he was dead . . . I heard you speaking . . .'

'To my shame I didn't tell her. I knew she would always hanker for him if she thought he was alive.'

In the beat of the silence, truth suddenly dawns on Wilf: 'Alive?'

Victor sighs, a long and painful sound. 'It is possible. That's why I need you to know. I didn't want you finding out if he ever came back. Or if anyone else told you . . .'

'Who else knows?'

'Your uncle Robbo suspected something when your ma lost her job. But apart from him, only Master Frederick.'

'He knew?'

'Not for certain at first. He first guessed something were amiss when the countess thought she recognised you . . .'

Pieces of a puzzle start to fall into place: Wilf thinks of the toy car on his windowsill. The kindness of Freddie helping him ride. He reddens with shame and fury. 'How could you have worked for them after what his brother did? How could you take up the position?'

'We did it for you. The viscount never promised me employment. We made it up when we heard of another batman working for his captain after the war. I didn't believe they'd fall for it, but your ma was sure they would. She thought you would have a better life there.'

Wilf stands and begins to pace around the kitchen. 'But they're bullies . . . fascists . . .'

'It's up to God to make the final judgement. But your ma saw something good in the viscount, and out in France, he were a fine officer. He taught me to ride. To shoot. To fight. He gave me self-respect.'

'And Master Frederick? He treated you no better than an animal, even when you say he knew?'

424

'He made a promise to look after you. That night by the lake . . . when your ma . . .'

Wilf snorts to cut him off. He remembers the two men shouting at each other, but he cannot bear to think of that night. 'Promises count for nothing with those people,' he says.

'He wants to make amends . . . He's been good to me since you left. And he's been helping look for you. He offered a reward for information. He had no idea about any of it before me and your ma turned up . . .'

'I won't accept it.'

'You must, or a part of you will always be missing. You'll never be whole.'

But now Victor is gulping for air, his hands in front of his mouth, flecked with blood, and he is bent over, and on the floor, and there is more blood, and the terrible sound of a creature in pain, and Wilf remembers a time long ago when he was crouched over a broken horse with his father so strong and gentle beside him. And he wishes he could go back to that time, when his da was still his da, and the sobs rise in his chest. 'I'm sorry. Don't go. Da. Please . . .'

But Victor has already gone, to a place where Wilf's words cannot reach.

425

CHAPTER 53

Celia walks slowly, savouring the chilly dawn air on her skin, the feel of the long grass on her fingertips. A pair of turtle doves are purring to each other in the apple trees. A great spotted woodpecker is drumming in the woods. She stops to lean on a gate to watch the cattle. Their rhythmic chewing is deeply calming.

She turns back to the house, calling Hope to come away from the molehill she is inspecting. The morning cart will soon be arriving with the outpatients from the village.

She hasn't been back to London since she left, and she has no desire to return. It took almost two years to set up the Littlecombe Centre for Ex-Servicemen, but it has been running successfully for almost a year now. It still astonishes her that Freddie as good as gave his cottages to the charity – charging a nominal rent, before disappearing, travelling abroad away from Coombe, away from his family for months. By the time he came back, her father had renovated the lot, transforming the entire village, with their new thatch, and neat baskets hanging outside the front porches. But still some of the locals do not like change, and they do not like having patients in the village.

As she enters the yard, Hope running ahead of her, she is surprised to see only the centre's full-time residents: Samuel with his strange hopping gait and Roy with his twitches and incoherent shouting. 'Any sign of Nurse Davies?' she asks Nurse Powell.

But the nurse shakes her head, knits her eyebrows together. 'They should be back by now . . . she left on time.'

Celia glances up the drive, but it is empty. She moves to help two of the men who are loading a handcart with tools to take down to the vegetable patch, checking that they have what they need. Samuel leads the old bull in from the top field; he is a different man whenever he takes charge of the animals, his trajectory straighter, his strides more determined. Roy is busy checking on the pig who is due to farrow any day now.

Suddenly John Harris comes tearing into the yard, his face slick with sweat, his breath coming in great gasps. He is shaking, something Celia has not seen him do for years, for his spasms have all but disappeared. 'You need to get down to the village. There's been an accident.'

'What sort of accident?'

He shakes his head, bent double, with his hands on his knees. 'You need to go . . .'

Joseph Cottam collects the car and they drive fast down the lane, the hedges banked up high around them, the road twisting and turning with her stomach. There is no need to ask where. A crowd of people has gathered outside the door. Before her father has even stopped the car, she has stepped into the road. 'Celia, wait! Let me . . .'

She ignores her father's calls, and the angry glares of the villagers as they part to let her through.

Two of the Littlecombe veterans are standing guard at the door, eyes darting in fear. 'What's happened?' she says, but neither of them is able to speak; they just stand aside. She steps into the dark of the corridor, and is surprised to see Freddie Hembury on the threshold of the front room. Since his return from his travels, they have become adept at avoiding each other.

Now he holds up his hands to block her moving forward. 'You really shouldn't see this,' he says.

'Let me through,' she answers, pushing his arm out of the way.

As she steps into the room she sees Nurse Davies on the floor next to a body, and the world crashes around her.

Rupert has not managed to kill himself. His legs are twitching uncontrollably. His breathing is shallow, and he is moaning like a wounded animal on every out-breath through his blue lips. A livid welt scoured into his neck is slowly turning purple.

Celia staggers and Freddie steadies her as they back out into the corridor.

'He'll be all right,' says Freddie. 'I sent my man for the doctor. He should be here any moment.'

'How . . .'

'I was sending a telegram, and Reid's wife ran to collect me . . . they still assume I'm in charge . . . You know what it's like . . .'

She gazes at him as if in a dream. 'No,' she says. 'I mean, how did he . . .'

Freddie swallows. 'He put a rope over one of the beams . . .'

Celia's legs are so weak that she has to rely on Freddie to keep her upright. He seems reluctant to touch her, but she cannot let go, because that night at the hospital in Bristol all those years ago is playing through her mind. With it comes all the shame and the guilt – and then the self-loathing when the major was found, with the same welt around his neck, but all life gone from his body.

'Celia!' Freddie clicks his fingers in front of her face. 'Come. Sit down . . .'

'I can't do this . . .'

He looks at her, eyebrows furrowed. 'You can. Of course you can.'

'I'm not strong enough.' It's as if she's doomed to repeat a vicious cycle for ever.

'You're the strongest person I know . . .'

'You don't understand. Something happened . . . years ago . . .'

'I know.'

'What? What do you know?'

He glances away. 'I know that one of your patients killed himself. Your father told me.'

'Do you know why?'

Freddie shakes his head.

'He did it because of me . . .'

'You cannot blame yourself for the actions of others . . .'

'But it was my fault. He tried to force himself on me, and couldn't live with what he'd done.'

Freddie gasps and steps away. 'Oh God,' he says. 'And then you had me . . .' He cannot meet her eye. He presses the palm of his hand against his forehead. 'I behaved appallingly. I shall never forgive myself for as long as I live . . . and now I find it is even worse, for you to have suffered at the hands of two men. I'm so sorry . . . But sorry will never be enough.' He looks across at her, his back against the wall. He gestures into the room. 'But this isn't related to that. And none of it is your fault. Not then, not now. It is the exact opposite . . . You must see that? All you are guilty of is trying to help these people. As you tried to help me . . .'

And as he says it, she realises that he is right. She is no different to the men she has aided over the years: damaged by something that was beyond her control. She sees her young self, so helpless and overwhelmed, and she wants to tell that girl that it wasn't her fault. And she feels a great weight lifting, a rush of relief, as she stands and leans back against the wall too. She is aware of Freddie next to her, and of a feeling of gratitude that his perceptions provide the unlikely solution to her long misery.

Her father appears at the front door, Dr Bickersteth at his side. 'Cee, are you all right?'

She nods. 'Yes. Really, I am . . .'

Freddie advances, as if grateful to have something to focus on. He indicates for the doctor to go through. 'He's in there,' he says.

430

'Have you seen the crowd?' asks Joseph Cottam, pointing at the front door.

'They would have pushed their way in,' says Freddie, 'but I got your men to stand guard.'

Celia gathers herself. 'They'll call for us to be closed,' she says. 'They've been trying to shut us down since day one.'

'Let's concentrate on this poor chap first.'

They stand in the doorway. The nurse moves away to give the doctor space. 'Thank goodness for the earl,' she says to Celia. 'I'd never have been able to get him down myself. He's that heavy . . .'

Celia shudders.

Dr Bickersteth summons the nurse to help the patient before coming to talk to the Cottams. He tips his hat at Freddie. 'Your driver made short work of those lanes.'

'He knows them well.'

'Rupert needs to be taken to the hospital for observation.'

'I'll tell my man to take you both there.'

'I could do that,' says Mr Cottam.

'It's no trouble. He's there. Ready.'

Freddie takes a step away from the group, as if suddenly realising he's in the wrong place. 'I'll leave you to it . . .'

Celia follows him to the door. It seems as if the entire village is outside the gate. They stop on the threshold, and as Freddie begins to move away, Celia is as exposed as if she were standing on a stage. She sees the glowering faces of the villagers, senses the anger in the air. 'What's going on in there?' yells someone.

'This place ain't safe,' shouts another.

'What if one of the children had seen him?'

'Those men aren't right in the head . . .'

Freddie has stopped at the gate. Suddenly his voice rings out. 'Enough of this nonsense!' he says. 'It's time you all left. Go home and tend to your own problems.'

'How can we sleep safe knowing these people are here?' someone cries.

Freddie's voice is filled with anger: 'These men fought

431

exactly so that you *can* sleep in your beds at night without fear. So that you have a life of freedom – and so that your children have one too. This man could just as easily be your father or uncle. Or my own brother . . . Edward. Have you really forgotten? Go on, go home and think on that.'

The people turn, chastened, bowing their heads as they shuffle away.

Freddie turns around to look at Celia. He places his hat firmly on his head. 'Tell your father I'll see him tomorrow,' he says.

Celia nods, and watches as he makes his way across the street to his parked car. She sees him instruct the driver, pointing back at the cottage, before turning on foot to walk away up the hill, and she is surprised to find the village seems emptier without him.

CHAPTER 54

S pring slips into summer, and there is barely a chance for Celia to notice the blood red poppies scattered along the edges of the barley fields, or the brown butterflies that flutter among them. But today Dr Bickersteth is delayed, and she is able to spend some time with her father, and her brother and sister-in-law, Barbara, who are living at Littlecombe while they search for a house nearby.

The four of them are having lunch outside, on the terrace that looks out across the valley, towards the distant village, across the fields that are yellowing in the sun. Barbara is pregnant with their second child. Their first, Joe, is helping Rupert search for eggs, for the chickens that scratch around in the dust are adept at laying in the strangest of places. Joe has a mop of unruly russet hair and an enthusiasm that reminds Celia of George at that age. She is filled with dread that he will experience the same turbulence of their own early years, cannot believe that war may come again.

The boy stretches on his tiptoes to look into an ornamental urn. Rupert, who still insists on wearing a scarf to hide the faint scar around his neck, lifts the child so he can reach inside, and they both turn to the group at the table, grinning triumphantly as Joe holds up a small brown egg. They move on across the garden hand-in-hand, the gentle giant and the innocent child.

George addresses Celia. 'You really have built up something to be proud of, Cee.'

She smiles. 'Our father had no small part . . .'

Joseph Cottam pours a glass of wine and leans back in his chair. 'I always said business is the key. We are a capitalist nation built on an industrial revolution that happened long before any other country. Working makes us thrive. Earning our way gives us confidence. And it leads to charity.'

'Don't let the men hear you say that. They don't want charity. They just want to return to normal.'

George picks at the cheese. 'Sounds like Freddie Hembury came up trumps,' he says. 'I have to say I was surprised when he let you the cottages, and at such a low rate.'

'It works for us both. We keep them in good repair; he retains the assets but doesn't have to maintain them.'

'We wouldn't be where we are without them,' says Celia.

'And he wouldn't exactly be where he is without us,' adds Joseph Cottam.

Celia glances at him, and he smiles. 'I do know about your loan,' he says.

She opens her mouth in shock. 'But how?'

'Freddie told me. I don't know why you look so embarrassed. It was a sound investment. I would have done the same if the boy had come to me!'

'Speak of the Devil . . .'

Celia follows her brother's line of sight, to where Freddie is waiting self-consciously in the yard. Joseph Cottam stands. 'If you'll excuse me . . .'

'He's back again?' says George. 'What are you two cooking up together?'

Their father's rosy cheeks seem to grow rosier. 'You'll find out soon enough.'

Celia watches him approach Freddie. Those days of their youthful dreams seem so long ago that it makes her feel old. But they have come through fire, and she is sure they could be friends now.

She takes some more salad, watches Freddie and her father from the corner of her eye.

'Did you hear that Miles is out of prison?' asks George.

'Yes. Thank goodness.'

'No thanks to Raymond, I'm afraid.'

'I can't believe the party is still supporting the Russians now that we know about Stalin's purges.'

'And the rest,' adds Barbara, shivering. 'It's not good that Italy has joined Germany against the Communists either. Everyone's at loggerheads.'

'Why does there always have to be a war . . . ?'

A cloud crosses the sun and a shadow falls across the lawn. Barbara pulls her shawl closer around her shoulders. Celia watches the light and dark chase each other across the valley. There is only one topic of conversation that is on everybody's minds.

'They're calling for volunteers to train as wardens in case of air raid attacks,' says George.

'Are you thinking of doing it?' asks Celia.

'It seems impossible to believe that it could happen all over again,' says Barbara.

'Why won't people compromise?' They all look at George as he says this, and Celia starts to laugh. 'I don't know why you're laughing,' he says, 'but it reminds me, I heard an MP speak the other day – his name is Churchill. The talk was arranged by the TUC, although he's a Tory. He was very stirring. Talking about the last few men who are still suffering the mental effects of war. I'll put you in touch. And I hear the British Legion are interested in what you're doing. Who knows . . . perhaps you could apply for royal patronage. I have friends who can help with that.'

'Whatever next, George. Hunting?'

George throws his napkin at Celia as Joseph Cottam returns to the table. Freddie has already disappeared. Her father reaches out for both of their hands. 'I'm glad I've got you both back,' he says.

Dr Bickersteth's car is pulling into the yard when Celia returns to her office. She watches him park, and retrieve his bag from

435

the back seat, just as Dr Rogers did all those years ago when he came to visit her mother. How times have changed. The doctor is due to discharge three of the men. Of the first fourteen patients at Littlecombe, eight have so far gone home to successfully resume lives they thought they had lost for ever. Others are mid-treatment, while some are likely to remain for years.

Dr Bickersteth greets her. They watch Samuel hammer in a post while Roy holds it in place. Private and lieutenant working side by side. Samuel's aim is true, much to the relief of Roy, whose grip is also steady.

'And all without one electric shock,' says the doctor.

'Or a frozen bath!'

'When you think of how we treated them in the past . . . those men who were executed for being cowards, for having no moral fibre . . .'

Celia shakes her head. 'I can't.'

'And how are you getting on convincing the locals?'

'The incident with Rupert set us back a bit.'

'You couldn't have known. He did a sterling job at hiding his symptoms.'

'The villagers are still angry. Or perhaps it would be fairer to say they're afraid.'

The doctor nods. 'Most anger stems from fear.'

'If only they could see . . . understand . . .'

'Why don't you have an open day? I've heard of a place near Exeter that's done the same. I'm sure Alan Hayne would come, and he's such a bigwig these days, working with the Ministry of Health, that it would be bound to draw publicity. One of the Bristol newspapers, perhaps? It would be a chance to show everyone that there is nothing to be afraid of.'

They choose a weekend in autumn, when the orchard is fat with apples hanging from the branches like Christmas baubles. Her father is waiting in the yard, and the residents are already up and about, oiling machinery, mucking out barns, polishing ironwork, shining hooves, rubbing down leather. She is as worried for them as she is for herself. John Harris smiles at her, his face calm. She smiles back. 'Ready?' she asks.

'Always,' he answers. 'The question is, are they?'

Celia is nervous. There has been no more egg-throwing in the village, no more refusal to serve her men in the shop, but recently there have been small incidents at the farm again: milk going missing as well as vegetables dug up. She prays the open day will set everyone's minds at rest.

John carries on adjusting the bunting that the men made out of old and worn clothes, as Nurse Davies arrives from the village with her charges. The nurse now lives in one of the estate cottages so that she is always on hand in case any of the men need her, though they look far from it as they jump down from the cart, fresh-faced and smiling. But Celia knows each of them hides his own ailment from the dark years of soldiering.

The men set to work carrying bottles down to the cider barn, and delivering the bread to the kitchen. The inpatients put the finishing touches to their tables, displaying the spoons and chairs they have made, the vegetables they have grown, brushing the last bits of dust from the animals they are showing. Rupert brings his sign, stammering a greeting. He has more to face than anyone today, and his nerves are showing. 'Perfect,' says Celia.

'Wh-where shall I put it?'

'Get John to show you. It needs to be in the middle so it points to the vegetable plot as well as the carpentry and the apple juice.'

By nine o'clock Dr Hayne is here, as well as a representative from the British Legion, and a journalist from the *Evening Post* in Bristol – none of which helps allay Celia's fears. She feels hands on her shoulders, and recognises the warm and comforting smell of her father. 'Your mother is looking down and smiling with delight. You have achieved more than we ever could. I'm so proud.'

They are ready. The bunting flutters in the wind. The piglets squeal with excitement as someone fills their trough with leftovers from the kitchen. Celia walks around the yard once more. She stops by Rupert, who is twisting his hands together, pretending to rearrange his trays of eggs. 'N-no-no one's coming . . .' he says. 'It's my fault. Mrs Greenslade made her children c-c-cross the road to avoid me again yesterday.'

'She shouldn't have done that,' says Celia forcefully. 'But she'll come today, and so will plenty of others, even if it's just to stir up trouble. And then we can show them how wrong they are.'

She can hear the journalist scratching in his notebook. She can sense the eyes of the British Legion representative boring into her back.

'Look!' Joseph Cottam strides forward. 'Our first visitor.'

Freddie waves a greeting from a distance, and Celia feels a needle of sadness that just once he might come to her. Her father strides away to welcome him warmly, before introducing him to the journalist. Celia watches as Freddie switches smoothly into discussions with the waiting men, and silently thanks whatever gene it is in the aristocracy that makes them so good at polite conversation.

John coughs, to catch her attention. She hears a bicycle bell and looks up to see the schoolmistress, Miss Prescott, whose own father struggled when he returned from the war, cycling towards them, followed by more people on bicycles. The schoolmistress's cheeks are rosy with effort, and she wipes the perspiration from her forehead with a handkerchief. 'I told them they had to come – and bring their parents – or there'd be extra cod liver oil for all of next week.'

'Bless you,' says Celia as Miss Prescott props the bike against a wall.

'Come on, then,' says the teacher, linking her arm through Celia's. 'Let's see what you've been up to.'

After Miss Prescott and the bicycles, more people start to arrive, some on foot, and even a few in motor cars. John shows them where to park to keep out of the way, and the farm yard starts to fill.

Dr Hayne, his hair grey and his back stooped, fights his way through the crowd to reach her. 'Congratulations,' he says. 'An inordinate success, I'd say.'

'You should claim some of the credit. It was your methods that got us here.'

He frowns. 'When I think how far you've come since those early days. It was a bad business how we treated our young women after the war. And, to my eternal shame, you suffered more than most.'

'What's past is past.'

'You know, I did put your return to the hospital board, but they rejected it. I believe they were worried it might reflect badly on them if what happened ever came out. I should have put up more of a fight, though. It was cowardly, but I felt I was partly to blame.'

'None of it was your fault. It was an unfortunate combination of things.'

He pats her arm gratefully. 'It seems you didn't need me to make a success of yourself anyway.'

They are distracted by a commotion at one of the tables, where two women are tutting loudly and shaking their heads. Celia excuses herself.

'Mrs Huxtable. Can I help?'

'This is dead.' Mrs Huxtable waves a wilting plant at her.

'It just needs water – it's been in the sun all morning, as I'm sure Samuel would have told you if you'd asked him.'

Samuel nods politely, but Mrs Huxtable puts her hand to her mouth. 'Oh, I couldn't go near one. What if he . . .'

'If he what?'

'We still can't be sure they're safe. Maud Greenslade says one of them looked at her daughter funny.'

'I'm sure you can't mean that.'

'And Jeannie says they come into the shop and don't buy nothing. Just walk out. Probably stealing . . .'

'That's got more to do with the way Jeannie treats them. I've seen her moving things from the shelf.'

'What about that one in Briar Cottage? I've seen him tapping. It's not right. And there's that foreign-looking one who never says a word. What if he's a spy? You know there's another war coming . . .'

Celia has heard enough. She cannot, will not take any more of this. She hushes Mrs Huxtable with one hand, and then calls out above the crowd. 'Could everyone gather around, please.'

Mrs Huxtable opens her mouth, but Celia shushes her again, and this time claps her hands, and the neat little woman clamps her teeth together in vexation. Dr Hayne joins the calls for attention, and soon the news spreads from one group to the next that Celia is about to say something. An expectant hush descends.

Celia takes a deep breath. 'First, I'd like to thank you for coming to our first open day. It means a lot to me and to my father. But most of all, it means a lot to the men. So from them, a hearty thank you.'

A voice she recognises as Mrs Huxtable's mutters loud enough for all to hear, 'It's dangerous, if you ask me. I can't understand why they aren't locked safely away. That's what usually happens in an asylum.'

'As I've explained to you before, Mrs Huxtable, this is not an asylum, and these men are here of their own volition. They are volunteering for treatment, and we are giving it.'

'But—'

Celia raises her hand. 'Enough, Mrs Huxtable! Please!' Slowly the whisperings die away. 'It is time for you all to start behaving in a way I know you are capable of.' She ignores the tuts of disapproval. 'You must open your hearts to these men. I can assure you the only thing wrong with them is that they have been forgotten by the very people who should remember them most. They gave their young lives, and here they are, twenty years later, unable to work, ill, rejected by their own communities, loved by their families who despair at what to do. Every other country – America, Canada, France, New Zealand – even Germany and Italy – takes care of its disabled veterans better than we do. It is time we redressed the balance.'

The man from the British Legion looks around, nodding his head. The journalist scribbles. Her father and Freddie both smile in encouragement.

'But why does it have to be here?' The crowd looks at Mrs Huxtable – who will not relinquish her position as their mouth-piece – then back to Celia.

'A moment ago, you told me that Maud Greenslade said one of our men looked at her daughter in a peculiar way, but Maud is happy to take our laundry for us. In fact, she's making enough money to employ extra staff to do so. Staff found among you and your children in the village. And I know that the Hartnells' forge is up and running full time again. And the Stonemans have had to build another oven to keep up with orders. And as for you, Mrs Huxtable, I'd have thought the fact that Nurse Davies is engaged to your son, who may well end up living with her in one of our cottages, might have been enough for you to see what a boon it's been for our village. You should all be proud to be associated with the Centre, and with our men. If you cannot be proud, then please leave while the rest of us enjoy our day. Thank you very much.'

There is shocked silence as the women glance at each other, and at the ground, and then Freddie starts to clap, and so do George and Barbara, and Joseph Cottam, Dr Hayne, the jour-nalist, the representative, and finally everyone else, and Celia can sense there is a shift in the mood as the people begin to disperse, and she even catches sight of one or two engaging in conversation with the veterans as they wander around again.

Freddie is saying goodbye to Joseph Cottam when Celia approaches. 'Would you like a full tour before you leave?' she asks.

He glances at her, hesitant, then says curtly, 'That would be lovely. Thank you.'

They follow the people meandering from the vegetable patch to the baskets that they make. A toddler runs past them chasing a chicken. One of the men is showing some children where the sow likes best to be scratched, and John is demonstrating turning a bowl on the lathe.

'No Elizabeth?' asks Celia.

'She's in London.'

'What about the girls?'

'She's packed them off to boarding school. Wycombe Abbey. It's miles away.' Freddie looks pained.

'You must miss them?'

'I hate not having them around.'

They end up in the cider barn, where the vicar is playing billiards with some of the men. She points at the bookshelves on the walls. 'Donated by you, I believe,' she says.

'We had plenty to spare.'

'You must be pleased that Ceylon turned out so well. I didn't realise you'd kept it going.'

'It's all thanks to my business partner, really.' He pauses. 'And to you, of course.'

She reddens. She is not looking for his gratitude. 'My father says it's down to your solid plan, as well as expanding your sales to other countries.'

'Your father is being generous, as always. I had the easy part. I am lucky that Matthew is so capable. If you think farming here is difficult, you should try it abroad.'

'And the cottages? We cannot expect to pay a peppercorn rent for ever.'

'I won't be putting it up.'

'I don't understand; it doesn't make financial sense.'

'You had to spend a lot of money making those cottages fit for habitation. Besides, I owed you from a long time ago.'

'I never expected the money back.'

'I want to reimburse you.'

'There's no need . . .'

'I'd give them to you if I could, but my brother . . . well . . . you know they may not even be mine.'

They have stopped next to the old cider press at one end of the barn. The giant screws have been cleaned ready for this season's apples, and the black ironwork gleams.

'I remember when you used to make cider,' says Freddie.

She smiles at the recollection. 'It seems a lifetime ago. No demand for it now that we don't need to attract those casual labourers.'

'No. The world is very different to when you first arrived.' He inspects his hands as if he cannot bear to look at her.

'We make apple juice now. We've been selling it to a couple of shops in London. A taste of the West Country . . . The farm as a business is doing really well. It should help keep the charity open.'

'Hopefully that's not all that will help.'

'What do you mean?'

'I've said too much for now. You'll find out when the paperwork is signed . . .'

Finally their eyes meet, and she feels that old spark crackle between them, undimmed by the years.

CHAPTER 55

The clouds are thickening, great dark cumulonimbus sweeping in from the south, rain pooling in the potholes of the road, and streaming off the roof of the cow shed. Celia sits on the window seat in her bedroom, trying to escape the talk of gas masks and blackout curtains. Though the papers are still full of appeasement, there is a growing sense that something terrible is coming, rolling across Europe like the clouds that bump and press above her now.

Celia hears her father calling her down to the front room. She is surprised to see Freddie there, dark patches on his shoulders where the rain has soaked into his clothes.

Her father speaks as soon as she enters. 'Ah, Celia. I need you to hear this. It is the next step in your journey.'

'What step? What do you mean?'

Her father looks between them. Freddie nods, as if giving some signal. 'Why don't you say?' asks Mr Cottam.

But Freddie shakes his head.

'Very well.' Celia's father turns to her: 'Freddie is turning the Hall over to us. To use as a hospital to treat men with neurological complaints.'

'A hospital?'

Freddie's thick hair is shiny with raindrops. He rubs the back of his neck. 'Yes. The government will need to requisition places for training troops, for hospitals, for schools. I want to offer Coombe to you and your father as a place for men to recover from the coming war . . .'

'You really believe it will happen?'

'I am certain of it.'

'As am I,' adds her father.

'It will be more important than ever that you are there to help. For the men now . . . For the men in the future . . .'

Celia stares at them both blankly. 'But what about you?' she eventually asks Freddie. 'Where will you live?'

'I have plans. But for now, I'm going to fight.'

'You can't. You're too old.'

He laughs for the first time she can recall in a long while. 'I'm 39. Not past it yet. They need soldiers. And I want to protect the things I hold dear . . . my daughters, my country . . . Besides, there's something else I must do.'

'Father, tell him he can't.'

But Joseph Cottam shrugs, 'We've talked about it many times.'

'Do neither of you remember what happened in the last war?' she says, aware that her voice is rising, along with the realisation that having regained his friendship, she can't bear the thought of losing Freddie again. 'How many men we lost. How many men never recovered. It's all here if you don't. Right in front of you!' She points to the window, and then her hand drops as she wonders how on earth she will explain to those ex-soldiers that it is all going to start again.

'I can't dissuade him,' says her father.

'Then you haven't tried hard enough.'

'This is something I need to do,' says Freddie quietly.

She appeals to her father once more, but Joseph Cottam stands. 'I believe you two must talk,' he says. 'Alone.' He gives a short bow, and leaves the room.

Celia and Freddie stand self-consciously until she crosses to the window, and looks out across the sodden valley. 'You were so determined to make Coombe work,' she says without turning. 'It was your family duty . . .'

'And look where it got me.'

'What does Elizabeth say?'

'I don't know. She's still in London. She's not coming back. We're divorcing. She keeps her title, and the house in Cadogan Square for her lifetime. She seems happy enough.'

'I'm sorry.' Still, she cannot turn to face him. 'The girls?'

He pauses for a second, and she can hear the pain in his voice. 'They will live with Elizabeth. Their mother is hardly destitute. Her shares will recover eventually. I've sold my half of the business in Ceylon. I enjoyed my time out there, but it's becoming too unstable. With Gandhi in India, the locals are becoming obsessed with independence, and then there's the war. It's so close to Japan. I don't feel safe having so much money tied up out there. There was enough to set up trusts for the girls with the proceeds, as well as put some away for myself. I'll be maximising the farming on the estate. I have no doubt the government will be pushing us to produce more food when things hot up.'

'But the plantation was your dream.'

'And you made it possible.' His voice is quiet with emotion. 'I hope that Coombe might go some way to helping you fulfil yours.'

'But what about you?'

'The children are my focus now. I want to provide for them. I'll still be on the board of Carrington and Thorneycoombe, and the main thing is that I've kept Coombe going to pass on to Dilly if she wants it. Perhaps she will think of something to do with it after the war. Perhaps she will continue to let you use it. Perhaps she will sell it. Whatever happens, they will both be wealthy in their own right. Most importantly, they must follow their own dreams. I will not pressure Dilly into keeping Coombe going if that is not what she wants.'

'And what does your mother think?'

'My mother . . .' His voice chokes a bit, and at last she turns. Freddie is staring at her own mother's old chair and desk. He picks up one of the paintings that are still propped up against the ink stand. 'I hope she might move into the old coach house. I can join her there once war is over. Of course, she may not want that, once she knows . . .' He puts the canvas down, runs his hand over his face. 'Does a mother forgive her child everything?' he asks glumly.

And Celia suddenly realises that they have come full circle. The brother was the cause, the brother is the solution.

'Have you told her that Edward may be alive?'

'I'm going to wait until I have proof. She has suffered enough. The shock could set her back years.'

'And have you found any proof?'

'Your father has been helping me. He put me in touch with your Dr Hayne, who put me in touch with another doctor who worked with disfigured patients on the Front. From what Bolt told me, Edward would have needed specialist surgery. Dr Hayne's doctor knew of a woman in Paris who worked with men to reconstruct their faces. That's why I was abroad for so long. I went to her old workshop.' He shudders at the recollection. 'I can't explain what it was like, those casts still covering the wall. The faces of men destroyed and rebuilt. And among them the spitting image of Edward . . . I hardly dare hope. It's terrible how we inflict such damage on each other . . .'

'And now we're set to do it again . . .' Celia adds grimly. 'And you are planning to join the carnage.'

'That is why I want to make my peace with everyone I've wronged. My mother. And . . . my nephew – Wilf. Although he has proved impossible to trace. Bolt never returned from London the last time he went up. It's been a year since. He heard something about the boy being involved with those Communist friends of yours, but people only clam up when I ask questions.'

'Is it surprising? You set the police on Wilf.'

'I know.' He looks miserable. 'I was wrong to do that . . .' He suddenly crosses the room to kneel in front of her, bending his head. 'But most of all, I was wrong to . . . to try to take advantage of you that day in the woods.'

'Don't . . .'

'I must. I'm more ashamed about how I behaved . . . than about anything I've ever done in my life.'

'You weren't yourself.'

'I have promised myself – and others – that I will never touch a drop again. It's a battle every day.' He looks up, deep into her eyes. 'But it would be easy to blame it solely on the alcohol. In reality there are no excuses. I am sorry. For it all. For before then . . . For thinking I can take what I want.'

'Stand up, please. I forgive you. Really, I do.'

He gets to his feet, eyes still locked on hers. He takes her hand. 'Before I leave, I just want you to know that I wish I'd followed my heart from the moment I fell for you, when you walked into the Hall all those years ago, on another wet day very much like today . . .'

Outside the rain pours in sheets across the yard. Inside, his touch is so delicate that it makes her heart stop, and she knows she does not want him to go.

CHAPTER 56

The rain does not let up over the next few weeks. The coloured carpet of fallen leaves in the woods has turned to mud, and bare branches fracture the sky.

Freddie looks around Joseph Cottam's office. It is strange to think that a decade ago he would have felt awkward here. Now the man is like a father to him.

Mr Cottam removes his glasses. 'I think we've got everything tied up,' he says. His brow is creased with wrinkles, and Freddie notices there are other lines that crisscross his face, fanning out from his eyes and mouth.

Freddie nods. 'There is only one thing outstanding. As you know, I had hoped to find Wilf Bolt before I left. Can I trust that you will ensure my wishes are carried out if he ever returns?'

'Of course.'

'I have to say, I was surprised – and upset – that Victor never came back. I thought we had reached an understanding.'

'We can never truly know what goes on in another's mind.'

'No.' Freddie sighs. 'All I do know is there is another war coming, and that means there will be another War Agriculture Executive Committee. They'll be dictating what we grow and where if we don't have a plan.'

'And we have a plan. So don't worry. I'm grateful for your expertise.'

'And I'm grateful for yours. Sharing the machinery makes sense. And the land will be more productive combined.'

'We'll be able to accommodate a lot of men in the Hall.'

'Use it however you need. There will certainly be plenty of outdoor work for the men who are able.'

Joseph Cottam pinches his nose, his glasses in his hand. 'Are you happy if we still allow men to stay down by the river?'

Freddie nods. 'It's your side. I rarely see anyone there these days.'

'They still come sometimes. Just not so many. But I'll make sure it's undisturbed.'

'I trust you of all people will be bold enough to stand up to the committee.'

'Bravery or stubbornness?' Celia's father laughs. 'I'll let you decide.'

Freddie relaxes; he knows the estate will be safe with the Cottams overseeing it. 'Well,' he says, pushing himself to his feet. 'I'd better go. It's already getting dark.'

'I can run you back in the car?'

'No. Thank you. I'd like to walk. I enjoy these wild nights.' He also wants to make the most of the countryside he loves before he leaves. He knows there is a chance he may not come back.

'Do drop in on Celia on your way. She's in the cider barn. Some of the men have a reading group.'

Freddie bows his head as he rests his hands on the back of the chair. 'I will.' He leaves Joseph Cottam in the glow of the fire, the warm light flickering on his ageing face.

It is cold outside. One of the large doors of the cider barn is partly open, and Freddie can see Celia, seated at the table with some of the men. Lamps burn in the hollows in the walls, as well as on the tabletop. One veteran is standing in front of the lit stove, reading from an open book.

Freddie cannot bring himself to enter. He watches as Celia claps and smiles up as the man makes his way back to the table. Her warmth and spirit seem to shine a light on all around her. He wishes he could turn back time to when they first met. He aches to be with her, to make good all the hurt, to start afresh. Why did he have to hit rock bottom before he understood what really matters? His shame at how he has treated her is overwhelming. He knows he does not deserve another chance. It's one of the reasons he's leaving. He gazes at her once more, and then he slips away into the night. Only the pale face of a barn owl sheltering in the owl hole sees him go.

As soon as he steps away from the barn, its comforting light is sucked away. He curses and wishes he'd brought a light. There is a strong breeze, and he can hear the crack and thwack of some canvas that must have come loose. On the periphery of his vision, at the edge of the yard, the hayricks squat wetly, like small cottages.

He crosses the lane. The north wind bites through the wool of his jacket. He can just make out the old lodge house, a black mass by the entrance to the drive. Its little wooden gate is banging in the wind, the latch missing the catch every time. He advances to try to remedy the situation, fumbling in the dark. His hand finally finds metal, and he is about to shut the gate, when he is surprised to notice a soft light in one of the downstairs rooms of the house. Hardly there. Is it his imagination?

He creeps through the gate, turning to latch it quietly now. Something moves in the corner of his vision. He snaps round. A shadow within shadows, a furry shape, a tail. A cat. He berates himself. He is being ridiculous. There is nothing out here but creatures of the night.

But then his eyes catch the light again, moving to another room. Who on earth would be in there at this time of night?

The light suddenly goes out.

He feels his way around the house, first stone beneath his hands, then a window ledge. He peers carefully into the glass, but all is dark. Suddenly he senses a presence. He is sure he can hear breathing below the sound of the wind. He freezes and turns, feels the lodge house at his back, knows someone is watching him.

'Who's there?' he says, hoping his voice sounds strong.

Nobody answers. The ghosts of the past brush past him: Victor and Aggie. Wilf. The wind has chased the clouds away and for a moment a crescent moon illuminates the little garden.

He is a handsome young man, tall and chiselled, still with a faint look of Edward about his face. 'Wilf?' whispers Freddie.

The young man looks as if he might throw a punch, and Freddie braces himself, but it does not come. The silver-laced clouds scud over the moon. Everything has a magical, unreal look in the pale light. Wilf just stares.

Myriad thoughts tumble through Freddie's mind: this is Wilf, who he thought he might never see again; Wilf, his brother's child; Wilf, who has every reason to hate him. He has been thinking about this moment for years. He must take charge of the situation.

'How long have you been here?' he asks.

Wilf shrugs. 'A few weeks.'

Freddie can see the boy is too thin, his shoulders angular, his cheeks sunken. 'Why didn't you show yourself?'

'I didn't think I'd be welcome.' Wilf's voice is low, hardly discernible.

'You're wrong. I'm glad you're here.'

The boy snorts, tossing his head and turning away. Freddie can smell his clothes, see they are tattered and dirty.

He calls after him. 'Where have you been these last couple of years? We've been looking for you everywhere.'

Wilf ignores him.

Freddie steps after him. 'Did your father find you?'

Now Wilf stops. 'My father?' He turns to face Freddie again. His teeth glint in the darkness. 'Don't speak to me of my father.' Anger laces every word. Secrets are pushing their way towards the light.

Freddie stands his ground. 'We must talk.'

'What good would that do? It's your fault . . . you pushed us out . . . even when you knew . . . even when you knew . . .'

Freddie balks at his rage, turning his face, remembering his split cheek.

Wilf laughs sourly. 'Oh, I won't hurt you again. I've seen enough of that. I understand how my da felt. You ask me where I've been? I went to Spain to fight cruel men. But the men I were fighting for were just as cruel. There ain't no difference between people who think they're right: communists kill the same way as fascists – with hate in their hearts. And fascists die the same way as communists – crying for their mothers. We're all the same, and death don't care whose side you're on.'

He stops, and they stand for a while, listening to the wind whistle and moan around the chimney, until Wilf's teeth begin to chatter.

'Come to the Hall,' says Freddie, 'I can give you dry clothes. We can talk . . .'

'I won't set foot in there. It's poison. Your family are poison.'

Freddie thinks of the conversations he's had with Joseph in the past. 'Then come to Littlecombe?' he says. 'I know there is warmth in Miss Cottam's barn. She won't mind you sharing it.'

Wilf doesn't answer.

Freddie tries again. 'Just a cup of hot tea. You don't have to stay for long . . .'

They walk in silence back to Littlecombe. Joseph Cottam is surprised to see Freddie again so soon, but he understands when he sees Wilf a few steps behind. They have talked about this moment before. Celia's father agreed with her that if Wilf did ever return, it would be best to talk on neutral ground.

'I wondered if we might be able to sit in the cider barn,' says Freddie, as if nothing is planned.

Mr Cottam nods. 'I believe Celia is there at the moment.

Let me go ahead and inform her. We can put the kettle on.'
He shrugs on a coat while Wilf hangs back.

Freddie leans in so they can talk out of earshot. 'I need you
to help me keep him there. I've got to get him to listen.'

'I hope you know what you're doing,' says Mr Cottam,
fastening his buttons.

'I've got to give it a try.'

The old man digs his hands into his pockets and hurries
ahead. 'Give us five minutes,' he says.

When Freddie and Wilf enter the cider barn the veterans are
gone, and Celia is rekindling the stove.

In the light of the lamps Freddie can see how like Edward
Wilf is. He must be older than Edward was when he left.
Freddie wonders briefly what his brother might look like now,
how he might have aged.

Wilf regards him suspiciously, moving to sit at the far end
of the table, where Joseph Cottam is setting some soup and
bread.

Freddie removes his hat. He moves slowly, as he would
with a flighty horse. He sits without taking his eyes off Wilf.

He waits for Wilf to finish the soup. He does not have to
wait long: the young man is obviously starving. The bread
disappears quickly too. Celia and her father hang back, giving
them space, but they do not leave. Freddie has told Mr Cottam
that should this day ever come, he would need witnesses.

Freddie clears his throat. 'I just want to talk,' he says.

Wilf looks at him as he wipes his mouth with the back of
his hand.

'I don't want to talk. I'll be going now.' He stands.

'Please?'

'You said I didn't have to stay.'

'And you don't. But I want you to listen before you make
up your mind . . .'

Wilf leaps to his feet. He glances at the Cottams, then back
at Freddie. 'Why should I listen to you? Why should I listen

454

to any of you? You're all liars!' He backs away as he points a finger around the room until it lands on Freddie. 'And you. You've lied to me from the beginning.'

Freddie holds up his hands. 'I accept the charge,' he says. 'I didn't know what to do. When I found out who you were, I was as confused as you.'

Wilf puts his hands over his ears, a child again. 'I don't want to hear it. I don't want to hear more poison.'

'I know I have acted shamefully. Let me make amends. We were close once.'

Wilf rolls his eyes, shakes his head as if trying to block the idea from his mind.

'I didn't imagine it,' adds Freddie. 'I know we were. I was genuinely fond of you.' He feels a stab of guilt as he sees the hurt flutter across Wilf's face, and he knows he is right, despite Wilf's attempt to pretend otherwise.

'It's too late.' Wilf has reached the wide doors on one side of the barn, but the great iron bar that holds them closed is down on the other side. He rattles it, but to no avail. He spins to look to the other door, but Celia and Joseph Cottam are standing in front of it.

Wilf's eyes dart around, searching for another way out, but there are no options. He appeals to Celia: 'Please, let me out. Let me go,' he says.

Celia winces. Freddie knows she does not want to be party to this, but she also knows how important it is for Wilf. And for Freddie. 'You need to acknowledge the truth,' she says. 'It's the only way.'

'How long have you known?' cries Wilf, and Freddie sees that the boy is wounded again as he realises that Celia is party to the lies.

Celia glances at her hands, ashamed, but before she can answer, Wilf adds with contempt, 'I can't trust you anyway. You're as bad as him. I saw you once. I saw you together. By the cow barn.'

She blushes, and for a second Freddie wonders whether

the recollection gives pleasure or shame. 'Then you know that not everything is black and white,' she says quietly.

'How can you forgive him for how he behaved in the woods . . . for taking advantage of you just as his brother took advantage of my mother all those years ago. It's what they do. How could you forgive them?'

Freddie's heart is pounding; his behaviour is on display for all to hear. He senses Joseph Cottam's kind but probing eyes on him, dreads the man's disappointment.

'I have learnt that acceptance and forgiveness are the only way we can move forward with our lives,' says Celia. 'It is true for me. It is true for you too.' Freddie glances over at her. She is looking straight back at him, and for the first time, he feels hope that she really might have forgiven him. But then she adds, 'And I mean forgiveness of ourselves as well as of others.'

Freddie frowns, and he and Wilf regard each other.

There is a long silence. Wilf suddenly sits down, with his head in his hands. 'I'm so tired,' he says. 'I'm tired of running. Of fighting . . . of wondering where I belong . . . Bristol, Coombe, London, Spain . . .'

Freddie places his palms flat on the table, almost reaching out. 'You don't have to run,' he says calmly. 'Stay.'

Wilf looks up, and as they gaze at each other across the table, Freddie knows in that instant that Wilf is listening, and that he has to keep him listening: it is his only chance to put things right. He takes a deep breath. 'I didn't want to believe you were Edward's son. Not because I was ashamed of you, but because I was ashamed of him. Of what it meant he'd done. He's my older brother, and I knew well what he was capable of. And I couldn't understand why he wasn't here, to face up to things. And why he wasn't here to perform his duty. To take charge of Coombe. Always leaving me to pick up the pieces, to deal with the fall-out . . .

'But then I realised this is about us – not him. We cannot be responsible for his behaviour, only our own. And I know

456

that you can still love someone even if they have behaved badly. No one should be defined by their past actions, and nor should they be defined by where they come from. You have guts and spirit; you're a better horseman than I am; and the girls always adored you.'

Wilf is watching him warily, but still listening.

'I knew you were Edward's from the very minute my mother knew too. When she found you with the toy car. I mean, who could doubt it? You look just like him. You walk like him. You smile like him.'

Wilf leans his elbows on the table and hides his face in his hands.

'And despite how he behaved, Edward wasn't all bad. Loyal, brave, impetuous. I loved him. He was . . . *is* . . . my brother . . . And God knows, we've all done things in the past that we're ashamed of.'

He blushes here, deep crimson, glancing at Wilf first, then Celia, who doesn't look away, but encourages him on with a small smile.

'In fact, there is only one man I know for whom that doesn't hold true: the man who brought you up as his own.'

Wilf takes his hands away from his face and stares at Freddie.

'Victor is a good man. I treated him badly. I thought he was after something, because that's how most people operate around my family. But all he was looking for was a better life, somewhere to rest after the horrors he'd seen in the war, somewhere you might have prospects.' He pauses to swallow. 'If it helps at all, I did apologise to him, and I like to think he has forgiven me. He came to me the day you left. He said he didn't care what I did to him, but that you weren't to blame. That you were suffering from the loss of your mother, that you'd always had a feeling of being out of place, that you loved the children – and Coombe – but you'd taken a wrong path. All things I knew, of course. Miss Cottam had already shown me what an unbearable ogre I had become, but as I talked to Victor, I remembered how much I'd liked him when he first came. How much I still like him. He seemed to harbour no ill thoughts. He was so kind about Edward, despite everything. It became evident that he wasn't after anything but a quiet and peaceful life, with money on the table and a roof over his head. He made me realise that all my problems were of my own making.

'We tried to find you. We even put up a reward. Victor travelled up and down to London once a month, and then one time he didn't come back. I assumed he'd found you and you'd set up home together.'

'Well we didn't. He's dead,' says Wilf. 'They put him in a pauper's grave. Buried him with strangers, and no stone to mark he'd ever been on this earth.' He sniffs and rubs at his eyes.

'I am so very sorry to hear that. He was not in good shape for that last year before he left. But I hope he found some comfort knowing that I promised I would look after you if ever we found you.' Freddie stops and looks at his hands, remembering he made that promise once before, by the lake . . . but this time it has been witnessed by Joseph Cottam, and he knows anyway that he won't go back on it.

'I went to Ceylon when Victor didn't return. It was something I'd wanted to do since I was your age – younger.' He smiles at the memory; to finally have seen the elephants at Kandy, the bougainvillea, and the neat rows of tea before he sold. He had pictured the life he could have had, with Celia.

'While I was out there I did a lot of thinking. I'd been trying to leave here for so long I didn't appreciate what I had. But I also realised something else: that I needed to find my brother. I want to know why he didn't come back. What is going through his mind. I won't be judging him for it, just trying to understand. Life cannot be about what everyone else expects.

'Which brings me to you. When war comes I'm going to France with the artillery. I'd like you to take over the upkeep of the estate: the gardens, the stables, the woods, the fields.

458

You know it so well already. The Cottams will deal with the house. I would sell the whole damn thing if I could, but it's not mine to sell. If Edward is still alive . . . well . . . we shall see. One day, I will move into the coach house. The lodge house – where you used to live – is yours, if you want it. And I will need someone to liaise with the land manager . . .'

Wilf gazes at him in exhausted confusion. 'And we play happy families, is it? Do Miss Dilly and Miss Anne know?'

'Would you like them to know? Because I would be happy to tell them. In fact, you can tell whoever you want. I am fed up with secrets. No doubt you are too. There won't be anything formal, but I will make sure you are provided for.'

Wilf glances at Celia, and back to Freddie, as if he can't believe what he is hearing. 'But . . . but if I accept your offer . . . I don't know about upkeep . . . I don't know how to liaise . . .'

'I have a feeling you will be quick to learn.' Freddie grabs at the chance that Wilf is at least contemplating his proposal.

'And I'll help,' says Joseph Cottam, stepping forward. 'Littlecombe and Coombe Hall will be working together . . .'

'And what about . . . the . . . the captain?' says Wilf, as if he still cannot say the name. 'What will he say?'

Freddie shrugs. 'I have no idea, but I give you my word that you will have my support, whatever it is.'

'I don't know,' says Wilf. 'I don't know what to say.'

'You can stay here while you decide,' says Celia, moving closer as well. 'There is room for you. You can work with the men . . .'

Freddie can see that Wilf is wavering. 'What have you got to lose?' he adds gently.

And there is no answer to that, for Wilf has nothing.

CHAPTER 57

'There is an Englishman asking for you.' Edward looks up from the desk. Madame Sauveur is slower these days, as she shuffles into the room, but her bright make-up is still intact, the powder smoothed over the crinkles in her face, the lipstick as red as ever.

'What Englishman?'

She shrugs. 'He asks for someone – not James Cooke . . . Edward . . .'

Edward clutches the desk as the room sways. 'I can't . . .' he stutters. He pushes himself to his feet, glances towards the window.

'You must. It is time for the English soldier to face his past.'

In a daze Edward walks into the hall, and to the wide front door, towards the daylight. He can feel the heat of the sun reflected from the drive; he can hear the crickets whirring in the borders. At the bottom of the steps is parked an Army vehicle, one man at the wheel, his elbow resting on the window ledge as he stares out across the fields; the other standing, his back to the vehicle, his face squinting up at the house.

Edward hears footsteps behind him and feels Aurélie's hand on his shoulder. But Madame tugs the girl away. '*Non. Laisses-les.*'

Aurélie's fingers retract, and he knows that he is alone. He begins his descent.

* * *

461

Freddie looks up. He sees a man walking towards him, and at first he feels anger that this man has kept himself hidden for more than twenty years, expecting Freddie to run his affairs, to live his life for him, but the anger turns to guilt, for the man must have endured much to have kept hidden all these years. The man has reached the bottom of the steps, and though one half of him is misshapen, the hair patchy, the skin scarred, the face does not shock Freddie, for he can see that this really is his brother. This is Edward.

Edward stops in front of him. They stare at each other for a moment, and those blue eyes with the pupil bleeding from the centre are nursery food, and toy soldiers, and running with the dogs through the long grass, and splashing after each other on horses through the river, and blossom falling like snow.

'I'm taller than you,' says Freddie in surprise. And then they are both reaching out for each other, and Edward does not smell like Edward, but of sweat and earth, and he does not feel like Edward, for his back is broader, his hands are rougher, and his muscles more powerful: he is a man forged by physical labour. And it is only then that Freddie understands that this man is something more than the older brother who rode to war all those years ago.

Edward too is wondering at his younger brother, who is now a man, with an unfamiliar bearing of confidence, far from the chaotic, dishevelled boy he used to be. The questioning energy that Freddie always had has been fused with a sadness, but as Edward stands back and looks into the grey eyes, he sees the spirit is still there, the daring that is sailing over a forbidden fence, and climbing the clock tower, and jumping off the haystacks – and he cannot help smiling back.

'How . . . what are you doing here?' says Edward.

'We're off to help the French dig defences along the Belgian border.'

'You've joined the artillery?'

Freddie salutes. 'For king and country.'

'But how did you find me?'

'It wasn't easy . . .'

'You always were a dogged little bugger.'

'Why didn't you let us know you were alive?'

Edward bows his head, puts a hand up to his face, fingers the shrivelled skin, the scars.

'Did you really think anyone would care about that? We just wanted you to come home.'

Edward shakes his head. 'Edward Damerel does not exist any more.'

'I don't understand.'

'How could I go back to . . . that life . . . to being the young heir, when all those men – so many who used to work for us – lost their lives? How could anyone back home ever understand that?'

'You never even let us try.'

'I couldn't . . .'

'What about Coombe? It is yours . . .'

'No. I forgo all claim on it. My life is here now. This is my family.'

'You have a family in England.'

Edward kicks his foot in the dust, and turns away, exasperated. 'I don't want to come back. Can't you see? My life was a waste before. Now I have some kind of purpose.'

It is Freddie's turn to vent his frustration. 'So you just abandoned all of us? Papa? Mama? Ginny? Me? Without a moment's thought?'

'Of course I think about you. I've carried you with me always.' Edward reaches into his shirt and pulls out something tied around his neck. It glints gold in the sunlight. His signet ring.

Freddie catches hold of it, feels the warmth in the metal, sees the coat-of-arms, the noble eagle, the intrepid wild boar. 'You broke Mama's heart.'

'I regret that. But I won't go back.'

'You broke Papa's too. He is dead.'

'I am sorry to hear it, but I too have died in my own way.'

463

Freddie understands there is no point in trying to persuade Edward otherwise; he does not doubt this man is different to the boy who left Coombe two decades ago. He glances over Edward's shoulder at the willowy girl standing next to the painted old lady. 'I see you have a child,' he says.

'She's not mine by blood, though she feels like mine.'

Freddie snorts, and looks at the ground.

'Have you any children?' asks Edward.

'Two. Dilly and Anne.' Freddie looks up, stares into his eyes. 'And you have a son. He's 24.'

'What?'

'Parkfield.' There is no need for further explanation.

The memories flash through Edward's head. A fumbled rendezvous in the corridor at his uncle's house. The pretty little maid who had been so keen to please, who had smiled and flirted in the weeks before he left. It was not the first time he took what he wanted. Not the first time he enjoyed the fun without the responsibility in those heady, frightening days before they were deployed.

Freddie sighs. 'Her name was Agatha. Agatha Bolt.'

'Bolt?' The name sears through him. 'But Bolt . . . I had no idea they were related. I thought they were simply friends.'

'Not related. Childhood sweethearts. They married soon after. He wanted to make sure she wasn't shamed by an illegitimate baby.'

More images flicker in his mind: of Bolt cleaning his tack, falling with a thud as he learnt to ride, bringing his morning tea, whistling through his teeth as he groomed the horses. 'I had no idea.' He shudders. 'All those months and he never said a thing. He saved me, you know . . . Twice.'

Freddie nods, curtly. 'He's dead now too.'

'I am sorry to hear that. He was a good man. A good soldier.' The truth of the situation bites into his chest. 'And the child?' His voice is almost a whisper.

'Wilf. He looks like you. He's good with horses . . .' How do you explain a lifetime in a few short minutes?

464

'You've cared for him?'

'To a certain extent. It's a long story.'

'Is he . . . does he . . . ?'

'He knows. Everyone who matters knows.'

They stare at each other, and the world does not disintegrate: the wind still blows through the golden barley, the dogs still pant in the shade.

Edward struggles to take the ring from around his neck. He holds it out to his brother. 'Give this to him.'

'You can give it to him yourself.'

It is only then that Edward realises that the driver has got out of the car. He is a young man, tall, broad, hesitant. He starts to walk towards Edward as Freddie steps away.

Freddie watches as Wilf passes. He has pulled strings for them both to get here. He hopes it will be worth it: with another war in the offing, they must all make peace with their past.

Wilf walks slowly, calmly, but Freddie knows he is churning inside. With a jolt, he realises he has known his nephew since the boy was five years old: a lifetime. Wilf pauses a distance from his father, and now Freddie can see the differences as well as the similarities. Wilf is darker, though the tips of his hair have lightened in the French sun. He is fine-boned like Edward, though broader, and they have similar gestures, a similar gait, though Wilf has lost that confident bearing that is for ever ingrained in Edward.

The two men face each other, their movements measured, precise, as the late-summer sun bathes them in light. Edward starts the conversation. Freddie hears Wilf respond. He sees Edward look into Wilf's eyes, expecting to see the monster that he has created, and he sees Wilf look into Edward's eyes, expecting to see the monster that created him, and he knows that they only see each other.

Far away, Freddie hears the calls of children and adults finishing for the day. He sees them move through the shimmering fields, their hands spread out so that their palms touch the swaying heads of the crop. A flock of doves rises high on thermals, spinning in the air before settling back on the *pigeonnier*. Freddie remembers his last meeting with Celia. He remembers the weight of her leaning on his arm, her auburn hair brushing his shoulder, her smile, and he knows that at last he has something to fight for. He remembers his daughters, prim in their school uniform, but with fire in their hearts, and he knows that they will be fine. And he sees his brother and his nephew, their heads bent together, their quiet acknowledgement of each other. And suddenly everything is so clear: the rustling of the leaves in the trees, the heat of the sun on his face, the blue of the azure sky, and he has to narrow his eyes against the brightness of it.

AUTHOR'S NOTE

This novel has not come easily, although its theme is one I've always wanted to write about.

My father died when I was young, having taken a very different path to the one marked out for him. On the face of it, he'd started out with everything that mattered to people in those days: money, status, education. Yet he died living the opposite life to that which had been within reach.

But why? My instinct is that he did not feel able to live up to what was expected of him, something that can happen to everyone, anywhere, at one time or another: the coal miner who wants to be a ballet dancer; the girl who is expected to be a natural mother; the boy who hides the empty gin bottles for his mother when his friends visit; the athlete who wants to come out.

Family, society, even our inner demons all put the weight of expectation on us – make us fearful of just being who we are.

At least in a novel, it's easier to break free.

I am not very good at letting people read as I go along – so there are only a handful of people that I can thank for that: first and foremost my editor Susan Watt. Her ability to suggest things without denting morale is second only to her ability to be able to reread for a third time without appearing bored. I wouldn't be here without her.

Then there are the quiet technicians working behind the

scenes – chiefly Charlotte Webb – a copy-editor who deserves to have her name on the front cover – and the galvanisers, like my agent Heather Holden-Brown, and Kirsty Ennever, the only other person who read an early draft.

But the support doesn't just come from the readers. My heartfelt thanks to everyone involved with this book at HarperCollins. Just like family, it's a large team – some of whom I've never met – but I am grateful for their faith in me.

Front of house, it's the independent booksellers who have helped me so much: Emma at Hungerford Bookshop, and Jackie and Kayleigh at Liznojan in Tiverton. Support like theirs is a lifeline – not only in promoting a novel, but in the confidence they boost by doing so (not to mention making me feel like a bona fide author).

However, I don't think they have sold as many of my books as my mother, whose book emojis indicating another sale seem to ping on to my phone almost weekly. She is the spearhead of a phalanx of siblings, step-parents, in-laws and cousins who miraculously keep persuading people to read my first novel, as well as signing me up for book clubs, and constantly asking when the next one is coming out. As they all know, I'm rubbish at public displays of affection, but I thank them all from the bottom of my heart.

But mostly I'd like to thank my husband, Luke – who puts up with me – and my children, Amelia, Nancy and Joey, who are the least judgemental people that I know. I hope they won't ever feel torn between where they come from and where they want to be. I urge them to follow their dreams and be proud of who they are, no matter what anyone else says.

If you enjoyed *A Time to Live*, don't miss
Vanessa de Haan's epic, heart-rending debut,
The Restless Sea

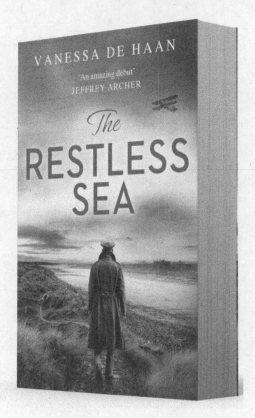

'A rich and skilful novel dramatizing how
the war changed so many lives'
Elizabeth Buchan